Jacob Grimm was born in Hanau, Germany, in 1785, his brother, Wilhelm, the following year. Obeying the wish of their father, who had died when they were children, they attended the University of Marburg, where they studied law. It was there that they first encountered the rising tide of German national consciousness and the growing interest in the country's historical roots; it was this intellectual current that was to shape their careers. Pursuing scholarly roles, first as librarians, then as university lecturers in Berlin, the brothers remained inseparable throughout their lives; not even Wilhelm's marriage disturbed their singular personal and professional harmony. Together they pioneered in the study of German philology and medieval history, making lasting scholarly contributions. Their greatest fame, however, came through their collections of folk tales, *Kinder- und Hausmärchen* (1812–1815) and *Deutsche Sagen* (1816–1818), both later revised several times, principally by Wilhelm, who, of the two, possessed the more striking literary talent. The brothers' final project was their monumental German dictionary on which they were still engaged when they died, Wilhelm in 1859 and Jacob in 1863.

Alfred David is a professor of English at Indiana University. Mary Elizabeth Meek is a professor of English at the University of Pittsburgh.

THE FROG KING
and other tales of
The Brothers Grimm

A NEW SELECTION AND TRANSLATION
WITH AN AFTERWORD BY
ALFRED DAVID AND
MARY ELIZABETH MEEK

ILLUSTRATED BY
SHEILA GREENWALD

A SIGNET CLASSIC

NEW AMERICAN LIBRARY

A DIVISION OF PENGUIN BOOKS USA INC., NEW YORK
PUBLISHED IN CANADA BY
PENGUIN BOOKS CANADA LIMITED, MARKHAM, ONTARIO

SIGNET CLASSIC TRADEMARK REG. U.S. PAT. OFF. AND FOREIGN COUNTRIES
REGISTERED TRADEMARK—MARCA REGISTRADA
HECHO EN DRESDEN, TN, U.S.A.

SIGNET, SIGNET CLASSIC, MENTOR, ONYX, PLUME, MERIDIAN
and NAL BOOKS are published *in the United States* by New American Library,
a division of Penguin Books USA Inc.,
1633 Broadway, New York, New York 10019,
in Canada by Penguin Books Canada Limited,
2801 John Street, Markham, Ontario L3R 1B4

First Printing, August, 1964

3   4   5   6   7   8   9   10   11

PRINTED IN THE UNITED STATES OF AMERICA

CONTENTS

THE FROG KING
and other tales of
The Brothers Grimm

THE FROG KING

or

IRON HENRY

I n the old days, when wishes still came true, there lived
a king whose daughters were all beautiful, but the
youngest was so beautiful that the sun itself, who
has seen so many things, marveled every time it shone
on her face. Close to the king's castle lay a large, dark
forest, and in the forest beneath an old linden tree there
was a well. Whenever the day was very hot, the king's
daughter went out into the forest and sat at the edge of
the cool well, and when she got bored, she took a gold
ball, threw it up in the air, and caught it again. That was
her favorite game.

Now it happened one time that the gold ball missed
her outstretched little hand, and instead bounced along
the ground and rolled directly into the water. The king's
daughter followed it with her eyes, but the ball disappeared, and the well was deep—so deep that one
couldn't see the bottom. Then she began to cry, and
cried louder and louder, and simply could not be consoled.

As she was carrying on like that, someone called out
to her, "What's the matter, king's daughter? Your crying
would move a stone to pity."

She looked around to see where the voice had come
from and saw a frog sticking its ugly thick head out of
the water. "Oh, it's you, old water-splasher," she said.
"I'm crying because I let my gold ball fall into the well."

"Be still and don't cry," answered the frog. "I guess

I can help you out, but what will you give me if I bring your plaything up again?"

"Whatever you want, dear frog," she said. "My clothes, my pearls and jewels, and even the gold crown I have on."

The frog answered, "I don't want your clothes, your pearls and jewels, or your gold crown. But if you will

love me and let me be your friend and playmate, and let me sit beside you at your little table, eat from your little gold plate, drink from your little cup, and sleep in your little bed—if you promise me that, I'll go down and fetch up your gold ball."

"Oh yes," she said, "I'll promise whatever you like if only you'll bring back my ball." She was thinking, "What nonsense the silly frog is talking. It sits in the water with its kind and croaks—it can't live among people."

When the frog had her promise, it ducked its head under the water, dived down, and after a little while came paddling back up. It had the gold ball in its mouth and threw it on the grass.

The king's daughter was overjoyed to see her beautiful plaything again, picked it up, and ran away with it.

"Wait, wait," cried the frog, "take me with you. I can't run as fast as you." But what good did it do for it to cry out after her at the top of its voice, "Croak, croak!" She didn't listen, hurried home, and had soon forgotten the poor frog, who had to crawl back down into its well.

The next day, as she was sitting at table with the king and all the court, and eating from her little gold plate, something came crawling up the marble steps: Plip, plop, plip, plop. And when it got to the top, there was a knocking at the door, and someone called, "Oh, king's youngest daughter, let me in."

She ran to see who was out there, but when she opened the door, the frog was sitting in front of it. Quickly she slammed the door, sat down at the table again, and she was very frightened.

The king saw that her heart was beating very fast, and said, "My child, why are you frightened? There's not a giant at the door wanting to take you away, is there?"

"Oh no," she answered, "it's not a giant but a horrible frog."

"What does the frog want from you?"

"Oh, dear Father, yesterday as I was playing beside the well in the forest, my ball fell into the water. And because I cried so much, the frog got it back for me, and because it insisted, I promised to be its friend. I never thought that it could get out of the water. Now it's out there and wants to come to me."

At that very moment there was a second knocking, and someone called:

> "Oh, king's youngest daughter,
> Let me in.
> Don't you remember yesterday,
> What you promised
> By the cool well water?
> Oh, king's youngest daughter,
> Let me in."

The king said, "Whatever you promised, you have to do. Now go and let it in."

She went and opened the door, and the frog came hopping in, following her to her chair. There it sat and called, "Lift me up beside you."

She hesitated until finally the king ordered her to do it. When the frog was on the chair, it wanted to be up on the table next, and when it was sitting there, it said, "Now push your little gold plate closer so that we can eat together." She did it, but it was easy to see that she didn't do it willingly. The frog enjoyed its meal, but practically every bite stuck in her throat.

Finally the frog said, "I've eaten my fill and I'm tired Now carry me to your little bedroom and put the silk covers on your little bed, and let us lie down beside each other to sleep."

The king's daughter started crying because she was afraid of the cold frog, which she couldn't bear to touch, and which now was supposed to sleep in her nice clean bed. But the king got angry and said, "If anyone helps you when you are in need, you have no right to scorn him afterward." So she picked up the frog with two fingers, carried it upstairs, and set it down in a corner. But when she was in bed, it came crawling up and said, "I'm tired. I'd like to sleep just like you. Pick me up, or I'll tell your father."

Then she got furious, picked it up, and threw it against the wall with all her strength. "Now you'll be able to sleep, you horrible frog."

But when it fell down, it was no frog but a king's son with a beautiful and kindly smile. He was to be her friend and husband according to her father's will. Then he told her that he had been put under a spell by an evil witch, and no one could have freed him from the well except her, and tomorrow they would travel together to his own kingdom.

Then they went to sleep, and the next morning, when the sun woke them, a carriage drove up, pulled by eight white horses with white ostrich plumes on their heads, and harnessed in gold traces. Riding behind stood the young king's servant who was called Faithful Henry. Faithful Henry had become so sad when his lord was turned into a frog that he had had three iron bands fastened around his heart to prevent it from breaking in pain and sorrow.

The carriage had come to fetch the young king to his country. Faithful Henry lifted them both inside and got up behind again, and he was overjoyed that the spell had been broken. And after they had driven a little way, the king's son heard a snapping noise behind him, as though something had broken. He turned around and called:

> "Henry, the coach is breaking down."
> "No, lord, the coach is driving on.
> It is a band around my heart,
> That suffered bitter pain and smart,
> While you were under the spell
> As a frog inside the well."

Once more and still once more there was a snapping along the way, and the king's son kept thinking the carriage was breaking down, but it was only the bands snapping around Faithful Henry's heart because his lord had been set free and made happy.

OUR LADY'S CHILD

At the edge of a great forest lived a woodcutter and his wife. They had only one child, a little girl three years old. They were so poor, however, that they no longer had enough for their daily bread and didn't know how to find food for the child. One morning the woodcutter went off to work in the forest sorely troubled, and as he was chopping wood, suddenly a beautiful woman with a crown of shining stars on her head stood before him and said to him, "I am the Virgin Mary, the mother of the little Christ Child. You are poor and needy. Bring your child to me. I will take her with me, be her mother, and provide for her."

The woodcutter obeyed, fetched the child, and gave her to the Virgin Mary, who took her up to Heaven. There she had a good life: she ate cake and drank sweet milk, she wore clothes made of gold, and the little angels played with her.

When she had reached the age of fourteen, the Virgin Mary summoned her one day and said: "Dear child, I am going away on a long journey. There, take charge of the keys to the thirteen doors in the kingdom of Heaven. You may open twelve of them and look at the wonders inside, but the thirteenth, which this little key opens, is forbidden. Beware of opening it, or you will be very unhappy."

The girl promised to obey, and after the Virgin Mary had gone away, she began to look at the rooms in the kingdom of Heaven. Each day she opened one, until she had seen the twelve. In each an apostle was sitting in shining glory, and all the majesty and splendor made her happy, and the little angels, who always accompanied her, were happy too.

Now only the forbidden door was left. Then she felt a

great desire to know what was hidden behind it, and she said to the angels, "I won't open it all the way and I won't go inside, but I'll open it so that we can catch just a little glimpse through the crack."

"Oh no," said the little angels. "That would be sinful.

The Virgin Mary has forbidden it, and it could easily bring you misfortune." Then she was silent, but her secret longing would not be stilled, and chafed and goaded her heart and would not let her rest.

One time, when all the little angels were out, she thought, "Now I am all alone, and I could peek in because no one would see me do it." She picked out the key, and when she held it in her hand, she put it in the lock, and when she put it in the lock, she turned it. The door sprang open, and she saw the Trinity seated in fire and glory. She stood there a little while amazed, looking at everything. Then she just barely touched the glory with her finger, and the whole finger turned gold. Immediately she became terribly afraid, slammed the door, and ran away. But do what she might, the fear would not go away, and her heart beat rapidly and would not be quiet. The gold, too, remained on her finger and would not come off, no matter how much she washed and rubbed it.

It wasn't long before the Virgin Mary returned from her journey. She summoned the girl and told her to give back the keys of Heaven. As she handed back the bunch of keys, the Virgin Mary looked into her eyes and said, "You did not open the thirteenth door?"

"No," she answered.

Then the Virgin Mary laid her hand on the child's heart and felt how it was beating and beating, and she knew very well that she had disobeyed and opened the door. Then she said once again, "Are you certain you did not do it?"

"No," said the girl for the second time.

Then the Virgin Mary noticed the finger that had turned gold from touching the heavenly fire, saw very well that she had sinned, and said a third time, "You did not do it?"

"No," said the girl for the third time.

Then the Virgin Mary said, "You did not obey me, and you have told a lie besides. You don't deserve to stay in Heaven."

Then the girl fell into a deep sleep, and when she awoke she was lying in the middle of a wilderness down on earth. She wanted to cry out, but she could not make a sound. She sprang up and wanted to run away, but wherever she turned she was forced back by a thick hedge of thorns that she could not break through. In the wilderness where she was confined stood an old hollow tree; that is where she had to live. She crept there at night to sleep, and she found shelter there against the storm and the rain. But it was a wretched life, and when she remembered how beautiful it had been in Heaven and how the angels had played with her, she wept bitterly. Roots and wild berries were her only nourish-

ment, and she searched for them as far as it was possible for her to go. In the autumn she gathered the fallen leaves and nuts and carried them into the hollow tree. In winter the nuts provided her with food, and when the snow and ice came, she crept among the leaves like a poor little animal to keep from freezing. It wasn't long before her clothes were in tatters and fell away from her piece by piece. As soon as the warm sun was shining again, she came out to sit under the tree, and her long hair covered her completely like a cloak. She sat like that year after year and felt the grief and misery of the world.

One time, when the trees were fresh and green again, the king of that country was hunting in the forest, chasing a roe. It fled into the thicket around the clearing, so he dismounted, tore aside the briars, and hacked a path for himself with his sword. When he finally got to the other side, he saw a wondrously beautiful girl sitting under a tree. There she sat, and her golden hair covered her down to her toes. He stood still and gazed at her, struck with amazement. Then he spoke to her and said, "Who are you? Why are you sitting here in this wilderness?"

She did not answer because she could not open her mouth.

The king continued, "Would you like to go with me to my castle?"

Then she nodded her head slightly.

The king took her in his arms, placed her on his horse, and rode home with her; and when he came to his royal castle, he had her dressed in beautiful clothes and gave her everything in abundance. And even though she could not talk, she was so sweet and beautiful that he fell deeply in love with her, and it was not long before he married her.

When about a year had gone by, the queen gave birth to a son. The next night, as she was lying in her bed alone, the Virgin Mary appeared to her and said, "If you will tell the truth and confess that you opened the forbidden door, I will open your mouth and give back your speech, but if you continue to sin and to deny it stubbornly, I will take your newborn child away with me."

Then the queen was permitted to answer, but she remained obstinate and said, "No, I did not open the forbidden door," and the Virgin Mary took the newborn child out of her arms and disappeared with it.

The next morning, when the child was nowhere to be found, a rumor spread among the people that the queen ate human flesh and had killed her own child. She heard all and could say nothing to defend herself, but the king would not believe it because he loved her so much.

After a year the queen gave birth to a second son. During the night the Virgin Mary appeared again and said, "If you will confess that you opened the forbidden door, I will return your child and set your tongue free, but if you continue to sin and to deny it, I will take this newborn child too."

Then the queen said again, "No, I did not open the forbidden door," and the Virgin took the child out of her arms and carried it away with her to Heaven.

In the morning, when this child too had disappeared, the people said openly that the queen had devoured it, and the king's counselors demanded that she be brought to justice. But the king loved her so much that he would not believe it, and he commanded his counselors, as they valued their lives, not to speak of it again.

The next year the queen gave birth to a beautiful little daughter, and the Virgin Mary appeared for the third time at night and said, "Follow me!" She took her by the hand and led her to Heaven, and there she showed her the two older children, who were laughing and playing with the globe of the world. When the queen rejoiced at the sight, the Virgin Mary said, "Has your heart still not softened? If you confess that you opened the forbidden door, I will give back your two little sons."

But the queen answered for the third time, "No, I did not open the forbidden door." Then the Virgin let her sink down to earth again, and she took the third child away from her too.

The next morning, when the news spread, all the people cried out, "The queen is an ogress. She must be condemned," and the king could no longer overrule his counselors. She was put on trial, and since she could not answer to defend herself, she was sentenced to be burned at the stake. The wood was piled up, and as she was tied to the stake and the fire sprang up all around her, the stubborn pride that had frozen her heart melted. She was filled with remorse, and she thought, "If only I could confess before I die that I opened the door."

Then she recovered her voice and cried out, "Yes, Mary, I did do it!"

And immediately a rain fell from Heaven and put out

the flames, and a light blazed out above her, and the Virgin Mary came down with one little boy on each side and the newborn daughter in her arms. She said to her kindly, "Whoever is sorry for his sin and confesses it shall be forgiven," and she returned the three children, set free her tongue, and gave her happiness for the rest of her life.

THE STORY OF
THE BOY WHO WANTED TO
LEARN TO BE AFRAID

A father had two sons. The older one was bright and clever and managed to do everything right, but the younger was stupid and couldn't understand or learn anything. Whenever people saw him, they said, "That boy will turn out to be a burden to his father." If anything needed to be done, the oldest always had to do it. However, if the father asked him to fetch anything at a late hour, not to mention at night, and if the errand led past the churchyard or some other frightening place, he always replied, "Oh no, Father—I won't go there— it makes me shudder!" for he was afraid. At night when stories were told around the fire—the kind that make one's flesh crawl—the listeners sometimes said, "Oh, it makes me shudder!" The youngest sat in a corner listening to them and couldn't figure out what they were talking about. "They're always saying it makes me shudder, it makes me shudder! Nothing makes me shudder. I suppose that's another skill that I don't know about."

Now it happened one time that the father said to him, "Listen, you there in the corner. You're getting big and strong, but you're also going to have to learn something by which to earn a living. Look how hard your brother tries—but all your efforts are wasted."

"Why, Father," he answered, "I'd be glad to learn something. In fact, if it's possible, I'd like to learn something that would make me shudder. I don't know a thing about that."

The older brother laughed when he heard this, and thought, "Good gracious, what a numskull my brother is. He'll never amount to anything. Who would be a thorn must prick betimes."

The father sighed and answered, "You'll learn something that will make you shudder all right, but that won't help you earn your daily bread."

Not long after that the sexton paid a visit to the house. The father told him his troubles, how his youngest son was so ignorant in every way that he didn't know anything and wasn't learning. "Just imagine, when I asked him how he was going to earn a living, he asked to learn something that would make him shudder."

"If that's all he wants," answered the sexton, "I can teach him. Just leave him to me—I'll straighten him out."

The father agreed because he thought, "The boy will at least be trimmed up a bit."

The sexton took the boy home and set him to ringing the bell. After a few days the sexton woke him around midnight and told him to get up and climb the church steeple to ring the bell. "I'll make you shudder," he thought.

He sneaked up there ahead of him, and as the boy got to the top and turned around to seize the bell rope, he saw a white figure standing on the stair opposite the sound hole.

"Who's there?" he called, but the figure didn't answer and didn't move or stir.

"Answer me," cried the boy, "or see that you get out of here. You've got no business here in the middle of the night." But the sexton kept standing there without moving so that the boy would think it was a ghost.

The boy called out a second time, "What do you want here? Say something if you're an honest fellow, or I'll throw you down the stairs."

The sexton thought, "He's bluffing," didn't make a sound, and stood as though he were made of stone.

The boy called to him a third time, and when that didn't work either, he dashed across and pushed the ghost down the stairs so that it fell down ten steps and landed in a corner. Then he rang the bell, went home, and without saying a word to anyone, went to bed and slept.

The sexton's wife waited a long time for her husband, but he didn't come back. At last she became frightened, woke up the boy, and asked, "Have you any idea what became of my husband? He climbed up into the steeple before you did."

"No," answered the boy, "but someone was standing on the stairs opposite the sound hole, and because he wouldn't answer and wouldn't go away, I took him for a rascal and pushed him down the stairs. Just go, and you'll see whether it was him—I'd be sorry if it was."

The woman rushed over and found her husband lying in a corner, moaning because he had broken his leg. She carried him down and then hurried to the boy's father, making a dreadful clamor. "Your son," she cried, "has caused a terrible accident. He threw my husband down the stairs and broke his leg. Get that good-for-nothing out of our house."

The father was alarmed, ran over, and scolded the boy. "What sort of godforsaken tricks are these—the devil must have been teaching them to you."

"Just listen, Father," he answered. "It wasn't my fault at all. He was standing there in the middle of the night as though he were up to no good. I didn't know who it was and warned him three times to say something or to go away."

"Oh," said the father, "you only bring me bad luck. Get out of my sight—I never want to see you again."

"Well, Father, I'll be glad to. Just wait until morning. Then I'll set out to learn something that will make me shudder so I'll have some skill by which to earn a living."

"Learn anything you like," said the father, "it's all the same to me. Here's fifty thaler for you to go into the wide world, and don't tell a soul where you come from and who your father is, because I'm ashamed of you."

"Certainly, Father, just as you like. If that's all you want, I'll be able to remember easily."

When day came, the boy pocketed his fifty thaler, set out down the highway, and kept saying to himself, "If only something would make me shudder! If only something would make me shudder!"

A man came up and overheard the boy talking to himself. After they had gone on a way, they came in sight of a gallows. The man said to him, "Do you see that tree over there where seven men have gotten hitched to the ropemaker's daughter and are taking flying lessons? Sit down under it and wait until night comes, and you'll learn what makes one shudder."

"If that's all it takes," answered the boy, "that's easily done. And if I learn about shuddering as quickly as that, I'll give you my fifty thaler. Just come back to see me tomorrow morning."

Then the boy went to the gallows, sat down under it, and waited until evening came. He built a fire because he was chilly, but around midnight the wind blew so cold that he couldn't get warm in spite of the fire. And as the wind knocked the hanged men about so that they swung back and forth, he thought, "If I'm cold down here by the fire, how those fellows up there must be freezing and fidgeting." And because he was by nature compassionate, he set up the ladder, climbed to the top, untied them one after the other, and fetched all seven of them down. Then he poked the fire, blew on it, and arranged the seven in a circle around it so that they might warm themselves.

But they sat there without stirring, and their clothes caught on fire. "Look out, or I'll hang you up again," he said. But the dead men didn't hear him, said nothing, and let their rags burn. Then he got angry and said, "If you won't look out for yourselves, I can't help you—I'm not going to burn up with you." And one after another, he hung them up again.

Finally he sat down again beside his fire, and the next morning the man came back to collect his fifty thaler.

"Well," he said, "have you found out what makes one shudder?"

"No," he answered, "how should I? Those fellows up there didn't open their mouths, and they're so stupid that they were letting the fire burn up the few rags they have on."

The man realized that he wasn't going to earn fifty thaler that day and went off saying, "I've never met one like that."

The boy also went his way and started talking to himself again. "Oh, if only something would make me shudder! If only something would make me shudder!"

A carter, who was walking along behind him, heard him and asked, "Who are you?"

"I don't know," answered the boy.

The carter kept on asking questions: "Where are you from?"

"I don't know."

"Who is your father?"

"I'm not supposed to tell."

"What is it that you keep muttering in your beard?"

"Well," the boy answered, "I want something to make me shudder, but no one can teach me what to do."

"Stop your silly nonsense," said the carter. "Come along with me. I'll see to it that someone looks after you."

The boy went with the carter, and in the evening they arrived at an inn where they planned to stay overnight. As they came into the taproom, the boy said again very audibly, "If only something would make me shudder! If only something would make me shudder!"

The innkeeper, who heard him, laughed and said, "If that's all you're hankering for, you'll certainly get your chance here."

"Oh, keep still," said the innkeeper's wife. "A lot of nosy fellows have paid for their curiosity with their lives, and it would be a crime and a shame if those fine eyes of his were never to see the light of day again."

But the boy said, "I don't care how hard it is, I'm going to learn. After all, that's why I left home." And he gave the innkeeper no peace until the latter told him that not far away there was a haunted castle where anyone could count on learning what makes one shudder if he'd agree to keep watch there for three nights. The king had promised his daughter in marriage to the person who would risk it, and she was the most beautiful girl under the sun. Moreover, inside the castle there were great treasures guarded by evil spirits, and if the spell was broken, there would be enough to make a poor man rich. Many had gone in there, but so far no one had ever come out again.

The next morning the boy appeared before the king and said, "With your permission, I'd like to keep watch for three nights in the haunted castle."

The king looked him over, and because he had taken a fancy to the boy, he said, "You may ask for three things, as long as they're not living things, and you may take them into the castle with you."

He answered, "In that case, I'll ask for a fire, a turning lathe, and a carpenter's bench and knife."

The king had all of these things carried into the castle for him during the day. As night was falling, the boy went upstairs and made a bright fire in one of the rooms. Next to it he placed the carpenter's bench with the knife, and he sat down at the lathe. "Oh, if only something would make me shudder!" he said. "But I probably won't learn any more about it here."

Around midnight he wanted to stir up the fire, and as he was blowing on it, something suddenly cried out in a corner, "Miaow, miaow! How cold we are!"

"You fools," he called, "what are you crying for? If you're cold, come sit beside the fire and get warm." As soon as he had spoken, two big black cats came over in an enormous leap and sat down on either side of him, glaring at him savagely with their fiery eyes.

In a little while, after they had gotten warm, they said, "How about a game of cards, comrade?"

"Why not?" he answered. "But let me have a look at your paws."

Then they stretched out their claws.

"My," he said, "what long nails you have! Wait, I'll have to trim them first." With that he grabbed them by the neck, lifted them up onto the carpenter's bench, and screwed their paws firmly into a vice.

"I've had a sharp look at your hands," he said, "and now I don't feel like playing cards anymore." He killed them with a blow and tossed them outside into the water.

But when he had put the two of them to rest and was just about to sit down by the fire again, black cats and black dogs on red-hot chains came out of every nook and corner, more and more of them, until he couldn't fend them off. They howled in a ghastly fashion, trampled on his fire, pulled it apart, and were starting to put it out.

He looked on calmly for a while, but when it got too much for him, he took his knife and shouted, "Get out, you rabble," and he started hitting them. A few escaped, and the rest he beat to death and threw them into the pond. When he returned, he blew on the sparks to make his fire blaze up afresh and warmed himself. And as he was sitting there like that, he couldn't keep his eyes open any longer and became sleepy. He looked around and saw a large bed standing in the corner. "That's just what I need," he said, and he lay down on it.

But as he was closing his eyes, the bed began rolling of its own accord, and it rolled him through the whole castle. "That's all right," he said, "the faster the better." Then the bed began to roll as though six horses were hitched to it, over thresholds and up and down the stairs. Suddenly—flip-flop—it turned bottom up so that it covered him like a mountain. But he flung the covers and pillows into the air, climbed out from under, and said, "Now whoever feels like it can take the next ride." And he lay down beside the fire and slept until it was day.

In the morning the king came, and when he saw him lying on the ground, he thought the ghosts had murdered him and that he was dead. "What a pity," he said, "such a handsome young man."

The boy heard him, sat up, and said, "Things aren't that bad yet!"

The king was astonished, but he was glad and asked how it had gone.

"Not bad," answered the boy. "The first night is over, and the other two will also pass."

The innkeeper couldn't believe his eyes when he saw him come back. "I never thought that I'd ever see you alive again," he said. "Now do you know what makes one shudder?"

"No," he said, "nothing seems to do any good—if only someone could explain it to me!"

The second night he again went upstairs in the old castle, sat down beside the fire, and started the same old song, "If only something would make me shudder!" Around midnight a noise and rumbling began, first softly, then louder; then it was quiet for a while, and finally, with a piercing shriek, half a man came down the chimney and landed at his feet. "Hey there!" cried

the boy, "one half is missing. There isn't enough of you."

Then the noise started all over, there was a raging and howling, and the second half came down too. "Wait," the boy said, "first let me blow on the fire a bit." When he had done that and turned around again, the two pieces had joined, and a horrible man was sitting on his bench.

"That wasn't part of the wager," said the boy. "The bench belongs to me." The man tried to crowd him off, but the boy wouldn't stand for that, shoved him violently aside, and resumed his own place.

Then several other men came falling down, one after another. They fetched nine leg bones and two skulls, set them up, and played ninepins. The boy also wanted to play, and asked, "Listen, may I play too?"

"Yes, if you have money."

"I've got plenty of money," he answered, "but your

balls aren't quite round." He took the skulls, fastened them in the lathe, and rounded them off. "There, now they'll roll better," he said. "Hurrah! now for some fun!" He played with them and lost a little money, but at the stroke of midnight everything vanished before his eyes. He lay down and went quietly to sleep.

The next morning the king came to find out what had happened. "How did it go this time?" he asked.

"I played at ninepins," he answered, "and lost a few pennies."

"Didn't anything make you shudder?"

"Not at all," he said. "I was having a good time. If only I knew what shuddering was."

The third night he sat down at his bench and said very gloomily, "If only something would make me shudder!"

When it grew late, six big men came, carrying a bier.

"Aha," he said, "I'll bet that's my cousin who died a few days ago." He motioned with his finger and called, "Come, cousin, come!"

They set the coffin down, and he went over and lifted the lid. A dead man was lying inside. He felt the face with his hand, but it was as cold as ice. "Wait," he said, "I'm going to warm you a bit." He went over to the fire, warmed his hand, and laid it on the face of the corpse, but it stayed cold.

Then he lifted the corpse out, deposited it by the fire, and took it in his lap. And he massaged its arms to start the circulation again.

When that didn't work either, he remembered, "When two bodies lie in the same bed, they warm each other." He carried him to a bed, covered him up, and lay down beside him. After a little while the dead man got warm too and began to stir.

"See there, cousin," said the boy, "that comes from my warming you!"

But the dead man shouted, "Now I'm going to strangle you!"

"What," he said, "is that all the thanks I get? Back into the coffin with you." He picked him up, threw him inside, and closed the lid. Then the six men came and carried him away again. "Nothing is making me shudder," he said. "I'll never learn even if I stay here for the rest of my life."

Then a man came in who was bigger than all the rest and horrible to look at, but he was old and had a long white beard. "Oh, you miserable creature," he cried, "now I'll soon make you shudder, for you are about to die."

"Not so fast," said the boy. "If I'm going to die, you'll have to reckon with me."

"I'll get my hands on you all right," said the monster.

"Easy, easy, don't puff yourself up so much. I'm as strong as you and probably even stronger."

"We'll see about that," said the old man. "If you are stronger than I am, I'll let you go. Come on, let's try it."

Then he led him through dark passageways to a forge, took an ax, and with one blow drove one of the anvils into the ground.

"I can do better than that," said the boy, and went to the other anvil. The old man stood beside him to watch, and his white beard was hanging down. The boy grabbed the ax, split the anvil with one blow, and caught the old man's beard in the crack.

"Now I've got you," said the boy. "Now it's your turn to die." Then he took an iron bar and began beating the old man until he whimpered and begged him to stop, promising to give him great riches. The boy pulled out the ax and let him go.

The old man led him back into the castle, and in a cellar showed him three chests full of gold. "One third of this," he said, "is for the poor, one third for the king, and the rest is yours." Right then it struck twelve, and the ghost disappeared, so that the boy was left standing in the dark.

"I'll find my way out all right," he said, felt around, and found the way back to the room, and there he went to sleep beside the fire.

The next morning the king came and said, "Now I suppose you've learned what makes people shudder?"

"No," he answered, "how should I? My dead cousin was here, and a bearded man came and showed me a lot of money down there, but nobody told me what shuddering is."

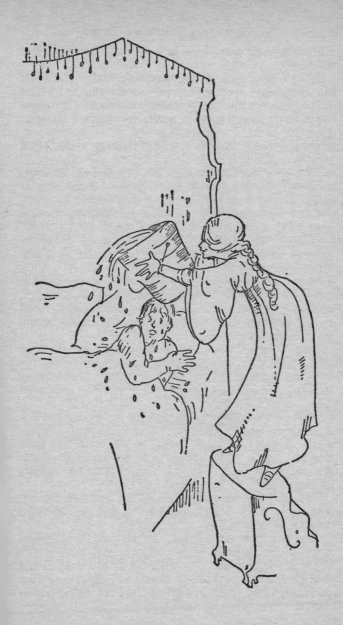

Then the king said, "You have broken the spell on the castle, and you shall marry my daughter."

"That's all very fine," he answered, "but I still don't know anything that will make me shudder."

The gold was brought up, and the wedding was celebrated, but the young king, dearly as he loved his wife and happy as he was, still kept saying, "If only something would make me shudder, if only something would make me shudder."

Finally she couldn't stand it any longer. Her chambermaid said, "I know what to do. I'll make him shudder all right." She went to the brook that ran through the garden and fetched a whole bucketful of minnows.

At night, as the young king was sleeping, his wife took the covers off and emptied the cold water and the minnows all over him so that the little fish wriggled over his whole body. Then he woke up and cried, "Oh, dear wife, it makes me shudder all over, it makes me shudder all over! Yes, now I know what shuddering is."

THE WOLF AND
THE SEVEN KIDS

Once upon a time there was an old nanny goat who had seven kids, and she loved them as a mother loves her children. One day she was going out into the forest to fetch food, and she called all seven to her and said, "Dear children, I am going out into the forest. Watch out for the wolf. If he gets in he'll eat you all, skin and bones. The villain often pretends to be someone else, but you can recognize him right away by his gruff voice and his black feet."

The kids said, "Dear Mother, we'll certainly be careful. You needn't worry about leaving us alone." Then the

mother bleated, and started on her way with an easy
mind.

It wasn't long before someone knocked at the front
door and called, "Open up, dear children, it's your mother, and I've brought each of you a present."

The kids knew by the gruff voice that it was the wolf.
"We won't open the door," they cried. "You're not our
mother. She has a soft, sweet voice, but your voice is
gruff: you're the wolf."

Then the wolf went to a grocer and bought a big piece
of chalk. He ate it and so made his voice soft. Then he
went back, knocked on the front door, and called, "Open
up, dear children, it's your mother, and I've brought each
of you a present."

But the wolf had put his black paw in the window.
The children saw it and cried, "We won't open the door.
Our mother doesn't have a black foot like you: you're
the wolf."

Then the wolf ran to a baker and said, "I've bumped

my foot—spread some dough on it." And when the baker had spread dough on his paw, he ran to the miller and said, "Sprinkle some white flour on my paw."

The miller thought, "The wolf wants to trick somebody," and refused, but the wolf said, "If you don't do it, I'll eat you up." Then the miller was afraid and made the paw white. Yes, that's the way of the world.

Now the villain went to the front door a third time, knocked, and said, "Open the door for me, children. Your dear mother has come home, and I've brought each of you a present."

The kids cried, "First show us your paw, so that we can be sure that you are our dear mother." Then he put his paw in the window, and when they saw that it was white, they believed all he said was true and opened the door.

But who should come in but the wolf. They were terrified and tried to hide. One jumped under the table, the second into bed, the third into the stove, the fourth into the kitchen, the fifth into the cupboard, the sixth under the washbasin, the seventh into the cabinet of the clock on the wall. But the wolf found them and made short work of them. He gulped them down one after another except for the youngest in the clock cabinet—that one he missed.

When the wolf had satisfied his hunger, he strolled off, stretched out in the green meadow under a tree, and went to sleep.

Soon afterward the old nanny goat returned home from the forest. Oh, what a sight greeted her eyes! The front door was standing wide open. The table and the chairs and benches had been overturned, the washbasin lay shattered into a thousand pieces, the covers and pillows had been yanked off the bed. She searched for her children and couldn't find a single one. She called their names in order, but no one answered. Finally, when she got to the youngest, a small voice called, "Dear Mother, I'm hiding in the clock cabinet." She got him out, and he told how the wolf had come and eaten all the others. You can imagine how she wept over her poor children.

Finally in her sorrow she went out, with the youngest kid running at her side. When they came to the meadow, they found the wolf lying there, snoring so that the branches were shaking. They examined him from all sides and noticed that something was stirring and struggling inside his swollen stomach.

"Oh, heavens," she thought, "could my poor children, whom he crammed down for his supper, still be alive?" The kid was sent home to fetch scissors, needle, and thread. Then she cut open the monster's belly, and she had hardly taken a snip when right away a kid stuck his head out, and as she continued cutting, all six sprang out one after another. They were still alive and had not even been hurt, because in his greed the monster had swallowed them whole.

What joy! They hugged their dear mother and skipped around like a tailor dancing at his wedding. However, she said, "Now go and look for stones. We'll fill up the wicked beast's stomach with them while he's still asleep." Then very hurriedly the seven kids hauled stones and put them in the wolf's stomach, as many as would go in. Then the mother sewed him up as quickly as she could, so that he didn't notice anything and didn't even move.

When the wolf had finally slept enough, he got up, and because the stones in his stomach made him very thirsty, he started for the well in order to take a drink. But as he began walking and moving about, the stones in his stomach banged together and rattled around. Then he cried,

> "What's rumbling and tumbling
> Around in my belly?
> Weren't there six kids before?
> Now it's six stones or more."

When he got to the well and bent over the water to drink, the heavy stones pulled him in, and he drowned miserably.

When the seven kids saw that, they came running, crying noisily, "The wolf is dead! The wolf is dead!" And in joy they and their mother danced round about the well.

FAITHFUL JOHN

O nce upon a time an old king was sick and thought, "The bed on which I am lying will probably be my deathbed." Then he said, "Send Faithful John in to me." Faithful John was his favorite servant, and he was called that because all his life he had been so loyal to the king. Now when he appeared at the bedside, the king said to him, "My dearest Faithful John, I feel that my end is near, and I have no worry except for my son. He is still a boy and will not always know how to help himself. Unless you promise me to instruct him in all the things he needs to know and to be his foster-father, I will not be able to close my eyes in peace."

Then Faithful John answered, "I will not leave him, and I will serve him loyally, even if it should cost me my life."

The old king said, "Now I shall die in peace and good comfort." And then he continued, "After my death you must show him the entire castle, all of the rooms, halls, and vaults, and all the treasures in them. But you must not show him the room at the end of the long corridor in which is hidden the portrait of the daughter of the King of the Golden Roof. Should he see her picture, he will fall violently in love with her. He will fall unconscious, and for her sake will come into great danger. You must protect him against this." And after Faithful John had once more given the old king his hand upon it, the latter was silent, laid his head upon his pillow, and died.

After the old king had been carried to his grave, Faithful John told the young king what he had promised his father on his deathbed and said, "This I will surely keep, and I will be as loyal to you as I was to him, even if it should cost me my life." When the period of mourning had passed, Faithful John said to him, "Now the time has come for you to see your inheritance. I shall show you your ancestral castle." Then he led him about everywhere, up and down, and let him see all the treasures and magnificent rooms. Only the one room containing the dangerous portrait he did not open. The picture was placed in such a way that one could see it as soon as the door was opened, and it was so wonderfully wrought that one thought that it lived and breathed and that there was nothing lovelier or more beautiful in the whole world.

The young king saw very well that Faithful John always passed by one door, and he said, "Why do you never open this one for me?"

"There is something inside," he said, "that would frighten you."

The king, however, answered, "I have seen the entire castle, and now I also want to know what is in there." And he proceeded to try to force open the door.

Faithful John held him back and said, "I promised your father before his death that you should not see what is inside that room. It could mean a terrible misfortune for you and for me."

"Oh no," answered the young king. "If I cannot go in, it will mean my certain destruction. I would not rest day and night until I had seen it with my own eyes. I will not move from this spot until you unlock the door."

Then Faithful John realized that it could not be prevented, and with a heavy heart and many a sigh he picked the key out of the great bunch. When he opened the door, he went in first, thinking that he would cover the portrait before the king could see it. But what good did that do? The king stood on tiptoe and looked over his shoulder. And as soon as he had seen the portrait of the girl, which was so marvelous and glittered with gold and jewels, he fell to the ground unconscious. Faithful John lifted him up and carried him to his bed, thinking in great sorrow, "The misfortune has occurred. Heaven knows what will come of it!"

Then he gave the king wine to revive his strength so that he regained consciousness. The first words he spoke were, "Oh! Who is the beautiful girl in the picture?"

"That is the daughter of the King of the Golden Roof," answered Faithful John.

"I love her so much," the king continued, "that if all the leaves on the trees were tongues, they could not express it. I will stake my life to win her. You are my dearest Faithful John. You must help me."

The faithful servant pondered for a long time how to go about the business, for it was difficult even to get into the presence of the king's daughter. Finally he hit upon a way and said to the king, "Everything about her is made of gold—tables, chairs, dishes, cups, bowls, and all the household articles. You have five tons of gold in your treasury. Let the goldsmiths of the kingdom use one ton to make all kinds of vessels and implements and all sorts of birds, wild game, and fabulous beasts—that will please her. With these things we shall sail there to try our luck."

The king had all the goldsmiths summoned, and they had to work day and night until finally the most magnificent objects were ready. After everything had been loaded on a ship, Faithful John dressed himself like a merchant, and the king had to do the same to disguise himself completely. Then they sailed over the ocean, and sailed until they came to the city where the daughter of the King of the Golden Roof lived.

Faithful John told the king to stay aboard ship and to wait for him. "Perhaps," he said, "I will come back with the king's daughter; therefore, see to it that everything is ready. Have the golden vessels put on display and have the whole ship decked out." Thereupon he picked out a number of the golden objects to put in his apron, disembarked, and went straight to the king's castle.

As he arrived in the courtyard, a beautiful girl was standing beside the well, holding two golden buckets with which she was drawing water. When she turned around to carry away the sparkling water, she saw the stranger and asked who he was.

He answered, "I am a merchant," and opened his apron to let her look into it.

She cried, "My, what beautiful goldware!" And she set down her buckets and examined one piece after another. Then she said, "The king's daughter must see these. She is so fond of gold objects that she will buy all that you have." She took him by the hand and led him upstairs, for she was the chambermaid.

When the king's daughter saw the wares, she was delighted and said, "The workmanship is so fine that I will buy everything you have."

But Faithful John said, "I am only the servant of a rich merchant. What I have here is nothing compared to what my master has aboard his ship—the most cunning and precious work that has ever been done in gold."

She wanted to have it all brought up, but he said, "That would take many days—there is such a quantity—and so many rooms to display it all that there would not be enough space in your apartments."

Then her curiosity and longing were aroused more and more, until finally she said, "Take me to your ship. I will go myself to look at your master's treasures."

Then Faithful John was very glad and led her to the ship; and the king, when he looked at her, saw that she was even more beautiful than her portrait; and he was sure that his heart would burst. She came aboard the ship, and the king escorted her inside. But Faithful

John remained behind with the helmsman and gave orders to get the ship under way: "Set full sail so she will fly like a bird."

Meanwhile, inside, the king was showing the girl the golden trinkets, each one in turn—the vessels, cups, bowls, the birds, the wild game, and the fabulous beasts. Many hours passed while she was looking at it all, and in her pleasure she did not notice that the ship was moving. After she had seen the last one, she thanked the merchant and wanted to go home. But when she came to the rail, she saw that the ship was going over the high seas far from land and rushing ahead under full sail. "Oh," she cried out in fear, "I have been betrayed. I have been stolen away and have fallen into the power of a merchant. I would rather die!"

But the king took her hand and said, "I am no merchant but a king and no lower of birth than you. But I have stolen you away through cunning because I was too much in love with you. The first time I saw your portrait I fell to the ground unconscious." When the daughter of the King of the Golden Roof heard this, she took comfort, and her heart inclined toward him so that she gladly consented to become his wife.

It happened, however, that as they were sailing over the high seas Faithful John, who was sitting at the prow playing upon an instrument, saw three ravens in the sky flying toward them. Then he stopped playing and listened to what they were saying to each other, for he could understand them well.

The first one cried, "Look, he is taking home the daughter of the King of the Golden Roof."

"Yes," answered the second, "but she isn't his yet."

"But he does have her," said the third. "There she is on his ship."

Then the first began again and cried, "What good will that do him! As soon as they land, a bay horse will gallop up to meet him. He'll want to mount it, and if he does, it will run away with him right into the clouds so that he'll never see his bride again."

"Is there no remedy?" asked the second.

"Oh yes, if someone else quickly jumps on first, pulls out the gun that will be in the holster, and shoots the horse dead, then the young king will be saved. But who knows about that! And whoever does know and tells him will turn to stone from his toes to his knees."

Then the second said, "I know still more. Even if the horse is killed, the young king won't get to keep his bride. When they arrive at the castle together, a wedding shirt will be laid out in a dish all ready, looking as though it were woven of gold and silver. But it's really only sulphur and pitch. If he puts it on, his flesh will be burned right down to the bone and marrow."

"Is there no remedy at all?" asked the third.

"Oh yes," answered the second. "If someone seizes the shirt with gloves and throws it into the fire so that it burns up, the young king will be saved. But what's the use! Anyone who knows this and tells him will turn to stone from his knees to his heart."

Then the third said, "I know still more. Even if the wedding shirt is burned, the young king still won't have his bride. When the dancing after the wedding begins and the young queen is dancing, she will suddenly turn pale and fall down as if dead. And if someone doesn't lift her up, suck three drops of blood out of her right breast, and spit them out again, she will die. But if anyone knows this and tells, his whole body will turn to stone from top to toe."

When the ravens had talked about these things together, they flew away, and Faithful John had understood all of it very well. From that moment he was silent and sad. If he did not tell his master what he had heard, misfortune would overtake him. If he revealed it to him, he would have to pay for it with his own life. Finally he said to himself, "I will save my master, even if I should perish in the act."

When they came to land, it happened as the raven had prophesied, and a splendid bay steed galloped to meet them. "Good," said the king, "it shall carry me to my castle." He wanted to get on, but Faithful John got ahead of him, quickly vaulted into the saddle, pulled the gun out of the holster, and shot the horse dead.

Then the king's other servants, who disliked Faithful John, cried, "What a disgrace to kill the splendid animal that was supposed to carry the king to his castle!"

But the king said, "Be silent and leave him alone. He is my dearest Faithful John. Who knows what good end it may serve!"

Then they went to the castle, and in the hall stood a dish with a wedding shirt laid out all ready, looking as though it were made of gold and silver. The young king went to pick it up, but Faithful John pushed him aside, seized it with gloves, and quickly carried it over to the fire and burned it.

Again the other servants began complaining and said, "Look! Now he is even burning up the king's wedding shirt."

But the young king said, "Who knows what good end it may serve! Leave him alone. He is my dearest Faithful John."

Now the wedding was celebrated. The dancing began, and the bride also joined in. Faithful John paid close attention and watched her face. Suddenly she turned pale and fell to the ground as if she were dead. He rushed to the spot, lifted her up, and carried her to her chamber.

There he put her down, got on his knees, and sucked three drops of blood out of her right breast and spit them out. Immediately she began breathing again and revived. But the young king had been watching, and since he did not know why Faithful John had done it, he was angry and cried, "Throw him into prison."

The next morning Faithful John was sentenced and led to the gallows. When he was standing up there about to be executed, he said, "Every condemned prisoner is allowed to say a few words before his death. Will you also grant me this right?"

"Yes," answered the king, "it shall be granted to you."

Then Faithful John said, "I have been condemned unjustly and have always remained faithful to you." And he told how at sea he had overheard the conversation of the ravens, and how he had been forced to do everything in order to save his master.

· Then the king cried, "Oh, my dearest Faithful John, pardon! Pardon! Take him down." But with the last word he had spoken Faithful John had fallen down lifeless and had turned to stone.

The king and queen suffered great sorrow, and the king said, "Oh, how ill I have rewarded such great loyalty!" And he had the stone image taken up and placed in his bedroom beside his bed. Every time he looked at it, he wept and said, "Oh, if I could only bring you back to life, my dearest Faithful John."

After a certain time the queen gave birth to twins, two little sons who grew up and were their pride and joy. One time when the queen had gone to church and the two children were with their father, playing, the latter looked at the stone image again, full of sorrow, sighed, and said, "Oh, if I could only bring you back to life, my dearest Faithful John."

Then the stone began to speak and said, "Yes, you can bring me back to life if you are willing to sacrifice what is dearest to you."

Then the king cried, "For you I would give up everything that I have in this world."

The stone continued to speak. "If with your own hand you will strike off the heads of your two children and smear me with their blood, I will return to life."

The king was horrified when he heard that he himself had to kill his dearest children. But he thought of Faithful John's great loyalty and of how he had died for him, drew his sword, and with his own hand struck off the heads of his children. And when he had smeared the stone with their blood, life returned, and Faithful John stood before him again, hale and hearty.

"Your loyalty shall not go unrewarded," he said to the king, and he took the children's heads, set them on again, smeared the wounds with their blood, and in the twinkling of an eye they were whole again and frolicked about in their play as though nothing had happened to them.

The king was overjoyed, and when he saw the queen coming, he hid Faithful John and the two children in a large wardrobe. When she came in, he asked her, "Did you pray in church?"

"Yes," she answered, "but I was thinking all the time of Faithful John and the great misery he suffered for our sake."

Then he said, "Dear wife, we can restore him to life, but it will cost us both of our little sons. We have to sacrifice them."

The queen turned pale and her heart was afraid, but she said, "We owe it to him because of his great loyalty."

Then the king was glad that she thought as he had. He went and opened the wardrobe and let out the children and Faithful John. "God be praised," he said, "he is redeemed, and our sons, too, have been restored to us." And he told her how it had all come about. And they lived happily together for the rest of their lives.

THE TWELVE BROTHERS

░░░

Once upon a time a king and queen were living peacefully together, and they had twelve children, all of them boys. Now the king said to his wife, "If the thirteenth child you bring into the world turns out to be a girl, the twelve brothers shall die so that she will have a great fortune and will inherit the kingdom alone." He had twelve coffins made, and they were filled with wood shavings, and each was provided with a coffin pillow. He had them carried into a locked room, then gave the keys to the queen, and ordered her not to tell anyone.

Now the mother sat sorrowing all day long until the youngest son, who never left her side and whom she had named after the Benjamin in the Bible, said to her, "Dear Mother, why are you so sad?"

"Dear child," she answered, "I may not tell you." But he gave her no peace until she went and unlocked the room and showed him the twelve coffins already filled with shavings. Then she said, "My dearest Benjamin, your father had these coffins made for you and your eleven brothers, for if I have a daughter you are all to be killed and buried in them."

She was weeping while she was telling him this, but her son consoled her and said, "Dear Mother, don't cry —we will save ourselves by going away."

But she said, "Go into the forest with your eleven brothers, and one of you must always sit at the top of the tallest tree you can find to keep watch and observe the castle tower. If I give birth to a son, I shall run up a white flag, and then you may come back. If I give birth to a daughter, I will run up a red flag, and then you must flee as fast as you can, and may God protect you. I will get up each night to pray for you, in the wintertime that you may be warm by a fire, and in summer that you may not suffer in the heat."

And so when she had blessed her sons, they went out into the forest. They took turns sitting on top of the tallest oak and keeping watch on the tower. After eleven days had gone by, it was Benjamin's turn, and he saw a flag being raised. But instead of the white one it was the blood-red flag, letting them know that they were all to die. When the brothers heard about it, they were angry and said, "Are we to die for the sake of a girl! We swear that we will take revenge—wherever we meet with a girl, her red blood shall be spilled."

Then they went deeper into the forest, and in the very heart, where it was darkest, they found an enchanted cottage standing empty. "Let us stay here," they said, "and you, Benjamin, because you are the youngest and weakest, shall stay home and keep house, while the rest of us go out to provide food." And they went into the forest and shot hares, wild deer, birds, doves, and whatever was fit to eat. They brought it home to Benjamin, who had to prepare it for them to appease their hunger. In this cottage they lived together for ten years, and the time passed quickly for them.

Meanwhile, the little daughter their mother the queen had given birth to was growing up. She was kindhearted and beautiful, and she had a gold star on her forehead. One time when there was a great deal of laundry, she noticed twelve men's shirts among the things and asked her mother, "Whose are those twelve shirts—aren't they much too small for Father?"

Her mother replied with a heavy heart, "Dear child, they belong to your twelve brothers."

The girl said, "Where are my twelve brothers? I've never heard of them."

She answered, "Heaven knows where they are. They are wandering through the world." Then she took the girl and unlocked the room and showed her the twelve coffins with the shavings and the coffin pillows. "These coffins," she said, "were made for your brothers, but they stole away secretly before you were born." And she told how it had all happened.

"Dear Mother," said the girl, "don't weep. I shall go in search of my brothers."

She took the twelve shirts and went directly into the great forest. She walked all day long, and in the evening she came to the enchanted cottage. She entered and found a young boy, who asked her, "Where do you come from and where are you going?" And he was astonished at her beauty, at her royal clothes, and at the star on her forehead.

"I am a king's daughter," she answered, "and I am looking for my twelve brothers and shall go as far as the sky is blue until I find them." And she showed him the twelve shirts belonging to them.

Then Benjamin knew that she was his sister and said, "I am Benjamin, your youngest brother." And they both wept with joy and kissed and embraced with great love.

Then he said, "Dear sister, there is still one difficulty —we have agreed that every girl who meets with us must die, because we have had to leave our kingdom for the sake of a girl."

"I would gladly die," she said, "if that way I could redeem my twelve brothers."

"No," he answered, "you shall not die. Hide under this tub until my eleven brothers come, and I'll manage to work it out with them."

That is what she did, and at nightfall the others returned from the chase, and their meal was ready. As they were sitting around the table eating, they asked, "What news is there?"

"Don't you know of any?" said Benjamin.

"No," they answered.

"You've been in the forest," he continued, "and I've had to stay home, but I still know more than you do."

"Tell us," they cried.

He answered, "Will you promise that the first girl we meet shall not be killed?"

"Yes," they all cried, "she shall have mercy—only tell us."

Then he said, "Our sister is here." And he lifted the tub. The king's daughter came out in her royal clothes with the gold star on her forehead, and she was very beautiful, tender, and graceful. Then they were all glad, embraced and kissed her, and took her to their hearts.

She stayed at home with Benjamin and helped him with the housework. The eleven others went into the forest and caught game, deer, birds, and doves to provide food, and their sister and Benjamin saw to it that it was prepared for them. She gathered wood for the stove and herbs for vegetables. She put the pots on the fire so that dinner was always ready by eleven o'clock when the eleven brothers came home. She also kept the house in order and made up the beds with fresh white sheets. The brothers were always content and lived with her in complete harmony.

One time the two at home had prepared a good meal, and after they were all together, they sat down and ate and drank, and they were full of merriment. Beside the enchanted cottage there was a small garden in which grew twelve lilies—the kind that are also called "student lilies." * Wishing to please her brothers, she thought that she would put one on each plate. But the very moment she picked the flowers, the twelve brothers were turned into twelve ravens and flew away over the forest, and the cottage and garden vanished too.

Now the poor girl was alone in the wild forest, and when she looked about, an old woman was standing at her side, who said, "My child, what have you done? Why didn't you leave the twelve white flowers alone? Those were your brothers, who have now been changed forever into ravens."

The girl said, weeping, "Is there no way to redeem them?"

"No," said the old woman, "there is no way in all the world but one, and that is so hard that you will never manage to set them free. For you must be silent for seven years, you may neither speak nor laugh, and if you were to say a single word—though only one hour of the seven years was lacking—everything would have been in vain, and that one word would kill your brothers."

But the girl said in her heart, "I know for certain that I shall redeem my brothers." And she searched

* That is, not a real lily but a small flower so-called because university students were fond of wearing them as boutonnieres.

out a tall tree, and sat in it spinning, and she did not speak or laugh.

Now it came to pass that a king was hunting in the forest. He had a big greyhound that ran to the tree in which the girl was sitting, and it jumped around and yelped and barked up at her. The king came along and saw the beautiful king's daughter with the gold star on her forehead, and he was so smitten with her beauty that he called up to her to ask whether she wanted to be his wife.

She didn't answer, but nodded her head slightly. He climbed the tree himself, carried her down, set her on his horse, and led her home. The wedding was celebrated with great splendor and joy, but the bride did not speak or laugh.

After they had lived happily together a few years, the king's mother, who was a wicked woman, began to slander the young queen, and said to the king, "You've brought home a common beggar girl. Who knows what wickedness she is practicing in secret? Even if she is mute and cannot speak, she might at least laugh occasionally. Anyone who never laughs must have a bad conscience."

At first the king did not want to believe her, but the old woman carried on for so long and accused her of so many evil things that the king finally let himself be convinced, and he condemned the young queen to death.

A great fire was lit in the courtyard in which she was to be burned to death. The king stood at the window above, watching with tears in his eyes because he still loved her very much. And when she was already tied to the stake and the red tongues of flame were licking at her clothes—just then the seven years were up. A beating of wings was heard in the air, and the twelve ravens appeared in the sky and descended. And as they touched the ground, they turned into the twelve brothers whom she had redeemed.

They scattered the brands, extinguished the fire, set their dear sister free, and kissed and embraced her. Now that she could open her mouth to speak, she told the king why she had remained mute and had never laughed. The king was happy to hear that she was innocent, and

from that time on they all lived happily together until they died.

The wicked stepmother was brought to trial and put in a barrel filled with boiling oil and poisonous snakes, and she died a horrible death.

BROTHER AND SISTER

░░

B rother took his little sister by the hand and said, "Since Mother died, we haven't spent a happy hour. Our stepmother beats us every day, and when we come to her, she kicks us away. We have to eat the hard leftover crusts, and the little dog under the table fares better than we do, for she sometimes tosses it a good morsel. God be merciful—if our mother could know this! Come, let us go out into the wide world together."

They walked the whole day over meadow, field, and stone, and when it rained, Sister said, "God and our hearts are weeping together!" At night they came to a great forest, and they were so tired from hunger and misery and the long journey that they crept into a hollow tree and went to sleep.

The next morning when they woke up, the sun had already climbed high in the heavens, and its hot beams were shining into the tree. Brother said, "Sister, I'm thirsty. If I knew where to find a spring, I'd go there and drink. I think I can hear one murmuring." Brother rose, took Sister by the hand, and they went looking for the spring. But the wicked stepmother was a witch and had seen the children starting out. She had sneaked after them—stealthily, the way witches creep—and had bewitched all the springs in the forest.

They found a little spring sparkling brightly as it bubbled over the stones, and Brother wanted to drink from it. But Sister heard how it was saying as it babbled on, "Whoever drinks from me will turn into a tiger; whoever drinks from me will turn into a tiger."

Then Sister called, "I beg you, Brother, do not drink, or you will turn into a wild animal and tear me to pieces."

Brother didn't drink, even though he was terribly thirsty, and said, "I'll wait until we come to the next spring."

When they came to the second little spring, Sister heard how this one too was saying, "Whoever drinks from me will turn into a wolf; whoever drinks from me will turn into a wolf."

Then Sister called, "Brother, I beg you, do not drink, or you will turn into a wolf and eat me."

Brother didn't drink and said, "I'll wait until we come to the next spring, but then I shall have to drink, no matter what you say. I'm so terribly thirsty."

And as they came to the third little spring, Sister heard how it was saying as it babbled on, "Whoever drinks from me will turn into a fawn; whoever drinks from me will turn into a fawn."

Sister said, "Oh, Brother, I beg you, do not drink, or you will turn into a fawn and run off and leave me." But right away Brother knelt beside the spring, bent down, and drank from the water, and as soon as the first drop touched his lips, he lay there in the shape of a fawn.

Now Sister wept over poor Brother in his enchantment, and the fawn wept too and sat very sadly at her side. At last the girl said, "Be quiet, dear fawn, for I will never leave you." Then she took off her golden garter and tied it around the fawn's neck, and she pulled up some rushes and plaited them into a soft cord. To this she attached the little creature and led it along, going ever deeper into the forest.

After they had gone a long, long time, they finally came to a little hut. The girl looked in, and because it was empty, she thought, "We can stay and live here." Then she searched for leaves and moss to make a soft bed for the fawn, and each morning she gathered roots, berries, and nuts, and for the fawn she brought tender grass, which he ate from her hand, and he was happy and played in front of her. At night when Sister was tired and had said her prayers, she laid her head on the fawn's back—that was her pillow—and went gently to sleep. And if only Brother had had his human shape, they would have led a wonderful life.

Thus they lived all alone for a while in the wilderness. But it happened that the king of that country held a great hunt in the forest. Then the blowing of the horns, the baying of the hounds, and the merry shouts of the hunters resounded among the trees, and the fawn heard them and wanted very much to take part too. "Oh," he said to Sister, "let me out to join the hunt. I can't stand it any longer." And he pleaded until she gave her consent.

"But be sure to come home in the evening," she said to him. "I will bar the door against the rough huntsmen, and in order that I may recognize you, you must knock and say, 'Sister dear, let me in here.' And if you don't say it, I won't unbar the door."

Then the fawn sprang outside, and he felt so good and was so happy to be out in the open air. The king and his huntsmen saw the fine animal and pursued him, but they couldn't catch him, and each time they were sure they had him, he leaped over the bushes and was gone. When darkness fell, he ran to the hut, knocked and said, "Sister dear, let me in here." Then the little door was opened to admit him, and he sprang inside and rested all night on his soft bed.

The next morning the hunt began anew, and when the fawn again heard the hunting horn and the Heigh-ho! of the hunters, he had no peace and said, "Sister, let me out. I have to go out."

Sister opened the door for him and said, "But in the evening you have to be back and you must say your little rhyme."

When the king and the huntsmen again saw the fawn with the golden collar, they all rode after him, but he was too swift and nimble for them. This went on the whole day, but finally in the evening the hunters surrounded him, and one of them wounded him slightly in the leg so that he had to limp and run away slowly. One of the hunters stalked him to the hut and overheard him calling, "Sister dear, let me in here." And he saw that the door was opened for the fawn and was shut again right away. The hunter took good note of everything, went to the king, and told him what he had seen and heard. Then the king said, "Tomorrow we shall hunt once more."

Sister, however, got a terrible shock when she saw that the fawn was wounded. She washed off the blood, applied herbs to the wound, and said, "Lie down on your bed, dear fawn, so that you will get well again."

But the wound was so slight that the next morning the fawn could not even feel it. And when he again heard the merry hunt going on outside, he said, "I can't stand it; I have to go along. They won't catch me so easily."

Sister wept and said, "This time they will kill you, and I shall be alone in the forest and abandoned by all the world. I shan't let you out."

"Then I shall die here of sorrow," answered the fawn. "When I hear the hunting horn, I feel as though I had to jump out of my shoes!" Then Sister couldn't do other-

wise, and with a heavy heart she opened the door for
him, and the fawn ran into the forest, all well again
and gay.

When the king saw him, he said to his huntsmen,
"Chase after him the whole day until night, but let no
one harm him." As soon as the sun had set, the king
said to the huntsman, "Now come and show me the forest
hut." And when he got to the door, he knocked and
called, "Sister dear, let me in here." The door opened,
and the king stepped inside, and there stood a girl, the
most beautiful he had ever seen. The girl was afraid
when instead of the fawn she saw a man coming in
with a golden crown on his head. But the king looked
at her kindly, gave her his hand, and said, "Will you
go with me to my castle and become my wife?"

"Oh yes," answered the girl, "but the fawn must come
along too. I won't abandon him."

The king said, "He shall stay with you as long as you
live, and he shall lack nothing." At that moment he
came bounding in. Sister tied him to the rush cord and
went with him from the forest hut.

The king took the beautiful girl on his horse and led
her to the castle, where the wedding was celebrated with
great pomp, and now she was queen, and they lived together happily for a long time. The fawn was pampered
in every way, and frolicked about in the garden of the
castle. But the wicked stepmother, on whose account the
children had set out into the world, had no idea but
that Sister had been torn to pieces by the wild animals
in the forest and that Brother in the shape of a fawn
had been shot to death by the hunters. When now she
heard that they were so happy and so well off, envy
and jealousy stirred in her heart and gave her no peace,
and her only thought was how she might still bring misfortune upon both of them.

Her own daughter, who was as ugly as the night and
had only one eye, reproached her. "To be a queen—
that should have been my fortune by rights."

"Just be quiet," said the old woman, and spoke sooth-
ing words to her. "When the moment is right, I'll go
to work, you may be sure."

When the time came that the queen gave birth to a

handsome little boy and the king happened to be out hunting, the old witch took the appearance of the maid-in-waiting and entered the room where the queen was lying. She said to the sick girl, "Come, your bath is ready. That will do you good and give you new strength. Quick, before it cools off." Her daughter too was on hand, and they carried the queen in her weak state to the bathroom and placed her in the tub. Then they locked the door and ran off. But they had made the fire in the bathroom so terribly hot that the beautiful young queen soon suffocated.

Having accomplished this, the old woman took her daughter, placed a nightcap on her head, and laid her in bed in the queen's place. She also gave her the shape and appearance of the queen, except that she couldn't give her back the lost eye. In order that the king wouldn't notice, however, she had to lie on the side where the eye was missing.

When he came home at night and heard that a little son had been born to him, he was glad with all his heart and went over to his dear wife's bed to see how she was. The old woman quickly called out, "Take care, and don't open the bed-curtains. The queen can't stand any light yet and has to rest." The king went away again without finding out that there was a false queen in the bed.

At midnight when everyone was asleep, the nurse, who was sitting by the cradle in the nursery and was the only person still awake, saw the door open and the true queen come in. She lifted the child out of the cradle, held it in her arms, and nursed it. Then she shook up its little pillow, put it back again, and spread the cover-let over it. She didn't forget about the fawn either, but went over to the corner where he was lying and stroked his back. Then she went out the door again in complete silence.

The next morning the nurse asked the watchmen if anyone had come into the castle during the night, but they answered, "No, we didn't see anyone." The queen came like this many nights and never said a word. The nurse saw her each time but didn't dare tell anyone.

After a time had passed in this manner, the queen began to speak in the night and said,

> "How is my baby? How is my fawn?
> I'll come twice more and never again."

The nurse did not answer, but when the queen had left, she went to the king and told him everything. The king said, "Dear heaven, what can it be! I will keep watch by the child tonight."

In the evening he went to the nursery, and at midnight the queen appeared again and said,

> "How is my baby? How is my fawn?
> I'll come once more and never again."

Then she nursed the child as she always did before she disappeared again.

The king did not dare speak to her, but he kept watch again the following night. Again she spoke:

> "How is my baby? How is my fawn?
> I'll come this time and never again."

Then the king could not hold back, ran to her, and said, "You can be none other than my dear wife."

She answered, "Yes, I am your dear wife." And in that moment through God's grace she came back to life, and she was fresh, rosy, and healthy.

Then she told the king about the crime that the wicked witch and her daughter had committed against her. The king had them both brought to trial, and they were sentenced. The daughter was taken out into the forest where the wild animals tore her to pieces, but the witch was brought to the stake and burned up miserably. And when she had been burned to ashes, the fawn received back his human shape, and Brother and Sister lived happily together for the rest of their lives.

RAPUNZEL

▪▪▪

Once upon a time there lived a man and his wife who for a long time had wished in vain for a child, and at last the woman had reason to believe that the good Lord would fulfill her wish. The couple had a little window at the back of their house from which they could see a splendid garden full of the loveliest flowers and vegetables, but it was surrounded by a high wall, and no one dared to go inside because it belonged to a very powerful witch of whom everyone was afraid.

One day the woman was standing at the window and looking down into the garden. There she caught sight of a bed planted with the most beautiful rapunzels,* and they looked so fresh and green that her mouth began to water, and she felt a very great longing to eat some of them. Her longing increased every day, and because she realized that she could not have any, she pined away and looked pale and miserable. Her husband took fright and asked, "What ails you, dear wife?"

"Oh," she said, "if I don't get some of the rapunzels from the garden behind our house, I shall die." Her husband, who loved her, thought to himself, "Rather than let my wife die, I'll bring her some of those rapunzels, no matter what it may cost." And so at dusk he climbed over the wall into the witch's garden, hastily picked a handful of rapunzels, and brought them to his wife. She immediately made a salad and ate it ravenously. But it tasted so awfully good that the next day her desire was three

* A European lettucelike vegetable used in salads. Its English name is "rampion," but since the word is almost as unfamiliar to American readers as the German "Rapunzel," the latter has been retained to show where Rapunzel gets her name.

times as great. If she was to have peace, her husband had to climb into the garden a second time. He went back again at dusk, but as he climbed over the wall, he was terrified to see the witch standing in front of him.

"How dare you," she said with a savage look, "climb into my garden and steal my rapunzels like a thief? This is going to have disagreeable consequences for you."

"Oh," he replied, "temper justice with mercy. I would not have dared if I hadn't had to do it. My wife saw your rapunzels from the window, and she has such a longing to eat some that she will die if she can't have any."

The witch became a little less angry and said to him, "If it is as you say, I will allow you to take as many rapunzels as you want, but on one condition—you must give me the child that your wife is about to bring into the world. It will be well treated, and I will give it a mother's care." The man was so afraid that he agreed to everything, and as soon as the baby was born, the witch appeared, named the child Rapunzel, and took it away with her.

Rapunzel was the most beautiful child under the sun. When she turned twelve, the witch shut her up in a tower in a forest. The tower had neither stairs nor doors; there was only a tiny little window at the very top. Whenever the witch wanted to get in, she stood below and cried:

> "Rapunzel, Rapunzel,
> Let down your hair."

Rapunzel had magnificent long hair, as fine as spun gold. When she heard the witch's voice, she would undo her braids and wind them around a window hook, and then her hair would drop twenty yards down to the ground, and the witch would climb up by it.

After several years it happened that the king's son was riding through the forest and passed by the tower. He heard singing that was so lovely that he stood still and listened. It was Rapunzel, who in her loneliness passed the time singing sweetly to herself. The king's son wanted to climb up to her and looked for a door in the tower, but he could not find one. He rode home, but the

song had so touched his heart that every day he went
out into the forest to listen.

One time, as he was standing behind a tree, he saw the
witch coming and heard her call up:

> "Rapunzel, Rapunzel,
> Let down your hair."

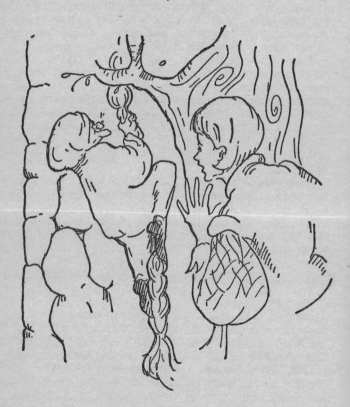

Then Rapunzel let down her braids, and the witch
climbed up to her.

"If that's the ladder one climbs up on, I'll try my luck."
And the following day as it was getting dark, he went to
the tower and called:

"Rapunzel, Rapunzel,
Let down your hair."

Right away the hair was let down, and the king's son climbed up.

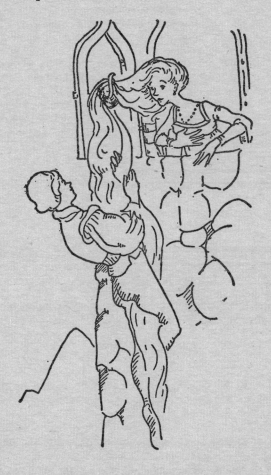

At first Rapunzel was terribly frightened to see a man enter, because she had never seen one before. But the

king's son began to talk to her kindly and told her that
her song had touched his heart so much that he could
not rest until he had seen her. Then Rapunzel was no
longer afraid, and when he asked her if she would marry
him and she saw that he was young and handsome, she
thought, "He'll love me better than my old godmother," and she said yes and laid her hand in his hand. She
said, "I would gladly go with you, but I don't know how
to get down. Each time you come, bring a skein of silk
with you and I'll twist it into a ladder, and when it's
ready I'll climb down, and you will take me away
on your horse."

They arranged for him to come every evening because
the old woman came in the daytime. The witch suspected
nothing until Rapunzel said to her one day, "Do tell me,
Godmother, why are you so much heavier to pull up
than the young king's son—he's up in a flash."

"Oh, you wicked child," cried the witch, "what are you
saying? I thought I had shut you away from all the world,
and still you have deceived me." In her rage she seized
Rapunzel's beautiful hair, wound it a few times around
her left hand, grabbed a pair of scissors with her right,
and snip, snap, cut it off. And the beautiful braids were
lying on the floor. Moreover, she was so heartless that
she took poor Rapunzel to a desert place where she had
to live in great sorrow and misery.

On the same day, however, on which she had banished
Rapunzel, the witch tied the braids to the window hook,
and when the king's son came and cried:

> "Rapunzel, Rapunzel,
> Let down your hair,"

she let the hair down. The king's son climbed up, but
instead of finding his beloved Rapunzel, he found the
witch, who glared at him spitefully.

"Aha," she cried mockingly, "you've come to take
away your lady love, but the beautiful bird is no longer
sitting in the nest singing. The cat has got it, and what's
more, is going to scratch out your eyes. You've lost
Rapunzel, and you'll never see her again."

The king's son was beside himself with grief, and in

his despair he leaped from the tower. He escaped with his life, but the brambles he fell into put out his eyes. He wandered blind through the forest and ate nothing but roots and berries, and he did nothing except to moan and weep over the loss of his beloved wife.

So he wandered for several years in misery and happened at last upon the desert place where Rapunzel lived in sorrow with the twins she had borne—a boy and a girl. He heard her voice, and it seemed very familiar to him. He went toward the voice, and when he approached, Rapunzel recognized him, and she embraced him and wept. Two of her tears fell upon his eyes and moistened them so that they became clear again and he could see as well as before. He took her to his kingdom, where he was received joyfully, and they lived for many more years in happiness and contentment.

THE THREE SPINNERS

There was a girl who was lazy and didn't want to spin, and her mother might say what she would—she couldn't get her to do it. One time the mother finally lost her patience and her temper and started hitting the girl so that she began howling. The queen happened to be driving past, and when she heard the girl's cries, she stopped, went into the house, and asked the mother why she was hitting her daughter so that her crying could be heard out in the street. The woman was ashamed to confess to her daughter's laziness and said, "I can't get her to stop spinning. She wants to spin all the time, and I am poor and can't provide the flax."

The queen answered, "I like nothing better than to hear the sound of spinning, and I'm never happier than when the wheels are humming. Let me take your daughter to

the castle. I have plenty of flax, and there she can spin
as much as she likes."

The mother consented with all her heart, and the
queen took the girl with her. When they got to the castle
she led her upstairs to three rooms that were filled
from floor to ceiling with the finest flax. "Now spin this
flax for me," she said, "and if you can finish it, you shall
have my oldest son for your husband. Even though you
are poor, that doesn't matter to me. Your tireless in-
dustry is dowry enough."

The girl was secretly afraid, for she couldn't spin the
flax, and she couldn't have if she had lived three hundred years and had worked at it every day from morning till evening. When she was left alone, she began to
cry and sat there like this for three days without lifting
a finger. On the third day the queen came, and when she
saw that nothing had been spun yet, she wondered at it,
but the girl excused herself by saying that she hadn't
been able to start because she was sad at being away
from her mother's house. The queen put up with it,
but said as she was leaving, "Tomorrow you have to start
work."

When the girl was alone again, she was at her wits'
end, and in her sorrow she went over to the window.
She saw three women coming. The first had a broad
splayfoot, the second had such a big lower lip that it
hung down below her chin, and the third had a splayed
thumb. They stopped under the window, looked up, and
asked the girl what was troubling her. She told them her
predicament, and they offered her their help and said,
"If you will invite us to the wedding and won't be
ashamed of us and will say that we're your aunts and
also let us sit at your table, we'll spin the flax for you,
and it won't take long."

"With all my heart," she answered. "Please come in
and start to work right away."

Then she let the three strange women in and cleared
a space in the first room, where they sat down and
began spinning. The first pulled out the thread and
pushed the treadle; the second moistened the thread; the
third twisted it and rapped the table with her finger, and

every time she rapped, a reel of yarn dropped on the floor, as finely spun as could be.

The girl concealed the three spinners from the queen and showed her the quantity of spun yarn every time she came so that the queen couldn't praise her enough. When the first room was empty, they started on the second, and finally on the third, and that too was soon cleared. Then the three women took their leave and said to the girl, "Don't forget what you promised us. It will make your fortune."

When the girl showed the queen the empty rooms and the huge pile of yarn, the queen arranged for the wed-

ding. The bridegroom was glad that he was getting such a skillful and diligent wife, and he praised her to the skies.

"I have three aunts," said the girl, "and because they have been very kind to me, I wouldn't like to forget them in my good fortune. Please let me invite them to the wedding and let them sit at the table with me."

The queen and the bridegroom said, "Why shouldn't we allow it?"

When the feast began, the three old maids came in

dressed in outlandish clothes, and the bride said, "Welcome, my dear aunts."

"Oh," said the bridegroom, "how do you come to have such hideous kinsfolk?" Then he went up to the one with the broad splayfoot and asked, "How did you get such a splayed foot?"

"From treadling," she answered, "from treadling."

The bridegroom went up to the second and said, "How did you get your hanging lip?"

"From licking the thread," she answered, "from licking the thread."

Then he asked the third, "How did you get your splayed thumb?"

"From twisting the thread," she answered, "from twisting the thread."

At this the king's son became afraid and said, "In that case my lovely bride shall never again touch a spinning wheel."

And so she was done with the nasty spinning.

HANSEL AND GRETEL

A t the edge of a great forest lived a poor woodcutter with his wife and two children—a boy called Hansel and a girl called Gretel. He had little enough for them to eat, and once when there was a great famine in the land, he could not even keep on providing their daily bread. One night as he lay in bed brooding and tossing and turning from care, he sighed and said to his wife, "What will become of us? How are we going to feed our children, now that we no longer have enough for ourselves?"

"Do you know what, husband?" his wife answered. "Tomorrow let us take the children to the wildest part of the forest. There we will build a fire and give each of them one more little piece of bread. Then we will go about our work and leave them alone. They won't find the way home, and we'll be rid of them."

"No, wife," said the husband. "I will not do such a thing. How could I find it in my heart to abandon my children in the forest? The wild beasts would soon come and tear them to pieces."

"Oh, you fool," she said, "then all four of us will die of hunger: you might as well start smoothing the boards for our coffins." And she gave him no peace until he agreed.

"All the same, I pity the poor children," he said.

The children, too, had not been able to sleep for hunger and had overheard what their stepmother said to their father. Gretel shed bitter tears and said to Hansel, "Now it's all over with us."

"Never mind, Gretel," said Hansel, "don't grieve. I'll find some way to save us."

When the parents had gone to sleep, he got up, put on his little jacket, opened the bottom panel of the door, and stole outside. The moon was shining very brightly, and the pebbles in front of the house gleamed like so many silver pennies. Hansel bent down and stuffed as many as he could into the little pocket of his coat. Then he went back and said to Gretel, "Don't worry, dear sister, and sleep in peace. God will not forsake us." And he went back to bed.

At daybreak, even before the sun had risen, the woman was already up to wake the two children. "Get up, lazybones, we're going into the forest to fetch wood." Then she gave each of them a little piece of bread and said, "There's something for your noon meal, but don't eat it up before, because that's all you'll get." Gretel carried the bread under her apron because Hansel's pocket was full of pebbles. Then they all set out together into the forest.

After they had gone a little way, Hansel stopped and looked back at the house, and he did this again and again. His father said, "Hansel, what are you gaping at and why are you lagging behind? Pay attention and step along."

"Oh, Father," said Hansel, "I'm looking at my white kitten sitting on the roof to tell me good-bye."

"That's not your kitten, stupid," said the woman. "It's the morning sun shining on the chimney." But Hansel wasn't looking at the kitten—each time he had taken a shiny pebble out of his pocket and dropped it on the path.

When they got to the middle of the forest, the father said, "Now gather wood, children; I'm going to build a fire so you won't be cold." Hansel and Gretel gathered twigs, a whole pile of them. The twigs were kindled, and when the fire blazed up, the woman said, "Lie down now beside the fire, children, and rest. We're going into the forest to cut wood. When we're finished, we'll come back and get you."

Hansel and Gretel sat beside the fire, and at noon they ate their little pieces of bread. Hearing the blows of the ax, they thought that their father was close by. It wasn't the ax, though, but a branch he had tied to a dead tree, that the wind was blowing to and fro. After they had been sitting a very long time, the children's eyes closed from weariness, and they fell fast asleep.

When they woke at last, it was already pitch-black night. Gretel began to cry and said, "How shall we ever get out of the forest!"

But Hansel comforted her. "Wait a little while till the moon rises, and then we'll find the way all right." And when the moon had risen, Hansel took his little sister by the hand and followed the pebbles that glistened like newly minted silver pennies and pointed the way.

They walked all night and at daybreak reached their father's house. They knocked, and when the woman opened and saw that it was Hansel and Gretel, she said, "You bad children, why did you sleep so long in the forest—we thought you were never coming home." The father, however, was glad, because he repented in his heart that he had left his children all alone.

Soon harsh necessity closed in on them once more, and the children overheard the mother telling the father, "Everything has been eaten up again. There's half a loaf left, and when that's gone, we've reached the end of our rope. We have to get rid of the children. Let's take them deeper into the forest so that they can't find their way back. There's no other remedy."

It went sorely against the man's heart, and he thought, "Better to share one's last bite with one's children." But the woman refused to listen to a thing he said, scolded him, and reproached him. Whoever says "A" has to say "B," and because he had given way once, he had to give in again.

The children were still awake and had overheard the conversation. After the parents had gone to sleep, Hansel got up again and tried to go outside to collect pebbles as he had the time before, but the woman had locked the door and Hansel couldn't get out. But he consoled his little sister and said, "Don't cry, Gretel, and sleep in peace. God will surely help us."

Early in the morning the woman got the children out of bed. They received their little pieces of bread, but they were even smaller than the other time. On the way into the forest Hansel crumbled his bread in his pocket and stopped often to throw the crumbs on the ground. "Hansel, why are you standing there looking back?" said the father. "Come along."

"I'm looking back at my little pigeon sitting on the roof to tell me good-bye," answered Hansel.

"That's not your little pigeon, stupid," said the woman. "That's the morning sun shining on the chimney." Bit by bit, however, Hansel threw all the crumbs on the path.

The woman led the children still deeper into the forest, to a place where they had never been before. Once again they built a big fire, and the mother said, "Just stay here, children, and when you get tired, you may sleep a little. We're going into the forest to cut wood, and in the evening, when we've finished, we'll come and get you."

At noon Gretel shared her bread with Hansel, who had scattered his piece along the way. Then they went to sleep, and the evening passed, but no one came for the poor children. They didn't wake up until it was pitch-black night, and Hansel consoled his little sister and said, "Just wait, Gretel, until the moon rises—then we will be able to see the bread crumbs I scattered, and they'll show us the way home." When the moon rose, they set out, but they found no crumbs, for the many thousands of birds that fly over the fields and the forest had pecked them up.

Hansel said to Gretel, "We'll find the way all right," but they didn't find it. They walked all night and all the next day from morning until evening, but they did not find the way out of the forest, and they were very hungry because they had eaten nothing except for the few berries along the ground. When they were too tired to stand, they lay down under a tree and went to sleep.

Now it was already the third morning since they had left their father's house. They began walking, but they got deeper and deeper into the forest, and if help did not come soon, they would perish there.

At noon they saw a pretty snow-white bird perched on a branch, singing so beautifully that they stopped to listen. And when it finished, it fluttered its wings and flew ahead of them, and they followed it until they reached a little house.

The bird perched on the roof, and when they came closer, they saw that the little house was made of bread and covered with shingles made of cake, and the windows were made of clear sugar.

"Let's set to," said Hansel, "and have a good meal. I'm going to eat a piece of the roof, and you can start on the windows—they'll be sweet." Hansel reached up and broke off a bit of the roof to see what it would taste like, and Gretel stood nibbling at a windowpane.

Suddenly a shrill voice called out from inside:

> "Nibble, nibble, little mouse,
> Who is nibbling at my house?"

The children answered:

> "The wind on high,
> The child of the sky."

And they went right on eating without letting themselves be disturbed. Hansel, who liked the taste of the roof, tore off a large piece, and Gretel knocked out a round windowpane all in one piece and sat on the ground enjoying it.

All of a sudden the door opened, and an ancient woman, propping herself on a crutch, came creeping out. Hansel and Gretel were so terrified that they dropped everything. The old woman waggled her head and said, "Why, you dear children, who brought you here? Please come inside and stay with me; I won't do you any harm." She took them both by the hand and led them into her little house. A fine meal was set on the table—milk and sugared pancakes, apples and nuts. Next two beautiful little beds were made with clean white sheets, and Hansel and Gretel lay down on them and thought they were in Heaven.

But the old woman was only pretending to be so kind. She was a wicked witch who lay in wait for children, and the only reason she had built her little bread house was to lure them to her. Whenever she got one in her clutches, she killed it, cooked it, and ate it, and those were the days she celebrated. Witches have red eyes and are very nearsighted, but they have a keen sense of smell, like animals, and they know when human beings are approaching. When Hansel and Gretel came near her house, she gave a wicked laugh and said sarcastically, "Those two are mine. I won't let them escape from me."

She was already up early in the morning before the children were awake, and they were such a lovely sight asleep, with their round red cheeks, that she murmured to herself, "That will be a tasty morsel."

Then she seized Hansel with her wrinkled hand and carried him off to a little coop with a grated door and locked him in. He might scream as loud as he pleased—it didn't do him any good.

Then she went to Gretel, shook her awake, and cried, "Get up, lazybones, fetch water and cook something nice for your brother. He's outside in the coop, and he has to get fat. When he's fat, I'm going to eat him." Gretel began to cry bitterly, but it was all in vain. She had to do what the witch told her.

Now poor Hansel was served the best of everything, but Gretel got only crab shells. Every morning the witch crept out to the little coop and called out, "Hansel, put out your finger so I can feel whether you'll be fat soon."

But Hansel stuck out a little bone, and the old woman couldn't tell because of her bad eyesight and thought it was Hansel's finger. She was amazed that he didn't seem to get fat at all.

After four weeks passed and Hansel remained as skinny as ever, she lost patience and didn't want to wait any longer. "Hi there, Gretel!" she called to the girl. "Be quick and fetch water. I don't care whether Hansel is fat or skinny—tomorrow I'm going to slaughter him and eat him."

Oh, how the poor little sister grieved as she carried

the water, and how the tears rolled down her cheeks. "Dear God, please help us," she cried out. "If only the wild beasts in the forest had eaten us. Then at least we would have died together."

"Stop your blubbering," said the old woman. "Nothing is going to help you."

Early in the morning Gretel had to go out and hang up the kettle of water and light the fire. "Let's bake first," said the old woman. "I've already heated the oven and kneaded the dough." She pushed poor Gretel outside toward the oven—the flames were already shooting out of it.

"Crawl inside," said the witch, "and see if it's hot enough to put the bread in."

She meant to close the door as soon as Gretel was inside in order to roast her and eat her, too. But Gretel suspected what she had in mind and said, "I don't know how to do it—how do I get in?"

"Stupid goose," said the old woman, "the opening is big enough. See there, I could get in myself." She scrabbled up and put her head into the oven.

Gretel gave her a shove so that she tumbled all the way in, closed the iron door, and threw the bolt. Ugh! How hideously she screamed. But Gretel ran off, and the wicked witch burned to death miserably.

Gretel ran straight as an arrow to Hansel, opened the little coop, and cried, "Hansel, we're saved! The old witch is dead." Hansel hopped out like a bird out of the cage when someone opens the door. How happy they were, how they fell on each other's neck, skipped around, and kissed! And now that there was nothing to be afraid of, they went into the witch's house, where there were boxes full of pearls and diamonds in every nook and corner.

"These are better than pebbles," said Hansel, and put as many as he could into his pockets, and Gretel said, "I'll take some home, too," and she filled her apron. "And now let's go," said Hansel, "so that we get out of this haunted forest."

When they had walked for a few hours, they reached a wide stream. "We can't get across," said Hansel. "I don't see any plank or bridge."

"And there's no little ferryboat either," answered Gretel, "but look at the white duck swimming there. If I ask her, she'll help us to get across." And she called:

"Little duck, little duck,
Here stand Hansel and Gretel.
No plank, no bridge to get across.
On your white back please carry us."

The little duck swam over, and Hansel got on and asked his little sister to join him. "No," answered Gretel, "that would be too heavy for the little duck. Let it take us over one at a time."

The helpful little animal did it, and when they were safely across and had gone on a little way farther, the forest became more and more familiar, and finally they saw their father's house from a distance. Then they started to run, rushed into the room, and threw their arms around their father's neck.

The man had not spent a happy moment since leaving the children in the forest, and the woman had died.

Gretel emptied her apron so that the pearls and diamonds skipped around the room, and Hansel threw down one handful after another from his pocket. Now all their worries were over, and they lived together in perfect happiness.

My tale is done—see the mouse run. Whoever catches it can make himself a great big fur cap out of it.

THE STRAW,
THE COAL,
AND THE BEAN

I n a village there lived a poor old woman who had gathered a dish of beans and was about to cook them. So she prepared a fire on her hearth, and to make it burn faster she kindled it with a handful of straw. As she was pouring the beans into the pot, one of them got away from her unnoticed and landed beside a straw. Soon a glowing coal hopped down from the hearth and joined them.

The straw began and said, "My dear friends, where did you come from?"

The coal answered, "I had the good fortune to escape the fire, and if I hadn't pushed myself forward, it would have meant certain death."

The bean said, "I also got away with a whole skin, but if the old woman had gotten me into the pot, I would have been mercilessly cooked into a mash along with my fellows."

"Would my fate have been any better?" said the straw. "The old woman let all of my brothers go up in

fire and smoke. She seized sixty at one time and took their lives. Fortunately I slipped between her fingers."

"What shall we do now?" said the coal.

"I think," answered the bean, "since we escaped death through such lucky chance, we should stay together as loyal companions, and in order to avoid some new catastrophe here, emigrate to a foreign country."

The other two liked the proposal, and they set out together. However, they soon reached a little brook, and since there was no bridge or plank, they didn't know how to get across.

The straw thought of a good plan and said, "I will stretch myself straight across, and you can use me as a bridge."

And so the straw stretched itself from one bank to the other, and the coal, which was by nature hot-headed, skipped out onto the new bridge quite boldly. But when it got to the middle and heard the roar of the water below, it got scared: it stopped in its tracks and didn't dare take another step.

However, the straw started to burn, broke in two, and fell into the brook. The coal slid after it, hissed as it fell into the water, and gave up the ghost.

The bean, which had cautiously stayed behind on the bank, had to laugh at the affair, couldn't stop, and finally laughed so hard that it split.

Now it too would have been done for if by good fortune a journeyman tailor had not been resting on the bank. Because he had a kind heart, he got out his needle and thread and sewed the bean together.

The bean thanked him most graciously. However, the tailor used black thread, and since that day all beans have had a black seam.

THE FISHERMAN
AND HIS WIFE

O nce upon a time there were a fisherman and his wife living together in a shack beside the sea, and the fisherman went every day to fish, and he fished and he fished. That's how he happened to be sitting once beside his line looking into the clear water, and he sat and he sat. Suddenly the line sank down, deep down, and when he pulled it in, he hauled out a big flounder.

The flounder said to him, "Listen, fisherman, I beg you, let me live. I'm not a real flounder; I'm an enchanted prince. What good would it do you to kill me? I wouldn't taste right to you anyway. Throw me back in the water and let me swim."

"Well, now," said the man, "you don't have to make a long speech about it. I guess I'd have thrown back a talking flounder anyhow." With that he put it back into the clear water, and the flounder dived down, leaving a long trail of blood. And the fisherman got up and went back to his wife in the shack.

"Husband," said the wife, "didn't you catch anything today?"

"No," said the man, "I caught a flounder that said it was an enchanted prince, so I threw it back."

"Didn't you make a wish?" said the wife.

"No," said the man. "What should I wish for?"

"Oh," said the wife, "it's not nice living in a shack all the time—it smells and it's so nasty. You could have wished for a little cottage. Just go back and call it: tell it we'd like to have a little cottage. It'll surely do that."

"Oh," said the man, "what's the use of going back there again?"

"Pooh," said the wife, "didn't you catch it and throw it back? It'll surely do it. Go right now." The man still didn't really want to, but he didn't want to quarrel with his wife either, and he went down to the sea.

When he got there, the sea was all green and yellow and not nearly so clear. He stood there and said:

> "Mannikin, mannikin, Dimpy, Dee,
> Flounder, flounder, in the sea,
> My old woman Ilsebill
> Has a wish against my will."

Then the flounder came swimming up and said, "Well, what does she want?"

"Oh," said the man, "I did catch you, you know, and now my wife says I should have made a wish. She doesn't want to live in a shack anymore. She wants to have a cottage."

"Just go back," said the flounder. "She already has it."

Then the man went home, and his wife was no longer sitting in the shack. A little cottage was standing there, and his wife was sitting on a bench in front of the door. She took him by the hand and said to him, "Come on inside. Look, isn't this a lot better?"

Then they went in, and inside the cottage was a little entryway and a lovely little parlor and a bedroom with a bed for them and a kitchen and pantry, and all the utensils that belong there, tinware and brass, the best of everything, hanging up as neat as could be. In the rear there was a little yard with chickens and ducks, and a little garden with fruit and vegetables. "See," said the wife, "isn't that nice?"

"Yes," said the man. "Let's keep it that way. Now we'll lead an easy life."

"We'll see about that," said the wife. And then they had a bite to eat and went to bed.

Thus it went for a week or two until the wife said, "Listen, husband, the cottage is really too small, and the yard and the garden are so tiny. The flounder could

just as well have given us a bigger house. I'd rather live
in a big stone castle."

"Oh, wife," said the man, "the cottage is good enough.
What do we want to live in a castle for?"

"Pooh," said the woman, "just you go back. The
flounder can still do it."

"No, wife," said the man. "The flounder has already
given us a cottage. I don't want to go back—it might
make the flounder angry."

"Just go," said the wife. "It's no trouble for it, and
it'll be glad to do it. You just go there." The man's
heart was very heavy, and he didn't want to. He said to
himself, "It's not right," but he went anyway.

When he got to the shore, the water was all purple
and dark blue and murky and not nearly so green and
yellow, but it was still calm. He stood there and said:

> "Mannikin, mannikin, Dimpy, Dee,
> Flounder, flounder, in the sea,
> My old woman Ilsebill
> Has a wish against my will."

"Well, what does she want?" said the flounder.

"Oh," said the man very uncomfortably, "she wants
to live in a big stone castle."

"Just go back. She's standing in front of the door,"
said the flounder.

Then the man went back and thought he was going
home, but when he got there, there stood a big stone
palace, and his wife was standing on the stairway about
to go in. Then she took him by the hand and said,
"Come on inside."

So he went in with her, and inside the castle there
was a great entrance hall paved with marble; and there
were lots of servants who threw open the big doors; and
the walls were all bright and hung with beautiful tapes-
tries; and in the rooms all the chairs and tables were of
gold; and crystal chandeliers hung from the ceilings;
and every room and chamber was carpeted; and the
tables looked as if they were going to collapse under
all the food and the best wines. Behind the house there
was a big courtyard with stables and cow sheds and

the finest coaches; and there was a big, beautiful garden with the loveliest flowers and splendid fruit trees, and a park about half a mile long with stags and roe and hares and everything one could wish for.

"Well," said the wife, "isn't that lovely?"

"Oh yes," said the man. "Let's keep it that way. From now on let's live in the beautiful castle and be content."

"We'll see about that," said the wife. "Let's sleep on it." With that they went to bed.

The next morning the wife was the first to wake up, just at daybreak, and from the bed she could see the wonderful countryside spread out before her. The man was still stretching, so she poked him in the ribs with her elbow and said, "Husband, get up and take a look out the window. See, couldn't we become king over all that land? Go back to the flounder—we want to be king."

"Oh, wife," said the man. "What do you want to be king for? I don't want to be king."

"Well," said the wife, "if you don't want to be king, I'll be king."

"Oh, wife," said the man. "What do you want to be king for? I don't want to tell it that."

"Why not?" said the wife. "Go straight to it—I must be king."

Then the man went back, greatly embarrassed that his wife wanted to be king. "It isn't right, it isn't right," the man thought. He didn't want to go, but finally he did.

And when he got to the shore, the sea was all dark gray, and the water boiled up from below and gave off a foul stench. He stood there and said:

> "Mannikin, mannikin, Dimpy, Dee,
> Flounder, flounder, in the sea,
> My old woman Ilsebill
> Has a wish against my will."

"Well, what does she want?" said the flounder.

"Oh," said the man, "she wants to be king."

"Just go back," said the flounder. "She already is."

Then the man went back, and when he came near the palace, it had become much bigger, with a big, splendidly

decorated tower; and a sentry was standing in front of
the door; and there were lots of soldiers and drums and
trumpets; and when he came inside, everything was
made of pure marble with gold; and there were velvet
covers with big gold tassels. Then the doors opened upon
the room where the whole court was assembled; his wife
was sitting high on a throne of gold and diamond; and
she had on a big gold crown and was holding a scepter
of solid gold and jewels; on either side of her six ladies-
in-waiting were lined up, each one a head shorter than
the next.

He stood there and said, "Well, wife, are you king
now?"

"Yes," said his wife, "now I'm king."

He stood there looking at her, and after looking at
her awhile that way, he said, "Oh, wife, how grand it
is, your being king! And now we won't wish for anything
more."

"No, husband," said the wife, and she was terribly
restless, "I'm already tired of this. I can't stand it anymore. Go back to the flounder. I'm king—now I must
be emperor too."

"Oh, wife," said the man, "what do you want to be
emperor for?"

"Husband," she said, "go to the flounder. I want to
be emperor."

"Oh, wife," said the man, "it can't make you emperor.
I don't want to tell the flounder that. There's only one
emperor in the empire. The flounder can't make you
emperor—and if it can't, it can't."

"What," said the wife, "I'm king, and you're my husband. Will you go there this instant! Go immediately—
if it can make a king, it can make an emperor too. I
want to be emperor. Go right away."

So he had to go. However, on the way there he was
very much afraid, and as he was going along he thought
to himself, "No good can come of it. Emperor—that's
too much. The flounder will get sick of it at last."

With that he got to the shore, and the sea was still
all black and murky, and began to boil up from below
so that it made bubbles, and a stiff gale blew over it,

churning it up. And the man shuddered. He stood there and said:

> "Mannikin, mannikin, Dimpy, Dee,
> Flounder, flounder, in the sea,
> My old woman Ilsebill
> Has a wish against my will."

"Well, what does she want?" said the flounder.

"Oh, flounder," he said, "my wife wants to be emperor."

"Just go back," said the flounder. "She already is."

Then the man went back, and when he got there, the whole castle was of polished marble with alabaster statues and gold ornaments; soldiers were marching up and down in front of the door blowing trumpets and beating drums and kettle drums; inside, barons, counts, and dukes were wandering around as servants; and they opened the doors for him, which were made entirely of gold. And as he entered, there was his wife sitting on a throne made out of one solid piece of gold; and it was about two miles high; and she had on a great gold crown about three yards high set with diamonds and rubies; in one hand she was holding the scepter and in the other the imperial orb; and on either side of her stood the retainers in two rows, each one smaller than the next, from the biggest giant, who was about two miles tall, to the littlest dwarf, who was as tall as my little finger. And in front of her stood a lot of princes and dukes.

The man stood there among them and said, "Wife, are you emperor?"

"Yes," she said, "I'm emperor."

Then he stood looking at her, and after looking at her awhile, he said, "Oh, wife, how grand it is, your being emperor."

"Husband," she said, "why are you standing there? Now that I'm emperor, I want to be pope too. Go back to the flounder."

"Oh, wife," said the man, "what more do you want? You can't be pope. There's only one pope in Christendom—it certainly can't make you that."

"Husband," she said, "I want to be pope. Go back right away—I've got to be pope this very day."

"No, wife," said the man, "I don't want to tell it that. No good can come of it. That's too much. The flounder can't make you pope."

"What rubbish, husband!" said the wife. "If it can make an emperor, it can make a pope too. Go back quickly. I'm emperor and you're my husband—I'm telling you to go."

Then he was afraid and went back, but he was ready to faint, and he was shivering and trembling, and his knees and his calves were shaking. A tremendous gale was blowing over the land, and the clouds were flying as it grew dark. The leaves were blown from the trees, and the water roared as though it were boiling and pounded the shore. In the distance he saw ships firing distress signals and dancing and tossing on the waves. However, there was still a bit of blue in the middle of the sky, but the horizon had turned a somber red as when a bad storm is brewing. He approached very timidly in his fright and stood there and said:

> "Mannikin, mannikin, Dimpy, Dee,
> Flounder, flounder, in the sea,
> My old woman Ilsebill
> Has a wish against my will."

"Well, what does she want now?" said the flounder.

"Oh," said the man, "she wants to be pope."

"Just go back. She already is," said the flounder.

Then he went back, and when he got there, there was a great church surrounded by many palaces. He pushed his way through the crowd. Inside all was lighted with thousands upon thousands of candles; and his wife was clothed entirely in gold and was sitting upon a throne that was a lot bigger still; and she had on three gold crowns; and she was all surrounded by prelates; and on either side of her stood rows of candles, the largest as tall and as thick as the biggest tower down to the tiniest candle stump; and all the emperors and kings were down on their knees in front of her, kissing her slipper.

"Wife," said the man, staring at her, "are you pope now?"

"Yes," she said, "I'm pope."

He stood there staring at her, and it was like looking into the bright sun. When he had looked at her like that for a while, he said, "Oh, wife, how grand it is, your being pope!"

But she was sitting as stiff as a ramrod, without moving or stirring.

Then he said, "Wife, now be satisfied. Now that you're pope, you can't become anything higher."

"I'll think about that," said the wife. With that they both went to bed, but her greed didn't let her sleep; she kept thinking about what she still wanted to be.

The man had a good night's sleep, for he had done a lot of running that day, but his wife simply couldn't go to sleep and tossed and turned all night, thinking all the time of what she might still be, and she just couldn't think of anything higher. Now the sun was about to rise, and when she saw the dawn, she sat up in bed to look at it, and when she saw the rising sun through the window, she thought, "Ha! couldn't I, too, make the sun and moon rise?"

"Husband," she said, and poked him in the ribs with her elbow, "wake up. Go back to the flounder—I want to be God Almighty."

The man was still asleep, but he got such a shock that he fell out of bed. He thought he hadn't heard right and rubbed his eyes and said, "Oh, wife, what did you say?"

"Husband," she said, "if I can't make the sun and moon rise and if I'm forced to look on when the sun and moon are rising—I won't be able to stand it, and I won't have a quiet moment unless I can make them rise myself." Then she gave him such an awful look that he shuddered. "Go back right away. I want to be God Almighty."

"Oh, wife," said the man, falling on his knees in front of her, "the flounder can't do it. He can make an emperor and a pope. I beg you, control yourself and stay pope."

Then she flew into a rage, and her hair streamed

wildly around her head. She tore open her bodice, gave him a kick, and screamed, "I can't bear it, I can't bear it any longer—will you get started!" Then he put on his trousers and ran off like a madman.

Outside, however, the storm was blowing so that he could hardly keep on his feet. Houses and trees were being blown over, the mountains were trembling, and boulders were rolling down the cliffs into the sea. The sky was as black as pitch, the thunder rolled and the lightning flashed, and the sea rose up in black waves as high as church steeples and mountains, and each had a white crest of foam at the top. He shouted without being able to hear his own words:

> "Mannikin, mannikin, Dimpy, Dee,
> Flounder, flounder, in the sea,
> My old woman Ilsebill
> Has a wish against my will."

"Well, what does she want?" said the flounder.

"Oh," he said, "she wants to be God Almighty."

"Just go home. She's already there in the shack."

And that's where the two of them are still sitting to this very day.

THE BRAVE
LITTLE TAILOR

O ne summer morning a little tailor was sitting on his work table by the window, feeling in high spirits and sewing with all his might. A farm woman came down the street calling out, "Good jam for sale! Good jam for sale!" The sound was music to the little tailor's ears, and he stuck his puny head out of the window and shouted, "Up here, my good woman. Here's the place to get rid of your wares."

With her heavy basket the woman walked up the three flights of stairs to the tailor's, and he made her unpack every single one of her jars. He inspected them all, picked them up, sniffed them, and finally said, "This jam seems all right to me. Measure me out three ounces, my good woman, and if it come to a quarter of a pound, I shan't be particular." The woman, who had hoped to make a good sale, gave him what he asked for but went away angry and grumbling.

"Well, God bless the jam," cried the little tailor, "and may it give me strength and energy." He fetched the bread out of the cupboard, cut a whole slice from the loaf, and spread it with jam. "That won't taste bad," he said, "but before biting into it, I'll finish this jacket." He laid the bread aside, kept on sewing, and out of sheer exuberance made bigger and bigger stitches.

Meanwhile, the odor of the sweet jam rose up along the wall where great numbers of flies were sitting. It attracted them and brought them down in swarms.

"Hey there, who invited you?" said the little tailor, and drove off the unbidden guests. But the flies, who couldn't understand English, wouldn't be put off and kept coming back in an ever-increasing company. At last it got the tailor's goat, as the saying goes. He reached into his tailor's hell * for a piece of cloth. "Just wait, I'll give it to you!" And he brought the cloth down on top of them unmercifully. When he pulled it away and counted, at least seven were lying dead before him with their toes turned up.

"Is that the kind of fellow I am?" he said, and he had to admire his own courage. "The whole town shall know about it." And the little tailor hastily cut out a belt, sewed it together, and stitched on it in large letters: "SEVEN AT ONE BLOW!" "The town, pooh!" he continued. "Let the whole world know it!" And his heart bobbed up and down for joy like a lamb's tail.

The tailor fastened the belt around his waist, intending to go out into the world because he considered

---

* A place under a tailor's worktable where leftover shreds and pieces of material are kept.

the workshop too small to contain his courage. Before setting off, he looked around the house to see if there wasn't anything for him to take along, but he found nothing but an old cheese that he put in his pocket. Before the gate he noticed a bird caught in the shrubbery, and it was obliged to join the cheese.

Then he marched bravely down the road, and since he was light and nimble, he didn't get tired.

The road went up a mountain, and when he got to the highest peak, an enormous giant was sitting there looking around placidly. The little tailor marched up to him boldly and said, "Good morning, comrade, you're sitting there gazing out into the great big world, aren't you? I'm just on my way there to try my luck. Would you like to come along?"

The giant looked at the tailor contemptuously and said, "You urchin! You miserable creature!"

"Really?" answered the little tailor. He unbuttoned his coat and showed the giant the belt. "There you can read what a man I am."

The giant read: "SEVEN AT ONE BLOW." He thought it meant people whom the tailor had killed, and he conceived a bit of respect for the little fellow. But first he wanted to test him, so he picked up a stone and squeezed it so that the water oozed out. "Let's see you do that," said the giant, "if you're so strong."

"Is that all?" said the little tailor. "That's child's play for someone like me." He reached into his pocket, took out the soft cheese, and squeezed it so that the whey ran out. "That was more like it, wasn't it?" he said.

The giant didn't know what to say and couldn't believe the little man had it in him. Then the giant picked up a stone and threw it up so high that the eye could hardly follow it. "Well, you runt, let's see you do that."

"Nice throw," said the tailor, "but the stone did come back to earth. I'll throw one that won't come back at all." He reached into his pocket, took the bird, and threw it into the air. The bird, glad to be free, soared up, flew off, and didn't return. "How did you like that little trick, comrade?" asked the tailor.

"You've got a good arm," said the giant, "but now let's see if you're able to carry a decent load." He led the little tailor to a huge oak which had been cut down and said, "If you're strong enough, help me carry this tree out of the forest."

"Gladly," answered the little man. "Just take the trunk on your shoulder. I'll lift and carry the branches and twigs, since that's the heaviest part."

The giant took the trunk across his shoulder, but the tailor sat down on a branch, and the giant, who couldn't see behind him, had to carry the whole tree and the little tailor besides. The latter, at the rear, was cheerful and gay, whistling the tune "Three tailors were riding through the gate," as though carrying trees were child's play. The giant, after lugging the heavy load for a little way, couldn't keep it up, and cried, "Look out, I have to drop the tree!"

The tailor hopped down nimbly, put his arms around the tree as though he'd been carrying it, and said to the giant, "You're such a big fellow, and you can't even carry this tree."

They went on together, and as they came past a cherry tree, the giant took hold of the top where the ripest fruit was hanging, bent it down, put it in the tailor's hand, and told him to eat. The tailor was much too weak to hold on to the tree, and when the giant let go, the tree sprang back up and the little tailor was catapulted through the air. When he came down again unhurt, the giant said, "What's the trouble? Aren't you strong enough to hold on to this feeble twig?"

"It's not because I lack the strength," the tailor answered. "Do you think that would be difficult for one who felled seven with one blow? I jumped over the tree because the hunters down there are firing into the thicket. Let's see you jump if you can."

The giant tried but couldn't get over the tree. He got caught in the branches instead, and so once again the little tailor had the best of it.

The giant said, "Since you're such a brave fellow, come along to our cave and spend the night with us." The tailor agreed and followed him. When they got to the cave, several other giants were sitting by the fire, each holding a roasted sheep in his hand and eating it. The little tailor looked around and thought, "This is certainly grander than my workshop."

The giant showed him a bed and told him to climb in and get a good night's sleep. But the bed was too big for the little tailor, so he didn't get in but crawled into a corner instead. When it got to be midnight and the giant felt sure that the tailor was asleep, he got up, took a big iron bar, and split the bed with one blow, thinking that he had finished off that grasshopper.

As soon as it was morning, the giants went into the forest, having forgotten all about the little tailor, when suddenly there he came striding along as bold and merry as you please. The giants were frightened, and fearing that he would kill them all, fled in haste.

The little tailor traveled on, always following his pointed nose. After he had wandered for a long time, he came to the courtyard of a king's palace, and because he was tired, he lay down in the grass and went to sleep. As he was lying there, people came, examined him all over, and read on the belt: "SEVEN AT ONE BLOW."

"Oh," they said, "why has this great warrior come here in time of peace? This must be a powerful lord."

They went to tell the king and said that if war were to break out, this would be an important and valuable man, who should at no cost be permitted to go away. The advice pleased the king, and he sent one of his courtiers to the little tailor to offer him a military post as soon as he should wake up.

The messenger remained standing at the sleeper's side until the latter began stretching his limbs and opened his eyes, and then the man stated his errand. "That's exactly what I came for," was the answer. "I'm ready to enter the king's service." And so he was received with honors, and a special apartment was assigned to him.

The soldiery, however, had no use for the little tailor and wished him a thousand miles away. "What will happen," they said to each other, "if we quarrel with him and he starts to fight? Seven will fall at each blow. Our sort can't compete against that." So they made a resolve, went in a body to the king, and asked for their discharge. "We're not made of the stuff it takes to hold out against someone who kills seven at one blow."

The king was sorry that he was going to lose all of his trusty servants for the sake of one man. He wished that he had never set eyes on him and would gladly have been rid of him. But he was afraid to discharge the tailor because he feared that he might kill him and all his court and take over the throne. He thought about it for a long time and finally hit on a plan.

He sent to the tailor to tell him that he had an offer to make him because he was such a great warrior. Two giants were living in one of the forests of his country, creating havoc by robbing, murdering, burning and devastating the land. Nobody could come near them without risking his life. If he overcame and killed these two giants, he should have the king's only daughter for his wife and half the kingdom for dowry. Besides, a hundred horsemen should go along to stand by him.

"That would be something for a man like me," thought the little tailor. "One isn't offered a beautiful king's daughter and half a kingdom every day."

"Yes, indeed," he answered, "I'll take care of those giants, and I won't need a hundred horsemen for that.

One who fells seven at one blow doesn't need to be afraid of two."

The little tailor set out with the hundred horsemen following him. When he got to the edge of the forest,

he told his escort, "Just stop here—I'll finish off the giants alone." Then he ran into the forest and looked around to the right and left. After a little while he saw both giants: they were lying asleep under a tree and snoring so that the branches rose and fell.

The little tailor, wasting no time, filled his pockets with stones and climbed the tree. Halfway up he slid out on a branch until he was sitting directly over the sleepers, and began dropping stones, one after another, on the chest of one giant. For a long time the giant didn't feel anything, but finally he woke up, poked his companion, and said, "What are you hitting me for?"

"You're dreaming," said the other. "I'm not hitting you."

They went back to sleep, and the tailor dropped a stone on the second. "What's the meaning of this?" cried the second. "Why are you throwing things at me?"

"I'm not throwing anything at you," answered the first, grumbling. They argued for a while, but because they were tired they didn't make an issue out of it, and their eyes fell shut again.

The little tailor began the game all over again, picked out the biggest stone, and threw it as hard as he could against the chest of the first giant.

"This is too much!" he cried, jumped up like a madman, and shoved his companion against the tree so that it trembled. The other paid him back in the same coin, and they got into such a rage that they uprooted trees and battered away at each other until finally they both fell down dead at the same instant.

Now the little tailor scrambled down. "It's certainly lucky," he said, "that they didn't uproot the tree I was sitting on, or I would have had to spring to another one like a squirrel. But I'm the flighty type!"

He drew his sword and gave each one a few hearty stabs in the chest. Then he went out to the horsemen and said, "The work is done. I finished off the two of them, but it was a struggle. They tore up trees in desperation in order to defend themselves, but all that does no good against someone like me who kills seven at one blow."

"Weren't you wounded?" asked the horsemen.

"It's all right," answered the tailor. "They didn't harm a hair on my head."

The horsemen wouldn't believe him and rode into the forest: there they found the giants bathed in their own blood with the uprooted trees lying all around.

The little tailor demanded the promised reward from

the king, but the latter regretted his promise and pondered again how he might get rid of the hero. "Before you get my daughter and half of the kingdom," he said, "you have to perform one more heroic deed. A unicorn is loose in the forest causing great damage—you have to catch it first."

"A unicorn scares me even less than two giants. Seven at one blow—that's my job."

He took a rope and an ax and went into the forest, once again ordering his escort to wait outside. He didn't have to search long. The unicorn soon came running and dashed straight at the little tailor as though it meant to spear him without any trouble at all.

"Easy, easy," he said, "you won't get me that fast." He stood waiting until the beast was nearly on top of him, then hopped nimbly behind the tree. The unicorn ran into the tree with all its might and rammed its horn so deep into the trunk that it didn't have strength enough to pull it back out. And so it was caught.

"Now I've caught my bird," said the tailor. He came out from behind the tree, first tied the rope around the unicorn's neck, then cut the horn out of the tree with the ax. When all was taken care of, he led the beast away and brought it to the king.

The king didn't want to make good his pledge and made a third demand. Before the wedding the tailor must catch a wild boar that was causing great damage in the forest. The huntsmen were to help him.

"Gladly," said the tailor, "that's child's play." He didn't take the huntsmen into the forest, and they were probably just as glad, for on several occasions the boar had given them such a welcome that they had no desire to lie in wait for it.

When the boar saw the tailor, it rushed at him, foaming at the mouth and gnashing its tusks, trying to knock him to the ground. But the light-footed hero sprang into a nearby chapel and out again by a high window in one leap. The boar had pursued him, but he ran around the outside and slammed the door on it. And so the raging beast, which was far too heavy and clumsy to jump out of the window, was caught.

The little tailor called the huntsmen to the spot to

see the prisoner with their own eyes. The hero, however, went to the king, who now, whether he liked it or not, had to keep his promise and give him his daughter and half the kingdom. Had he known that a tailor instead of a war hero was standing before him, he would have been even sorrier. And thus the wedding was celebrated with much pomp but little joy, and a tailor was transformed into a king.

After a time the young queen heard her husband talking in his sleep at night. "Fix that jacket, my lad, and patch those trousers, or I'll beat you over the ears with the yardstick." Then she realized what station the young gentleman had been born to, and the next morning she told her father to get rid of her husband who was no better than a tailor.

The king consoled her and said, "Leave the bedroom door open tonight. My servants will wait outside, and when he's asleep, they'll come in, tie him up, and put him on a ship that will carry him into the wide world."

The girl was satisfied, but the king's squire, who had overheard everything, was well disposed toward the young lord and reported the whole plot.

"We'll put a spoke in their wheel," said the little tailor.

At night he went to bed with his wife at the usual hour. When she thought that he had fallen asleep, she got up, opened the door, and lay down again.

The little tailor, who was only pretending to be asleep, began to cry out in a loud voice, "Fix that jacket, my lad, and patch those trousers, or I'll beat you over the ears with the yardstick! I killed seven at one blow, slew two giants and led off a unicorn, caught a wild boar, and I'm supposed to be afraid of those people outside the bedroom door!"

When they heard the tailor talking like that, a terrible fear came over them, and they ran as though the Wild Hunt * were after them, and none of them dared come near him again. And so the little tailor remained a king for the rest of his life.

* In Germanic legend, a band of ghosts condemned to ride wildly through the sky at night as if hunting.

CINDERELLA

The wife of a rich man fell sick, and when she felt that her end was near, she summoned her only daughter to her bedside and said, "Dear child, be devout and good, and the dear Lord will always stand by you, and I shall look down on you from Heaven and shall be near you." And then she closed her eyes and died.

The girl went out to her mother's grave every day and wept, and she remained devout and good. When winter came, the snow spread a white coverlet over the grave, and in the spring when the sun had removed it again, the man took another wife.

The woman brought two daughters into the house who were fair and beautiful of face but foul and black at heart. Now hard times began for the poor stepchild. "Are we going to let that stupid goose sit in the parlor with us?" they said. "Whoever wants to eat has to work: off to the kitchen with her." They took away her beautiful clothes, dressed her in an old gray smock, and gave her wooden shoes. "See how grand she looks, the proud princess," they cried, laughing, and they led her to the kitchen.

There she had to toil from morning till night. She had to get up before dawn, carry water, light the fire, cook, and wash. Besides that, her sisters tormented her in every way they could think of. They made fun of her and scattered peas and lentils into the ashes so that she had to sit there and pick them out again. At night, when she was worn out from work, she was not allowed to sleep in a bed but had to lie in the cinders beside the hearth. And so, because she always looked dusty and dirty, they called her Cinderella.

It happened one time that the father was going to the fair, and he asked the two stepdaughters what he should bring them. "Beautiful clothes," said the one. "Pearls and jewels," said the other.

"How about you, Cinderella?" he said. "What would you like?"

"Father, the first twig that brushes against your hat on your way home—break it off for me."

He bought beautiful clothes, pearls, and jewels for the stepdaughters, and on the way home, as he was riding through a green thicket, a twig of hazel brushed against him and knocked off his hat, so he broke it off and took it along. When he got home, he gave the stepdaughters what they had asked for, and he gave the hazel twig to Cinderella.

Cinderella thanked him and went to her mother's grave, and there she planted the twig. She wept so much that she watered it with her tears, and it grew into a beautiful tree.

Cinderella went there three times a day to weep and pray, and each time a little white bird came to the tree, and whenever she wished for anything, the little bird threw down what she had wished for.

Now it happened that the king proclaimed a feast that was to last three days and to which all the beautiful maidens in the land were invited so that his son might choose a bride. When the two stepdaughters heard that they had been invited, they were in high spirits, and called Cinderella and said, "Comb our hair, polish our shoes, and fasten our buckles—we're going to the feast at the king's castle."

Cinderella obeyed, but she cried because she too should have liked to go to the ball, and she asked her stepmother for permission.

"You, Cinderella," she said, "you're covered with dust and dirt, and you want to go to the feast! You have no proper clothes and no shoes, and you want to go dancing!"

But when Cinderella kept on pleading, she finally said, "There, I've scattered a dish of lentils into the ashes— if you can pick them out in two hours, you may come along."

The girl went out the back door into the garden and called, "Gentle doves, turtledoves, all you birds beneath the sky, come and help me sort out lentils:

> The good ones in the pot,
> The bad ones down the throat."

And two white doves came in the kitchen windows, and then the turtledoves, and finally all the birds beneath the sky came whirring and swarming and settled around the ashes. The doves nodded their heads and started to peck, peck, peck, peck, and the rest also started to peck, peck, peck, peck, and they put all the good grains into the bowl. In barely an hour they had finished, and they all flew away.

The girl carried the bowl to her stepmother, thinking happily that now she would be allowed to go to the feast. But the stepmother said, "No, Cinderella, you have no clothes, and you don't know how to dance: you'll only make everyone laugh at you." But when the girl burst into tears, she said, "If you can sort out two bowls of lentils from the ashes in one hour, then you may come along," thinking, "She'll never manage that."

When the woman had scattered two bowls of lentils into the ashes, Cinderella went out the back door into the garden and called, "Gentle doves, turtledoves, all you birds beneath the sky, come and help me sort out lentils:

> The good ones in the pot,
> The bad ones down the throat."

Then two white doves came in the kitchen windows, and then the turtledoves, and finally all the birds beneath the sky came in and settled around the ashes. And the doves nodded their heads and started to peck, peck, peck, peck, and the rest also started to peck, peck, peck, peck, and they put all the good grains into the bowls. And in less than a half hour they were finished, and they all flew out again.

The girl carried the bowls to her stepmother, happy because she thought that now she would be allowed to go to the feast. But the stepmother said, "It won't do you any good: you can't come along because you haven't any clothes and you don't know how to dance—we'd be ashamed of you." With that, she turned her back and hurried off with her two proud daughters.

Now when everyone had left, Cinderella went to her mother's grave and stood under the hazel tree and called:

> "Shake yourself, shake yourself, little tree,
> Throw gold and silver down on me."

Then the bird threw down a dress of silver and gold and slippers embroidered with silk and silver. Cinderella put on the dress as fast as she could and went to the feast.

Her sisters and stepmother didn't recognize her and thought that she must be a foreign princess, she looked so beautiful in the gold dress. Cinderella never entered their mind because they thought that she was sitting home in the dirt, picking lentils out of the ashes.

The king's son came to meet her, took her by the hand, and danced with her. He refused to dance with anyone else and never let go her hand. When anyone else came to ask her to dance, he said, "She's my partner."

She danced until evening, when she wanted to go home. But the king's son said, "I'll come along to escort you," for he wanted to find out where the beautiful girl came from. However, she slipped away from him and jumped into the dovecote.

The king's son waited there until her father came and then told him that the unknown girl had jumped into the dovecote. The old man thought, "What if it were Cinderella?" and he called for an ax and mattock in order to break open the dovecote. But there was no one inside.

When everyone got to the house, Cinderella in her dirty clothes was lying in the ashes, and a dim oil lamp was burning in the fireplace. For Cinderella had quickly jumped down from the other side of the dovecote and run to the hazel tree. There she had taken off the beautiful clothes and laid them on the grave, and the bird had taken them away. Then she had sat down among the ashes in her little gray smock.

The next day, when the feast began again, and her parents and stepsisters had gone, Cinderella went to the hazel tree and said:

> "Shake yourself, shake yourself, little tree,
> Throw gold and silver down on me."

The bird threw down a dress that was far more splendid than the first one. And when Cinderella appeared at the feast in this dress, everyone was amazed at her beauty. The king's son, who had been waiting for her to come, immediately took her by the hand and danced only with her. When anyone else came to ask her to dance, he said, "She's my partner."

When it was evening, she wanted to leave, and the king's son followed her in order to see what house she might enter. But she sprang away into the garden behind the house. A large and beautiful tree was standing there full of the most gorgeous pears, and she climbed into the branches as nimbly as a squirrel so that the king's son didn't know where she had disappeared to.

But he waited until her father came, and told him, "The unknown girl escaped from me, and I believe she jumped up into the pear tree."

The father thought, "What if it were Cinderella?" He had an ax brought and cut the tree down. But there was no one in it. And when everyone came into the kitchen, Cinderella was lying in the ashes as usual, for she had jumped down on the other side of the tree, taken the beautiful clothes back to the bird in the hazel tree, and put her gray smock back on.

On the third day, after the parents and sisters had gone, Cinderella went once more to her mother's grave and said to the tree:

> "Shake yourself, shake yourself, little tree,
> Throw gold and silver down on me."

This time the bird threw down a dress more sparkling and magnificent than the others, and the slippers were made of pure gold.

When she arrived at the feast dressed like that, everyone was speechless with wonder. The king's son danced only with her, and when anyone else asked her to dance, he said, "She's my partner."

When it was evening, Cinderella wanted to leave, and the king's son wanted to accompany her, but she ran away so fast that he couldn't keep up. However, the king's son had thought of a device and had had the whole stairway coated with pitch. As the girl ran down, her left slipper remained stuck. The king's son picked it up, and it was small and shapely and made entirely of gold.

The next morning he carried it to the man and said to him, "No one shall be my bride except the one whose foot this gold shoe fits."

The two sisters were glad because they had pretty feet. The older one took the shoe to the bedroom to try it on, and her mother was standing at her side. But her big toe wouldn't fit in, and the shoe was too small for her. Her mother handed her a knife and said, "Chop off your toe: when you're queen, you won't need to walk anymore."

The girl chopped off the toe, forced her foot into the shoe, suppressed the pain, and went out to the king's son. He took her up on his horse as his bride and rode off with her. But they had to pass by the grave where two doves were sitting on the hazel tree, calling:

> "Look you, look you,
> There's blood in the shoe,
> The shoe is too small.
> The true bride is waiting at home in her hall."

Then he looked at her foot and saw the blood oozing out. He turned his horse around and brought the false bride back home and said that she wasn't the right one —let the other sister try on the shoe.

The other sister went into the bedroom and got her toes in without trouble, but the heel was too big. Her mother gave her a knife and said, "Chop off a piece of your heel: when you're queen, you won't need to walk anymore."

The girl chopped off a piece of her heel, forced the

foot into the shoe, suppressed the pain, and went out
to the king's son. And he took her up on his horse as his
bride and rode off with her. As they passed by the hazel
tree, though, the two little doves were sitting on it, calling:

> "Look you, look you,
> There's blood in the shoe,
> The shoe is too small.
> The true bride is waiting at home in her hall."

He looked down at her foot and saw how the blood
was oozing out of the shoe and how the red had mounted

up on her white stockings. So he turned his horse around
and brought the false bride back home.

"That's not the right one either," he said. "Have you
no other daughter?"

"No," said the man, "except for a runty little Cinderella, the child of my dead wife—she couldn't possibly be
the bride."

The king's son told him to have her sent up, but the mother answered, "Oh no, she's much too dirty to be presentable." But he insisted on seeing her, and they had to call Cinderella.

First she washed her hands and her face. Then she went and curtsied before the king's son, who handed her the gold shoe. She sat down on a stool, stepped out of her heavy wooden shoe, and put her foot into the slipper, and it fit perfectly. And when she got up, the king's son looked at her face and recognized the beautiful girl who had danced with him. And he cried, "She is the true bride!"

The stepmother and the two sisters were frightened and turned pale with anger. But he took Cinderella up on his horse and rode off with her. When they passed the hazel tree, the two little doves called:

> "Look you, look you,
> There's no blood in the shoe,
> The shoe's not too small.
> The true bride is going home to your hall."

And when they had said it, they both came flying down and perched on Cinderella's shoulders, one on the right, the other on the left, and there they stayed.

When her wedding with the king's son was to be celebrated, the false sisters came to curry favor and to share her good fortune. As they were going to church with the bride and groom, the older one was on the right and the younger on the left, and the doves pecked out an eye from each. On the way out, the older one was on the left and the younger on the right, and the doves pecked out the other eyes. And so they were blind for the rest of their lives as punishment for their wickedness and treachery.

FRAU HOLLE

||||||||||||||||||||||||||||||||||||||||||||||||||||||||||||||||||||||||||||||||||

A widow had two daughters, one of whom was beautiful and hard-working, the other, ugly and lazy. But she liked the ugly and lazy one much better because she was her own daughter, and the other had to do all the work and serve as cinder girl. The poor girl had to sit every day on the street beside a well, and there she had to spin until her fingers bled.

Now it happened one day that the bobbin had become all bloody, so she reached down into the well to wash it off. The bobbin slipped out of her hand and fell in. She cried, ran to her stepmother, and told her about the accident. But the stepmother scolded her so harshly and was so merciless that she said, "Because you dropped the bobbin into the well, you have to bring it up again!"

Then the girl went back to the well and didn't know what to do. And in her terror she jumped into the well to get the bobbin. She lost consciousness, and when she woke up again, she was in a beautiful meadow in the sunshine among many thousands of flowers. She walked in the meadow until she came to an oven full of bread.

The bread called out, "Oh, take me out, take me out, or I'll burn up! I've been done for a long time!" Then the girl stepped up and pulled out the loaves one after another with a baker's shovel.

She went on, and next she came to a tree full of apples, which called out to her, "Oh, shake me, shake me! We apples are all ripe!"

Then she shook the tree so that the apples poured down as though it were raining, and she shook until not one remained on the tree. And when she had made a pile of them, she went on.

At last she came to a little house. An old woman was looking out, and because she had such big teeth, the girl was afraid and wanted to run away. But the old

woman called after her, "What are you afraid of, my child? Stay with me. If you do all the housework properly, you'll be well taken care of. Just be sure to do a good job making my featherbed and shake it thoroughly so that the feathers fly—that's what makes it snow on earth. I'm Frau Holle."

Because the old woman spoke so kindly, the girl took heart, consented, and entered her service. She did everything to the old woman's satisfaction and always shook out her bed so hard that the feathers flew like snowflakes. In return, she had a good life, never a harsh word, and good things to eat all day long.

When she had been with Frau Holle for a while, she became sad, and at first she herself didn't know what was the matter. At last she realized that she was homesick. In spite of the fact that she was a thousand times better off than at home, she still had a longing to go back. Finally she said to Frau Holle, "I have a longing for home, and no matter how well you treat me down here, I still want to go back up to my people."

Frau Holle said, "I'm pleased that you want to go back home, and because you've served me so faithfully, I'll take you up myself."

She took her by the hand and led her before a large gate. When the gate opened and the girl was standing directly under it, a shower of gold fell down, and all the gold stuck to her, so that she was completely covered by it. "That's your reward for working so hard," said Frau Holle, as she also gave her back the bobbin she had dropped into the well.

Then the gate closed and the girl found herself up in the world, not far from her mother's house. And when she came into the farmyard, the cock was sitting on the well and cried:

> "Cock-a-doodle-doo,
> Our golden girl is back home!"

She went in to her mother, and she and her sister welcomed her because she was covered with gold.

The girl told all that had happened to her, and when the mother heard how she had come by her great riches, she wanted her ugly and lazy daughter to have the same good fortune. She had to sit down by the well and spin, and in order to make the bobbin bloody she pricked her fingers and thrust her hand into a hedge of thorns. Then she threw the bobbin into the well and jumped after it.

Like her sister, she came to the same meadow and followed the same path. When she reached the oven, the bread called again, "Oh, take me out, take me out, or I'll burn up. I've been done for a long time." But the lazy girl answered, "Do you think I want to get myself dirty!" And she went her way.

Soon she came to the apple tree, which called, "Oh, shake me, shake me! We apples are all ripe!" But she answered, "You've got nerve! One of them might hit me on the head!" And she went her way.

When she reached Frau Holle's house, she wasn't afraid, because she had been told about her big teeth, and she agreed to serve her right away. The first day she forced herself to work hard and obeyed whenever Frau Holle gave her instructions, because she was thinking about all the gold that she would be given. But on the second day she already began to loaf, and on the third morning she didn't even want to get up. She also didn't make Frau Holle's bed the way she was supposed to, and didn't shake it hard enough to make the feathers fly.

Frau Holle soon got tired of that and gave her notice. The lazy girl was well satisfied and thought that now the gold shower would begin. Frau Holle led her to the gate. When she was standing under it, instead of gold, a great kettle of pitch was poured out. "That's the reward for your service," said Frau Holle, and shut the gate.

So the lazy girl came home all covered with pitch, and when the cock on the well saw her, he cried:

> "Cock-a-doodle-doo,
> Our dirty girl is back home!"

The pitch stuck fast to her and wouldn't come off as long as she lived.

LITTLE
RED RIDING HOOD

Once upon a time there was a sweet little girl. Everyone who so much as set eyes on her adored her, but her grandmother loved her most of all and couldn't think of enough things to give the child. Once she gave her a little hood made of red velvet, and because it was so becoming to her that she

would never wear any other, she was always called Little Red Riding Hood.

One day her mother said to her, "Come, Red Riding

Hood, here is a piece of cake and a bottle of wine: take them to your grandmother. She is feeble and sick, and they'll do her good. Start before it gets hot, and when you get outside, see that you go like a good little girl and don't stray from the path, or you'll fall down and break the bottle, and Grandmother won't get anything. And when you come into her bedroom, don't forget to say good morning, and don't peer into all the corners first."

"I promise to do everything right," Little Red Riding Hood said to her mother, and gave her her hand on it.

The grandmother, however, lived out in the forest a half hour from the village. Just as Red Riding Hood was entering the forest, she met the wolf. But Red Riding Hood didn't know what a wicked animal he was, and she wasn't afraid of him.

"Good morning, Red Riding Hood," he said.

"Thank you very much, wolf."

"Where are you off to so early, Red Riding Hood?"

"To Grandmother's."

"What are you carrying under your apron?"

"Cake and wine. Yesterday we baked, and Grandmother, who is sick and feeble, is to have something to do her good and help her get stronger."

"Where does your grandmother live, Red Riding Hood?"

"Another quarter of an hour farther into the forest," said Red Riding Hood. "Her house stands under the three big oaks with the hazel bushes beneath—surely you know where that is."

The wolf thought to himself, "A tender young thing who will make a juicy morsel. She'll taste even better than the old woman. I'll have to proceed cunningly to catch both of them." For a little while he walked along with Red Riding Hood, and he said, "Red Riding Hood, just look at the pretty flowers growing everywhere. Why aren't you looking around? I believe you aren't even listening to the lovely singing of the birds. Why, you're walking along as though you were on your way to school, and it's so delightful out here in the forest."

Red Riding Hood looked around, and when she saw the sunbeams dancing in the foliage and the pretty

but had glared at her in such an evil way: "If it hadn't been right out in the open, he would have eaten me up."

"Come," said the grandmother, "let's lock the door so he can't get in."

Soon after that the wolf knocked and cried, "Open the door, Grandmother, it's Red Riding Hood, bringing you some cake." But they kept quiet and didn't open the door.

Old grizzly-head sneaked several times around the house and finally jumped up on the roof to wait until Red Riding Hood would go home in the evening. Then he meant to creep after her and eat her in the dark.

But the grandmother guessed what was in his mind. There happened to be a big stone trough in front of the house. "Take a bucket, Red Riding Hood," she said to the child. "Yesterday I made sausage. Take the water it cooked in and empty it into the trough." Red Riding Hood carried water until the big trough was completely full.

The aroma of sausage was wafted up into the wolf's nose. He sniffed, peered down, and finally craned his neck until he lost his hold and began sliding. He slid off the roof straight into the big trough and drowned.

But Red Riding Hood went merrily home, and nobody tried to harm her.

THE BREMEN
TOWN MUSICIANS

A certain man owned a donkey that for many long years had cheerfully borne sacks of grain to the mill, but now his strength was giving out so that he became less and less fit for work. His master decided to save the cost of his fodder, but the donkey suspected

that the man was up to no good, ran away, and set out
on the road to Bremen; he thought that there he could
become a town musician.

After he had gone along for a little while, he found
a hunting dog lying across the path, panting like an exhausted runner. "Well, what are you panting like that
for, Hound Dog?" asked the donkey.

"Oh," sighed the dog, "because I'm old and get feebler
day by day and can't keep up with the hunt anymore,
my master wanted to get rid of me, so I took off. But
how am I going to earn my bread now?"

"Do you know what?" said the donkey. "I'm on my
way to Bremen to become a town musician. Come along,
and you too can take up the music business. I'll play the
guitar and you can beat the drums."

The dog liked the plan, and they went on together. It
wasn't long before they met a cat sitting at the roadside, making a face as gloomy as three rainy days. "Well,
what's rubbed you the wrong way, Whiskers?" said the
donkey.

"Who can be cheerful when he's about to get it in the
neck?" answered the cat. "Because I'm getting along in
years and my teeth are becoming blunt and I prefer
sitting behind the stove and purring to chasing after
mice, my mistress wanted to drown me. I managed to
get away all right, but now I'm at a loss—where shall I
go?"

"Come along with us to Bremen. You're a good sere-
nader and you can become a town musician there." The
cat thought this was a good idea and went along.

Next the three fugitives passed a farmyard where the
cock was sitting on the gate and crowing with all his
might. "You're crowing loud enough to split one's ear-
drums," said the donkey. "What are you up to?"

"I've just forecast fair weather," said the cock, "because it's the feast day of Our Lady, the day she washes
the little shirts of the Christ Child and hangs them out
to dry. But the mistress of the house has no mercy,
and because guests are coming for Sunday dinner tomorrow, she told the cook that she wants to eat me in the
stew. So tonight I'm supposed to get my head chopped
off. Now I'm crowing with all my might while I still can."

"Nonsense, Redhead," said the donkey. "Better come along with us—we're going to Bremen. No matter where you go, you can find something better than getting yourself killed. You've got a good voice, and when we make music together, it's bound to have style." The cock took the advice, and all four set off together.

But they couldn't reach Bremen in one day, and in the evening they came to a forest, where they decided to spend the night. The donkey and the dog lay down under a big tree. The cat and the cock got up into the branches, but the cock flew to the very top, where he felt more at home. Before he went to sleep, he looked around once again in all four directions. It seemed to him that he saw a little spark of light in the distance, and he called down to his companions that there must be a house nearby because a light was shining.

The donkey said, "We'll have to get up again and go there—these are poor accommodations." The dog observed that a few bones with some meat on them would do him good. So they set out in the direction of the light and soon saw it gleaming brighter, and it got bigger and bigger, until they came up to a brightly lit house, which belonged to a gang of robbers.

The donkey, because he was the tallest, went up to the window and looked in. "What do you see, Old Gray Nag?" asked the cock.

"What do I see?" answered the donkey. "A table spread with good food and drink, and the robbers are sitting there having a good time."

"That would be something for us," said the cock.

"Yes, indeed, I wish we were inside," said the donkey. Then the animals held a council to see how they might chase out the robbers, and at last they found a way. The donkey put his two front hooves on the windowsill, the dog jumped onto the donkey's back, the cat climbed on top of the dog, and finally the cock flew up and sat on the head of the cat. When they had done this, at a

signal they all began to make music together. The donkey brayed, the dog barked, the cat meowed, and the cock crowed. Then they plunged through the window into the room so that the panes rattled. The robbers jumped up at the ghastly noise. They were sure a ghost was coming in and fled into the forest in a panic. And now the companions sat down at the table, helped themselves with gusto to what was left, and ate as if they were going to starve for a month.

When the four performers had finished, they put out the light and looked for a place to sleep, each one where his kind would be most comfortable. The donkey stretched out on the manure pile, the dog behind the door, and the cat on the hearth beside the warm ashes, and the cock perched on the roof beam. And being tired after their long journey, they soon went to sleep.

After midnight the robbers saw from a distance that the light had gone out in the house and that everything seemed quiet. The captain said, "We were fools to let ourselves be scared off," and he ordered one of his men to go and investigate the house.

The man he sent found that all was quiet. He went into the kitchen to get a light, and mistaking the glowing, fiery eyes of the cat for live coals, he held a match to them. But the cat was not in a playful mood and sprang in his face, spitting and scratching. The man was terrified and ran to get out the back door, but the dog, who was lying there, jumped up and bit him on the leg, and as he ran through the yard past the manure pile, the donkey gave him a solid kick with his rear hoof, and the cock, who had been thoroughly aroused by the uproar, cried from the rafters: "Cock-a-doodle-doo."

The robber ran as fast as he could back to the captain and said, "Oh, there's a horrible witch in the house. She breathed in my face and scratched me with her long fingernails. There's a man with a knife standing by the door; he stabbed me in the leg. And there's a black monster lying in the yard; he started beating me with a club. And up on the roof, there sits the judge; he shouted, 'Bring the rascal to me!' So I got out of there."

From that time on, the robbers did not dare to enter the house, but the four Bremen town musicians liked it so much there that they decided never to leave.

And as for the person who just finished telling this story, his mouth is still watering.

THE SINGING BONE

‖‖‖

Once upon a time in a certain country there was great sorrow because of a wild boar which was devastating the farmers' fields, killing the cattle, and disemboweling men with its tusks. The king promised a large reward to anyone who would rid the country of this plague, but the beast was so big and strong that no one would venture near the forest in which it lived. Finally the king proclaimed that whoever caught or killed the wild boar should have his only daughter for a wife.

Now two brothers were living in that country, the sons of a poor man, and they volunteered to undertake the dangerous task. The oldest, who was cunning and clever, did so out of pride; the youngest, who was innocent and slow-witted, did so out of goodness of heart.

The king said, "In order to be sure of finding the beast, you must enter the forest from opposite directions." So the oldest entered from the west and the youngest from the east. After the youngest had gone a short way, he met a little man who was holding a black spear in his hand, who said, "I will give you this spear because your heart is innocent and good. With it you needn't be afraid to come near the boar—it can't hurt you."

He thanked the little man, laid the spear across his shoulder, and went forward unafraid. It wasn't long before he saw the beast, which rushed at him. But he held the spear in front of him, and in its blind fury the boar ran into it with such force that its heart was split in two. Then he lifted the monster on his shoulder and started home to bring it to the king.

As he came out on the other side of the forest, a

tavern stood at the entrance, where people were having a good time drinking and dancing. His older brother had turned in there, thinking the boar wouldn't run away from him, and that he'd boost his courage with a few drinks. Now when he saw his younger brother coming out of the forest loaded down with his prey, his envious and wicked heart gave him no peace. He called to him, "Come in here, dear brother; rest yourself and recover your strength with a cup of wine."

The youngest, suspecting no treachery, came in and told him about the good little man who had given him the spear with which he had killed the boar. The oldest made him stay till evening; then they left together.

It was dark when they came to a bridge over a stream, and the oldest let the youngest go first. And when he was halfway across the stream, he dealt him a blow from behind so that he fell down dead. He buried him under the bridge, took the boar, and brought it to the king with the story that he had killed it. When the youngest brother didn't come back, he said, "The boar must have torn him to pieces," and everyone believed it.

Because nothing remains hidden from God, however, this black deed, too, was destined to come to light. After many long years a shepherd was driving his flock across the bridge and saw a little snow-white bone lying in the sand below, and he thought that it would make a fine mouthpiece. Then he climbed down, picked it up,

and carved a mouthpiece for his horn. When he blew
into it for the first time, to the shepherd's great astonishment the little bone began to sing of its own accord:

> "Oh, shepherd, that tone
> You blew on my bone.
> My brother murdered me,
> Under the bridge he buried me,
> Made the wild boar his own,
> The king's daughter he won."

"What a strange little horn," the shepherd said, "playing by itself. I must bring it to my lord the king."

When he came before the king with it, the horn began
once more to sing its song. The king understood it very
well and had the ground under the bridge dug up. Then
the entire skeleton of the murdered man appeared. The
wicked brother could not deny the deed. He was sewn
into a sack alive and drowned. The bones of the murdered man, however, were laid to rest in a beautiful
grave in the churchyard.

THE DEVIL'S
THREE GOLDEN HAIRS

O nce upon a time there was a poor woman who
gave birth to a little son, and because he was
born with a caul, it was prophesied that when
he got to be fourteen he would marry the king's daughter. It happened that soon after that the king came to
the village, but no one knew that he was the king. When
he asked people for the latest news, they answered, "Not
long ago a child was born with a caul, and whatever
such a person sets out to do will turn out lucky. In-

deed, it has been prophesied that when he gets to be fourteen he'll marry the king's daughter."

The king, who had an evil heart, was angry at the prophecy. He went to the parents, made a show of friendliness, and said, "You poor people, give me the child to take care of and I'll provide for it!"

At first they refused, but when the stranger offered them solid gold, they thought, "It's a good-luck child; everything is bound to turn out for the best." So they finally consented and gave him the child.

The king put the child into a box and rode on with it until he came to a deep stream. There he threw the box into the water and thought, "I've helped my daughter get rid of this unexpected suitor."

But instead of sinking, the box floated like a little boat, and not a drop of water got inside. It floated to a point two miles above the king's capital where there was a mill, and it caught on the weir. One of the millhands, who was luckily standing there, noticed it and pulled it in with a hook, expecting to find it full of treasure. But when he opened it, there lay a handsome baby boy, lively and gay. He brought him to the miller and his wife, and because they had no children of their own, they were glad and said, "God has given him to us!" They took good care of the foundling, and as he grew up, all the virtues grew in him.

It came to pass one time that during a storm the king took shelter at the mill and asked the miller and his wife if that strapping lad were their son. "No," they answered, "he's a foundling. Fourteen years ago he floated up against the weir inside a box."

Then the king knew that this was none other than the good-luck child he had thrown into the stream, and he said, "Good people, could the boy bear a letter to the queen? I will give him two gold pieces as a reward."

"As your Majesty commands!" they answered, and told the boy to get ready.

Then the king wrote a letter to the queen, saying, "As soon as the boy delivers this letter, he is to be killed and buried, and all of this must be done before my return."

The boy started out with this letter, but he lost his

way and in the evening came to a large forest. He saw a small light in the darkness, went toward it, and came to a little house. As he entered, an old woman was sitting beside the fire all alone. She was frightened when she saw the boy and said, "Where do you come from and where are you going?"

"I'm coming from the mill," he answered, "and I'm going to the queen, to whom I'm supposed to take a letter. But I'd like to spend the night here because I've lost my way in the forest."

"You poor boy," said the woman. "You've come upon a house that belongs to a gang of robbers, and when they come home, they will kill you."

"Come what may," said the boy, "I'm not afraid. But I'm so tired that I can't go any farther." He stretched out on a bench and fell asleep.

Soon after that the robbers came and asked angrily who that strange boy lying there was. "Oh," said the old woman, "he's an innocent child who lost his way in the forest, and I took him in out of pity. He's supposed to take a letter to the queen."

The robbers opened the letter and read it, and it said that as soon as the boy arrived he was to be put to death. Then the hardhearted robbers took pity, and the captain tore up the letter and wrote another one, which said that as soon as the boy arrived he was to be married to the king's daughter. Then they let him sleep in peace on the bench until the next morning, and when he woke up, they gave him the letter and showed him the right way.

When the queen had received the letter and read it, she followed the instructions, ordered a splendid wedding, and so the king's daughter was married to the good-luck child. And because the young man was handsome and kind, she lived with him in happiness and contentment.

After a time the king returned to his castle and saw that the prophecy had been fulfilled and that the good-luck child had married his daughter. "How did this happen?" he said. "I gave a completely different order in my letter."

The queen handed him the letter and told him to see

for himself what it said. The king read the letter and
realized that his letter had been exchanged with another one. He asked the young man what had become of
the letter that had been entrusted to him and why he
had brought another in its place.

"I know nothing at all about it," he answered. "They
must have been exchanged at night while I was sleeping
in the forest."

"You can't get away with it that easily!" the king said
furiously. "Whoever wants to have my daughter will have
to go to Hell and fetch me three golden hairs from the
head of the Devil. If you bring me what I ask for, you
can keep my daughter." That way the king hoped to get
rid of him for good.

But the good-luck child answered, "I'll manage to
bring back the golden hairs—I'm not afraid of the
Devil." With that he took his leave and began his
travels.

His journey took him to a large city, where the watchman at the gate asked him what his trade was and what
he knew.

"I know everything," said the good-luck child.

"Then you can do us a favor," said the watchman, "if
you can tell us why the well in the marketplace that
used to produce wine has dried up and won't even yield
water any more."

"You'll find out," he answered. "Just wait until I come
back!" Then he went on and came to another town,
where the watchman at the gate again asked him what
his trade was and what he knew.

"I know everything," he answered.

"Then you can do us a favor and tell us why the tree
in our city that used to bear golden apples doesn't even
put out leaves anymore."

"You'll find out," he answered. "Just wait until I come
back!"

Then he went on and came to a great river that he
had to cross. The ferryman asked him what his trade
was and what he knew.

"I know everything," he answered.

"Then you can do me a favor," said the ferryman,

"and tell me why I have to go over and back all the time without any relief."

"You'll find out," he answered. "Just wait until I come back!"

When he had crossed the river, he found the entrance to Hell. Everything was black and sooty down there, and the Devil wasn't home, but his grandmother sat there in a large easy chair. "What do you want?" she said to him, but she didn't look so very fierce.

"I'd like very much to have three golden hairs from the head of the Devil," he answered, "or else I won't be able to keep my wife."

"That's asking a lot," she said. "If the Devil finds you when he comes home, that will be the end of you. But I feel sorry for you, and I'll see whether I can help you." She turned him into an ant and said, "Crawl into the folds of my skirt—you'll be safe there."

"All right," he said, "that's fine. But I'd still like to find out three things: why a well that used to produce wine has dried up and won't even yield water; why a tree that used to bear golden apples now won't even put out leaves; and why a ferryman has to go over and back all the time without any relief."

"Those are hard questions," she answered, "but just keep good and quiet and pay attention to what the Devil says when I pull out the three golden hairs."

As night was falling, the Devil came home. No sooner had he come inside than he noticed something strange in the air. "Sniff, sniff, I smell human flesh," he said. "Something is wrong here." Then he peeked into every corner and searched, but he couldn't find anything.

His grandmother scolded him: "I've just finished sweeping and putting the house in order," she said, "and there you go turning everything upside down again. You're always smelling human flesh! Sit down and eat your supper!"

After he had had enough to eat and drink, he was tired, laid his head in his grandmother's lap, and told her to pick a few lice out of his hair. It wasn't long before he fell asleep and snorted and snorted. Then the old woman took hold of a golden hair, pulled it out, and put it down beside her.

"Ouch!" cried the Devil. "What are you trying to do?"

"I was having a bad dream," answered the grandmother, "and happened to grab at your hair."

"What were you dreaming about?" asked the Devil.

"I dreamed that a well in the marketplace that used to produce wine has dried up and won't even yield water now. What could be the matter with it?"

"Ha, if they only knew!" answered the Devil. "There's a toad sitting under a stone in the well. If they kill it, the wine will flow again."

The grandmother picked out some more lice until he went to sleep again and snored so that the windows rattled. Then she pulled out the second hair.

"Ow! What are you doing?" the Devil cried furiously.

"Don't be angry!" she answered. "I did it in my dream."

"What were you dreaming about this time?" he asked.

"I dreamed that in a certain kingdom there stands a tree that used to bear golden apples and now won't even put out leaves. What could be the matter?"

"Ha, if they only knew!" answered the Devil. "There's a mouse gnawing at the roots. If they kill it, the tree will bear golden apples again, but if the mouse continues to gnaw much longer, the tree will die. But leave me alone, and if you disturb me one more time with your dreams, I'm going to slap your face!"

The grandmother spoke soothingly to him and picked more lice out of his hair until he went back to sleep and snored. Then she took hold of the third golden hair and pulled it out.

The Devil jumped up, howled, and was going to beat her, but she calmed him down again and said, "One can't help bad dreams!"

"What were you dreaming about?" he asked, for he was still curious.

"I dreamed about a ferryman who complains that he has to go over and back all the time without any relief. What could be the matter?"

"Ha, the idiot," answered the Devil. "When someone comes wanting to be taken across, he must put the pole into his hands. Then the other will have to be ferryman, and he'll be free."

Since the grandmother had pulled out the three golden hairs and he had answered the three questions, she left the old dragon in peace, and he slept until daybreak.

When the Devil was gone again, the old woman took the ant out of the folds of her skirt and restored the good-luck child's human shape. "There are the three golden hairs for you," she said, "and I suppose you heard the Devil's answers to the three questions?"

"Yes," he answered, "I heard, and I'll remember them."

"So now you've been helped," she said, "and you can be on your way."

He thanked the old woman for helping him in his need and left Hell, pleased that everything had turned out so lucky. When he came to the ferryman, he had to give the promised answer. "First take me across," said the good-luck child, "and I'll tell you how you can get someone to relieve you." When they got to the other side, he gave the ferryman the Devil's advice: "The next time someone wants to be taken across, just put the pole into his hands!"

He went on and came to the city where the barren tree stood, and there the watchman wanted his answer too. He told him just what he had heard the Devil say: "Kill the mouse gnawing at the roots, and the tree will bear golden apples again." The watchman thanked him and as a reward gave him two donkeys loaded with gold— they had to follow him.

Finally he came to the city whose well had dried up.

He told the watchman just what the Devil had said: "There's a toad under a stone in the well. You must find it and kill it, and then plenty of wine will flow again." The watchman thanked him, and he too gave him two donkeys loaded with gold.

At last the good-luck child got back home to his wife, who was heartily glad to see him again and to hear how well everything had turned out. He brought the king what he had demanded—the Devil's three golden hairs. When the king saw the four donkeys with the gold, he was delighted and said, "Now every condition has been fulfilled, and you can keep my daughter. But please tell me, my dear son-in-law, where did you get all that gold? That's an enormous treasure!"

"I crossed a river," he answered, "and that's where I picked it up—the bank on the far shore is covered with gold instead of sand."

"Can I get some too?" asked the king, and he was all eagerness.

"As much as you want," he answered. "There's a ferry-man on the river. Let him take you across, and then you can fill your sacks on the other side."

The greedy king set out in great haste, and when he came to the river, he signaled to the ferryman to take him across. The ferryman came and told him to get aboard, and when they reached the other side, he gave the pole to the king and jumped out. And from that time, the king had to run the ferry as punishment for his sins.

"Do you think he is still running it?"

"What do you think? Nobody is going to take the pole away from him."

THE TAILOR IN HEAVEN

I t happened one fine day that the Lord wanted to go for a walk in the Garden of Paradise and took along all the apostles and saints, so that no one was left in Heaven except for Saint Peter. The Lord had left orders that no one was to be let in while He was gone, so Peter was standing by the gate, keeping watch.

It wasn't long before someone knocked. Peter asked

who was there and what he wanted. "I'm a poor, honest tailor," a high voice answered, "and I'd like to be let in."

"Yes, honest—" said Peter, "honest as a thief on the gallows. You were sticky-fingered, and you kept back some of your customers' cloth. You won't get into Heaven. The Lord forbade me to let anyone in while He was out."

"Have pity," cried the tailor. "Little scraps that fall down from the table of their own accord aren't stolen property; they aren't worth mentioning. Just look, I'm limping—my feet got blistered coming here. I can't possibly turn back again. Just let me in, and I'll do any menial job. I'll carry the babies, wash the diapers, wipe and scrub the benches they've been playing on, and mend their torn clothes."

Saint Peter was won over out of pity and opened the gate of Heaven just enough to let the tailor's skinny body slip through. He ordered him to sit in a corner behind the door and to stay there quietly, lest the Lord should notice him on His return and get angry. The tailor obeyed, but one time when Saint Peter stepped out the door, he got up, and full of curiosity, went exploring in all the corners of Heaven, surveying the situation. Finally he came to a place where a great many beautiful and luxurious chairs were standing, and in the center was an easy chair of solid gold, decked with sparkling gems. It was taller than the rest of the chairs, too, and there was a golden footstool in front of it. That was the chair on which the Lord Himself sat when He was at home, and from which He could see everything that was happening on earth.

The tailor stopped and looked at the chair for quite a while because he liked it better than anything else. Finally his curiosity got the better of him, and he climbed up and sat down in the chair. Then he was able to see everything that was happening on earth, and he noticed an ugly old woman standing beside a brook doing some washing, and she was stealthily putting aside a couple of veils. This sight made the tailor so angry that he grabbed the golden footstool and hurled it down from Heaven to earth at the thieving old woman. But since he couldn't fetch the footstool back up again, he stole softly out of the chair, resumed his place behind the door, and acted as though he hadn't been doing a thing.

When the Lord and Master returned with His heavenly band, He didn't notice the tailor behind the door, but when He sat down in His chair, He missed His footstool. He asked Saint Peter what had become of the footstool, but he didn't know. Then He asked him if he had let anyone in.

"I can't think of anyone who could have been here," answered Peter, "except for a lame tailor who is still sitting behind the door."

Then the Lord summoned the tailor into His presence and asked him if he had taken the footstool and what he had done with it.

"Oh, Lord," answered the tailor gleefully, "in my wrath I threw it at an old woman on earth whom I saw stealing two veils out of the wash."

"Oh, you rogue," said the Lord. "If I were to judge as you judge, what do you think would have happened to you long ago? I would long since have run out of stools, benches, chairs, and wouldn't have so much as a poker left—everything would have been thrown at sinners. After this you can't stay in Heaven—out the gate you go again. There you can find yourself someplace to go. Here no one has the right to mete out punishment except for me, the Lord."

Peter had to escort him out of Heaven again, and because his shoes were torn and his feet all blistered, he took his stick in hand and set off to Waitawhile, which is the place where pious soldiers stay and make merry.

TABLE-SET-YOURSELF,
THE GOLD-DONKEY, AND
CUDGEL-OUT-OF-THE-SACK

▬▬▬▬▬▬▬▬▬▬▬▬▬▬▬▬▬▬▬▬▬▬▬

Once upon a time there was a tailor who had three sons and only one goat. Because the goat provided all three of them with milk, it had to have good fodder and had to be led out to pasture every day, and the sons took turns doing this.

One time the oldest took it to the churchyard where the loveliest plants were growing, and there he let it graze and gambol about. In the evening when it was time to go home, he asked, Goat, are you full?"

The goat answered,

> "So full I can't
> Crop another plant: meh! meh!"

"Then come on home," said the boy, took it by the halter, led it to the stable, and tied it up.

"Well," said the old tailor, did the goat get plenty to eat?"

"Oh," answered the son, it's so full it can't crop another plant."

But the father wanted to see for himself, went down to the stable, petted the good animal, and asked, "Goat, are you sure that you're full?"

The goat answered,

> "How that could be I can't make out!
> Among the graves I skipped about
> And couldn't find a single sprout: meh! meh!"

"What's this I hear!" cried the tailor, ran upstairs, and said to the boy, "Eh, you liar! Telling me the goat is full after letting it starve?" And in his wrath he took the yard-stick down from the wall and drove him out with blows.

The next day it was the second son's turn. He picked out a place near the garden hedge where many fine plants were growing, and the goat cropped them to the ground. In the evening, when the boy was ready to go home, he asked, "Goat, are you full?"

The goat answered,

> "So full I can't
> Crop another plant: meh! meh!"

"Then come on home," said the boy, led it back, and tied it up in the stable.

"Well," said the old tailor, "did the goat get plenty to eat?"

"Oh," answered the son, "it's so full it can't crop another plant."

The tailor wouldn't take his word for it, went down to the stable, and asked, "Goat, are you sure you're full?"

The goat answered,

> "How that could be I can't make out!
> Among the graves I skipped about
> And couldn't find a single sprout: meh! meh!"

"The wicked scoundrel!" cried the tailor. "Letting such a good animal go hungry!" He ran upstairs, and with the yardstick he drove the boy out the front door.

Now it was the third son's turn. He wanted to do the job right, picked out some brush with the most beautiful foliage, and let the goat graze on it. In the evening, when he was ready to go home, he asked, "Goat, are you sure you're full?"

The goat answered,

> "So full I can't
> Crop another plant: meh! meh!"

The tailor didn't trust his son, went down, and asked, "Goat, are you sure you're full?"

The malicious animal answered,

> "How that could be I can't make out!
> Among the graves I skipped about
> And couldn't find a single sprout: meh! meh!"

"Oh, what a pack of liars!" cried the tailor, "one as rascally and undutiful as the next! You won't make a fool of me anymore!" Utterly beside himself with rage, he bounded upstairs, and with the yardstick flayed the poor boy's back so savagely that he dashed out of the house.

Now the old tailor was left alone with his goat. The next morning he went down to the stable, fondled the goat, and said, "Come, my pet, I'll take you to pasture myself." He took it by the halter and led it to green hedges and yarrow and whatever else goats like to eat. "There now, for once you can eat to your heart's content," he told it, and he let it graze until evening. Then he asked, "Goat, are you full?"

It answered,

> "So full I can't
> Crop another plant: meh! meh!"

"Then come on home," said the tailor, led it to the stable, and tied it up. As he was leaving, he turned around once more and said, "Well, for once you really are full!"

But the goat made no exception of him and cried,

> "How that could be I can't make out!
> Among the graves I skipped about
> And couldn't find a single sprout: meh! meh!"

When the tailor heard that, he stopped short, and he realized that he had driven off his three sons without cause. "Just you wait," he cried, "you ungrateful creature! Driving you away would be too mild. I'll fix you so that you won't dare show yourself among respectable tailor folk."

He ran upstairs in haste to fetch his razor. Then he lathered the goat's head and shaved it as smooth as his palm. And because it was not worthy of the yardstick, he fetched the whip and gave it such a thrashing that it rushed away with leaps and bounds.

Sitting all alone in his house, the tailor became very sad and would have liked to have had his sons back, but no one knew what had become of them.

The oldest had apprenticed himself to a joiner. He learned diligently and eagerly, and when the time arrived for him to become a journeyman, the master presented him with a little table. It was nothing special to look at and was made of ordinary wood, but it had one good property. If one put it down and said, "Table, set your-

self," the good little table would suddenly be spread with a clean cloth and set with a plate and a knife and fork beside it. There would be dishes of good things to eat, as many as there was room for, and there'd be a glass of red wine glowing so as to gladden one's heart.

The young journeyman thought, "That should take care of me for the rest of my life." He set out into the world in high spirits, never caring whether an inn was good or bad or whether anything was to be had there. Whenever he felt like it, he didn't bother to turn in some place; but in field, forest, or meadow, according to his fancy, he took the table off his back, put it down in front of him, and said, "Set yourself." And there would be all that his heart desired.

At last the thought of returning to his father occurred to him—his father's wrath would have cooled by now, and he'd be glad to take him back with the table-set-yourself.

It happened that one evening on his way home he came to a crowded inn. The other guests bade him welcome and invited him to sit down and eat with them, for otherwise he would hardly get anything to eat at that hour.

"No," answered the joiner, "I won't deprive you of such scanty rations. I'd rather have you be my guests."

They laughed, thinking he was joking with them. But he put down his wooden table right in the middle of the room and said, "Table, set yourself!" Immediately it was spread with better provisions than any the innkeeper could have produced, and a delicious aroma was wafted to the noses of the guests.

"Fall to, good friends," said the joiner, and the guests, seeing that he had been in earnest, took their places, pulled out their knives, and helped themselves stoutly. What amazed them most of all was that as soon as one dish was empty, a full one immediately appeared in its place.

The innkeeper was standing in a corner watching this thing. He didn't know what to say, but he thought, "I could use a cook like that in my business." The joiner and his party made merry until late into the night. Finally they lay down to sleep, and the young journeyman also went to bed and set his wishing-table against the wall.

The innkeeper's thoughts, however, wouldn't let him sleep. He remembered that in his storage room there was a table that looked exactly like this one. Softly he went to fetch it and exchanged it for the wishing-table.

The next morning the joiner paid for his night's lodging, picked up his table, never thinking that it might be the wrong one, and went his way. At noon he arrived at his father's house and was received by him with great joy. "Well, my dear son, what have you learned?" his father said to him.

"Father, I've become a joiner."

"A worthy profession," replied the old man, "but what

have you brought back from your travels as a journey-man?"

"Father, the best thing I've brought with me is this little table."

The tailor examined the table on all sides and said, "You didn't turn out a masterpiece when you made that—it's an old and decrepit table."

"But it's a table that sets itself," answered the son. "When I put it down and tell it to set itself, then right away it's covered with the finest dishes and wine with it to warm one's heart. Just invite over all of our friends and kinfolk. Give them a real treat for a change, because the table will provide plenty for everyone."

When all the company was assembled, he placed the table in the middle of the room and said, "Table, set yourself." But the table didn't budge and remained as empty as any other table that can't understand speech. Then the poor journeyman realized that someone had ex-changed tables with him, and he was ashamed to be stand-ing there like a liar. The kinfolk, however, laughed him to scorn, and they had to return home without getting anything to eat or drink. The father got his cloth out again and kept on tailoring, and the son found work with a master joiner.

The second son had become apprenticed to a miller. When his term was up, the master said, "Because you have done so well, I am going to give you a very special kind of donkey, which won't pull a cart or carry sacks."

"Then what good is it?" asked the young journeyman.

"It spits gold," answered the miller. "When you set it on a cloth and say 'Bricklebrit,' the good animal spits out gold pieces in front and in the rear."

"That's a fine thing," said the journeyman, thanked the master, and set out into the world. Whenever he needed gold, all he had to do was to say "Bricklebrit" to the donkey. Then it rained gold pieces, and the only effort it cost him was to pick them up off the ground. Wherever he went, the best was none too good, and the costlier the better, for his purse was always full.

After he had spent some time seeing a bit of the world, he thought, "I should look up my father. When I bring him the gold-donkey, he'll get over his anger and welcome me back."

By chance he happened upon the same inn where his brother's table had been exchanged. He was leading the donkey, and the innkeeper wanted to relieve him of the animal and to tie it up. But the young journeyman said, "Don't trouble yourself—I'll take my donkey to the stable and tie it up myself, because I have to know where it is."

This struck the innkeeper as strange, and he thought that anyone who looked after his own donkey couldn't have much to spend. However, when the stranger reached into his pocket, took out two gold pieces, and told him to lay in something special for him, the innkeeper was wide-eyed with astonishment, and he ran to hunt up the best things he could get.

After dinner the guest asked how much he owed. The innkeeper had no scruples about charging double and said it would cost him another two gold pieces. The journeyman reached into his pocket, but his gold had just run out. "Wait a moment, Sir Host," he said, "I'll just go out to fetch some gold." And he took along the tablecloth.

The innkeeper couldn't imagine what was going on. He was curious, stole after him, and when the guest bolted the stable door, the innkeeper peeked through a knothole. The stranger spread out the cloth under the donkey, cried "Bricklebrit," and immediately it began to spit gold in front and in back so that it fairly showered to the ground. "Great heavens," said the innkeeper, "that's a fast way to coin ducats! A purse like that wouldn't be a bad thing!"

The guest paid his reckoning and went to bed, but the innkeeper sneaked down to the stable during the night, led away the master of the mint, and tied up another donkey in its place.

Early the next morning the journeyman left with the donkey, thinking that it was his gold-donkey. At noon he arrived at his father's house, and the latter was glad to see him again and made him welcome.

"What have you become, my son?" asked the old man.

"A miller, dear Father," he answered.

"What did you bring back from your travels as a journeyman?"

"Only a donkey."

"We've got plenty of donkeys around here," said the father. "In that case, I would have preferred a nice goat."

"Yes," answered the son, "but this is no ordinary donkey but a gold-donkey. Whenever I say 'Bricklebrit' to the good animal it spits out a whole clothful of gold pieces. Just invite all of our kinfolk, and I'll make them all rich."

"That I wouldn't mind a bit," said the tailor. "Then I won't have to work my fingers to the bone with my needle anymore." He himself ran off to invite all the kinfolk over.

As soon as they were assembled, the miller told them to stand back, spread the cloth, and led the donkey into the room. "Now pay attention," he said, and cried, "Bricklebrit," but it dropped something other than gold pieces; and it turned out that the beast was ignorant of the art, for not every donkey is so far advanced.

Then the poor miller pulled a long face, realized that he had been swindled, and asked forgiveness of his kin, who had to return home as poor as they started. There was no help except for the old man to take up his needle again and for the young man to hire himself out to a miller.

The third brother had been apprenticed to a turner, and because this is a highly skilled craft, he had to study longest. However, his brothers wrote to him in a letter how badly they had fared, and how the innkeeper on the very last night had cheated them out of their fine wishing things.

When the turner had finished his apprenticeship and was to begin his travels, his master presented him with a sack because he had done so well and said, "There's a cudgel inside."

"The sack I can hang over my shoulder, and it can do me good service, but what's the cudgel doing in there? It just makes it heavy."

"That I'll tell you," answered the master. "Whenever anyone does you an injury, just say, 'Cudgel, out of the sack,' and the cudgel will jump out among those people and dance so merrily on their backs that they won't be able to move or stir for eight days. And it won't leave off until you say, 'Cudgel, back in the sack.'"

The journeyman thanked him, slung the sack over his shoulder, and whenever anyone tried to lay hands on him, he said, "Cudgel, out of the sack." Immediately the cudgel jumped out and started beating the dust out of people's coats and jackets one after another, without waiting for anyone to take them off first. And it all happened so fast that before a person knew what was happening, it was already his turn.

It was toward evening when the young turner arrived at the inn where his brothers had been cheated. He put his sack on the table and started to tell about all the marvelous things that he had seen in the world. "Yes," he said, "it's possible to find a table-set-yourself and a gold-donkey and similar things. All good articles, and I don't look down on them. But nothing can compare with the treasure I've acquired and am carrying in my sack."

The innkeeper pricked up his ears. "What in the world could it be?" he thought. "The sack must be full of jewels. I ought to be able to make a cheap purchase of that, too, for good things always come in threes."

When it was time to sleep, the guest stretched out on the bench and used his sack as a pillow. When the innkeeper thought that the guest was fast asleep, he approached, and tugged and pulled at the sack very softly and carefully to see if he could get it out from under and put another one in its place.

But the turner had been lying in wait for him quite a while, and as the innkeeper was just about to give a hearty pull, he cried, "Cudgel, out of the sack." Immediately the cudgel rushed out, set upon the innkeeper, and tickled his ribs in no uncertain fashion.

The innkeeper cried pitifully, but the louder he cried, the harder the cudgel beat time on his back, until finally he fell to the ground exhausted.

Then the turner said, "If you don't give back the table-set-yourself and the gold-donkey, the dance will start all over."

"Oh no," the innkeeper cried very humbly. "I'll gladly give back everything, only make that cursed demon crawl back into the sack."

"I will temper justice with mercy," said the journeyman,

"but watch out for your skin!" Then he cried, "Cudgel, back in the sack!" And he let it stay there.

The next morning the turner set out for his father's house with the table-set-yourself and the gold-donkey. The tailor was glad to see him again and asked what he had learned while he was away from home.

"Dear Father, I've become a turner."

"A very skilled craft," said the father. "What have you brought back from your travels as a journeyman?"

"A precious thing, dear Father," answered the son. "A cudgel in the sack."

"What!" cried the father, "a cudgel! That's worth some trouble! You can cut one from every tree."

"It's not one of those, dear Father. When I say, 'Cudgel, out of the sack,' the cudgel jumps out and leads anyone who intends you harm a sorry dance and won't leave off

until he's lying on the ground begging you to stop. Do you see, with the cudgel I've gotten back the table-set-yourself and the gold-donkey which the thieving innkeeper took from my brothers. Now call both of them and invite all our kinfolk. I want to wine and dine them and fill their pockets with gold besides."

The old tailor didn't quite dare to believe him, but nevertheless he gathered together all the kin. Then the turner spread a cloth in the room, led in the gold-donkey, and said to his brother, "Now, dear brother, speak to it." The miller said, "Bricklebrit," and immediately the gold pieces showered down on the cloth as though a thunderstorm had come, and the donkey didn't stop until everyone had as much as he could carry. (I see by your face that you wish you had been there too.)

Then the turner fetched the table and said, "Now, dear brother, speak to it." And hardly had the joiner said, "Table, set yourself," than it was set and plentifully provided with dishes of the finest food. Then they had such a meal as the good tailor had never had in his house before, and the entire family stayed until evening, and everyone was merry and cheerful. The tailor shut away needle and thread, yardstick and goose in the cupboard, and he lived with his three sons in joy and bliss.

But what happened to the goat whose fault it was that the tailor drove off his three sons? That I'll tell you. It was ashamed of its bald head, ran into a fox's den, and curled up inside. When the fox came home, a pair of big eyes flashed at it out of the dark, so that it took fright and ran away again.

The fox met the bear, who, seeing the fox looking all upset, said, "What's the matter, Brother Fox, why are you pulling such a face?"

"Oh," answered the red one, "a fierce animal is sitting in my den, and glared at me with its fiery eyes."

"We'll soon get rid of it," said the bear, and went to the den, and looked inside. But when it saw the fiery eyes, it too was overcome with fear. It wanted no part of the fierce animal and took to its heels.

The bee met it, and noticing that the bear was not feeling very well, said, "Bear, you're making an awfully sour face. What's become of your happy disposition?"

"It's easy for you to talk," answered the bear. "A fierce animal with glowing eyes is sitting in the red one's house, and we can't chase it out."

"I feel sorry for you, Bear," said the bee. "I'm a poor weak creature that you wouldn't deign to look at in the street, but I think I can help you out." It flew into the fox's den, landed on the goat's smoothly shorn head, and stung it so hard that it jumped up crying, "Meh! meh!" and ran in a frenzy out into the world. And nobody knows to this hour where it ran to.

TOM THUMB

One evening a poor farmer sat beside his hearth stirring up the fire, and his wife sat spinning. Then he said, "How sad it is that we have no children! It's so quiet at our house, whereas in other houses things are so noisy and gay."

"Yes," answered his wife, and sighed. "If there were just one, and even if it were terribly small, only the size of a thumb, I'd be satisfied. We would still love it with all our hearts."

Now it happened that the wife became sickly, and after seven months she bore a child that was perfectly proportioned in all its limbs but was no taller than a thumb. The parents said, "It is according to the wish we made, and he shall be our dear child." And they called him Tom Thumb because of his size. They gave him all the nourishment he needed, but the child did not grow bigger but remained as he had been the hour he was born. However, he had an intelligent expression in his eyes and soon proved to be a clever and nimble little thing, succeeding at whatever he tried.

One day the farmer was getting ready to go into the forest to cut wood, and he was talking away to himself: "I only wish someone were around to follow me with the cart."

"Oh, Father," Tom Thumb cried, "I'll bring the cart all right. Depend on me, it will be in the forest at the time you set."

The man laughed and said, "How can that be? You're much too small to guide the horse by the reins."

"That makes no difference, Father. If only Mother will hitch up the horse, I'll sit in its ear and call out the directions to it."

"Well," answered the father, "let's try it once."

When it was time, the mother hitched up the horse and set Tom Thumb in its ear, and the little fellow called out the directions to the horse: "Giddap! Whoa! Gee! Haw!" Then it went as though a master-hand were guiding it, and the cart took the right way toward the forest.

It happened that just as it was turning a corner and the tiny fellow was crying, "Gee, Gee," two strangers came up.

"Well, I'll be——" said the man, "what's that? There goes a cart, and a carter is calling to the horse, yet he's nowhere to be seen."

"There's something strange about this," said the second. "Let's follow the cart to see where it's going." The cart went all the way into the forest, right to the place where the wood was being cut.

When Tom Thumb saw his father, he called to him, "See, Father, here I am with the cart. Now help me down." The father took the horse with his left hand and with his right lifted his little son out of the ear, and the boy sat down very cheerfully on a blade of straw.

When the two strangers saw Tom Thumb, they were speechless with amazement. Then one of them took the other aside and said, "Listen, the little fellow could make our fortune if we were to exhibit him in a big city for money. Let's buy him." They went to the farmer and said, "Sell us the little man. We promise to treat him well."

"No," answered the father, "He's the apple of my eye, and he's not for sale for all the gold in the world."

Tom Thumb, however, hearing the offer, had crawled up the folds of his father's coat, stood on his shoulder, and whispered in his ear, "Father, go ahead and give me to them—I'll manage to come back all right." Then the father sold him to the two men for a pretty sum.

"Where would you like to sit?" they asked him.

"Oh, set me on the brim of your hat. There I can walk up and down and look at the scenery, and I won't fall off." They did as he wished, and after Tom Thumb had said goodbye to his father, they went off with him.

They traveled like that until it began to grow dark. Then the little fellow said, "Put me down for a second— it's urgent!"

"Stay right up there," said the man on whose head he was sitting. "It won't bother me. The birds also drop something on there now and then."

"No," said Tom Thumb, "I know what's proper. Please set me down quickly."

The man took off his hat and set the little fellow down in a field by the wayside. He jumped and crawled around

among the clods for a while, and suddenly slipped into a mousehole he had picked out. "Good night, gentlemen, you may go home without me," he called, and made fun of them.

They came running and poked sticks into the mouse hole, but it was wasted effort. Tom Thumb kept crawling in deeper, and since it soon got completely dark, they were forced to return home in an angry mood and with an empty purse.

When Tom Thumb saw that they were gone, he crawled back out of the underground passage. "It's dangerous walking in the fields after dark," he said. "One could break a leg or one's neck!" By good fortune he stumbled upon an empty snail's house. "Thank God," he said, "here I can spend the night safely." And he sat down inside.

Shortly after that, as he was just about to fall asleep, he heard two men going by, one of whom was saying, "How are we going to set about stealing the rich parson's money and silver?"

"I can tell you how," Tom Thumb broke in.

"What was that?" the thief said, startled. "I heard someone speak."

They stood still and listened, and Tom Thumb spoke again. "Take me along and I'll help you."

"Well, where are you?"

"Just look on the ground and follow the sound of my voice," he answered.

At last the thieves found him and picked him up. "You little creature, how could you help us!" they said.

"Don't you see," he answered, "I'll crawl into the parson's storeroom through the iron bars, and I'll hand out whatever you want."

"Very well," they said, "let's see what you can do."

When they got to the parsonage, Tom Thumb crept into the room, but immediately he bellowed with all his might, "Do you want everything in here?"

The thieves were frightened and said, "For heaven's sake, speak softly so that you don't wake someone."

But Tom Thumb pretended that he hadn't heard them and bellowed again, "What do you want? Do you want everything in here?"

The cook, who was sleeping next door, heard this, sat up in bed, and listened. But the thieves had run off a piece in their fright. Finally they took heart again and thought, "The little fellow is teasing us." They returned and whispered to him, "Now be serious about it and hand something out to us."

Then again Tom Thumb yelled as loud as he could, "But I want to give you everything. Just reach in with your hands."

The maidservant who was listening heard this very clearly, jumped out of bed, and stumbled through the door. The thieves took to their heels and ran as if the Wild

Huntsman * were after them. The maid, however, who couldn't see anything, went to light a candle. When she came back with it, Tom Thumb had escaped to the barn without being seen. The maid, after searching in every corner without finding anything, went back to bed at last, thinking that she must have been dreaming with open eyes and ears.

Tom Thumb clambered around in the hay until he found a good place to sleep. There he planned to rest until day and then return home to his parents. But that's not how it worked out! Yes, there's much grief and suffering in the world!

With the gray dawn the maid got up to feed the animals. Her first errand was to the barn, where she grabbed an armful of hay, the very one in which poor Tom Thumb was lying asleep. But he was sleeping so soundly that he noticed nothing until he woke up inside the mouth of a cow that had gobbled him up with the hay.

"Good Lord," he cried, "how did I get caught in a fulling mill!" But he soon realized where he was. Now he had to be careful not to be ground to pieces between the teeth, and finally he couldn't avoid sliding down into the stomach.

"They forgot to put windows in this cell," he said, "and the sun doesn't shine in here. They don't provide any candles, either." In every way he disliked the accommodations, and worst of all, more hay kept coming through the door and the space kept shrinking. At last, in terror, he cried as loud as he could, "Don't bring me any more fresh fodder. Don't bring me any more fresh fodder."

The maid was milking the cow at that very moment, and when she heard someone talking without seeing anyone, in the same voice as the one she had heard during the night, she got such a shock that she fell off the stool and spilled the milk.

She ran in great haste to her master and cried, "Oh, heavens, Parson, the cow spoke to me."

"You're mad," answered the parson, but he went to the stable himself to see what was going on there. But hardly

* The leader of the Wild Hunt, a band of ghosts condemned to ride wildly through the sky at night as if hunting.

had he set foot inside than Tom Thumb started to cry again, "Don't bring me any more fresh fodder. Don't bring me any more fresh fodder."

Then the parson himself was afraid. He thought that an evil spirit had entered the cow, and he gave orders for it to be killed. It was slaughtered, but the stomach, with Tom Thumb inside, was thrown on the manure pile.

Tom Thumb began to extricate himself with much pain and trouble, and he finally managed to find an opening. But just as he was about to stick his head outside, another misfortune occurred. A hungry wolf ran up and swallowed the whole stomach in one gulp.

Tom Thumb did not despair. "Maybe," he thought, "one could talk to the wolf." And he called to him from inside his belly, "Dear wolf, I know where you can have a wonderful feed."

"Where is that?" said the wolf.

"In such and such a house. You have to crawl in through the drain, and you'll find cake and bacon and sausage, as much as you can eat." And he gave the wolf a minute description of his father's house.

The wolf didn't need to be told twice. At night it squeezed in through the drain and ate in the pantry to its heart's content. When it had had enough, it tried to get away, but had become so fat that it couldn't get out again the same way.

Tom Thumb had counted on this, and now he started making a terrible racket inside the wolf's stomach, shouting for all he was worth.

"Will you be quiet!" said the wolf. "You're waking up the household."

"So what," the little fellow answered, "You've eaten your fill, and now I want to have my fun." And he started again to shout with all his might.

At last the noise woke his father and mother, who came running to the pantry and looked in through a crack. When they saw a wolf in there, they ran off, the man to fetch the ax and his wife the scythe.

"Stand back," said the man as they entered the room. "If I don't kill him with the first blow, you strike at him and slice him through the middle."

Tom Thumb heard his father's voice and cried, "Dear Father, I'm here inside the wolf's belly."

The father said with great joy, "Praise God, our child has been found." And he told his wife to put the scythe away so that Tom Thumb would not be hurt.

Then he hauled off and struck the wolf such a blow on the head that it fell down dead. They went looking for knives and scissors, cut open the stomach, and freed the little fellow.

"Oh," said the father, "how we have worried about you!"

"Yes, Father, I've seen a lot of the world. God be praised that I can breathe fresh air again!"

"What are all the places you've been to?"

"Oh, Father, I was in a mousehole, the stomach of a cow, and the belly of a wolf. Now I shall stay with you."

"And we're not going to sell you again for all the riches in the world," said his parents, and they hugged and kissed their darling Tom Thumb. They gave him something to eat and drink, and had new clothes made for him because his old ones had been spoiled on his travels.

MISTRESS FOX'S WEDDING

Once upon a time there was an old fox with nine tails who suspected that his wife was unfaithful and decided to test her. He stretched out under the bench, didn't move a muscle, and pretended to be stone dead. Mistress Fox went up to her room, locked herself in, and her maid, Miss Cat, sat on the hearth cooking.

When the news got around that the old fox was dead, the suitors came calling. The maid heard someone knock-

ing at the front door. She went to open the door, and it
was a young fox, who said,

> "How do you do, Miss Cat?
> Is it sleeping or waking you're at?"

She answered,

> "Not asleep, but waking,
> Cooking and baking.
> I'm brewing some hot buttered beer.
> Would you care to be my guest, kind sir?"

"No thank you, miss!" said the fox. "What is Mistress
Fox doing?"
The maid answered,

> "She's gone to her room
> In sorrow and gloom.
> She's wept until her eyes are red
> Because old Mister Fox is dead."

"Tell her, please, miss, there's a young fox here who
would like to pay court to her."
"Very well, young gentleman."

The cat went up the trip-trap;
The door banged with a clip-clap.
"Mistress Fox, are you in?"
"Yes, kitty, I am."
"There's a suitor down there."
"What does he look like, my dear?

"Does he have nine bushy tails as beautiful as those
of the late Mister Fox?"
"Oh no," answered the cat. "He only has one."
"Then I don't want him."
Miss Cat went down and sent the suitor away. Soon
after that someone else knocked, and there was another
fox at the door who wanted to pay court to Mistress Fox.
He had two tails, but he had no better luck than the
first. After that others came, each with one more tail,
but they all got turned away until at last one came with
nine tails like old Mister Fox. When the widow heard that,
she said joyfully to the cat,

"Now open gate and doorway wide
And sweep old Mister Fox outside."

But just as the wedding was about to be celebrated,
old Mister Fox began to stir under the bench. He gave
the whole pack a good beating and chased them out of
the house, and Mistress Fox along with them.

THE ELVES

A shoemaker, through no fault of his own, had become so poor that all he had left was enough
leather to make a single pair of shoes. In the evening he cut out the shoes, intending to work on them the
next day. And because his conscience was clear he went

quietly to bed, commended himself to God, and fell asleep.

In the morning after he had said his prayers and was about to sit down to work, there stood the pair of shoes on the table all finished. He was greatly astonished

and didn't know what to make of it. He picked up the shoes to examine them more closely: the workmanship was so neat that every stitch was perfect, just as if the shoes had been intended for a masterpiece.*

Soon a customer appeared, and he liked the shoes so well that he paid more than the usual price for them, so that the shoemaker could afford the price of leather for two pairs of shoes. He cut them out in the evening and was going to start work the next morning with renewed spirits, but he didn't need to. When he got up, the shoes were all ready. Nor did the customers fail him, and they paid him enough money to buy leather for four pairs of shoes.

Early the next morning he found the four pairs finished too, and so it went on—whatever he cut out in the evening was finished in the morning, so that he soon was

---

* A journeyman must produce a "masterpiece" to become a master workman.

making a respectable living again and finally became a prosperous man.

Now it happened that one evening shortly before Christmas, as the man was cutting out shoes before going to bed, he said to his wife, "How would you like to stay up tonight to see who has been helping us so generously?" His wife agreed and lit a candle. Then they hid in the corner of the room behind some clothes hanging there and kept watch.

When it struck midnight, two pretty, naked little men appeared, sat down at the shoemaker's bench, took all of the leather that had been cut out, and with their little fingers they started to bore holes, to sew, and to hammer so nimbly and quickly that the shoemaker couldn't take his eyes off them in astonishment. They didn't stop until all the shoes were standing finished on the table. Then they sprang quickly away.

The next morning the wife said, "The little men have made us rich—we should do something for them in return. They are running around without a stitch of clothing on and must be freezing. Do you know what? I'm going to make them little shirts, coats, vests, and little trousers, and I'll knit each of them a pair of stockings, and you can make each of them a pair of little shoes."

Her husband said, "That's a fine idea." And at night when everything was ready, instead of the leather they put their presents on the table, and they hid in order to see what the little men would do.

At midnight they came skipping in and were going to begin work right away, but when instead of the leather they found the pretty little garments, they were astonished at first, and then they clearly showed that they were delighted. As quickly as possible they got dressed, smoothed down their fine new clothes, and sang:

> "Now we're such spruce and fine young men,
> Why should we make shoes again?"

Then they skipped and danced and jumped over the chairs and tables, and at last they danced out at the door.

They never came back, but the shoemaker remained a prosperous man for the rest of his life and succeeded in all of his undertakings.

THE JUNIPER TREE

This all happened long ago, it must be two thousand years. There was a rich man who had a beautiful and good wife, and they loved each other very dearly, but they had no children. However, they wanted some very much, and the woman prayed very often for some, day and night, but they didn't get any and didn't get any.

In front of the house was a yard in which there stood a juniper tree. Once in wintertime the woman was standing under it peeling an apple, and as she was peeling the apple, she cut her finger, and the blood fell upon the snow. "Oh," said the woman, sighing from the bottom of her heart, and she looked at the blood in front of her and was very sad. "If only I had a child as red as blood and as white as snow." And as she said this, she felt quite cheerful; she had a feeling that something would come of it.

She went back into the house, and a month passed and the snow melted; and two months, and things were green; and three months, and the flowers came out of the ground; and four months, and all the trees in the wood put out leaves and their green branches became entangled with each other—there the little birds sang so that the whole wood echoed and the blossoms fell from the trees. Then the fifth month was gone, and she stood under the juniper tree, which smelled so sweet, and her heart leaped and she fell on her knees and was carried away by joy. And when the sixth month had passed, the fruit got thick and heavy, and she became complete-

ly calm. And the seventh month, and she snatched at the
juniper berries and ate them very greedily, and she became sad and sick. Then the eighth month passed, and
she called her husband and wept and said, "If I should
die, bury me under the juniper tree." Then she was consoled and was glad until the ninth month had passed;
then she bore a child as white as snow and as red as
blood; and when she saw it she was so happy that she
died.

Her husband buried her under the juniper tree, and at
first he wept a great deal. After a while he wept somewhat less, and when he had wept a little longer, he
stopped. And after still some more time, he took another
wife.

By the second wife he had a daughter; the child of his
first wife, however, was a little son who was as red as
blood and as white as snow. Whenever the woman looked
at her daughter, she loved her very dearly, but then she
looked at the little boy, and this cut her to the heart, and
it seemed to her as though he were constantly in her
way. At such times she always considered how she
might get all the inheritance for her daughter. And the
Evil One filled her with anger against the little boy. She
pushed him around all over the house, and she shoved
him here and cuffed him there so that the poor child was
constantly afraid. When he got out of school, he had no
peace anywhere.

Once the woman went up to the storeroom, and her
little daughter came up too and said, "Mother, give me
an apple."

"Yes, my child," said the woman, and gave her a fine
apple out of the chest. The chest had a great, heavy lid
with a great, sharp lock.

"Mother," said the little girl, "can't Brother have one
too?"

This made the woman angry, but she said, "Yes,
when he gets out of school." And as she looked out of
the window and saw him coming it was just as though
the Evil One were taking possession of her, and she
snatched the apple back from her daughter and said,
"You won't get one before your brother does."

She threw the apple back into the chest and shut it.

And as the little boy came through the door, the Evil One made her say to him kindly, "My son, would you like an apple?" And she looked at him so spitefully.

"Mother," said the little boy, "how fierce you look! Yes, give me an apple."

Then it seemed to her as if she had to lead him on. "Come with me," she said, and raised the lid. "Take out an apple for yourself." And as the little boy put his head down into it, the Evil One prompted her. Crash! She slammed the lid down so that his head flew off and fell in among the red apples.

Then panic seized her, and she thought, "If I could only rid myself of the guilt for this!" She went up to her room to her dresser and took a white cloth out of the top drawer, and she set the head back on the neck and tied the neckerchief around it so that one couldn't notice anything. She set him down on a stool in front of the door and put the apple in his hand.

After that little Mary Ann came to her mother out in the kitchen where she was standing by the fire with a pot of hot water in front of her, which she was stirring constantly. "Mother," said Mary Ann, "Brother is sitting in front of the door and looks all white, and he's holding an apple in his hand. I asked him to give me the apple, but he didn't answer me, and then I got very scared."

"Go back again," said the mother, "and if he won't answer give him a box on the ear."

Then Mary Ann went back and said, "Brother, give me the apple." But he remained silent so she gave him a box on the ear, and his head fell off. She was so frightened at this that she began crying and screaming, and she ran to her mother and said, "Oh, Mother, I knocked off my brother's head." And she cried and cried and wouldn't be comforted.

"Mary Ann," said her mother, "what have you done! But just keep quiet so that no one will find out. It can't be helped now. We'll boil him in vinegar." Then she took the little boy and hacked him to pieces and boiled him in vinegar. Mary Ann stood there and cried and cried, and the tears all fell into the pot so that they didn't need to use any salt.

Then the father came home, sat down at the table, and asked, "Where is my son?"

The mother served up a great big dish of pickled meat, and Mary Ann was crying and couldn't stop.

The father said again, "Where is my son?"

"Oh," said the mother, "he's gone on a trip to Mother's great-uncle. He wants to stay there awhile."

"What's he doing there? He didn't even tell me good-bye!"

"Oh, he wanted to go very much and asked me if he could stay there six weeks. They'll take good care of him."

"Oh," said the man, "I'm very unhappy. After all, it's not right. He ought to have said good-bye to me." With that he began eating and said, "Mary Ann, why are you crying? Brother will surely come back."

"Oh, wife," he continued, "how good this meal tastes! Give me some more!" And the more he ate, the more he wanted, and he said, "Give me some more. You won't get any of it; it's as if it all belonged to me." And he ate and ate and threw all the bones under the table until he had eaten it all.

But Mary Ann went to her dresser and took her best silk scarf out of the bottom drawer, and she gathered up all the bones from under the table and tied them in the silk scarf and carried them outside, shedding blood-red tears. There she laid them down in the green grass under the juniper tree, and as she laid them down there, her spirits suddenly rose, and she stopped crying.

Then the juniper tree began to move, and the branches separated and joined just the way someone claps his hands when he is very happy. At the same time a cloud of mist went out from the tree, and in the center of the mist something was blazing like fire, and out of the fire flew a very beautiful bird that sang gloriously and flew high into the air. And when it had disappeared, the juniper tree was just as it had been before, and the scarf with the bones was gone. Mary Ann, however, was quite happy and gay, as if her brother were still alive. She went cheerfully back into the house to the table and ate.

But the bird flew off and perched upon a goldsmith's house and began to sing:

"My mother cut me up,
My father ate me up,
My sister Mary Ann has gone
And gathered each and every bone,
In a silk kerchief she tied them,
Under the juniper she laid them.
Chirrup, chirrup, what a pretty bird I am!"

The goldsmith was in his workshop making a golden chain. He heard the bird, which was sitting on his roof singing, and it sounded very beautiful to him. He got up, and as he was crossing the threshold, he lost one of his slippers. However, he went right out into the middle of the street with only one slipper and one sock on. He had on his apron, and was carrying the golden chain in one hand and the tongs in the other. And the sun was shining very bright upon the street. He stood there looking at the bird. "Bird," he said, "how beautifully you can sing! Sing that song again."

"No," said the bird, "I won't sing twice for nothing. If you will give me the golden chain, I will sing again."

"There," said the goldsmith, "take the golden chain. Now sing it again for me."

Then the bird came and took the golden chain in its right claw and came to the goldsmith and sang:

"My mother cut me up,
My father ate me up,
My sister Mary Ann has gone
And gathered each and every bone,
In a silk kerchief she tied them,
Under the juniper she laid them.
Chirrup, chirrup, what a pretty bird I am!"

Then the bird flew off to a shoemaker and perched on his roof and sang:

"My mother cut me up,
My father ate me up,
My sister Mary Ann has gone
And gathered each and every bone,
In a silk kerchief she tied them,
Under the juniper she laid them.
Chirrup, chirrup, what a pretty bird I am!"

The shoemaker heard it and ran out the door in shirt-sleeves. He looked up at the roof and had to shade his eyes with his hand in order not to be blinded by the sun. "Bird," he said, "how beautifully you can sing." Then he called through the door into the house, "Wife, come out for a moment and see the bird, how beautifully it can sing." Then he called his daughter and children, and his workmen, and the apprentice and the maid; and they all came out on the street to see the bird, how beautiful it was. It had such red and green feathers, and it seemed

to be pure gold around the neck, and its eyes sparkled in its head like stars.

"Bird," said the shoemaker, "now sing me that song again."

"No," said the bird, "I won't sing twice for nothing. You'll have to give me something."

"Wife," said the man, "go up, and on the top shelf there's a pair of red shoes. Bring them down here." Then the woman went and fetched the shoes. "There, bird," said the man, "now sing me that song again."

Then the bird came and took the shoes in its left claw and flew back up to the roof and sang:

"My mother cut me up,
My father ate me up,
My sister Mary Ann has gone
And gathered each and every bone,
In a silk kerchief she tied them,
Under the juniper she laid them.
Chirrup, chirrup, what a pretty bird I am!"

And when it had finished the song, it flew away. It had the chain in its right claw and the shoes in its left. And it flew away to a mill that went, "Clickety-clack, clickety-clack, clickety-clack." And inside the mill twenty mill-hands were shaping a millstone, and they chipped away at it, "Hick-hack, hick-hack, hick-hack," while the mill went, "Clickety-clack, clickety-clack, clickety-clack." Then the bird went and perched on a linden tree that was standing in front of the mill and sang:

"My mother cut me up,"

then one of them stopped;

"My father ate me up,"

then two more stopped and listened;

"My sister Mary Ann has gone"

then another four stopped;

"And gathered each and every bone,
In a silk kerchief she tied them,"

now only eight were chipping away;

"Under the juniper"

now only five;

"She laid them."

now only one;

"Chirrup, chirrup, what a pretty bird I am!"

Then the last stopped, too, and heard the last bit. "Bird," he said, "how beautifully you sing! Let me hear it too. Sing me that again."

"No," said the bird, "I won't sing twice for nothing. If you will give me the millstone, I will sing it again."

"Yes," he said, "if it belonged just to me, you should have it."

"Yes," said the others, "if it will sing again, let the bird have it."

Then the bird flew down, and all twenty of the mill-hands pried the stone up with boards: "Heave-ho-up, heave-ho-up, heave-ho-up!" The bird put its neck through the hole, wore it like a collar, flew back up into the tree, and sang:

"My mother cut me up,
My father ate me up,
My sister Mary Ann has gone
And gathered each and every bone,
In a silk kerchief she tied them,
Under the juniper she laid them.
Chirrup, chirrup, what a pretty bird I am!"

And when it had finished the song, it spread its wings, and in its right claw it had the chain and in its left the shoes and around its neck the millstone, and it flew back to its father's house.

The father, the mother, and Mary Ann were sitting in the room at the table. The father said, "Oh, how happy I am; I'm in such good spirits."

"No," said the mother, "I'm as afraid as if a terrible storm were coming."

Mary Ann, however, sat there crying and crying.

The bird came flying up, and when it perched on the roof, the father said, "Oh, I'm so happy, and the sun outside is shining so beautifully. I feel just as though I were going to see an old friend again."

"No," said the woman, "I'm so afraid that my teeth are chattering, and I feel as though there were a fire in my veins." And she tore at her bodice to open it some more.

But Mary Ann was sitting in the corner crying, and held her plate in front of her eyes and got it all wet with her tears.

The bird perched on the juniper tree and sang:

"My mother cut me up."

The mother covered her ears and shut her eyes tight and didn't want to see or hear, but there was a roaring in her ears like the most violent storm, and a burning and flashing in her eyes like lightning.

"My father ate me up."

"Oh, Mother," said the man, "there's a bird singing so wonderfully. The sun is shining so warm, and the air smells as though it were full of cinnamon."

"My sister Mary Ann has gone."

Then Mary Ann laid her head upon her knees and kept sobbing, but the man said, "I'm going outside. I've got to get a closer look at the bird."

"Oh, don't go," said the woman, "I feel as if the house were trembling and going up in flames."

But the man went out to look at the bird.

"And gathered each and every bone,
In a silk kerchief she tied them,
Under the juniper she laid them.
Chirrup, chirrup, what a pretty bird I am!"

With that the bird dropped the golden chain, and it fell around the man's neck so very neatly that it fit just right. He went inside and said, "See what a nice bird it is. It gave me such a beautiful golden chain and looks so beautiful."

But the woman was afraid and fell flat on the floor, and her cap fell off her head. Then the bird sang again:

"My mother cut me up."

"Oh, I wish I were a thousand fathoms under the earth so that I couldn't hear it!"

"My father ate me up."

The woman collapsed as if dead.

"My sister Mary Ann has gone."

"Oh," said Mary Ann, "I want to go out too, to see if the bird will give me something." And she went outside.

"And gathered each and every bone,
In a silk kerchief she tied them."

Then it threw down the shoes to her.

"Under the juniper she laid them.
Chirrup, chirrup, what a pretty bird I am!"

Then she was so gay and cheerful. She put on her new red shoes and came dancing and skipping in. "Oh," she said, "I was so sad when I went out, and now I'm so gay. That's a wonderful bird. It gave me a pair of red shoes."

"No," said the woman, and jumped up with her hair standing like flames of fire. "I feel as if the world were coming to an end. I want to go out too, to see if it will make me feel better."

And when she came out the door—Crash!—the bird dropped the millstone on her head so that she was completely crushed.

The father and Mary Ann heard it and went out. Steam and flames and fire came up from that place, and when this ceased, there stood the little brother. He took his father and Mary Ann by the hand, and all three were very happy and went into the house to the table and sat down to eat.

BRIAR ROSE

Once upon a time there were a king and queen who said each day, "Oh, if we only had a child!" but they never got one. Once while the queen was bathing, a frog crawled out of the water to the shore and said to her, "Before a year is up, you will give birth to a daughter."

It happened as the frog had said: the queen had a daughter who was so beautiful that the king was overjoyed and ordered a great feast. He invited not only his kinsfolk, his friends, and his acquaintances, but also the wise women so they would be gracious and kind to the child. There were thirteen of them in his kingdom, but because he had only twelve golden plates for them to eat from, one of them had to stay home.

The feast was celebrated with all magnificence, and when it was over, the wise women presented the child with their magic gifts—one with virtue, the second with beauty, the third with riches, and so on, with everything in the world one could wish for.

After eleven of them had pronounced their blessings, the thirteenth suddenly entered. She wanted to avenge herself for not having been invited, and without a greeting or so much as a look for anyone, she cried in a loud voice: "In her fifteenth year, the king's daughter shall prick herself with a spindle and shall fall down dead." Without another word, she turned her back and left the hall.

Everyone was horrified, but the twelfth, who still had her wish, came forward. Since she could not revoke the curse but could only mitigate it, she said, "The king's daughter shall not die but shall fall into a deep sleep that shall last for a hundred years." The king, who wished

to guard his beloved child against this misfortune, had
orders given that all the spindles in the entire kingdom were to be burned.

All the gifts of the wise women were fulfilled in the girl.
She was so beautiful, virtuous, kind, and intelligent that
she won the hearts of all who looked on her.

It happened that on her fifteenth birthday the king and
queen were away from home, and the girl stayed behind all alone in the castle. She went about wherever she
pleased, looking at the rooms and chambers, and came
at last to an old tower. She climbed the narrow spiral
staircase and arrived at a little door. A rusty key was
in the lock, and when she turned it, the door sprang
open. There in a little room sat an old woman with a
spindle, busily spinning flax.

"How do you do, Granny," said the king's daughter.
"What are you doing?"

"I'm spinning," said the old woman, nodding her head.

"What is that thing that bobs up and down so merrily?" asked the king's daughter, and took the spindle
because she wanted to spin too. But she had hardly
touched the spindle when the magic spell was fulfilled,
and she pricked her finger.

The very moment she felt the prick, she fell down on
a bed that was standing there, and lay in a deep sleep.

And the sleep spread throughout the castle. The king
and queen, who had just come home and entered the hall,
fell asleep, and with them the entire court. The horses
went to sleep in the stable, the dogs in the courtyard, the

pigeons on the roof, the flies on the wall—yes, even the fire flickering on the hearth grew still and slept, and the roast stopped sizzling, and the cook, who was about to pull the scullery boy's hair for some mistake, let him go and slept. The wind dropped, and not a leaf stirred on the trees in front of the castle.

A briar hedge began to grow around the castle. It got bigger each year, until at last it surrounded the castle completely and covered it so that nothing of the castle could be seen anymore, not even the flag on the roof. But a legend arose in the land about the beautiful sleeping Briar Rose, for that is what they called the king's daughter, so that from time to time kings' sons came and tried to break through the hedge into the castle. But it was impossible because the briars clung tightly together as though they had hands, and the young men got caught in them and could not get free again, so that they perished miserably.

After many long years another king's son came into the land and heard an old man telling about the briar hedge: there was supposed to be a castle behind it in which a wondrously beautiful king's daughter called Briar Rose had been sleeping for a hundred years, and with her slept the king and queen and the entire court. His grandfather had told him that many kings' sons had already tried to penetrate the briar hedge, but they had got caught in it and died a wretched death. "I am not afraid," said the young man; "I will try to see the beautiful Briar Rose." No matter how much the good old man tried to warn him against it, he did not listen to him.

Now the hundred years was just up, and the day had come on which Briar Rose was to wake up again. When the king's son approached the briar hedge, it had become a mass of large and beautiful flowers that separated of themselves to let him pass unharmed, then closed behind him like a hedge.

In the courtyard he saw the horses and the spotted hunting dogs lying asleep. On the roof the pigeons perched with their little heads nestled under their wings. And when he came into the house, the flies were asleep on the walls, the cook in the kitchen still held out his hand to grab the boy, and the kitchen maid was sitting before the black hen that she had to pluck. He continued on, and in the hall the entire court were lying asleep, and above them next to the throne lay the king and queen. He went still further on, and everything was so quiet that he could hear the sound of his own breathing.

Finally he came to the tower and opened the door to the little room where Briar Rose was sleeping. There she lay, so beautiful that he could not take his eyes from her, and he bent down and kissed her. At the touch of his kiss, Briar Rose opened her eyes, awoke, and looked at him very tenderly.

Together they went down, and the king and queen and the entire court woke up and looked at each other wide-eyed with astonishment. The horses in the courtyard got up and shook themselves; the hunting dogs jumped and wagged their tails; the pigeons on the roof pulled their heads out from under their wings, looked around, and flew off to the fields. The flies began to crawl along the walls; the fire in the kitchen blazed up and flickered and cooked the dinner; the roast started to sizzle again;

the cook slapped the boy so that he cried out; and the kitchen maid finished plucking the hen.

And then the wedding of the king's son and Briar Rose was celebrated with all magnificence, and they lived happily for the rest of their lives.

SNOW WHITE

O nce upon a time in deep winter, when the snow-flakes were falling like feathers from the sky, a queen was sitting at a window with a black ebony frame, and she was sewing. And as she looked up from her sewing at the snow, she pricked her finger with the needle, and three drops of blood fell upon the snow. And because the red looked so beautiful against the white snow, she thought to herself, "If I might have a child as white as snow, as red as blood, and as black as the wood in the frame." Soon after that, she bore a little daughter who was as white as snow and as red as blood and had hair as black as ebony, and therefore she was called Snow White. And when the child was born, the queen died.

After a year the king took a second wife. She was a beautiful woman, but she was proud and disdainful, and she could not bear that anyone should excel her in beauty. She owned a wonderful mirror, and when she stepped in front of it to look at herself, she said:

> "Mirror, mirror, on the wall,
> Who is the fairest one of all?"

And the mirror replied:

> "Lady Queen, you are the fairest one of all."

Then she was content, for she knew that the mirror told the truth.

Snow White grew up and became ever more beautiful, and when she was seven, she was as beautiful as the bright day and more beautiful than the queen herself. One time when the queen asked her mirror:

> "Mirror, mirror, on the wall,
> Who is the fairest one of all?"

it answered:

> "Lady Queen, you are fairest here, it's true,
> But Snow White is a thousand times more fair than you."

The queen started back, and she was yellow and green with envy. From that hour, whenever she saw Snow White she felt a violent pang in her heart, she hated the girl so much. And the envy and pride in her heart grew like weeds, ever higher, so that day and night she had no peace.

At last she summoned a huntsman and said, "Take the child out into the forest. I never want to set eyes on her again. You are to kill her and to bring me her lungs and her liver as proof."

The huntsman obeyed and led her away, but when he had drawn his hunting knife and was about to pierce Snow White's innocent heart, she began to weep, and said, "Oh, dear huntsman, spare my life. I shall run into the wild forest and never come home again."

And because she was so beautiful the huntsman took pity and said, "Run away, then, you poor child." He was thinking, "The wild beasts will soon devour you," but nevertheless it was as if a stone had been rolled from his heart because he did not have to kill her.

At that moment a young boar came rushing by, and he killed it, cut out the lungs and the liver, and took them to the queen as proof. The cook boiled them in salt, and the wicked woman ate them, thinking that she was eating Snow White's lungs and liver.

Now the poor child was left all forlorn in the great forest, and she was so frightened that she stared anxiously at all the leaves on the trees, and she didn't know what to do. Then she started running and ran over the sharp stones and through the brambles, and the wild beasts sprang past her but did her no harm. She ran as long as she could still take a step, until night began to fall. At last she saw a tiny little house and went inside to rest herself.

Everything in the little house was small, but neater and cleaner than words can tell. There stood a little table with a white cloth and seven little plates, each with its little spoon, and seven little knives and forks and seven little cups. Against the wall stood seven little beds in a row, covered with snowy-white sheets.

Snow White was so hungry and thirsty that she ate a few greens and a bit of bread from each little plate and drank a drop of wine from each little cup, for she did not want to take everything away from any single one. Next, because she was so tired, she lay down in a bed, but not one of them suited her; one was too long, the other too short, until finally the seventh was just right. There she remained, said her prayers, and fell asleep.

When it had grown quite dark, the owners of the little house returned. They were the seven dwarfs who quarried and mined for ore in the mountains. They lit their seven little candles, and when it became light in the house, they realized that someone had been there, for nothing was in the same order as they had left it.

The first one said, "Who has been sitting on my chair?"

The second, "Who has been eating from my plate?"

The third, "Who has taken some of my bread?"

The fourth, "Who has eaten some of my greens?"

The fifth, "Who has been using my fork?"

The sixth, "Who has been cutting with my knife?"

The seventh, "Who has been drinking out of my cup?"

Then the first turned around and saw a little crease

in his bed, and he said, "Who has been lying on my bed?" The others came running and cried, "Someone has been lying on mine too."

But the seventh, when he looked at his bed, saw Snow White lying there asleep. He called to the others, who ran up with cries of astonishment, fetched their seven little candles, and shone them on Snow White. "Ah, dear God! Ah, dear God!" they exclaimed. "How beautiful the child is!" And they were so overjoyed that they did not wake her but let her go on sleeping in the bed. The seventh dwarf slept one hour with each of his comrades, and then the night was over.

In the morning Snow White awoke, and when she

saw the seven dwarfs, she was frightened. But they were friendly and asked, "What is your name?"

She answered, "My name is Snow White."

"How did you get to our house?" continued the dwarfs.

So she told them that her stepmother had wanted her killed but that the huntsman had spared her life, and that she had run the whole day until at last she had found their little house.

The dwarfs said, "If you will look after our household, do the cooking, make our beds, do the washing, the sewing, and the knitting, and keep everything neat and clean, you may stay with us, and you shall lack nothing."

"Yes," said Snow White, "with all my heart." And she stayed with them and kept their house in order. In the morning they went into the mountains to look for ore and gold; in the evening they returned, and their supper had to be ready. Because she had to spend the whole day alone, the good little dwarfs warned her and said, "Beware of your stepmother—she will soon find out where you are. Do not let anyone in."

The queen, believing that she had eaten Snow White's lungs and liver, was certain that she was again supreme and that she was the most beautiful of all. She stepped in front of her mirror and said:

> "Mirror, mirror, on the wall,
> Who is the fairest one of all?"

And the mirror answered:

> "Lady Queen, you are fairest here, it's true,
> But over the mountains far away,
> Where the seven dwarfs stay,
> Snow White is a thousand times more fair than you."

She started back, for she knew that the mirror never lied, and she realized that the huntsman had deceived her and that Snow White was still alive. Then once again she thought and thought how she might kill her, for so long as she was not the most beautiful in the whole land, her envy gave her no peace.

Finally she hit on a plan. She smeared paint on her face

and dressed herself like an old peddler woman so that no one could recognize her. In this disguise she went over the seven mountains to the house of the seven dwarfs. She knocked at the door and called out, "Fine wares for sale! Fine wares for sale!"

Snow White looked out of the window and called out, "Good day to you, my good woman; what are you selling?"

"Fine wares, pretty wares," she answered. "Laces of every color." And she got out one woven out of many gaily colored silks.

"I can let in this honest woman," thought Snow White, so she unbarred the door and purchased the pretty lace.

"Child," said the old woman, "just look at you! Come here and let me lace you up properly for once!" Snow White, who suspected nothing, stood in front of her to let herself be laced up with the new lace. But the old woman laced her so quickly and so tight that Snow White could not breathe and fell down as if dead. "Now you *were* the most beautiful," the queen said, and hurried away.

Not long after that, toward evening, the seven dwarfs came home, but what a shock they got to see their beloved Snow White lying upon the ground without any motion or sign of life. They lifted her up, and seeing that she had been laced too tight, they cut the lace. Then she began to breathe faintly, and bit by bit she came back to life. When the dwarfs heard what had happened, they said, "The old peddler woman was none other than the evil queen. Beware, and don't let a soul into the house while we are away."

The wicked woman, as soon as she got home, went in front of her mirror and asked:

> "Mirror, mirror, on the wall,
> Who is the fairest one of all?"

And it answered as before:

> "Lady Queen, you are fairest here, it's true,
> But over the mountains far away,
> Where the seven dwarfs stay,
> Snow White is a thousand times more fair than you."

When she heard that, she was so startled that all the blood ran to her heart, for she realized that Snow White had come to life again.

"This time," she said, "I will think of something that will destroy you," and with witch's art, in which she was skilled, she made a poisoned comb. Then she disguised herself as a different old woman. Thus she went over the seven mountains to the house of the seven dwarfs. She knocked at the door and called out, "Fine wares for sale! Fine wares for sale!"

Snow White looked out and said, "You might as well go your way. I'm not allowed to let anyone in."

"Surely you are at least allowed to look," said the old woman, and she took out the poisoned comb and held it up. The child liked it so well that she let herself be taken in, and she opened the door.

When they had agreed on the price, the old woman said, "Now I'm going to comb you properly for once." Poor Snow White, suspecting nothing, let the old woman have her way. But no sooner had she stuck the comb into her hair than the poison began to work and the girl fell down unconscious. "You paragon of beauty," said the wicked woman, "now it's all over with you." And she went away.

Fortunately it was close to evening, when the seven dwarfs always came home. When they saw Snow White lying dead on the ground, they immediately suspected the stepmother, examined her, and found the poisoned comb. Hardly had they taken it out when Snow White came to herself and told what had happened. They warned her once more to be careful and not to open the door to anyone.

At home the queen stepped in front of the mirror and said:

> "Mirror, mirror, on the wall,
> Who is the fairest one of all?"

And it answered as it had before:

> "Lady Queen, you are fairest here, it's true,
> But over the mountains far away,
> Where the seven dwarfs stay,
> Snow White is a thousand times more fair than you."

When she heard what the mirror said, she trembled and quivered with rage. "Snow White must die," she cried, "if it costs me my life!"

With that, she went to a secret and lonely room where no one else ever entered, and there she made a poisoned apple. It was a beautiful sight, white with red cheeks, so that whoever saw it desired it, but whoever took just one little bite had to die. When the apple was finished, she daubed paint on her face and disguised her-

self as a farm woman. Thus she went over the seven mountains to the house of the seven dwarfs. She knocked, and Snow White put her head out the window and said, "I may not let anyone in. The seven dwarfs have forbidden it."

"Suits me just as well," answered the farm woman. "I'll have no trouble selling my apples. There, let me give you one."

"No," said Snow White, "I dare not accept anything."

"Are you afraid of poison?" said the old woman. "Look, I'll cut the apple in two—you eat the red half, and I'll eat the white half." However, the apple had been so skillfully made that only the red half was poisoned.

Snow White's mouth watered for the beautiful apple, and when she saw the farm woman eating part of it, she could resist no longer. She put out her hand and took the poisoned half. No sooner had she taken the first bite than she fell to the ground dead.

The queen leered at her horribly. She laughed scornfully and said, "White as snow, red as blood, black as ebony! This time the dwarfs can't revive you again."

And at home when she asked the mirror:

> "Mirror, mirror, on the wall,
> Who is the fairest one of all?"

it finally answered:

> "Lady Queen, you are the fairest one of all."

Then at last her jealous heart was at peace, so far as a jealous heart can ever be at peace.

When the dwarfs came home in the evening, they found Snow White lying on the ground. No breath came from her lips, and she was dead. They lifted her up and searched for a poisoned object, unlaced her, combed her hair, washed her with water and wine, but nothing did any good. The dear child was dead and stayed dead.

They laid her upon a bier and all seven of them sat around it mourning her, and they wept for three days. Then they started to bury her, but she still looked just as if she were alive, and she still had her beautiful red cheeks. They said: "We cannot lower her into the black earth." And they had a transparent coffin made of glass so that she could be seen from all sides. They laid her inside, and on it they inscribed her name in gold letters and that she was the daughter of a king. They placed the coffin on the mountain, and one of them always remained there to keep watch over it. And the birds came, too, and wept over Snow White, first the owl, then the raven, and last the dove.

Snow White lay a long time in the coffin, and her freshness did not fade; rather she looked as if she were

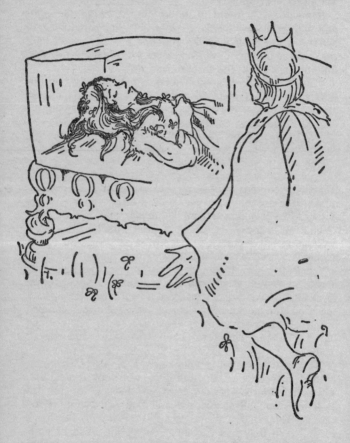

asleep, for she remained as white as snow and as red as blood, and her hair was as black as ebony. It came to pass that a king's son wandered into the forest and came to the dwarfs' house to spend the night. On the mountain he saw the coffin and beautiful Snow White within it, and he read the gold-lettered inscription.

He said to the dwarfs, "Let me have the coffin. I will pay you whatever you ask."

But the dwarfs answered, "We would not exchange it for all the gold in the world."

He said, "Then give it to me as a present, for I cannot live without seeing Snow White. I will honor and cherish her as my dearest possession."

When he spoke in such a way, the good little dwarfs took pity on him and gave him the coffin. The king's son had it carried off on his servants' shoulders. Now it happened that they tripped over a shrub, and the jar caused the piece of poisoned apple Snow White had bitten off to fly out of her throat. In a little while she opened her eyes, raised the lid of the coffin, sat up, and was alive again.

"Dear heaven, where am I?" she exclaimed.

The king's son said with great joy, "You are with me." He told her what had happened and said, "I love you more than anything in the world. Come with me to my father's castle, and you shall be my wife." And Snow White fell in love with him and went with him, and their wedding was celebrated with great pomp and magnificence.

Snow White's wicked stepmother was also asked to the feast. When she had dressed herself gorgeously, she stepped in front of the mirror and said:

> "Mirror, mirror, on the wall,
> Who is the fairest one of all?"

The mirror answered:

> "Lady Queen, you are fairest here, it's true,
> But the young queen is a thousand times more fair than
> you."

Then the wicked woman cursed and became so afraid, so terribly afraid, that she could not control herself. At first she did not even want to go to the wedding, but she had no peace: she had to go and see the young queen. When she entered, she recognized Snow White, and she stood there frozen with fear and terror. But already a pair of iron slippers had been placed on a charcoal fire. They were carried in with tongs and set down in front of her. And she had to step into the red-hot shoes and dance until she fell down dead to the ground.

RUMPELSTILTSKIN

O nce upon a time there was a miller who was poor but who had a beautiful daughter. Now it happened that he got to talk with the king, and in order to make himself seem important, he told him, "I have a daughter who can spin straw into gold."

The king said to the miller, "That's an art that appeals to me. If your daughter is as skilled as you say, bring her to my castle in the morning. I'd like to put her to the test."

When the girl came, he led her into a room that was completely filled with straw, gave her a wheel and spindle, and said, "Now get to work! You have the night, and if by tomorrow morning you haven't spun this straw into gold, you must die." With that, he himself locked the room, and she was left all alone.

There sat the poor miller's daughter and didn't know how to help herself, for she hadn't the least idea how one goes about spinning straw into gold. She became more and more frightened until at last she burst into tears.

Suddenly the door opened, and a little man came in and said, "Good evening, miller's daughter, why are you crying so hard?"

"Oh," answered the girl, "I'm supposed to spin straw into gold, and I don't know how."

The little man said, "What will you give me if I spin it for you?"

"My necklace," said the girl.

The little man took the necklace, sat down in front of the wheel, and whir, whir, whir—three pulls—and the bobbin was full. Then he set up another one, and whir, whir, whir—three pulls—and the second was full too. And so it went until morning, when all the straw had been spun and all the bobbins were full of gold.

At sunrise the king was already there, and when he saw all the gold, he was amazed and delighted, but his heart lusted all the more after gold. He had the miller's daughter taken into another room filled with straw—a much bigger one—and ordered her to spin that, too, in one night, if she valued her life.

The girl didn't know what to do, and she was crying when the door opened again and the little man appeared and asked, "What will you give me if I spin the straw into gold for you?"

"The ring on my finger," answered the girl.

The little man took the ring, and once more he started the wheel humming, and by morning he had spun all the straw into glittering gold.

The king was overjoyed at the sight, but his thirst for gold was still not satisfied. Instead, he had the miller's daughter taken into an even bigger room filled with straw and said, "You still have to spin all of this tonight; but if you succeed, you shall become my wife." "Even if she's just a miller's daughter," he thought, "I'd never find a richer woman in all the world."

When the girl was alone, the little man came for the third time and said, "What will you give me if I spin the straw for you one more time?"

"I haven't anything else to give you," answered the girl.

"Then promise me your first child if you become queen."

"Who knows what may come?" thought the miller's daughter, and, besides, she could think of no other way out of her predicament. She promised the little man what he asked, and he spun the straw into gold for her one more time. And in the morning, when the king saw that everything had gone as he wished, he married her, and the beautiful miller's daughter became a queen.

A year later she gave birth to a fine child. She had forgotten all about the little man when he suddenly came into her room and said, "Now give me what you promised."

The queen was afraid and offered the little man all the wealth in the kingdom if he would let her keep the child.

But the little man said, "No, I'd rather have a living thing than all the treasure on earth." Then the queen started to lament and weep so that the little man took pity on her and said, "I'll give you three days, and if you can find out my name in that time, you may keep the child."

Now the queen thought all night long of all the names

she had ever heard, and she sent a messenger through the land to inquire far and wide what other names there might be. When the little man came the next day, she started with Caspar, Melchior, and Balthazar, and she recited all the names that she knew, one after another. But after each one, the little man said, "That's not my name."

The second day she asked all around the neighborhood

what people were called, and she gave the little man the strangest and most unusual names—Beastlyribs, Muttonshanks, Bootlace—but the answer was always, "That's not my name."

The third day the messenger returned and reported, "I couldn't find a single new name, but as I was passing the edge of a forest near a high mountain, way out where the fox and hare say good night to each other, I saw a little house, and in front of the house a fire was blazing, and an absurd little man was hopping around the fire on one leg, shouting,

> 'I'll brew tomorrow, I'll bake today,
> On the third, I'll take the queen's child away.
> A good thing no one knows who I am,
> Because Rumpelstiltskin is my name!' "

You can imagine how glad the queen was when she heard the name, and as soon as the little man came again and asked, "Well, my Lady Queen, what is my name?" she asked first, "Is your name Conrad?"—"No" "Is your name Hal?"—"No."

"Could your name be Rumpelstiltskin?"

"The Devil told you that, the Devil told you that!" shrieked the little man, and he got so angry that he stamped his right foot into the ground so hard that it went in all the way up to his middle, and in his rage he grabbed his left foot with both hands and tore himself in two.

ROLAND, MY LOVE

Once upon a time there was a woman who was a witch, and she had two daughters, one ugly and wicked whom she loved because she was her own daughter, and one beautiful and good whom she hated because she was her stepdaughter. One time the stepdaughter had a pretty apron to which the other one had taken a fancy. She became jealous and said to her mother that she wanted the apron and had to have it.

"Be quiet, my child," said the old woman. "You'll get it all right. Your stepsister has long deserved to die. Tonight, while she is asleep, I will come and chop off her head. Just make sure that you get to lie on the far side of the bed and push her well toward the front."

That would have been the end of the poor girl if she had not by chance been standing in a corner and overheard everything. She wasn't allowed to go outside all day, and at bedtime her stepsister got into bed first in order to lie on the far side. But when the latter had gone to sleep, she pushed her gently to the front and took her place on the far side against the wall. During the night the old woman stole in. She was holding an ax in her right hand, and with her left she felt around first to see whether one of them was lying toward the front. Then she grasped the ax with both hands, brought it down, and cut off the head of her own child.

When she had gone away, the girl got up to go and see her love, whose name was Roland, and knocked at his door. When he came out, she said to him, "Listen, Roland, my love, we must flee quickly. My stepmother tried to kill me but hit her own child. As soon as day comes and she sees what she's done, we'll be lost."

"I advise you to take along her magic wand, though,"

said Roland. "Otherwise we won't be able to save ourselves when she starts after us and pursues us."

The girl got the magic wand, and then she took the
dead girl's head and let three drops of blood trickle on
the ground—one by the bed, one in the kitchen, and
one on the steps. Then she hurried away with her love.

When the old witch got up in the morning, she called
her daughter, wanting to give her the apron, but the
girl didn't come. Then the old witch called, "Where are
you?"

"Here I am, sweeping the steps," answered the first
drop of blood.

The old woman went out but didn't see anyone on the
steps and called again, "Where are you?"

"Here I am in the kitchen, getting warm," cried the
second drop of blood.

She went to the kitchen but didn't find anyone. Then
she called once more, "Where are you?"

"Oh, here I am in bed, sleeping," cried the third drop
of blood.

She went to the bedroom and to the bed. What did
she see there? Her own child, bathed in its own blood,
and she herself had cut off its head.

The witch fell into a rage, ran to the window, and
since she had the power to see far into the distance, she
saw her stepdaughter hurrying away with her love
Roland. "That won't do you any good," she cried. "Even
though you're already far off, you still won't escape me."

She put on her seven-league boots in which she could
go one hour's distance with each step, and before long
she had caught up with them.

But when the girl saw the old woman come striding
behind them, with the magic wand she turned her love
Roland into a lake and herself into a duck swimming in
the middle of the lake. The witch stood on the shore,
tossed in bits of bread, and did all she could to coax
the duck to her. But the duck wouldn't come, and at
night the old woman had to turn back, foiled in her
purpose.

Thereupon the girl and her love Roland took back
their natural shapes and traveled on the whole night
until dawn. Then the girl turned herself into a beautiful

flower growing in the middle of a briar hedge and her love Roland into a fiddler.

Soon the witch came striding along and said to the fiddler, "Friend fiddler, may I please break off the beautiful flower?"

"Oh yes, " he answered, "I'll play a tune while you do it."

She hastily crawled inside the briar hedge to break off the flower—for she knew who the flower was—and he struck up a tune. And she had to dance, whether she would or no, for it was a magic tune. The faster he played, the more wildly she had to leap about, and the thorns tore the clothes from her body and scratched her until she was cut and bleeding; and since he didn't stop, she had to keep dancing until she lay there dead.

When they were saved, Roland said, "Now I'll go to my father to arrange about the wedding."

"I'll wait for you here in the meantime," said the girl, "and so that no one will recognize me, I'll turn myself into a red stone."

Then Roland went away, and the girl stayed as a red stone in the field, waiting for her love.

But when Roland returned home, he was ensnared by another woman, who succeeded in making him forget the girl. The poor girl waited a long time, but at last when he didn't come back at all, she grew sad and turned herself into a flower, thinking, "Someone will surely come along and step on me."

But it happened that a shepherd was keeping his sheep in the field and saw the flower, and because it was so beautiful, he picked it and took it along to put in his box.

From that time on strange things began happening in the shepherd's house. When he got up in the morning, the work was already done. The room had been swept, the table and benches had been dusted, the fire was going on the hearth, and the water had been brought in. And when he came home at noon, the table had been set and a good meal had been served. He couldn't imagine how this happened because he never saw anyone in his house, and, besides, no one could have been hiding in his little cottage. He was pleased with the fine service, of course, but at last he did get frightened and went to seek the advice of a wise woman.

The wise woman said, "There is magic behind it. Very early some morning keep a close watch to see if anything stirs in the room, and when you see something stirring, no matter what it is, quickly throw a white cloth over it, and the magic won't work."

The shepherd did as she had said, and the next morning, as day was just breaking, he saw the box opening itself and the flower coming out of it. He ran quickly and threw a white cloth over it. Right away the enchantment was at an end and a beautiful girl was standing before him. She confessed that she had been the

flower and had been keeping house for him. She told him her fate, and since he liked her, he asked her to marry him. But she said no because she wanted to remain true to her love Roland even though he had forsaken her. But she promised not to leave him and to continue to keep house for him.

Now the time of Roland's wedding approached. It was proclaimed that, according to an ancient custom of the land, all maidens had to assemble to sing in honor of the bridal couple. When the faithful girl heard about this, she was so sad that she thought her heart would break, and she didn't want to go, but the others came to fetch her.

But every time her turn came to sing, she hung back, until she alone was left, and then she couldn't get out of it. But when she started to sing and Roland heard her, he jumped up and cried, "I know that voice. She is the true bride and I don't want any other." His heart suddenly remembered all that had been forgotten and that had vanished from his mind. Then the faithful girl was married to her love Roland: her sorrows were over and her happiness began.

THE GOLDEN GOOSE

T here was a man who had three sons. The youngest of them was called Dumbbell, and he was despised and ridiculed and put down on every occasion.

It happened that the oldest wanted to go into the forest to cut wood, and before he went, his mother gave him a nice fine cake and a bottle of wine so that he wouldn't be hungry or thirsty. As he got to the forest, he met a gray-haired little man who wished him good day and said, "Won't you give me a piece of the cake in your bag and let me drink a drop of your wine? I'm so hungry and thirsty."

But the clever son answered, "If I give you my cake and my wine, there won't be any for me. Go about your business." He left the little man standing there and went on his way. Now as he started to cut down a tree, it wasn't long before he missed his stroke, and the ax cut into his arm so that he had to go home to have it bandaged. However, it was the gray little man who had caused that.

Thereupon the second son went into the forest, and

his mother gave him a cake and a bottle of wine like the oldest. The gray little old man met him, too, and asked him for a piece of cake and a drink of wine. But the second son also said very sensibly, "Whatever I give you means so much the less for me. Go about your business." He left the little man standing there and went on his way. The punishment didn't fail. After striking a couple of blows at the tree, he hit his leg and had to be carried home.

Then Dumbbell said, "Father, let me go out once to cut wood."

"Your brothers got hurt doing it," answered the father. "Leave it alone. You don't know anything about it." But Dumbbell pleaded so long that he finally said, "Go ahead, then; misfortune will make you wise." The mother gave him a cake made with water and baked in the ashes, and a bottle of sour beer besides.

When he got to the forest, the gray little old man met him, too, greeted him, and said, "Give me a piece of your cake and a drink out of your bottle. I'm so hungry and thirsty."

"All I have is an ashcake and sour beer," answered Dumbbell. "If you don't mind that, let's sit down and eat."

So they sat down, and when Dumbbell got out his ashcake, it was a fine cake, and the sour beer was an excellent wine. Then they ate and drank and afterward the little man said, "Because you have a kind heart and gladly share what is yours with others, I shall give you good fortune. There is an old tree over there. Cut it down, and you will find something among the roots." Then the little man took his leave.

Dumbbell went and cut down the tree, and when it fell, a goose was sitting among the roots, and its feathers were pure gold. He picked it up, took it along, and went to an inn where he wanted to spend the night.

However, the innkeeper had three daughters who saw the goose. They wondered what sort of rare bird it might be, and they would have liked to get one of the golden feathers. The oldest thought, "I'm sure to have a chance to pluck out a feather," and when Dumbbell happened to leave the room, she grabbed the goose by the wing, but her finger and hand remained stuck.

Soon the second came along with the same idea, to pluck herself a golden feather. Hardly had she touched her sister than she was stuck.

Finally the third came with the same intention. The others cried to her, "Keep off, for heaven's sake, keep off." But she couldn't see why she should keep off and thought, "If they're at it, I can be at it too." She ran up, and when she touched her sister, she stuck to her. So they were forced to spend the night with the goose.

The next morning Dumbbell took the goose under his arm and went away without paying any attention to the three girls sticking to it. They had to run after him all the way, left, right, whatever direction took his fancy.

Out in the fields the parson met them, and when he saw the procession, he said, "Shame on you, you brazen hussies, chasing a young man across the fields. Is that the way to behave?" With that he grabbed the youngest by the hand in order to hold her back. But as he touched her, he, too, was stuck and had to run after them himself.

After a little while the sexton came up and saw the parson following hard upon the heels of three girls. He was amazed and cried, "Why, Parson, where are you going in such a rush? Don't forget that we have a christening today." He ran after him, caught hold of his sleeve, and also was stuck.

As the five of them were trotting after each other, two farmers came out of the fields with their hoes. The parson called out to them to get him and the sexton loose. But they had no sooner touched the sexton than they were stuck, and now there were seven running after Dumbbell and his goose.

Next he came to a city ruled by a king who had a daughter so solemn that nobody could get her to laugh. He had therefore issued a proclamation that whoever could make her laugh should marry her. When Dumbbell heard this, he went before the king's daughter with his goose and its following, and when she saw seven people running after each other, she burst into loud laughter and could hardly stop.

Dumbbell demanded her as his bride, but the king didn't like him for a son-in-law. He made all sorts of conditions, and said that first he'd have to bring a man who could drink up a whole cellar of wine.

Dumbbell remembered the gray little man—he'd surely be able to help. He went out into the forest, and on the spot where he had cut down the tree he saw a man sitting with a very sad expression on his face. Dumbbell asked what it was that he was taking so much to heart.

"I've got such a terrible thirst that I can't satisfy it," he answered. "Cold water doesn't agree with me, and though I've emptied a barrel of wine, what good is one drop on a hot stone?"

"In that case I can help you," said Dumbbell. "Just come with me and you'll get enough." Thereupon he led him to the king's wine cellar, and the man fell upon the great kegs, drank and drank till his sides ached, and before the day was over, he had drunk up the whole cellar.

Dumbbell again demanded his bride, but the king was vexed that a common fellow whom everyone called Dumbbell should carry off his daughter, and he made new conditions. He'd have to produce a man who could eat a mountain of bread.

Dumbbell didn't think long about it but went straight out into the forest. There sat a man in the same place who was tightening his belt and making a pathetic face. "I've eaten a whole ovenful of hard rolls," he said, "but what good is that to anyone as hungry as I am? My stomach is still empty, and I've got to tighten my belt if I don't want to die of hunger."

Dumbbell was pleased at this and said, "Pull yourself together and come with me. You'll get enough to eat." And he led him to the king's court. The latter had ordered all the flour in the whole kingdom to be carted to one place and to be baked into an enormous mountain of bread. However, the man from the forest stepped up to it, started eating, and in a single day the entire mountain had disappeared.

Dumbbell demanded his bride for the third time, but the king tried to get out of it once more and asked for a ship that could sail on both land and water. "As soon as you come sailing back in it," he said, "you shall immediately have my daughter for your wife."

Dumbbell went straight to the forest. There sat the gray little old man whom he had given some of his cake, and he said, "I've drunk for you and eaten for you, and I'll give you the ship too. I am doing all this because you took pity on me."

Then the man gave him the ship that could sail over land and water, and when the king saw it, he couldn't keep his daughter from Dumbbell any longer. The wedding was celebrated, and after the king died, Dumbbell inherited the kingdom and lived happily with his wife for a long time.

JORINDA AND JORINGEL

ᴵᴵ

Once upon a time there was an old castle in the middle of a great, dense forest in which an old woman was living all alone, and she was a notorious sorceress. During the day she changed herself into a cat or an owl, but in the evening she turned back into ordinary human shape. She knew how to lure wild animals and birds, and when she did, she slaughtered, cooked, and roasted them. Anyone who came within one hundred feet of the castle would freeze to the spot and could not move until she broke the spell. But whenever a pure maiden came into her circle, she would change her into a bird, put her in a basket, and carry the basket to a room in her castle. In the castle she had as many as seven thousand baskets with such rare birds.

Now there was a maiden called Jorinda who was more beautiful than any of the others. She was engaged to a very handsome young man called Joringel. It was shortly before their wedding, and their greatest pleasure was in each other. In order to converse alone together once, they went for a walk in the forest.

"Be careful," said Joringel, "that you don't go too near the castle." It was a lovely evening with the bright sunlight slanting between the tree trunks upon the dark green of the forest, and the turtledove was singing mournfully upon the old beech trees.

Jorinda was weeping now and then, and she sat down in the sunlight to grieve. Joringel too was grieving. They were as dismayed as though they were going to die. They looked around, and they had lost their way and didn't know how to get home. Half of the sun was still visible

over the mountaintops, and the other half had already disappeared. Joringel peered through the thicket and saw the old castle wall close by. He was startled and became deathly afraid. Jorinda was singing:

> "My little bird with ringlet red
> Sings sorrow, sorrow, sorrow:
> It tells the dove it will soon be dead.
> Sing sorrow, sor—tereu, tereu, tereu."

Joringel turned around to look at Jorinda. Jorinda had been changed into a nightingale, singing, "Tereu, tereu." An owl with glowing eyes flew around her three times and cried thrice, "Whoo-oo, whoo-oo, whoo-oo." Joringel could not stir. He stood there as though he were made of stone and could not speak or move hand or foot.

Then the sun went down. The owl flew into a bush, and straightway an old woman came out of it, stooped over, yellowish, and thin. She had big red eyes and a hook nose, the tip of which reached to her chin. Mumbling, she caught the nightingale and carried it away in her hand. Joringel could not speak or move from the spot. The nightingale was gone. Finally the woman came back and said in a muffled voice, "I greet you, Zachiel. When the moon shines in the basket, let go, Zachiel, when the time is right."

Then Joringel was free. He fell upon his knees before the woman and begged her to give him back his Jorinda, but she said that he should never have her again and went away. He cried out and wept and lamented, but all in vain. "Oh, what shall become of me?"

Joringel left home and finally came to a strange village; there he kept sheep for a long time. Often he walked around and around the castle, but not too close to it. Finally he dreamed one night of finding a blood-red flower at the center of which was a large and beautiful pearl. He picked the flower and went to the castle with it, and everything he touched with the flower was released from its spell. Moreover, he dreamed that by this means he won back Jorinda.

In the morning, after he woke up, he began to search over hill and dale for a flower like that. He searched until the ninth day, on which he found the blood-red flower early in the morning. At the center was a large dew drop as big as the most beautiful pearl. He carried this flower day and night until he reached the castle. When he came within one hundred feet of the castle, he did not freeze but went on up to the gate.

Joringel rejoiced and touched the gate with the flower, and it sprang open. He went inside, through the courtyard, listening for the sound of all the birds. At last he heard it. He went and found the hall where the sorceress was feeding the birds in the seven thousand baskets.

When she saw Joringel, she became angry, terribly angry, and hurled abuse and spit poison and gall at him, but she could not get within two feet of him.

He walked right past her, examining the baskets with the birds. But there were many hundreds of nightingales. How would he go about finding his Jorinda again? But while he was looking, he noticed the old woman stealthily taking one basket with a bird and heading for the door. Quickly he sprang after her, touched the basket with the flower, and the old woman too. Now she couldn't work her spells anymore, and Jorinda was standing there with her arms around his neck, as beautiful as ever. Then he turned all of the other birds back into maidens and returned home with his Jorinda, and they lived together happily for a long time.

BROTHER LUSTIG*

Once upon a time there was a great war, and when the war was over, many of the soldiers were discharged. Brother Lustig also got his discharge, and nothing else, except for a small loaf of army bread and four pennies in cash. With that he set off. However, Saint Peter had seated himself beside the road disguised as a poor beggar, and when Brother Lustig came along, he asked him for alms. "Friend beggar," he answered, "what can I give you? I've been a soldier and have got my discharge. And I haven't anything at all except for a bit of army bread and four pennies in cash. When that's gone, I'll have to beg just like you. All the same, I'll give

* Brother Lustig is a name for a jolly, devil-may-care, shrewd sort of fellow.

you something." Thereupon he divided his loaf into four parts and gave the apostle one of them, and also one penny.

Saint Peter said thank you, went on ahead, and disguised as another beggar, sat down again where the soldier would pass by. When the soldier came up, Saint Peter asked him for alms as he had the first time. Brother Lustig gave him the same answer and again let him have a fourth of the bread and one penny.

Saint Peter said thank you and went ahead, and he sat down beside the road a third time, disguised as still another beggar, and hailed Brother Lustig. Brother Lustig gave him the third quarter of the bread too, and the third penny.

Saint Peter said thank you, and Brother Lustig went on with only a quarter of a loaf and one penny to his name. With this he entered an inn, ate the bread, and ordered a penny's worth of beer to drink with it. When he had finished, he went on, and Saint Peter came to meet him disguised as another discharged soldier and spoke to him. "Hello there, comrade, can you spare a bit of bread and a penny for a drink?"

"Where would I get it from?" answered Brother Lustig. "I was handed my discharge and nothing else except for a loaf of army bread and four pennies in cash. Three beggars met me along the road, and I gave each of them a quarter of my bread and a penny of my money. The last quarter I ate at an inn and spent my last penny for something to wash it down. Now I'm cleaned out, and if you haven't got anything either, we can go begging together."

"No," answered Saint Peter, "it hasn't quite come to that. I know a little about medicine, and that way I'll manage to earn enough to get by on."

"Is that so?" said Brother Lustig. "I don't know a thing about that, so I'll have to go begging alone."

"Well, just come along," said Saint Peter. "If I earn anything, I'll give you half."

"That's all right with me," said Brother Lustig. So they set off together.

They came to a farmhouse and heard a terrible moaning and groaning within. They went in to find the master of the house lying critically ill and near the point of death and his wife weeping and wailing very loudly. "Stop your weeping and wailing," said Saint Peter. "I'll cure this man." He took a salve out of his pouch and cured the sick man in an instant so that he was able to get up and was completely well.

"How can we repay you?" the husband and wife said in great joy. "What shall we give you?" But Saint Peter wouldn't take anything, and the more the farmer and his wife insisted, the more he refused.

But Brother Lustig poked Saint Peter and said, "Go ahead and take something—after all, we need it."

Finally the farmer's wife fetched a lamb and told Saint Peter that he had to take it, but he refused. Then Brother Lustig poked Saint Peter in the ribs and said, "Take it, you silly devil—after all, we need it."

Saint Peter finally said, "Well, I'll take the lamb, but I won't carry it. If you want it, you'll have to carry it yourself."

"That's no problem," said Brother Lustig, "I'll carry it all right." And he lifted the lamb up on his shoulder.

They went on and came to a forest. Brother Lustig was getting tired of carrying the lamb. He was hungry, and so he said to Saint Peter, "Look, there's a good place where we can cook the lamb and eat it."

"That's all right as far as I'm concerned," answered Saint Peter, "but I don't know how to cook. If you're willing to cook, here's a kettle for you. I'll take a walk in the meantime until the lamb gets done. But you mustn't begin eating before I come back. I'll be sure to be back in time."

"Go ahead," said Brother Lustig, "I know how to cook. I'll take care of it all right."

Then Saint Peter went away, and Brother Lustig slaughtered the lamb, built a fire, tossed the meat into the kettle, and cooked. But when the lamb was done, the apostle still hadn't returned, so Brother Lustig took it out of the kettle, cut it up, and found the heart. "That's supposed to be the best part," he said, and tasted it, and at last he ate it all up.

Finally Saint Peter came back and said, "You can have the whole lamb for yourself. All I want is the heart. Give me that."

Brother Lustig took his knife and fork and pretended to be searching busily in the meat, but he wasn't able to find the heart. At last he said shortly, "There isn't one."

"Well, what could have become of it?" said the apostle.

"I don't know," answered Brother Lustig. "But see here, what fools we are! Here we're looking for the lamb's heart, and it doesn't occur to either one of us that of course a lamb doesn't have a heart!"

"Indeed!" said Saint Peter, "That's something altogether new. Every animal has a heart, so why shouldn't a lamb have a heart?"

"No indeed, brother, a lamb doesn't have a heart. Just try to think, and you'll remember. It really doesn't have one."

"Well, never mind," said Saint Peter, "if there isn't any heart, I don't need any part of the lamb. You can eat it all by yourself."

"Well, whatever I can't finish, I'll put in my knapsack,"

said Brother Lustig, and he ate half of the lamb and put the rest in his knapsack.

As they went on, Saint Peter caused a great river to flow directly across their path, and they had to ford it. "You go first," Saint Peter.

"No," answered Brother Lustig, "you go first." He was thinking, "If the water is too deep, I'll stay behind."

Then Saint Peter waded across, and the water only went up to his knees. Now Brother Lustig tried to wade across too, but the water became deeper and went up to his neck. Then he cried, "Help me, brother!"

Saint Peter said, "Will you confess that you ate the lamb's heart?"

"No," he answered, "I didn't eat it."

Then the water rose up still higher and came all the way up to his mouth. "Help me, brother," cried the soldier.

Saint Peter said again, "Will you confess that you ate the lamb's heart?"

"No," he answered, "I didn't eat it."

In spite of this Saint Peter didn't want to let him drown, so he made the water go down and helped him across.

Then they traveled on and came to a kingdom where they heard that the king's daughter was sick and dying. "Well now, brother," the soldier said to Saint Peter, "here's a break for us. If we can cure her, our worries are over for good."

Saint Peter didn't move quickly enough to suit him. "Now pick up your feet, brother dear," he said to him, "so that we'll get there in time." But Saint Peter walked more and more slowly no matter how much Brother Lustig urged and prodded him along, until finally they were told that the king's daughter had died. "That does it," said Brother Lustig. "This is what comes of dragging your feet."

"Just keep quiet," answered Saint Peter. "I can do more than cure the sick; I can also bring the dead back to life."

"Well, if that's the case," said Brother Lustig, "I'm not mad a bit. But for that you'll have to get us half the kingdom at the very least."

Then they entered the royal palace where everyone was in deep mourning. However, Saint Peter told the king that he would bring his daughter back to life. They took him to her, and he said, "Bring me a kettleful of water." And when they had brought it, he ordered everyone out of the room, and only Brother Lustig was allowed to stay with him.

Then he cut off the dead girl's limbs and threw them into the water, made a fire under the kettle, and boiled them. And when all the flesh had fallen off, he took out the lovely white bones, laid them out on the table, and arranged them in their natural order. When that was done, he stepped up and said three times, "In the name of the

Most Holy Trinity, dead woman, arise." And the third time the king's daughter stood up, alive, healthy, and beautiful.

The king was overjoyed at this and said to Saint Peter, "Name your reward, and if it should be half of my kingdom, I shall give it to you."

But Saint Peter answered, "I don't want anything for it."

"Oh, you fool!" Brother Lustig thought to himself, dug his comrade in the ribs, and said, "Don't be so stupid. If you don't want anything, I could use something." But Saint Peter didn't want anything. However, because the king saw that the other one would have liked to get something, he had the treasurer fill his knapsack with gold.

Thereupon they continued on their way, and when they came into a forest, Saint Peter said to Brother Lustig, "Now let's divide the gold."

"Yes," he answered, "let's do that."

Then Saint Peter divided the gold into three parts. "Here's another one of his crazy notions!" thought Brother Lustig. "He makes three shares even though there are only two of us."

But Saint Peter said, "Now I've divided it just right: one share for me, one share for you, and one for the one who ate the heart of the lamb."

"Oh, I ate that," answered Brother Lustig, and quickly gathered in the gold. "You can be certain of that."

"How could that be true," said Saint Peter, "since a lamb doesn't have a heart?"

"Nonsense brother, what are you thinking of! Of course a lamb has a heart, just like every other animal. Why should it alone not have one?"

"Well, never mind," said Saint Peter. "Keep the gold for yourself. But I won't travel with you any longer. I'll go my way alone."

"Just as you like, brother dear," answered the soldier. "Farewell."

Then Saint Peter took another road. But Brother Lustig thought, "It's just as well that he's gone trotting off. He certainly is a queer fish."

Now he had plenty of money, but he didn't know how to manage it. He spent it and gave it away, and after a time he was penniless again. Then he came to a country where he heard the king's daughter had died. "Well, now," he thought, "here's an opportunity. I'll bring her back to life and make them pay me for it properly." So he went to the king and offered to revive the dead girl. Now the king had heard that a discharged soldier was wandering about bringing the dead back to life, and he thought that Brother Lustig was the man. However, since he had no faith in him, he asked his councillors first, but they said he should risk it, since his daughter was dead anyway.

Now Brother Lustig had them bring him a kettleful of water, ordered everyone outside, cut off the limbs, threw them into the water, and made a fire under it, just as he had seen Saint Peter do it. The water began to boil, and when the flesh fell off the bones, he took them out and laid them on the table. But he didn't know the order in which to arrange them and got them all mixed up. Then he stood in front of them and said, "In the name of the Most Holy Trinity, dead woman, arise." He said it three times, but the bones did not sitir. Then he said it three more times with no better luck. "Stand up, you minx," he cried. "Stand up, or you'll be sorry."

When he had said this, Saint Peter suddenly came in through the window in his old disguise as a discharged soldier. "You scoundrel," he said, "what are you doing? How can the dead girl stand up when you've scrambled up her bones like that?"

"Brother dear, I did the best I could," he answered.

"This time I'll help you out of your predicament. But let me tell you, if you try something like this one more time, you'll suffer for it. Moreover, you mustn't ask for the slightest reward from the king for this." Thereupon Saint Peter put the bones in the right order, said to her three times, "In the name of the Most Holy Trinity, dead woman, arise," and the king's daughter got up and was as healthy and as beautiful as before.

Then Saint Peter went out through the window again. Brother Lustig was glad that everything had turned out so well, but he was annoyed that he wasn't allowed to take anything for it. "I'd like to know," he thought, "where he gets these crazy ideas, because whatever he gives with one hand, he takes away with the other. It doesn't make any sense." The king offered Brother Lustig whatever he desired, but he didn't dare accept anything. Nevertheless, through hints and cunning he managed to get the king to have his knapsack filled with gold, and with that he left.

As he was going out, Saint Peter was standing in front of the gate and said, "What sort of man are you! I for-

bade you to take anything, and now your knapsack is full of gold after all."

"How can I help it," said Brother Lustig, "if they fill it for me?"

"I'll tell you so you won't try such tricks another time, or else it will be the worse for you."

"Well, brother, don't worry. Now that I've got gold, why should I bother washing bones?"

"Yes," said Saint Peter, "the gold will last a long time! But to keep you from going astray again, I'll give your knapsack the power that whenever you make a wish to have something in it, in it goes. Farewell. You won't see me again."

"Good-bye," said Brother Lustig and thought, "I'm glad that you're going off, you queer fellow. I won't run after you." But he thought no more about the magic power of his knapsack.

Brother Lustig traveled about with his gold and spent and squandered it as he had the first time. When he was down to his last four pennies, he passed an inn and thought, "The money must go." And he ordered three pennies' worth of wine and one penny's worth of bread. As he was sitting there drinking, he smelled the aroma of roast goose. Brother Lustig pried and looked around and saw that the innkeeper was keeping two geese warm in the oven. Then he remembered what his comrade had told him: whatever he wished into his knapsack, in it went. "Well now, I'll have to try that with the geese."

He went outside, and in front of the door he said, "I wish the two roast geese out of the oven and into my knapsack." When he had said that, he unbuckled it and looked in, and there they both were. "Ah, that's fine," he said, "now my fortune is made." He went into a meadow and got out his roast.

As he was eating away heartily, two journeymen came along and looked hungrily at the goose he hadn't touched yet. Brother Lustig thought, "One will be enough for me." He called the two journeymen over and said, "Take the goose and eat it for the good of my health."

They thanked him and took it to the inn, where they ordered a half bottle of wine and a loaf of bread, unpacked the goose they'd been given, and started eating. The innkeeper's wife was watching and said to her husband, "Those two are eating a goose. Go look and make sure it's not one of those warming in the oven."

The innkeeper ran to see and found the oven empty. "What, you pack of thieves, you like to get your geese cheap! Pay me this instant, or I'll give you a tanning."

"We're not thieves," they both said. "A discharged soldier gave us this goose out there in the meadow."

"You can't pull the wool over my eyes. The soldier was here, but he walked through the door an honest man. I was keeping my eye on him. You're the thieves and you'll have to pay." But since they weren't able to pay, he took his cudgel and beat them out of the door.

Brother Lustig went his way and came to a place where there was a splendid castle and not far from it a common inn. He went to the inn and asked for a bed for the night, but the innkeeper turned him away and said, "There's no more room. All the accommodations have been taken by guests who are noblemen."

"I'm surprised," said Brother Lustig, "that they come to you instead of going to the splendid castle."

"Well," answered the innkeeper, "It's not so easy to stay overnight there. No one who has ever tried it has come out alive."

"If others have tried it," said Brother Lustig, "I'll try it too."

"Better leave it alone," said the innkeeper. "It will cost you your life."

"It won't cost my life right away," said Brother Lustig, "just give me the keys and plenty to eat and drink."

The innkeeper gave him the keys and food and drink, and with that Brother Lustig went to the castle, had a good meal, and when he finally got sleepy, he lay down on the ground because there was no bed.

He had no trouble going to sleep, but in the middle of the night he was awakened by a terrible racket, and as he came to, he saw nine ugly devils in the room who were dancing around him in a circle. "Dance as long as you like," said Brother Lustig, "but make sure that none of you comes too close to me."

But the devils kept coming closer and were practically stepping on his face with their horrible feet.

"Calm down, you fiends," he said, but they only carried on all the more.

Then Brother Lustig got angry, and cried, "Well, I'll soon quiet you down." He picked up the leg of a chair and lit right into them. But nine devils is too great odds even against one soldier, and while he was clubbing the one in front of him, the others grabbed his hair from behind and pulled it grievously.

"You pack of devils," he cried, "this is too much. Just wait, though! All nine of you into my knapsack!" Zip! they were inside, and then he buckled it and tossed it into a corner. Then it was suddenly still, and Brother Lustig lay down again and slept until it was broad daylight.

The innkeeper and the lord who owned the castle came to see how he had fared, and when they saw him hale and hearty, they were astonished and asked, "Didn't the ghosts do anything to you?"

"Not at all," answered Brother Lustig. "I've got all nine of them in my knapsack. You can move safely back into your castle; from now on no one is going to haunt it."

The lord thanked him, rewarded him bountifully, and asked him to enter his service. He promised to take care of him for the rest of his life.

"No," Brother Lustig answered, "I've grown used to traveling about. I'd like to move on."

Then Brother Lustig went away, entered a smithy, and laid the knapsack with the nine devils inside on the anvil and told the smith and his men to lay on. They pounded away with their big hammers as hard as they could, so that the devils set up a pitiful screeching. After that, eight were dead when Brother Lustig opened the knapsack, but one who had been sitting in a crease was still alive, slipped out, and plunged back down to Hell.

After this Brother Lustig wandered many more years all over the world, and whoever knows the story could tell a lot about it. But at last he got old and thought about his end. He went to a hermit who was well known as a holy man, and said to him, "I'm tired of wandering about, and now I'd like to see to it that I get into the Heavenly Kingdom."

"There are two ways," answered the hermit. "The first is broad and easy and leads to Hell. The second is rough and narrow and leads to Heaven."

"I'd have to be a fool to take the rough and narrow path," thought Brother Lustig. He set off on the broad and easy path and finally came to a big black gate, and that was the gate of Hell.

Brother Lustig knocked, and the gatekeeper looked out to see who was there. But when he saw Brother Lustig he was frightened, because he was that very ninth devil who had been along in the knapsack and had gotten off lightly. So he quickly shot the bolt again, ran to the commander of the devils, and said, "There's a fellow with a knapsack out there who wants to come in. But as you value your life, don't let him in, or else he'll wish all of Hell into his knapsack. One time I got a dreadful hammering in there." So they called out to Brother Lustig that he should go away again because they wouldn't let him in.

"If they don't want me here," he thought, "let's see if there's a place for me in Heaven. After all, I've got to stay somewhere." So he turned around went on until he came to the gate of Heaven, where he also knocked.

Saint Peter happened to be sitting there as gatekeeper. Brother Lustig recognized him at once and thought, "Here's an old friend. Now things will go better."

But Saint Peter said, "Am I really to believe that you'd like to get into Heaven?"

"Do let me in, brother. I have to turn in somewhere. If they'd taken me in Hell, I wouldn't have come here."

"No," said Saint Peter, "you won't get in here."

"Well, if you won't let me in, take back your knapsack. In that case, I don't want anything of yours," said Brother Lustig.

"Then give it to me," said Saint Peter.

Brother Lustig handed the knapsack through the bars into Heaven, and Saint Peter took it and hung it up next to his easy chair.

Then Brother Lustig said, "Now I wish myself into the knapsack." Zip! he was inside, and then he was in Heaven, and Saint Peter had to let him stay there.

THE GOOSEGIRL

〰〰〰〰〰〰〰〰〰〰〰〰〰〰〰〰〰〰〰〰〰〰〰〰〰〰〰〰

Once upon a time there lived an old queen whose husband had died many years ago, and she had a beautiful daughter. When she grew up, she was promised in marriage to a king's son far away. Now when the time came for her to be married and the child had to begin her journey to the foreign kingdom, the old queen packed up a great many costly dishes and jewels, gold and silver, goblets and trinkets—everything, in short, that belongs in a royal dowry—for she loved the child with all her heart. She also gave her a maid-in-waiting, who was supposed to ride along with her and to give the bride into the hands of the groom. Each one got a horse for the journey, but the princess's horse was called Falada, and it could talk.

When the hour of parting had come, the old mother went to her bedroom, took a little knife, and cut her fingers to make them bleed. She held a scrap of white cloth up to them and let three drops of blood trickle on it, gave them to her daughter, and said, "Dear child, take good care of them. You will have need of them on your way."

And so they sadly said good-bye to each other. The princess tucked the scrap of cloth into her bosom and got up on her horse, and then she set off to meet her bridegroom.

After they had ridden along for an hour, she became terribly thirsty and said to her maid, "Get down and fill the cup you've brought for me with water from the brook. I would like a drink."

"If you're thirsty," said the maid, "get down yourself and lie down by the water and drink. I don't want to wait on you."

The princess got off her horse because she was so very thirsty, stooped down to the water in the brook, and drank. She wasn't permitted to drink out of the gold cup. She said, "Dear heaven!" and the three drops of blood answered, "If your mother knew this, it would break her heart."

But the bride of the prince was meek. She said nothing and got back on her horse. Thus they rode a few miles farther, but it was a warm day, the sun burned down, and soon she was thirsty again. When they came to a stream, she called again to her maid, "Get down and fetch me a drink in my gold cup." For she had long since forgotten all of the unkind words.

But the maid said even more proudly, "If you want to drink, help yourself. I don't want to wait on you."

Then the princess got down because she was so

thirsty, and she leaned out over the flowing stream. She wept and said, "Dear heaven!" and again the drops of blood answered, "If your mother knew this, it would break her heart." And as she was drinking and leaning out over the bank as far as she could, the little scrap of cloth with the three drops fell out of her bosom and

was carried away by the water, and she was too frightened to notice. But the maid noticed and was glad to get the bride in her power, for by losing the drops of blood the princess had become weak and helpless.

When she wanted to get back on her horse, Falada, the maid said, "I belong on Falada, and you belong on my nag." And she had to put up with it. Then the maid harshly commanded her to take off her royal garments and to put on her mean ones instead, and last of all she had to swear before the face of Heaven that she would tell no one at court about it. And if she had refused to swear this oath, she would have been murdered on the spot. But Falada saw all that went on and paid close attention.

Now the maid mounted on Falada and the true bride got on the common nag, and so they went on until finally they arrived at the royal castle. There was great joy at their coming, and the prince ran to meet them.

He lifted the maid down from the horse and thought that she was his bride. She was escorted up the steps, but the true princess had to remain standing below.

The old king looked out of the window and saw her waiting in the courtyard and noticed that she was well bred, gentle, and very beautiful. He went straightway to the royal apartment and asked the bride about the girl she had brought with her who was standing down there in the courtyard—who might she be?

"She's someone I picked up along the way for company. Give the girl some work so that she won't stand there idle."

But the old king had no work for her and wasn't able to think of anything better than to say, "I've got a small boy who looks after the geese. She can help him."

The boy was called Curdy, and he was the one the true bride had to help tend geese.

Soon thereafter the false bride said to the young prince, "Dearest husband, let me beg you to do me a favor."

He replied, "I'll do it gladly."

"Well, then, have the knacker * summoned to cut off the head of the horse on which I rode here, because it made me angry on the journey." But the real reason was that she was afraid the horse might tell what she had done to the princess.

Thus it happened, and when the time had come for the faithful Falada to die, the real princess also heard about it, and she secretly promised the knacker a piece of money in return for a small favor. There was a large, dark gateway in the town through which she had to pass with the geese every morning and every evening. Would he please nail Falada's head up under the dark gateway so that she could see him again more than once? The knacker promised to do it, struck off the head, and nailed it up under the dark gateway.

Early in the morning, when she and Curdy were driving the geese out through the gateway, she said as she passed:

---

* Someone who buys and slaughters worn-out horses and sells their flesh as dog's meat, etc.

"O Falada, there you hang high."

And the head answered:

"O young princess, there you go by.
If your mother knew this,
It would break her heart."

Then she went still farther out of town, and they drove
the geese into the fields. When they came to the pasture,
she sat down and loosened her hair, which was pure gold.
Curdy saw it and was delighted at the way it gleamed,
and he wanted to pull out a few hairs. Then she said:

"Blow, wind, blow,
Make Curdy go
Chasing after his cap
Till I've done up my hair
And braided it fair."

And such a strong wind started up that it blew Curdy's cap all over the countryside, and he had to run after it. By the time he got back, she was all finished combing her hair and putting it back up, and he couldn't get any of it. That made Curdy angry, and he refused to speak to her. And so they tended the geese until evening. Then they went home.

The next morning, as they were driving the geese through the dark gateway, the girl said:

"O Falada, there you hang high."

Falada answered:

"O young princess, there you go by.
    If your mother knew this,
    It would break her heart."

Out in the fields she sat down in the grass again and started to comb out her hair, and Curdy came running up to grab at it. But she said quickly:

"Blow, wind, blow,
    Make Curdy go
    Chasing after his cap
    Till I've done up my hair
    And braided it fair."

Then the wind blew, and blew the cap right off his head, far away, so that Curdy had to run after it. And when he came back, she had long since finished putting her hair up, and he couldn't get hold of a single lock. And so they tended geese until evening.

But that night, after they got home, Curdy went to the old king and said, "I don't want to tend geese with that girl anymore."

"Why not?" asked the king.

"Oh, she makes me angry all day long."

The old king ordered him to tell what he found to be the matter with her.

Curdy said, "Every morning when we pass under the

dark gateway, there's a horse's head on the wall, and she
says to it:

> 'Falada, there you hang high.'

And the head answers:

> 'O young princess, there you go by.
> If your mother knew this,
> It would break her heart.' "

And so Curdy told the rest, what happened in the
pasture and how he had to run after his cap.

The old king ordered him to drive the geese out again
the next day, and in the morning he himself hid behind
the dark gate and overheard the girl talking with Falada's head. And he also followed her into the fields and
hid himself behind a bush in the meadow. Soon he saw
for himself where the goosegirl and the gooseboy came
driving the flock and how, after a while, she sat down
and unbraided her hair—it shone forth with a radiant
brightness. Right away she repeated:

> "Blow, wind, blow,
> Make Curdy go
> Chasing after his cap
> Till I've done up my hair
> And braided it fair."

A gust of wind came and carried off Curdy's cap so
that he had to run far away, and the girl calmly went on
combing and braiding her locks, while the old king observed everything.

He went away unnoticed, and when the goosegirl returned home that night, he called her aside and asked
her why she did all of these things.

"I cannot tell you, nor can I tell my sorrow to a soul,
for that is what I swore before the face of Heaven on
pain of losing my life."

He urged her and gave her no peace, but he could get
nothing out of her. Finally he said, "If you can't confide
in me, tell your sorrow to that iron stove," and he went
away.

She crawled into the iron stove and wept and complained and poured her heart out and said, "Here I sit forsaken by all the world although I am a king's daughter, and a false maid-in-waiting has forced me to take off my royal garments and has taken my place with my bridegroom, and I have to do menial service as a goosegirl. If my mother knew this, it would break her heart."

But the old king was standing outside by the stovepipe listening, and he heard what she said. Then he went back inside and told her to come out of the stove. He had her dressed in royal garments, and she was so beautiful that it seemed a miracle.

The old king called his son and revealed to him that he had the wrong bride: she was just a maid-in-waiting, but the true one—the former goosegirl—was standing right there. The young prince was as glad as he could be when he saw her beauty and virtue, and a great feast was ordered to which all the good friends and neighbors were invited. At the head of the table sat the bridegroom, with the princess on one side and the maid-in-waiting on the other, but the maid was dazzled by the princess's finery and didn't recognize her.

Now, when they had eaten and drunk and spirits ran high, the old king gave a riddle to the maid: What does a woman deserve who betrays her master in such and such a manner, and he went on to tell the whole affair, and asked, "What sentence would such a one deserve?"

The false bride said, "She deserves no better than to be stripped stark naked and put in a barrel studded inside with sharp nails, and two white horses should be hitched to it and should drag her from street to street until she is dead."

"That is you," said the old king. "You have pronounced judgment on yourself, and that is what shall be done to you."

And when the sentence had been carried out, the young prince married the right bride, and they both ruled the land in peace and happiness.

THE WATER OF LIFE

Once upon a time a king was sick, and no one expected him to live. He had three sons who grieved for him and who went down into the castle garden and wept. There they met an old man who asked them the reason for their sorrow. They answered that their father was so sick that he would probably die, for nothing seemed to help him. Then the old man said, "I know of another remedy: it's the Water of Life. If he drinks some of it, he will recover, but it is hard to find."

The oldest said, "I'll find it all right." He went to the sick king and asked him for permission to go and seek the Water of Life because that was the only thing that would cure him.

"No," said the king. "It's too dangerous. I'd rather die."

But he kept pleading until the king gave his consent. The prince thought in his heart, "If I bring back the Water of Life, my father will love me best, and I will inherit the kingdom."

So he set on his way, and when he had been riding along for a while, there was a dwarf standing beside the path who hailed him and said, "Where are you off to so fast?"

"You stupid runt," the prince said very proudly, "that's none of your business." And he rode on.

But the little man was angry and put a curse on him. Soon afterward the prince got into a mountain gorge, and the farther he rode, the more the mountains closed in on him, and finally the path became so narrow that he couldn't advance another step. It was impossible to turn the horse around or to climb out of the saddle, and he sat there like a prisoner.

The sick king waited a long time for him, but he didn't come. Then the second son said, "Father, let me set out and seek the Water." And he thought to himself, "If my brother is dead, I will inherit the kingdom."

At first the king didn't want to let him go either, but at last he gave in. And so the prince followed the same path as his brother and also met the dwarf, who stopped him and asked him where he was off to so fast. "You tiny runt," said the prince, "that's none of your business." And he rode on without a backward glance. But the dwarf put him under a spell so that he, like the other one, got into a mountain gorge and couldn't go forward or backward. That's what happens to the proud.

When the second son, too, did not come back, the youngest offered to go fetch the Water of Life, and at last the king had to let him go too. When he met the dwarf who asked him where he was off to so fast, he stopped and answered with these words: "I am seeking the Water of Life, for my father is sick and dying."

"And do you know where to find it?"

"No," said the prince.

"Because you have behaved properly and not proudly like your false brothers, I will give you directions and tell you how you can get the Water of Life. It flows from a fountain in the courtyard of an enchanted castle, but you won't get inside if I don't give you an iron rod and two little loaves of bread. With the rod you must strike the iron gate of the castle three times, and it will spring open. Two lions are lying inside with their jaws wide open, but if you throw each one a loaf, they'll be quiet. Then you must hurry and get some of the Water of Life before the stroke of twelve, or else the door will slam shut again and you will be imprisoned."

The prince thanked him, took the rod and the bread, and set on his way. When he got there, everything was as the dwarf had said. The door sprang open at the third blow from the rod, and when he had quieted the lions with the bread, he entered the castle and came into a large and beautiful hall. Some enchanted princes were sitting there, and he drew the rings from their fingers. He also brought away a sword and a loaf of bread that were lying there. He went on and came to a room in which a beautiful maiden was standing. She was glad when she saw him, kissed him, and told him that he had set her free and should have her whole kingdom. If he would come back after one year, they would celebrate their wedding. She also told him where to find the fountain with the Water of Life, but he must hurry to draw the Water from it before it struck twelve.

Then he went on and finally came to a room in which a fine bed was standing freshly made up, and because he was tired he wanted to rest a little first. So he lay down and went to sleep. As he woke up, it was striking a quarter to twelve. He jumped up, very much frightened, ran to the fountain, dipped out some of the Water with a

cup standing beside it, and made haste to get away. Just as he was going through the iron gate it struck twelve, and the gate slammed shut so hard that it took off a piece of his heel.

But he was glad to have the Water of Life, started on the way home, and passed the dwarf once more. When the latter saw the sword and the bread, he said, "With these you have gained things of great value. With the sword you can defeat whole armies, and the bread can never be used up."

The prince didn't want to go home to his father without his brothers, and said, "Dear dwarf, couldn't you tell me where my brothers are? They set out before me to seek the Water of Life, but they didn't come back."

"They're hemmed in between two mountains," said the dwarf. "I sent them there under a spell because of their pride." The prince begged until the dwarf set them free again, but he warned him, and said, "Beware of them—their hearts are evil."

When his brothers came, he was glad, and told them how he had fared, and how he had found the Water of Life and taken along a cup of it, and how he had set free a beautiful princess who was going to wait a year for him and then they would celebrate their wedding and he would get a large kingdom.

After that they rode off together and came to a country where there was famine and war, and the king believed that he must perish, his need was so great. The prince went to him and gave him the bread, with which he fed all of his people until they had had enough. And the prince also lent him the sword, with which he defeated the enemy armies, and then he was able to live in peace and quiet. Then the prince took back his loaf of bread and his sword, and the three brothers traveled on.

They came to two more countries where famine and war reigned, and each time the prince gave the king his loaf of bread and his sword, and thus he saved three kingdoms. After that they boarded a ship and sailed over the sea.

During the voyage the two older ones said to each other: "Instead of us, it's the youngest who's found the Water of Life, and in return our father will give him the kingdom, which should belong to us, and he will steal our fortune." Then they wanted revenge and plotted his ruin. They waited one time until he was fast asleep. Then they poured the Water of Life out of his cup and took it for themselves, but they refilled the cup with bitter salt water.

When they came home, the youngest took the cup to the sick king so that he might drink from it and get well.

Scarcely had he drunk a little of the bitter salt water than he became even sicker than he had been before. And as he was complaining about it, the two oldest sons came and accused the youngest of trying to poison him. They said they were bringing him the true Water of Life and handed it to him. Scarcely had he drunk from it than he felt his sickness passing from him, and he was as strong and healthy as in the days of his youth.

After that the two went to the youngest and mocked him, saying, "You may have found the Water of Life, but you had the labor and we have the reward. You should have been smarter and kept your eyes open. We took it from you at sea while you were asleep. And when the year is up, one of us will fetch the beautiful princess. But take care that you don't tell any of it. Our father won't believe you anyway, and if you breathe a single word, you'll lose your life as well. But if you keep quiet, we'll spare you."

The old king was angry at his youngest son, believing that he had plotted against his life. Therefore, he called the court together to pronounce sentence on him: he was to be shot and killed in secret.

One time when the prince went hunting, suspecting no evil, the king's huntsman was sent along. When they were all alone out in the forest, the huntsman was looking so sad that the prince said to him, "Dear huntsman, what is troubling you?"

"I cannot tell you," said the huntsman, "and yet I should."

"Come out with it, whatever it is. I will forgive you for it."

"Oh," said the huntsman, "I am supposed to shoot you. The king ordered me to."

Then the prince was afraid and said, "Dear huntsman, let me live. Here, take my royal clothes. Give me your poor ones in exchange."

"I will do it gladly," said the huntsman. "I couldn't have brought myself to shoot you anyway." Then they traded clothes and the huntsman went home, but the prince went deeper into the forest.

After a time, the old king received three wagonloads of gold and jewels for his youngest son. They had been

sent by the three kings who had defeated their enemies
with the prince's sword and fed their people with his
bread, and they wanted to show their gratitude. Then the
old king thought, "Could my son have been innocent?"
And he said to his servants, "If only he were still alive!
What a grief it is to me that I had him killed."

"He is still alive," said the huntsman. "I didn't have
the heart to carry out your command." And he told the
king what had happened. Then a weight lifted from the
king's heart, and he had it proclaimed through every
land that his son might return and that he was to be par-
doned.

The princess, meanwhile, had had a road all golden
and glittering built in front of her castle. She told her
servants that whoever came riding straight down the road
was the right one, and they should let him in. But whoever came along the side of the road wasn't the right
one, and they shouldn't let him in.

When the time was just about up, the oldest son
thought that he'd hurry up and go to the king's daughter
and pass himself off as her savior. Thus he would get her
for his wife, and the kingdom with her. So he rode off,
and when he reached the castle and saw the beautiful
golden road, he thought, "It would be a pity and shame
to ride on it." He turned aside and rode along the
right shoulder. But when he got to the gate, the servants told him to go away again—he wasn't the right one.

Soon thereafter the second prince set out, and when he
reached the golden road and his horse had just set one
foot on it, he thought, "It would be a pity and shame.
The horse might scuff off a bit of it." He turned aside
and rode along the left shoulder. But when he got to the
gate, the servants told him to go away again—he wasn't
the right one.

When the whole year had passed, the third son decided to leave the forest and ride to his beloved and
forget his sorrow with her. So he set out, thinking constantly of her and wishing he were already with her, and
he didn't even see the golden road. His horse went
straight up the middle, and when he got to the gate, it was
opened, and the king's daughter received him joyfully.
She said he was her savior and the lord of the kingdom,

and the wedding was celebrated with great happiness.

After it was over, she told him that his father had asked him to come back and had forgiven him. Then he rode home and told his father everything—how his brothers had betrayed him and how, nevertheless, he had kept silent about it. The old king wanted to punish them, but they had gone to sea and sailed away, and didn't come back for the rest of their lives.

DOCTOR KNOW-IT-ALL

Once upon a time there was a poor farmer called Fish, who drove a load of wood into town with his two oxen and sold it to a doctor for two thaler. When the money was being paid out to him, the doctor happened to be sitting down to dinner. The farmer saw how sumptuously he ate and drank, and his heart longed for such a life, and he would gladly have been a doctor too. So he stood there a little while longer and finally asked whether he might not also become a doctor.

"Certainly," said the doctor, "that's easily done."

"What must I do?" asked the farmer.

"First of all buy yourself an ABC book—it looks like this—with a picture of a rooster at the beginning. Second, convert your wagon and oxen into cash and get yourself the clothes and all the rest that's required for practicing medicine. Third, have a sign painted with the words: 'I am Doctor Know-it-all,' and have it nailed up over your front door."

The farmer did everything as he was told. After he had been practicing for a while, but not very much, a rich and important gentleman was robbed of some money. He was told about Doctor Know-it-all down in the village, who would surely know what had become of the money.

So the gentleman had his carriage hitched up, drove into the village, and asked him if he were Doctor Know-it-all.

Yes, that was he.

Then he must come along and get back the stolen money.

"Oh yes, but my wife Greta has to come along."

The gentleman didn't mind and allowed both of them to sit in the carriage, and they drove off together. When they arrived at the gentleman's estate, the table was set, and the doctor was first invited to eat.

"Yes, but my wife Greta too," he said, and sat down with her at the table.

Now when the first servant came in with a serving dish of fine food, the farmer nudged his wife and said, "Greta, that's the first one," meaning that it was the one bringing in the first course.

The servant, however, thought that he had meant, "That's the first thief," and since he really was, he was frightened and reported to his fellows, "The doctor knows all about it. We're in for it. He said that I was the first."

The second didn't even want to go in, but he had to anyway. Now when he came in with his dish, the farmer nudged his wife. "Greta, that's the second one." The servant was frightened also and saw to it that he got out of there. The third fared no better. The farmer said again, "Greta, that's the third."

The fourth had to carry in a covered dish, and the gentleman told the doctor to give a demonstration of his skill by guessing what was inside. It happened to be fish. The farmer looked at the dish, didn't know what to do, and said, "Oh me, poor Fish!"

When the gentleman heard that, he cried, "There! He knows, and so he's sure to know who has the money."

The servant, however, was terrified and signaled to the doctor to step outside for a moment. When he came out, all four confessed to him that they had stolen the money. They would be glad to give it back and to give him a large sum besides if he wouldn't expose them. Otherwise it would mean their necks. And they led him to the place where the money was hidden.

The doctor was satisfied, went back in, sat down at the table, and said, "Sir, now I'll look in my book to find out where the money is."

The fifth servant, however, had crawled into the stove to find out how much more the doctor might know. The latter opened his ABC book and thumbed around in it, looking for the rooster. Not being able to find it right away, he said, "I know you're in there, and you have to come out."

The man inside the stove thought this meant him and jumped out terribly frightened, crying, "The fellow knows everything."

Then Doctor Know-it-all showed the gentleman where his money was, but didn't tell who had stolen it. He received a lot of money as a reward from both parties and became a famous man.

BEARSKIN

O nce upon a time there was a young man who enlisted as a soldier, served bravely, and was always in front when it was raining bullets. While the war lasted all went well, but when peace was made, he got his discharge, and the captain told him that he could go wherever he pleased. His parents were dead and he no longer had a home, so he went to his brothers and asked them to support him until the war would start again. But the brothers were hard men and said, "What should we do with you? We can't use you. Figure out for yourself some way to get by."

The soldier had nothing left except his rifle. That he shouldered and set out into the world. He got to a great heath on which there was nothing to be seen except for a circle of trees. He sat down under them very sadly and thought about his lot. "I have no money," he thought, "I've learned no trade other than fighting, and now that peace has been made, they don't need me anymore. I see that I'll have to starve."

Suddenly he heard a rushing sound, and when he turned around, a strange man was standing before him. He was dressed in a green coat and looked very distinguished, but he had a horrible cloven foot. "I know what you need," said the man. "You shall have money and goods, as much as you can use up, no matter how hard you try, but first I've got to know that you're not afraid so that I won't be spending my money for nothing."

"A soldier and fear—what sort of combination is that?" he answered. "You can put me to the test."

"Very well," answered the man, "look out behind you!"

The soldier turned around and saw a large bear trotting toward him growling. "Oho," cried the soldier, "I'll tickle your nose so that you won't feel like growling anymore." He aimed and hit the bear in the snout so that it collapsed and never stirred again.

"I can see," said the stranger, "that you don't lack courage. But there's still one condition that you have to fulfill."

"As long as it doesn't endanger my salvation," answered the soldier, who realized whom he was dealing with, "otherwise I won't agree to anything."

"That you can judge for yourself," answered the man in the green coat. "For the next seven years you must not wash, you must not comb your beard or your hair, you must not cut your nails or say the Lord's Prayer. Moreover, I will give you a coat and a cloak that you must wear the whole time. If you should die during the seven years, you will be mine. If you survive, however, you shall be free and rich for the rest of your life."

The soldier thought about his great need, and since he had so often risked death, he decided to risk it this time, too, and agreed.

The Devil took off his green coat, handed it to the soldier, and said, "When you have this coat on and reach into the pocket, you will always get a fistful of gold." Then he skinned the bear and said, "This shall be your cloak and also your bed, for you must sleep on it and you may not get into any other bed. And because of this garb you shall be called Bearskin." Thereupon the Devil disappeared.

The soldier put on the coat, reached into the pocket right away, and established the truth of the matter. Then he draped the bearskin over himself, went out into the world, and had a good time, omitting nothing that would give him pleasure and make the money give out.

The first year he still got along after a fashion, but in the second he already looked like a monster. His hair practically covered his face, his beard looked like a piece of coarse felt, his fingers developed claws and his face was so covered with dirt that if one had sowed cress there, it would have sprouted. Everyone who saw him ran away; however, because he gave money to the poor everywhere to pray that he might not die during the seven years and because he paid well for everything, he still obtained lodging every place.

During the fourth year he came to an inn where the innkeeper wouldn't take him and wouldn't even give him a place in the stable because he was afraid it might make his horses skittish. But when Bearskin reached into his pocket and produced a handful of ducats, the innkeeper softened and let him have a room in the outbuilding. Even so, he made him promise not to show himself so that his inn would not get a bad reputation.

As Bearskin was sitting alone in the evening, wishing with all his heart that the seven years were up, he heard a loud lamentation next door. He had a compassionate heart, and so he opened the door and beheld an old man weeping bitterly and clutching his head in despair. Bearskin came closer, and the man jumped up, wanting to flee. At last, when he heard a human voice, he was reassured, and by means of kindly encouragement Bearskin managed to get the cause of his sorrow out of him. His fortune had dwindled little by little. He and his daughters no longer had enough to eat, and he was so poor that he couldn't even pay the innkeeper and was about to be put in jail.

"If you have no other worries," said Bearskin, "I've got plenty of money." He summoned the innkeeper, paid him off, and thrust another bag of money into the unfortunate man's pocket.

When the old man saw that his worries were over, he hardly knew how to show his gratitude. "Come with me," he said to him. "My daughters are all marvels of beauty. Choose one of them for your wife. When she hears what you have done for me, she will not refuse. It's true that your appearance is rather odd, but she'll manage to fix you up again."

Bearskin liked the idea and went with him. When the oldest daughter saw him, she was so terrified at his countenance that she screamed and ran away. The second didn't run away and looked him over from head to toe, but then she said, "How can I take a husband who doesn't have a human shape anymore? I would have preferred the shaved bear who was on show here once and claimed to be a man; it at least had on a hussar's fur cap and white gloves. If he were merely ugly, I could get used to him."

But the youngest said, "Dear Father, this must be a good man if he helped you in your need. If you promised him a bride in return, your word must be kept."

It was too bad that Bearskin's face was covered up with dirt and hair, or else one might have seen how his heart laughed within him when he heard these words. He removed a ring from his finger, broke it in two, and gave her one half and kept the other himself. Inside her half he inscribed his name, and in his half he inscribed her name, and he bade her to keep her piece of the ring carefully. Thereupon he took his leave and said, "I have to wander for three more years. If I return at that time, we will celebrate our wedding, but if I don't come back, you will be free, because in that case I'll be dead. But pray to God to preserve my life."

The poor bride dressed entirely in black, and when she thought of her bridegroom, tears came into her eyes. From her sisters she got only scorn and mockery. "Be careful," said the oldest, "when you give him your hand; he'll strike it with his paw." "Watch out," said the second, "bears love sweets, and if he likes you he'll eat you up." "You'll have to obey him all the time," the oldest began again, "or he'll start to growl." And the second

continued, "But you'll have a good time at your wedding
—bears are good dancers." The bride remained silent and didn't let herself be disconcerted.

But Bearskin traveled about in the world from place to
place, did good deeds wherever he could, and gave generously to the poor so that they would pray for him.
Finally, when the last day of the seven years had
come, he went out on the heath again and sat down
under the circle of trees.

It wasn't long until there was a gust of wind and the

Devil was standing before him, looking at him sourly.
Then he threw the soldier his old coat and demanded
his green one back.

"We're not ready for that yet," answered Bearskin.
"First you have to clean me up." Whether the Devil liked
it or not, he had to fetch water, wash Bearskin, comb
his hair, and cut his nails. When that was done, Bearskin looked like a brave warrior and was much more
handsome than ever before.

When he was happily rid of the Devil Bearskin felt
very lighthearted. He went to town, put on a magnificent
velvet coat, got into a carriage drawn by four white
horses, and drove to his bride's house. Nobody recognized
him. The father took him for a noble staff officer and
conducted him to the room where his daughters were.
He placed him between the two older ones, who poured
out the wine for him, gave him the choicest bits, and
thought that they had never seen a handsomer man in
this world.

But the bride sat opposite him dressed in black, never
raised her eyes, and never spoke a word. When he
finally asked the father if he might have one of the
daughters for a wife, the two older ones jumped up and
ran to their room, intending to put on magnificent clothes,
because each fancied she was his choice.

The stranger, as soon as he was alone with the bride,
got out his half of the ring and tossed it into a goblet
of wine, which he passed across the table. She took it,
but when she had emptied it and found the half of the
ring lying at the bottom, her heart beat faster. She got
out the other half, which she was wearing on a rib-
bon around her neck, matched it against his, and sure
enough the two parts fit perfectly.

Then he said, "I am your promised bridegroom. You
have seen me as Bearskin, but through God's grace I
have got back my human shape and am clean once more."

At this moment the two sisters entered in all their
finery, and when they learned that the handsome man
had fallen to the lot of the youngest and found out that
he was Bearskin, they ran outside filled with anger and
rage. One drowned herself in the well; the other hanged
herself from a tree.

At night someone knocked at the door, and when the
bridegroom opened it, it was the Devil in his green coat.
He said, "See there, now I've got two souls in exchange
for your one."

THE CLEVER PEOPLE

O ne day a farmer fetched his hickory stick out of the corner and said to his wife, "Kate, I'm going on a trip and won't be back for three days. If the cattle dealer pays us a call in the meantime and wants

to buy our three cows, you can get rid of them, but only for two hundred thaler, no less, do you hear?"

"Just go in God's name," answered the woman. "I'll take care of it all right."

"Yes, you!" said the man. "When you were a little girl you fell on your head once, and you never quite recovered from it. But let me tell you this: if you do anything stupid, I'll turn your back blue without any paint, just with this stick that I'm holding here in my hand, and the color will last for a whole year—that you can count on." Thereupon the man set out on his way.

The next morning the cattle dealer came, and the woman didn't have to bargain with him very long. When he had looked the cows over and had been told the price, he said, "I'll pay it gladly. They're worth that much among friends. I'll take the beasts along with me right now."

He untied them from their chains and drove them out of the stable. But as he was about to go out the farmyard gate, the woman caught him by the sleeve and said, "First you have to give me the two hundred thaler, or I can't let you go."

"Right you are," answered the man. "I forgot to buckle on my purse, though. But don't worry; I'll give you some security until I pay. I'll take along two of the cows, and I'll leave the third behind with you so that you'll have a good surety."

This made sense to the woman. She let the man depart with his cows, thinking, "How pleased Hans will be when he sees how clever I've been."

The farmer came home the third day, as he had said, and asked right away whether the cows had been sold.

"Yes, indeed, Hans dear," answered the woman, "and, just as you said, for two hundred thaler. They're hardly worth that, but the man took them without argument."

"Where is the money?" asked the farmer.

"I haven't got the money," answered the woman. "He just happened to have forgotten his purse, but he'll bring the money soon. He left behind a good surety."

"What sort of surety?" asked the man.

"One of the three cows. He won't get it until he's paid for the others. I did a clever thing—I kept the smallest because it eats the least."

The man was furious, raised his stick, and wanted to give her the promised beating. Suddenly he lowered it again and said, "You're the stupidest goose waddling about on God's earth, but I feel sorry for you. I'm going out on the highway, and I'll wait three days to see if I can find anyone simpler than you. If I succeed, I'll let you off, but if I don't find anyone, you'll get your well-earned payment in full."

He went out on the highway, sat down on a stone, and

waited for whatever might turn up. He saw a hay cart driving along with a woman standing up in the middle of it instead of sitting on the bundle of straw that was lying right there, or walking alongside leading the oxen. "She must be the type I'm looking for," thought the man. He jumped up and ran back and forth in front of the wagon like someone who isn't quite in his right mind.

"What do you want, friend?" the woman said to him. "I don't know who you are. Where are you from?"

"I fell out of Heaven," answered the man, "and I don't know how to get back! Couldn't you give me a lift up there?"

"No," said the woman, "I don't know the way. But if you're from Heaven, you can probably tell me how my husband is. He's already been there three years. Surely you've seen him?"

"I've seen him, all right, but it's impossible for everyone to do well. He's a shepherd, and those precious beasts are giving him a lot of trouble. They run up the mountains and stray into the wilderness, and he has to run after them and drive them together again. He's in rags, too, and pretty soon his clothes are going to fall right off. There aren't any tailors up there—Saint Peter won't let any in, as you know from the fairy tale."

"Who would have thought it!" cried the woman. "Do you know what? I'll go get his Sunday suit, which is still hanging up in the closet at home. He can wear it there and look respectable. You'll be so good as to take it along."

"That won't work," answered the farmer. "One isn't allowed to take clothes into Heaven. They take them away from you at the gate."

"Listen to me," said the woman. "Yesterday I sold my fine crop of wheat for a pretty sum. I'll send him that. If I stick the bag with the money into your pocket, no one will notice."

"If there's no other way," replied the farmer, "I'll do you the favor all right."

"Just stay sitting right there," she said. "I'll drive home and get the bag. I'll be back soon. I don't sit down on the bundle of straw but stand up on the cart so that the team will have it easier."

She started up her oxen, and the farmer thought, "She's a born idiot. If she really brings the money, my wife can count herself lucky, for she'll escape her beating." It wasn't long before she came running with the money and put it into his pocket herself. Before she went away she thanked him again a thousand times for being so obliging.

When the woman got home, she found her son who had come back from the fields. She told him what surprising things she had learned and added, "I'm very glad that I found an opportunity to send my poor husband something. Who would have thought that he'd be lacking anything in Heaven?"

Her son was vastly astonished. "Mother," he said, "someone like that from Heaven doesn't show up every day. I want to go out right away to see if I can still find the man. He'll have to tell me what it looks like up there, and what sort of work there is." He saddled the horse and rode off in great haste.

He came across the farmer, who was sitting under a willow tree getting ready to count the money in the bag. "Did you see the man from Heaven?" the boy called out to him.

"Yes," answered the farmer, "he set out on the way back and went up that mountain over there to take a shortcut. You can still catch him if you ride hard."

"Oh," said the boy, "I've been slaving away all day, and the ride here has worn me out completely. You know the man. Be so kind as to get on my horse and persuade the man to come back here."

"Aha," thought the farmer, "here's another one who hasn't got any wick for his lamp."

"Why not do you the favor?" he said, got on, and rode off at a stiff trot.

The boy sat there till nightfall, but the farmer didn't come back. "I'm sure," he thought, "that the man from Heaven was in a great hurry and didn't want to turn around, and the farmer gave him the horse to take along to my father."

He went home to tell his mother what had happened —he had sent the horse to his father so he wouldn't have to run around all the time. "You did well," she answered. "Your legs are still young, and you can go on foot."

When the farmer got home, he put the horse in the stable next to the cow that had been left as surety. Then he went to his wife and said, "Kate, you were in luck. I found two who were even more simpleminded fools than you are. This time you'll get off without blows. I'll save them up for another occasion." Then he lit his pipe, sat down in his easy chair, and said, "That was a good bargain—a sleek horse for two lean cows, and a large bag of money besides. If foolishness always brought in such a profit, I wouldn't mind respecting it."

That's what the farmer thought, but I bet you like the sillies better.

STORIES
ABOUT THE TOAD

Once upon a time there was a little child, and every afternoon its mother would give it a bowl of bread and milk. The child would sit down with it in the yard outside, and when it started to eat, a toad would come crawling out of a crack in the wall, put its little head into the milk, and eat too. This gave the child pleasure, and if the toad didn't come right away when it sat down with its little bowl, it called:

> "Toad, toad, come hurrying,
> Come and join me, little thing,
> You shall have your bread crusts, too,
> And drink some milk to nourish you."

Then the toad came running and enjoyed its meal. It showed its gratitude, too, for it brought the child all sorts of beautiful things from its secret treasure—glittering stones, pearls, and golden toys. However, the toad drank only the milk and left the bread.

One time the child took its little spoon, struck the toad gently on the head, and said, "Thing, eat the bread too." Its mother, who was in the kitchen, heard the child talking to someone, and when she saw it hitting a toad with its little spoon, she came running with a wooden slat and killed the good creature.

From that time a change came over the child. While

it had been eating with the toad, it had grown big and strong, but now its pretty rosy cheeks faded and it grew thin. It wasn't long before the bird of death began to screech at night and the robin to gather twigs and leaves for a funeral wreath, and soon after that the child was lying on its bier.

II

An orphan child was sitting beside the town wall, spinning, when she saw a toad coming out of an opening at the foot of the wall. Quickly she spread out her blue silk scarf—that is what toads like very much and it is the one thing they will crawl on. As soon as the toad saw it, it turned around, and came back carrying a little gold crown, put it on the scarf, and went away again.

The girl picked up the crown, which glittered and was made of delicate spun gold. It wasn't long before the toad came back a second time. But when it didn't see the crown anymore, it crawled up to the wall and beat its head against it in sorrow as long as its strength held out, until finally it lay dead.

If the girl had left the crown sitting there, the toad would probably have fetched more of its treasures out of its hole.

III

Toad calls, "Hoo-oo, hoo-oo." Child says, "Come out." The toad comes out, and the child asks about its little sister, "Haven't you seen Red-Stockings?" Toad says, "No, not me, have you? Hoo-oo, hoo-oo, hoo-oo."

ONE EYE,
TWO EYES,
AND THREE EYES

Once upon a time there was a woman who had three daughters. The oldest was called One Eye because she had only a single eye in the middle of her forehead; the second, Two Eyes because she had two eyes like other people; and the youngest, Three Eyes because she had three eyes, and she, too, had the third eye in the middle of her forehead. However, because Two Eyes looked no different from other human children, her sisters and her mother couldn't stand her. "With your two eyes you're no better than common folk," they said to her. "You don't belong to us." They pushed her around and threw her shabby clothes; they only gave her leftovers to eat and hurt her feelings in every way they could.

It happened that Two Eyes had to go out into the pasture to tend the goat, but she was still very hungry because her sisters had given her so little to eat. She sat down on a ridge in the field and broke into tears, and she wept so hard that two streams of tears ran down her cheeks. When in her misery she looked up once, a woman was standing beside her, and she asked, "Two Eyes, why are you crying?"

"Why shouldn't I cry?" answered Two Eyes. "Because I have two eyes like other people, my sisters and my mother can't stand me. They push me around all over the house, throw me old clothes, and only give me leftovers to eat. Today they gave me so little that I'm still very hungry."

"Dry your tears, Two Eyes," said the wise woman. "I will tell you something so that you won't have to go hungry anymore. Just say to your goat,

> 'Little goat, bleat;
> Little table, set,'

and there will be a nicely set little table before you with the loveliest things to eat on it, and you may eat as much as you please. And when you've had enough and don't need the table anymore, just say,

> 'Little goat, bleat;
> Little table, get,'

and it will disappear before your eyes." Thereupon the wise woman went away.

But Two Eyes thought, "I'll have to try it out right away to see if what she said is true, for I'm so terribly hungry." She said,

> "Little goat, bleat;
> Little table, set,"

and scarcely were the words out than a little table was standing there spread with a little white cloth, and on it was a plate with knife and fork and a silver spoon, and standing round about were the loveliest dishes, steaming and still as hot as if they had just come out of the kitchen.

Then Two Eyes said the shortest prayer she knew—"Dear Lord, be our guest at all times, Amen"—helped herself, and ate a hearty meal. And when she'd had enough, she said, as the wise woman had instructed her,

> "Little goat, bleat;
> Little table, get."

As soon as she had said it, the table and everything on it vanished. "That's a fine way to keep house," thought Two Eyes, and she was very happy and cheerful.

At night when she came home with the goat, she found a little earthenware bowl with food that her sisters had left there for her, but she didn't touch a thing. The next day she went out again with her goat and didn't touch the few scraps she had been given. The first and second times the sisters didn't even pay any attention, but when it happened every time, they took notice and said, "Something is wrong with Two Eyes. She never touches her food although she used to eat up everything we gave her. She must have found other ways and means." In order to get at the truth, One Eye was supposed to go along when Two Eyes drove the goat to pasture, and to pay close attention to what went on there, and to see whether perhaps someone was bringing her food and drink.

When Two Eyes got ready to go, One Eye came up to her and said, "I want to go out into the field with you to make sure that the goat is getting the proper care and is being driven out to where it gets plenty to eat."

But Two Eyes realized what One Eye had in mind, and drove the goat out into the tall grass and said, "Come, One Eye, let's sit down. I want to sing something for you." One Eye sat down, tired out from the unaccustomed walk and the heat of the sun, and Two Eyes kept singing,

> "One Eye, are you waking?
> One Eye, are you sleeping?"

Then One Eye closed her eye and went to sleep. And when Two Eyes saw that One Eye was fast asleep and couldn't betray her, she said,

> "Little goat, bleat;
> Little table, set,"

and she sat down at the little table and ate and drank until she'd had enough. Then she called again,

> "Little goat, bleat;
> Little table, get,"

and everything vanished in an instant. Two Eyes woke up One Eye and said, "One Eye, you'd like to tend goats and fall asleep doing it! The goat could have run off to the ends of the earth in the meantime. Come, let's go home."

Then they went home, and Two Eyes again didn't touch her little bowl, and One Eye couldn't tell their mother why Two Eyes wouldn't eat, and excused herself by saying, "I fell asleep out there."

The next day the mother said to Three Eyes, "This time you go along, and pay attention whether Two Eyes eats anything out there and whether anyone is bringing her food and drink, for she must be eating and drinking on the sly."

Then Three Eyes came up to Two Eyes and said, "I want to come along to make sure that the goat is getting the proper care and is being driven out to where it gets plenty to eat."

But Two Eyes realized what Three Eyes had in mind, and drove the goat out into the tall grass and said, "Let's sit down, Three Eyes. I want to sing something for you." Three Eyes sat down, tired out from the walk and the heat of the sun, and Two Eyes began the same song and sang,

> "Three Eyes, are you waking?"

But instead of singing as she should have,

> "Three Eyes, are you sleeping?"

she carelessly sang,

> "*Two* Eyes, are you sleeping?"

and kept singing,

> "Three Eyes, are you waking?
> *Two* Eyes, are you sleeping?"

Then two of Three Eyes' eyes fell shut and slept, but the third didn't go to sleep because the little charm had not spoken to it. Three Eyes did shut it, but only out of cunning to make it look as if the third eye, too, were asleep; but it wasn't all the way closed and could see everything very well.

When Two Eyes thought that Three Eyes was fast asleep, she said the charm:

> "Little goat, bleat;
> Little table, set."

She ate and drank to her heart's content and then commanded the little table to go away:

> "Little goat, bleat;
> Little table, get."

But Three Eyes had been watching it all.

Then Two Eyes came to wake her up and said, "Well, Three Eyes, did you fall asleep? You're a fine goatherd! Come, let's go home."

And when they got home, Two Eyes again ate nothing, and Three Eyes said to the mother, "I know why the proud thing won't eat. When she's out there and says to the goat,

> 'Little goat, bleat;
> Little table, set,'

a little table comes and stands in front of her. It's set with the best food, much better than we get here. And when she's had enough, she says,

> 'Little goat, bleat;
> Little table, get,'

and everything disappears again. I watched it all closely. She put two of my eyes to sleep with a charm, but the one on my forehead luckily stayed awake."

"Do you want to fare better than we do?" cried the envious mother. "You'll get over that!" She fetched a butcher knife and stabbed the goat in the heart so that it fell down dead.

When Two Eyes saw that, she went out very sadly, sat down on the ridge in the field, and wept bitter tears. Suddenly the wise woman was standing at her side again, and said, "Two Eyes, why are you crying?"

"Why shouldn't I cry?" she answered. "My mother stabbed to death the goat that set such a fine table for me every day when I repeated your charm. Now I'll have to suffer hunger and misery again."

"Two Eyes," said the wise woman, "I want to give you some good advice. Ask your sisters to let you have the innards of the slaughtered goat, and bury them outside the front door, and it will make your fortune."

Then she disappeared, and Two Eyes went home and said to her sisters, "Dear sisters, do give me something of my goat. I don't ask for much; just give me the innards."

They laughed and said, "If that's all you want, you can have them."

And Two Eyes took the innards, and following the wise woman's counsel, silently buried them at night before the front door.

The next morning when they all woke up and went out the front door, there stood a marvelous and magnificent tree that had silver leaves, with gold fruit hanging among them. It must have been the most beautiful and most precious thing in the whole world. They didn't know, though, how the tree had got there during the night. Only Two Eyes realized that it had grown out of the goat's innards, for it was standing on the exact spot where she had buried them.

The mother said to One Eye, "Climb up, my child, and pick the fruit from the tree for us." One Eye climbed up, but when she started to grab one of the golden apples, the branch jerked out of her hand, and this happened every time so that she couldn't pick a single apple, no matter how hard she tried.

Then the mother said, "Three Eyes, you climb up. With your three eyes you can look about you better than One Eye."

One Eye slid down and Three Eyes climbed up. But Three Eyes was no better at it, and look wherever she might, the golden apples always shrank back from her.

Finally the mother lost patience and climbed up herself, but she was no more able to grasp the fruit than One Eye and Three Eyes, and she kept clutching the empty air.

Then Two Eyes said, "I'll try once—perhaps I will have better luck."

The sisters cried, "You with your two eyes—what do you think you can do!"

But Two Eyes climbed up, and the golden apples did not shrink back from her but came into her hands of their own accord so that she was able to pick one after another and brought down a whole apronful. The mother took them from her, and instead of being nicer to poor Two Eyes, she and One Eye and Three Eyes were all the more jealous because Two Eyes was the only one who could pick the fruit, and they treated her even more harshly.

Once as they were standing together by the tree, a young knight happened to come by. "Quickly, Two Eyes," cried the two sisters, "crawl under here so that we needn't be ashamed of you," and in great haste they dumped an empty barrel, which was standing by the tree, on top of poor Two Eyes, and shoved the golden apples she'd picked under with her.

As the knight came closer, he turned out to be a handsome gentleman. He stopped to admire the splendid tree of gold and silver, and said to the two sisters, "Who owns this fine tree? Whoever will give me a branch of it may ask me for whatever she wants."

One Eye and Three Eyes answered that the tree belonged to them and that they'd be glad to break off a branch for him. They both tried very hard, but they weren't able to do it because the branches drew back from them every time.

The knight said, "It's certainly strange that the tree belongs to you, and yet you can't break anything off from it."

They insisted that the tree belonged to them. While they were saying this, however, Two Eyes rolled two golden apples out from under the barrel so that they rolled over to the knight's feet, for Two Eyes was angry that One Eye and Three Eyes weren't telling the truth. When the knight saw the apples, he was astonished and asked where they came from. One Eye and Three Eyes answered that they had another sister, but she didn't dare to show herself because she had only two eyes like common folk.

The knight, however, wanted to see her and called, "Two Eyes, come out." Then Two Eyes boldly came out from under the barrel, and the knight was amazed at her great beauty and said, "Surely, Two Eyes, you can break a branch from the tree for me."

"Yes," answered Two Eyes, "I'm sure I can, because the tree belongs to me." And she climbed up and with almost no effort broke off a branch with fine silver leaves and golden fruit and handed it to the knight.

The knight said, "Two Eyes, what shall I give you for it?"

"Oh," answered Two Eyes, "I suffer from hunger and thirst, misery and need, from early in the morning till late in the evening. If you would take me with you and set me free, I would be happy."

Then the knight took Two Eyes on his horse and brought her home to his father's castle. There he gave her beautiful clothes and as much to eat and drink as her heart desired, and because he loved her very much, they were married to each other, and the wedding was celebrated with great joy.

When Two Eyes was carried off by the handsome

knight, her two sisters envied her more than ever for her good fortune. "At least the wonderful tree stays with us," they thought. "Even if we can't break off any of the fruit, everyone will still stop in front of it and come to us to admire it. Who knows what good fortune may still be in store for us?" But the next morning the tree had disappeared and their hopes with it. And when Two Eyes looked out of her bedroom, to her great joy the tree had followed her and was standing outside.

Two Eyes lived happily for a long time. Once two poor women came to her in the castle begging for alms. Two Eyes looked at their faces and recognized her sisters One Eye and Three Eyes, who had fallen into such poverty that they had to go from door to door begging their bread. But Two Eyes made them welcome and treated them well and took care of them, so that they were both sincerely sorry for all the wrong they had done to their sister in their youth.

THE TWELVE
DANCING PRINCESSES

Once upon a time there was a king who had twelve daughters, each one more beautiful than the next. They slept together in a large room with their beds lined up in a row, and at night, after they had gone to bed, the king locked and bolted the door. But when he opened the door in the morning, he saw that their shoes were all worn out from dancing, and nobody could discover how this happened.

The king issued a proclamation that whoever could find out where they went dancing at night could choose one of them for his wife and succeed him as king; but anyone who volunteered and could not find out after three days and nights was to forfeit his life. It wasn't long until a king's son offered to take the risk. He was received with hospitality, and at night he was taken to a room that opened on the bedroom. His bed was made there, and he was supposed to see where they went dancing. And in order to keep them from playing any secret tricks or going out by some other way, the door to the bedroom was left open. But the eyes of the king's son suddenly felt like lead and he fell asleep, and when he woke up the next morning, all twelve had been to the dance, for there were their shoes with the soles worn right through. The second and third nights were just the same, and so his head was chopped off without pity. Many others followed him and offered to undertake the dangerous enterprise, but they all lost their lives.

Now it happened that a poor soldier, who had been wounded and was no longer fit for service, was on his way to the city where the king lived. He met an old woman who asked him where he was going. "I'm not very sure myself," he said, and he added jokingly, "I'd really like to find out where the king's daughters wear out their shoes dancing, and then get to be king."

"That's not so hard," said the old woman. "You mustn't drink the wine they bring you before you go to bed, and you must pretend that you're fast asleep." With that, she gave him a little cloak and said, "If you put this around your shoulders you'll be invisible, and then you can steal after the twelve princesses."

Having been so well advised, the soldier took the matter in good earnest, and so he screwed up his courage, went before the king, and volunteered to be a suitor. He was received with the same hospitality as the others, and given royal garments to wear.

At bedtime he was led to the anteroom, and when he got ready for bed, the oldest daughter brought him a goblet of wine. But he had tied a sponge under his chin and let the wine run into it so that he didn't drink a drop. Then he lay down, and after lying there a little while, he started snoring as if he were fast asleep.

The twelve princesses heard him and laughed. "That one shouldn't have risked his life either," said the oldest. Then they got up, opened wardrobes, chests, and boxes, and took out magnificent clothes. They primped in front of the mirrors, frolicked around the room, and joyfully looked forward to the dance—except for the youngest. She said, "I don't know, you can be gay if you like, but I have such a strange feeling—I'm sure something terrible is going to happen to us."

"You're a little goose," said the oldest. "You're always

afraid. Have you forgotten how many kings' sons have already been here and failed? As for the soldier, I wouldn't even have had to give him the sleeping potion—nothing would have wakened that lout."

When they were all ready, they first had a look at the soldier, but he had his eyes closed and didn't move a muscle, so they thought they were completely safe. The oldest one went to her bed and rapped on it. Immediately it sank through the floor, and they climbed through the opening, one after the other, with the oldest in the lead.

The soldier, who had watched everything, lost no time, put on his little cloak, and climbed down after the youngest. Halfway down the stairs he stepped lightly on her gown. She was frightened and called out, "What is it? Who is holding onto my gown?"

"Don't be such a simpleton," said the oldest. "You caught it on a nail."

Then they went all the way down, and when they got to the bottom, they were standing in a magnificent avenue of trees: all the leaves were of silver, and they shimmered and shone. The soldier thought, "I'd better take along some token as proof," and he broke off a branch. The tree gave a prodigious crack.

The youngest cried out again, "Something's the matter —did you hear that cracking?"

But the oldest said, "They're firing a victory salute because soon we shall have redeemed our princes."

Next they came to an avenue of trees with leaves of gold, and finally to a third where the leaves were of bright diamond. Each time he broke a branch, and each time there was a cracking that made the youngest start with alarm. But the oldest insisted they were victory salutes.

They went on and came to a big river. Twelve little boats were floating on the water, and in each boat sat a handsome prince. They had been waiting for the twelve princesses, and each took one in his boat. The soldier, however, went and sat by the youngest.

"I don't know what's wrong," said the prince. "The boat is much heavier tonight, and I've got to row with all my strength to move it along."

"It must be the hot weather," said the youngest. "I'm very warm myself."

On the other side of the river stood a beautiful castle brightly illuminated, from which the gay music of drums and trumpets was sounding. They rowed across and went inside, and each prince danced with his own sweetheart.

The soldier danced along invisibly, and each time a princess took a goblet of wine in her hand, he drank it so that it was empty when she raised it to her lips. The youngest was frightened at this, too, but the oldest always managed to silence her.

They danced until three o'clock the next morning, when all the shoes were worn out and they had to stop. The princes rowed them back across the river, and this time the soldier sat up front with the oldest. On the shore they said good-bye to the princes and promised to come again the next night. But when they reached the stairs, the soldier ran ahead and lay down on his bed, and when the twelve came up wearily dragging their feet, he was already snoring again loud enough for them to hear. "We don't have to worry about *him*," they said. They took off their beautiful clothes, put them away, placed the worn-out shoes under the beds, and lay down.

The next morning the soldier didn't want to tell right away because he wished to see a little more of these wonderful goings-on, and he went along for the second and third nights too. Everything was just the same as the first time, and each night they danced until their shoes fell apart. The third time he took away a goblet for proof.

When the hour had come for him to give his answer, he concealed the three branches and the goblet on his person and went before the king. The twelve princesses were listening behind the door to see what he would say.

When the king asked, "Where did my twelve daughters wear out their shoes dancing in the night?" he answered, "With twelve princes in an underground castle." And he told everything that happened and produced his evidence.

The king had his daughters summoned and asked them if the soldier had told the truth, and since they saw that their secret was out and that lying would do no good, they had to confess everything.

Next the king asked the soldier which one he wanted to marry. "I'm no longer a young man," he answered, "so give me the oldest."

The wedding was celebrated the same day, and he was promised the kingdom after the king's death. But the enchantment of the princes was extended one day for each night they had danced with the princesses.

THE SIX SERVANTS

Once upon a time there lived an old queen who was a witch, and her daughter was the most beautiful girl under the sun. The old woman, however, thought of nothing else but how she could lure men to their ruin, and whenever a suitor came, she told him that whoever wanted her daughter must first perform a task or die. Many were dazzled by the girl's beauty and undertook the risk, but they could not perform the tasks that the old woman set them, and then there was no mercy: they had to get down on their knees, and their heads were struck off.

A king's son who also had heard of the girl's beauty said to his father, "Let me go there. I want to try to win her."

"Never," answered the king. "If you go, then you will be going to your death."

Then the son lay down mortally sick, and he lay seven long years, and no physician could cure him. When the father saw that it was hopeless, he said to him with a sorrowful heart, "Go and try your luck. I know no other remedy for you." When the son heard this, he got up from his bed cured, and he set cheerfully on his way.

As he was riding across a heath, it happened that far off he saw something lying on the ground that looked like a great haystack, and as he came closer, he could tell that it was the stomach of a man who was lying flat but whose stomach looked like a small mountain. When the fat man saw the traveler, he sat up and said, "If you need anyone, let me become one of your servants."

The king's son answered, "How could I use a man with such an ungainly shape?"

"Oh," said the fat man, "this isn't much. When I

really unfold myself, I'm three thousand times as fat."

"If that's the case," said the king's son, "I can use you. Come with me."

So the fat man followed the king's son, and after a while they found another man lying on the ground, holding his ear to the grass. "What are you doing there?" asked the king's son.

"I'm listening," answered the man.

"What are you listening to so intently?"

"I'm listening to what's going on in the world, for there's not a sound that can escape my ear. I can even hear the grass growing."

"What do you hear going on at the court of the old queen with the beautiful daughter?" asked the king's son.

"I hear the whistling of the sword," he answered, "striking off the head of a suitor."

"I can use you," said the king's son. "Come with me."

They traveled on and saw a pair of feet lying on the ground, and part of the legs, too, but they couldn't see where they ended. After they had gone on a good piece, they came to the trunk, and finally to the head as well.

"My," said the king's son, "what a bean pole you are!"

"Oh," answered the tall man, "this is nothing. When I really stretch my limbs, I'm three thousand times as long, and taller than the highest mountain in the world. I'll be glad to serve you, if you will take me."

"Come along," said the king's son, "I can use you."

They traveled on and came across a man sitting by the roadside with a blindfold over his eyes. The king's son said to him, "Are your eyes so weak that they can't stand the light?"

"No," answered the man, "I can't take off the blindfold because everything I look at bursts into pieces, I've got such a piercing look. If that could be of any use to you, I will gladly serve you."

"Come along," said the king's son, "I can use you."

They traveled on and came across a man lying in the hot sun who was freezing and shivering all over so that not a single one of his limbs was still. "How can you be cold," said the king's son, "with the sun burning this way?"

"Oh," answered the man, "with me it's just the other way around. The hotter it is, the colder I get, and the frost penetrates right to my bones. The colder it gets, the hotter I am. I can't stand ice for the heat or fire for the cold."

"You're an extraordinary fellow," said the king's son, "but if you want to serve me, come along."

They traveled on and saw a man standing and stretching his neck, gazing all around him and looking over the mountaintops. The king's son said, "What are you so busy looking at?"

"I have such sharp eyes that I can see over field and forest and over hill and dale," answered the man, "and I can see everything in the whole world."

The king's son said, "If you like, come along with me, because I still need a man like you."

Now the king's son and his six servants entered the city where the old queen lived. He didn't say who he was, but he said, "If you will give me your beautiful daughter, I will do whatever you tell me."

The witch was glad that once again a handsome young man had fallen into her toils, and said, "I will set you three tasks. If you can solve them all, you shall be my daughter's lord and master."

"What is the first?" he asked.

"To bring me a ring that I dropped into the Red Sea."

Then the king's son went back to his servants and said, "The first problem isn't easy. We have to fetch a ring out of the Red Sea. Now say what's to be done."

The sharp-eyed man said, "I'll see where it is." He looked down into the sea and said, "There it hangs from a pointed rock."

The tall man carried them there and said, "I'd get it out all right if I could only see it."

"If that's all it takes!" the fat man cried, lay down, and put his mouth to the water. Then the waves poured in as though into an abyss, and he drank the whole sea until it was as dry as a meadow. The tall man bent over a little and fetched out the ring with his hand. The king's son was glad when he had the ring, and carried it to the old woman.

She was surprised and said, "Yes, that's the right ring. You've succeeded in solving the first problem, but now for the second. Do you see that meadow in front of my castle? Three hundred fat oxen are grazing there, and you have to eat them up with hide and hair, bones and horns. And down in the cellar there are three hundred barrels of wine for you to drink. And if one hair of an ox or one drop of wine is left over, your life will be forfeit to me."

"Can't I invite any guests?" said the king's son. "No meal tastes any good without company."

The old woman laughed spitefully and answered, "You can invite one for company, but that's all."

The king's son went back to his servants and said to the fat one, "Today you shall be my guest and eat your fill for once."

Then the fat man unfolded himself and ate the three hundred oxen until there wasn't a hair left, and asked if they weren't serving anything besides breakfast. He drank the wine directly out of the barrels without using a glass, and drank the last drop from his nail.* When the meal was over, the king's son went to the old woman and said that he had performed the second task.

She was astonished and said, "No one has ever gotten this far, but there's still one task left." She was thinking, "You won't escape me, and your head isn't going to stay on."

"Tonight," she said, "I shall bring my daughter to your room, and you must take her in your arms. And when you are sitting together, you must be careful not to fall asleep. I'll come at the stroke of midnight, and if at that time she is no longer in your arms, you will have lost."

The king's son thought, "This task is easy. I'll surely manage to keep my eyes open." Still, he called his servants and told them what the old woman had said. "Who knows what trick she may have up her sleeve?" he said. "We'd better be careful. Keep watch, and see to it that the girl doesn't get out of the room."

At nightfall the old woman came with her daughter and led her into the arms of the king's son. Then the tall man coiled around them, and the fat man stood in front of the door so not a living soul could get in. There sat the two of them, and the girl did not say one word, but the moon was shining through the window upon her face so that the king's son could see her marvelous beauty. He did nothing but look at her. He was filled with love and joy, and no weariness came over his eyes. This lasted until eleven o'clock, when the old woman cast a spell over all of them so that they went to sleep, and at that moment the girl vanished.

They slept soundly until a quarter to twelve, when the spell wore off and they all woke up again. "Oh, misery and misfortune," cried the king's son, "now I am lost!"

The faithful servants began lamenting too, but the sharp-eared man said, "Quiet! I want to listen." He listened for a moment, then said, "She's inside a cliff three hundred hours away, bewailing her fate. You're the only one who can do anything, tall man. If you stand up all the way, you can be there in a few steps."

* An old test to show that the last drop has been drunk is to invert the glass over the thumbnail to prove that it is empty.

"Yes," answered the tall man, "but the man with the piercing eyes must come along to get rid of the cliff." Then the tall man lifted the blindfolded man pickaback, and as quick as you can say Jack Robinson, they were in front of the enchanted cliff. The tall man immediately removed the blindfold from the other's eyes. He merely glanced around and the cliff shattered into a thousand pieces. Then the tall man took the girl in his arms and carried her back in an instant, returned for his comrade just as quickly, and before it struck twelve, they were all back in their places, merry and wide awake.

On the stroke of twelve the witch came creeping in with a mocking smile, as if to say, "Now he is mine." And she believed that her daughter was inside the cliff three hundred hours away. When she saw her daughter in the arms of the king's son, she was frightened and said, "Here is a man more powerful than I am." But she couldn't make excuses and had to give him the girl. But she whispered in her ear, "It is a disgrace to you that you have to obey common folk and that you can't choose a husband to your liking."

At that the girl's proud heart swelled with anger, and she plotted her revenge. The next morning she had three hundred cords of wood carted together, and told the king's son that even though he had performed the three tasks, she would not become his wife until someone was willing to sit in the middle of the woodpile and endure the fire. She was sure that none of the six servants would be willing to burn up for him and that out of love for her he would sit there himself, and then she would be free.

But the servants said, "We've all done something except for the frosty man. Now it's his turn." They placed him in the middle of the woodpile and set it on fire. The fire started to burn and burned for three days until all the wood was gone, and when the flames died down, the frosty man was standing among the ashes trembling like an aspen leaf. "I've never endured such cold in my life," he said, "and if it had lasted any longer, I'd have frozen to death."

Now there was no other way to get out of it: the beautiful girl had to take the unknown youth as her husband. But as they were driving to the church the old woman said, "I cannot bear the disgrace." And she sent her army after them to cut down everything that got in its way and to fetch back her daughter.

However, the sharp-eared man had kept an ear cocked and had overheard what the old woman was saying in her secret conversation. "What shall we do?" he asked the fat man. The latter had an idea. With part of the sea-water he had drunk he spit once or twice behind the coach, making a big lake in which the soldiers were trapped and drowned.

When the witch learned about this, she sent her armed horsemen, but the sharp-eared man heard the rattling of their armor and removed the blindfold from the man with the piercing eyes, who gave a somewhat hard look at the enemy, and they shattered like glass.

Now they drove on in peace, and when the couple had been married in church, the servants took their leave, saying to their master, "Your wishes have been fulfilled. You don't need us anymore, and we shall travel on to try our fortune."

Half an hour from the castle was a village, on the outskirts of which a swineherd was tending his pigs. When they got there, the king's son said to his wife, "Have you any idea who I am? I am no king's son but a swineherd, and the man with the herd over there is my father. The two of us will also have to go to work helping him."

Then he got off with her at an inn, and he secretly told the servants to take away her royal clothes during the night. When they woke up the next morning, she had nothing to put on, and the innkeeper's wife gave her an old gown and a pair of wool stockings. What's more, the woman acted as though it were a grand present and said, "If it weren't for your husband, I wouldn't have given them to you at all."

Then she believed that he really was a swineherd, and helped him tend pigs, thinking, "I have deserved it for my arrogance and pride." This went on for eight days, until she couldn't keep it up because her feet had gotten sore.

Then some men came and asked if she knew what her husband was. "Yes," she answered, "he is a swineherd and just stepped out to make a little money selling ribbons and laces."

But they said, "Come along and we will take you to him." And they led her to the castle. When they entered the room, her husband was standing there dressed in royal robes, but she did not recognize him until he embraced her and kissed her and said, "I suffered so much for you; now you also have had to suffer for me."

Only then was the wedding feast celebrated, and the person who has told the story wishes that he had been there too.

IRON HANS

ONCE upon a time a king owned a great forest that stood near his castle and contained all kinds of game. One day he sent out a huntsman to shoot a roe, but he didn't come back. "Perhaps something happened to him," said the king, and the next day he sent out two other huntsmen to search for him, but they didn't come back either. On the third day he summoned all of his huntsmen, and said, "Range over the whole forest, and don't give up until you have found all three of them." But none of them came home either, nor was any dog of the pack they had taken along ever seen again. From that day no one ever ventured into the forest again, and it lay there in deep silence and solitude, and one saw nothing except, now and then, an eagle or a hawk flying over it.

Many years passed, until a foreign huntsman, looking for a place, volunteered to go into the dangerous forest. But the king didn't want to permit it and said, "Something sinister is in there, and I'm afraid you won't fare any better than the others and will never come out again."

The huntsman answered, "Sire, I'll take it upon my own head. I don't know the meaning of fear."

And so the huntsman and his dog started into the forest. Before long the dog came upon the scent of game and wanted to follow it, but it had hardly run a few steps before it was stopped by a deep pool, and a naked arm rose out of the water, seized it, and dragged it beneath the surface.

When the huntsman saw that, he fetched three men and made them bring buckets to drain the pool. When they could see bottom, a wild man was lying there whose skin was as brown as rusty iron and whose hair hung down over his face all the way to his knees. They bound him with ropes and led him away to the castle. Everyone marveled at the wild man, and the king had him placed in the courtyard in an iron cage, and he forbade anyone, upon pain of death, to open the door. The queen herself took charge of the key. After that the forest was safe again for everyone.

The king had an eight-year-old son who was playing in the courtyard one time, and as he was playing, his golden ball happened to drop into the cage. The boy ran up and said, "Give me my ball."

"Not until you open the door for me," answered the man.

"No," said the boy, "I can't do that—the king has forbidden it." And he ran off.

The next day he returned and demanded his ball. The wild man said, "Open the door." But the boy refused.

On the third day the king had gone hunting, and the boy came back and said, "Even if I wanted to, I couldn't open the door because I don't have the key."

Then the wild man said, "It's lying beneath your mother's pillow—you can get it there."

The boy, who wanted his ball, threw all caution to the winds and fetched the key. The door was hard to open, and the boy jammed his finger. When the door did come open, the wild man stepped out, gave the boy the golden ball, and hurried away.

The boy became frightened and cried out after him, "Oh, wild man, don't go away, or I'll get a beating."

The wild man turned around, lifted him up on his

shoulders, and with rapid strides went into the forest.

When the king returned home, he saw the empty cage and asked the queen what had happened. She knew nothing about it and looked for the key, but it was gone. She called the boy, but no one answered. The king sent men out to look for him in the fields, but they didn't find him. Then it was easy to guess what must have happened, and there was deep sorrow at court.

When the wild man had once more reached the dark forest, he lifted the boy down from his shoulders and said to him. "You will never see your father and mother again, but I shall keep you with me because you set me free, and I feel sorry for you. If you do everything I tell you, things will go well with you. I have enough treasure and gold—more than anyone else in the world."

He made the boy a bed of moss on which he slept. The next morning the man led him to a spring and said, "Do you see how the spring of gold is bright and clear as crystal? You have to sit beside it and make sure that nothing falls in, or it will be polluted. I shall come every evening to see whether you have obeyed my command."

The boy sat down at the edge of the spring, and now and then he saw a golden fish or a golden snake appear, and he made sure that nothing fell in. One time as he was sitting there, he felt such a sharp pain in his finger that he couldn't keep from putting it in the water. He quickly pulled it back out, but he saw that it was already completely covered with gold, and no matter how hard he tried to rub the gold off, it was all in vain.

At night Iron Hans returned, looked into the boy's face, and said, "What happened to the spring?"

"Nothing, nothing." And he held the finger behind his back in order to hide it.

But the man said, "You have dipped your finger into the water. Let it pass this time, but beware of letting anything else fall in."

Early in the morning the boy was already sitting beside the spring keeping watch. The finger was hurting him again so that he brushed it across his head, and as ill luck would have it, a hair fell into the spring. He took it out right away, but it had already turned completely to gold.

Iron Hans returned and knew already what had hap-

pened. "You have let a hair fall into the spring," he said.
"I'll overlook it once more, but if it happens a third time
the spring will be polluted, and you can't stay with me
any longer."

On the third day the boy was sitting beside the spring,
and he didn't move his finger, no matter how much it
hurt. But he grew bored and was studying the reflection
of his face in the water. As he was bending further and
further forward in order to gaze into his eyes, his long
hair fell from his shoulders into the water. He straight-
ened up quickly, but all the hair on his head had already turned to gold and gleamed like the sun.

You can imagine how frightened the poor boy was. He
took his handkerchief and tied it around his head so that
the man would not see what had happened. When the man
came home, though, he knew everything already and said,
"Take off the handkerchief." Then the golden hair flowed
forth, and no matter what excuses the boy might make,
nothing could help him.

"You have failed the test and cannot stay here anymore.
Go out into the world, where you will learn what it means
to be poor. But because you do not have a wicked heart
and because I wish you well, I will grant you one thing: if
you ever are in need go to the forest and call out 'Iron
Hans,' and I will come to your aid. I have great power—
greater than you think, and I have gold and silver to
spare."

Now the king's son left the forest and traveled over
highways and byways until at last he came to a large
city. He looked for work but could find none, and, besides, he had learned nothing by which he could make his
way. Finally he went to the castle and asked whether they
had a place for him. The household servants didn't know
what work to give him, but they liked his looks and asked
him to stay. At last the cook gave him a job and told him
that he could carry wood and water and rake the ashes.

One time when no one else happened to be at hand, the
cook ordered him to wait on the king's table, but because
he wanted to hide his golden hair, he kept his cap on.
Nothing like that had ever happened to the king before,
and he said, "When you come to the king's table, you
must take off your hat."

"Oh, Sire," he answered, "I can't, because I have a bad case of scurf on my head."

The king sent for the cook, scolded him, and asked how he could have given a job to a boy like that—he should run him off right away. But the cook felt sorry for him and had him trade places with the gardener's boy.

In the garden the boy had to plant and water, to hoe and dig, and to suffer the wind and the rain. One time

during the summer, as he was working alone in the garden, the day was so hot that he removed his cap so the breeze might cool him. The sun shining on his hair made it glitter and flash so that the reflection fell into the bedroom of the king's daughter, and she jumped up to see what was wrong. She saw the boy and called out to him, "Boy, bring me a bunch of flowers."

In great haste he put on his cap, picked some wild flowers, and tied them in a bunch. As he was coming up the stairs with them, he met the gardener, who said, "How dare you bring the king's daughter a bunch of worthless flowers? Hurry, gather some others, and pick out the rarest and the most beautiful."

"Oh no," answered the boy, "the wild ones have a stronger scent, and she'll like them better."

When he came into the room, the king's daughter said, "Take your cap off—it's bad manners to keep it on in front of me."

Again he answered, "I mustn't, because my head is covered with scurf."

But she snatched away the cap, and then his golden hair fell down to his shoulders, and it was a splendid sight.

He wanted to run away, but she clung to his arm and gave him a handful of ducats. He took them, but he had no use for the gold and gave it to the gardener, saying, "Here's a present for your children to play with."

The next day the king's daughter called out to him again to bring her a bunch of wild flowers. As he came into the room with them, she reached out for the cap right away to take it from him, but he held on to it tightly with both hands. Again she gave him a handful of ducats, but he wouldn't keep them and gave them to the gardener for his children to play with.

The third day was just the same: she couldn't take away his cap and he didn't want her gold.

Soon after that the country was invaded. The king gathered his forces and didn't know whether he would be able to withstand the enemy, who was more powerful and had a large army. The gardener's boy said, "I've grown up and want to come along to fight—just give me a horse."

The others laughed and said, "After we've gone, go and find one. We'll leave one for you in the stables." After they had marched away, he went to the stables and led out the horse, which was lame in one foot and limped clumpety-clump, clumpety-clump. Nevertheless, he got on and rode off toward the dark forest.

When he came to the edge, he called three times, "Iron Hans," so loud that it echoed through the trees. Right away the wild man appeared and said, "What do you want?"

"I want a strong steed because I would like to go to war."

"You shall have it, and more than you ask."

Then the wild man went back into the forest, and soon a groom came out leading a stallion that snorted through its nostrils and could hardly be controlled. It was followed by a large band of warriors, armed all in iron, and their swords flashed in the sun.

The youth handed the groom his three-legged horse, mounted the other, and rode at the head of the troops. By the time he arrived on the battlefield, the greater part of the king's forces had fallen, and the others were near the point of fleeing.

The youth galloped up with his iron troops, fell upon the enemy like a thunderstorm, and cut down everything that resisted him. They wanted to flee, but the youth followed upon their heels, and didn't give up until not one man was left. However, instead of returning to the king, he led his troops over back ways to the forest and called Iron Hans.

"What do you want?" asked the wild man.

"Take back your stallion and your troops, and give me back my three-legged horse." All was done as he wished, and he rode home on his three-legged horse.

When the king returned to his castle, his daughter went to meet him to congratulate him on his victory. "I didn't win the victory," he said, "but it was an unknown knight who came to my aid with his troops." His daughter asked who the unknown knight might be, but the king did not know and said, "He gave chase to the enemy, and I did not see him again."

She asked the gardener about his boy. He laughed and said, "He just came home on his three-legged horse, and the others made fun of him and called out, 'Here comes old clumpety-clump back again!' And they asked him, 'What hedge have you been sleeping behind all this while?' But he said, 'I did the most, and without me things would have gone badly.' Then they laughed at him even harder."

The king said to his daughter, "I shall proclaim a great

feast that will last three days, and you are to throw a golden apple—perhaps the stranger will come."

When the feast was proclaimed, the youth went out to the forest and called Iron Hans.

"What do you want?" he asked.

"I want to catch the golden apple of the king's daughter."

"It's as good as yours," said Iron Hans, "and you shall have a red suit of armor besides, and ride upon a proud bay horse."

When the day arrived, the youth galloped up to take his place among the other knights. The king's daughter appeared before them and tossed out a golden apple. He alone caught it, but as soon as he had it, he galloped away.

On the second day Iron Hans fitted him out in white armor and gave him a white horse. Again he alone caught the apple, but he galloped off without pausing an instant.

The king was angry and said, "This is not allowed—he has to present himself to me and tell his name." He gave orders that if the knight rode off again after catching the apple, they should pursue him, and if he refused to come back of his own free will, they should stop him with thrusts and blows.

On the third day Iron Hans gave him a black horse, and he caught the apple again. When he galloped off with it, the king's men followed, and one of them came so close that he wounded the boy in the leg with the point of his sword. In spite of that he escaped from them, but his horse gave such a mighty leap that his helmet fell off, and they could see that he had golden hair. They rode back and reported everything to the king.

The next day the king's daughter asked the gardener about his boy. "He's working in the garden—the strange fellow was also at the feast and only got back last night. And he showed my children three golden apples that he won."

The king had him summoned into his presence, and when he appeared, he still had his cap on. But the king's daughter went up to him and took it off, and his golden hair fell down over his shoulders, and everyone was amazed at how handsome he was.

"Are you the knight who came to the feast every day

in a different color and who caught the golden apples?"
asked the king.

"Yes," he answered, "and here are the apples." He took
them out of his pocket and handed them to the king. "If
you want further proof, I can show you the wound that
your men gave me when they were pursuing me. And I'm
also the knight who helped you conquer your enemies."

"If you can perform such feats, then you are no gardener's boy. Tell me, who is your father?"

"My father is a powerful king, and I have gold in abundance—as much as I want."

"I see well," said the king, "that I owe you a debt of
gratitude. Is there any favor I could grant you?"

"Yes," he answered, "indeed you can. Give me your
daughter for my bride."

Then the girl laughed and said, "He doesn't stand on
ceremony! But I already saw from his golden hair that he
is no gardener's boy." And she went and kissed him.

His mother and father came to the wedding full of joy
because they had given up all hope of ever seeing their
dear son again. And as they were sitting at the wedding
banquet, the music suddenly stopped, the doors opened,
and a noble king entered with a large following. He went
up to the youth, embraced him, and said, "I am Iron
Hans and was changed into a wild man, but you have set
me free. All the treasures that I own shall be yours."

THE TALL TALE
OF DITMARSH

L et me tell you something. I saw two roast chickens
flying through the air; they were flying fast and
had their breasts pointed toward Heaven and their
backs toward Hell; and an anvil and a millstone were

floating over the Rhine, smooth, slow, and easy; and at
Whitsuntide a frog was gobbling a plowshare on the ice.

Three fellows on crutches and stilts went out to catch
a rabbit—the first was deaf, the second blind, the third
dumb, and the fourth couldn't stir a step. Do you want to
know how it happened? The blind man was the first to see
the hare running across the field; the dumb man called to
the lame one; and the lame man collared it.

Some people wanted to sail overland. They set the sails
to the wind, and sailed away over great open stretches.
Then they sailed over a high mountain and were miserably drowned.

A crab put a hare to flight, and a cow had climbed up
to the top of the roof and was lying down there. In that
part of the country the flies are as big as goats.

Open the window and let the lies out!

SNOW WHITE
AND ROSE RED

A poor widow was leading a solitary life in a small
cottage, and in front of the cottage was a garden
in which stood two rosebushes, one of which bore
white roses and the other red. And she had two children
who were like the two rosebushes, and the one was called
Snow White and the other Rose Red. They were as devout
and good, as diligent and as cheerful, as ever two children
were in the whole world. The only difference between them
was that Snow White was quieter and gentler than Rose
Red. Rose Red preferred running about the meadows
and fields, hunting for flowers and catching butterflies;
Snow White, on the other hand, used to sit home with
her mother, helped her with the housework, or read aloud
to her when there were no chores to be done. The two

children loved each other so much that whenever they went out together, they went hand in hand. And when Snow White said, "We shall never leave each other," Rose Red answered, "Not as long as we live," and the mother added, "Whatever one of you has, she should share with the other."

Many times they wandered through the forest alone and gathered red berries, but none of the animals did them any harm; instead they came up trustingly. The rabbit ate a cabbage leaf out of their hands, the roe grazed at their side, the stag sprang merrily past, and the birds remained sitting on the branches, singing for all they were worth.

No accident every happened to them. If they tarried too long in the forest and night overtook them, they lay down side by side on the moss and slept until it was morning, and their mother knew this and did not worry about them.

One time when they had spent the night in the forest and the dawn had awakened them, they saw a beautiful child in a shining white garment sitting beside their place of rest. It arose and looked at them very kindly but said nothing and went into the forest. And looking around, they saw that they had been sleeping on the edge of an abyss and would surely have fallen in had they gone on a few steps farther in the dark. Their mother told them it must have been the angel who watches over good children.

Snow White and Rose Red kept their mother's cottage so clean that it was a joy to look in. In summertime Rose Red looked after the house and placed a bunch of flowers beside her mother's bed every morning before she woke up. It contained one rose from each of the bushes. In wintertime Snow White kindled the fire and hung up the kettle on the pot hook; the kettle was brass but had been scrubbed so clean that it gleamed like gold. In the evening when the snowflakes were falling, the mother said, "Go and bolt the door, Snow White," and then they sat around the hearth, and the mother took her glasses and read to them out of a big book, and the two girls sat and listened and spun. Beside them a lamb lay on the floor, and behind them a white dove sat on its perch with its head tucked under its wing.

One evening as they were sitting so cozily together, someone knocked at the door as if he wished to come in. The mother said, "Quickly, Rose Red, open the door; it must be a traveler looking for shelter." Rose Red went and unbolted the door, expecting a poor man; however, a bear stuck its big black head through the door. Rose Red screamed and jumped back. The lamb bleated, the dove fluttered up, and Snow White hid behind the mother's bed. But the bear began to speak and said, "Do not be afraid— I shall not harm you. I am nearly frozen to death and only want to warm myself a bit with you."

"You poor bear," said the mother, "lie down close to the fire; only be careful not to singe your fur." Then she called, "Snow White, Rose Red, come out. The bear won't hurt you. It means no harm." Then they both approached, and little by little the lamb and the dove came closer too and weren't afraid of it.

The bear said, "Children, brush some of the snow out of my fur." And they fetched the broom and swept the bear's fur clean. It stretched out by the fire and growled very contentedly and comfortably. Before long they weren't a bit afraid and teased their clumsy visitor. They pulled its fur with their hands, put their feet against its back and tumbled it back and forth, or they took a hazel switch and started hitting it and laughing every time it growled. The bear didn't mind at all; only when they were too rough, it called out, "Children, don't kill me,

> Snow White, Rose Red,
> Don't strike your suitor dead."

When it was time to sleep and the others were going to bed, the mother said to the bear, "Stay here beside the fire in the name of God, and you will be protected against the cold and the weather." As soon as day dawned, the children let the bear out, and it trotted across the snow into the forest.

From that time on the bear came every evening at a regular time, lay down at the hearth, and let the children have their fun with it as much as they pleased. And they got so used to it that they never bolted the door until their black friend had arrived.

When spring came and everything outside turned green, the bear said to Snow White one morning, "Now I must go away and may not return for the whole summer."

"But where are you going, dear bear?" asked Snow White.

"I have to go into the forest to guard my treasures against the evil dwarfs. In the winter when the ground is frozen hard, they have to stay underground and can't work their way to the surface, but now when the sun has thawed out and warmed the earth, they break through and go prying and stealing. Everything that falls into their hands and comes to lie in their caves will not come to light again so easily."

It made Snow White very sad to say good-bye, and when she unbolted the door and the bear squeezed through, he got caught on the door hook and a piece of his hide ripped open, and it seemed to Snow White that she could see gold gleaming underneath. But she couldn't be sure about it. The bear ran off hastily and soon disappeared amid the trees.

After a time the mother sent the children into the forest to gather brushwood. Out there they found a big tree that had been cut down and was lying on the ground, and near the trunk something was jumping up and down in the grass, but they couldn't tell what it was. When they came closer, they saw a dwarf with an old wrinkled face and a snow-white beard that was a yard long. The end of the beard was caught in a cleft in the tree, and the little man jumped back and forth like a puppy on a leash and didn't know what to do. He glared at the girls with his fiery red eyes and screamed, "What are you standing there for? Can't you try to help me out?"

"What were you doing, little man?" asked Rose Red.

"You stupid, inquisitive goose," answered the dwarf, "I was trying to split the tree to get some small pieces of wood for my kitchen; with the big logs the bit of food my kind needs gets burned up right away. We don't gorge ourselves with such huge amounts as coarse and greedy folk like you. I'd already driven the wedge in all right and all would have gone as I wished, but the cursed wood was too slippery, and the wedge suddenly popped out, and the tree snapped close so quickly that I didn't have time to get out my beautiful white beard. Now it's stuck in there and I can't get away. Now they're laughing, the silly blank whey-faces! Pfui, how disgusting you are!"

The children tried as hard as they could, but they weren't able to get the beard out—it was stuck fast. "I'll run and get somebody," said Rose Red.

"You harebrained idiots," sputtered the dwarf, "running for help right away. You're two too many for me already. Can't you think of anything better than that?"

"Don't be so impatient," said Snow White. "I've got

an idea." She got some scissors out of her pocket and cut off the end of the beard.

As soon as the dwarf realized that he was loose, he reached for a sack full of gold that was lying among the roots of the tree and picked it up, murmuring, "Barbarians—to cut a piece off my magnificent beard! The fiend reward you for it!" With that, he threw the sack onto his back and went off without so much as looking at the children again.

Some time thereafter Snow White and Rose Red wanted to catch some fish for dinner. As they were approaching the brook, they saw something like a huge grasshopper hopping down toward the water as if it were going to jump in. They ran up and recognized the dwarf.

"Where are you going?" asked Rose Red. "You don't want to go into the water, do you?"

"I'm no such fool," screamed the dwarf. "Can't you see that the cursed fish is trying to pull me in?" The little man had been sitting there fishing, and unhappily the wind had tangled his beard with the fishing line. When immediately thereafter a large fish bit, the weak creature lacked the strength to haul it out. The fish was having the better of it and dragging the dwarf in. He was hanging on to the stalks and rushes, but this didn't help much. He had to follow the movements of the fish and was in constant danger of being pulled into the water.

The girls arrived just in time, held on to him tightly, and tried to disentangle the beard from the line, but in vain. The beard and the line were completely snarled. There was no remedy except to get out the little scissors and cut the beard loose. A small part of it got lost in the process.

When the dwarf saw this, he railed at them, "What kind of behavior is that, you vile creatures, spoiling people's faces? It's not enough that you clipped the end off my beard—now you cut off the best part of it. I don't even dare show myself before my own people. I'd like to see you forced to run barefoot!" Then he fetched a sack of pearls that was lying in the reeds, and without another word, he dragged it off and disappeared behind a stone.

It happened soon after that the mother sent the two girls to town to buy thread, needles, laces, and ribbons.

The way led across a heath over which great boulders were lying scattered here and there. They saw a large bird hovering in the air, circling slowly above them, and finally it swooped down on a nearby boulder. Immediately they heard a piercing and pitiful scream. They came running and were horrified to see that an eagle had seized their old friend the dwarf and was trying to carry him off. The compassionate children at once clung tightly to the little man and waged a tug-of-war with the eagle until finally he let go of his prey.

When the dwarf had recovered from the initial shock, he cried in his shrill voice, "Couldn't you have handled me more gently? You've pulled at my light little coat until it's ragged and full of holes—awkward, clumsy riffraff that you are!" Then he picked up a sack of jewels and slipped back under the boulder into his cave. The girls were already used to his ingratitude, continued on their way, and ran their errands in town.

On their way home across the heath they surprised the dwarf, who had emptied a sack of jewels in a little clear spot, not thinking that anyone might still be coming along so late. The evening sun was shining on the glistening stones, and they shimmered and glowed so splendidly in all colors that the children stopped to look at them.

"Why are you standing there with your mouths open?" screamed the dwarf, and his ash gray face turned brick red with rage. He was going to continue his stream of abuse, when a loud growling was heard, and a black bear came trotting out of the forest. The frightened dwarf jumped up, but he didn't have time to reach his retreat. The bear was already on top of him. Then he cried out in terror, "Good Sir Bear, spare me. I will give you all my treasures. Look at the beautiful jewels lying there. Grant me my life. What good would a small and puny fellow like me do you? You wouldn't even feel me between your teeth. Seize those two wicked girls there. They'd be tender morsels for you—fat as young quail. Eat them in God's name." The bear paid no attention to his words, struck the spiteful creature a single blow with its paw, and he didn't stir again.

The girls had run away, but the bear called after them, "Snow White and Rose Red, don't be afraid. Wait, I want to come with you." Then they recognized its voice and stopped, and when the bear caught up with them, its bearskin suddenly dropped off, and there stood a handsome man clothed entirely in gold. "I am a king's son," he said, "and the wicked dwarf, who stole my treasure, put me under a spell so that I had to run through the forest as a wild bear until I should be released by his death. Now he has received his well-earned punishment."

Snow White was married to him and Rose Red to his brother, and they shared the vast treasures the dwarf had accumulated in his cave. The old mother continued to live for many years in peace and happiness with her children. But she took along the two rosebushes, and they stood outside her window, and each year bore the most beautiful white and red roses.

THE MOON

Long ago there was a country where the nights were always dark and the sky was spread out over it like a black cloth, for the moon never rose there and not one star gleamed through the darkness. When the world was first created, there had been enough light at night without them.

One time four lads set out on their travels and got to another country where in the evening, after the sun had vanished behind the mountains, a shining globe appeared at the top of an oak, shedding a soft light far and wide. By this light it was possible to see and distinguish everything even though it wasn't as bright as the sun.

The travelers stopped and asked a farmer who was driving by in his cart what sort of light that might be. "That's the moon," he answered. "Our mayor bought it for three thaler and fastened it to the oak. He has to fill it with oil every day and keep it clean to make sure that it always shines brightly. For that we pay him a thaler a week."

When the farmer had driven off, one of the boys said, "We could use that lamp. We have an oak at home just as big, and we could hang it from that. What a joy it would be not to have to grope one's way about in the dark!"

"Do you know what?" said the second. "Let's get a wagon and horses and take the moon away with us. They can buy another one here."

"I'm good at climbing," said the third. "I'll bring it down all right."

The fourth fetched a wagon and horses, and the third climbed the tree, bored a hole through the moon, passed a rope through, and let it down. When the shining globe was lying on the wagon, they covered it with a cloth so that no one would notice the theft. They succeeded in getting it to their own country and attached it to the tall oak. Old and young rejoiced when the new lamp was shining over all the fields and filling the rooms and chambers with its light. The dwarfs emerged from their caves, and in the meadows the elves in their red jackets danced around in a ring.

The four supplied the moon with oil, cleaned the wick, and received a thaler a week. But they got to be very old men, and when one of them became sick and saw his end approaching, he declared that a quarter of the moon, which was his property, was to go with him into the grave. When he was dead, the mayor climbed the tree and cut off a quarter with the hedge shears, and it was laid in the coffin. The light of the moon grew dimmer, but not noticeably.

When the second died, he was given the second quarter to take along, and the light diminished. It became weaker still after the death of the third, who took his share too, and when the fourth was buried, the old darkness returned. At night when the people walked out without a lantern, they banged their heads together.

However, when the parts of the moon joined together again in the Underworld, down where darkness had always reigned, the dead were disturbed and awoke out of their sleep. They were amazed to be able to see once more. The moonlight was enough for them because their eyes had grown so weak they they wouldn't have been able to stand the brightness of the sun. They got up, grew merry, and resumed their old way of life. Some began gambling and dancing; others ran to the inns, where they ordered wine and got drunk. They carried on and quarreled and finally picked up their cudgels and started belaboring each other. The noise got worse and worse, and at last it could be heard all the way up to Heaven.

Saint Peter, who guards the gate of Heaven, thought that there must be an uprising in the Underworld, and he called out the Heavenly Hosts to drive back the wicked Enemy, if with his cohorts he should try to storm the abode of the blessed. But when they didn't come, he got on his horse and rode out through the gate of Heaven down to the Underworld. He made peace among the dead, ordered them to lie back down in their graves, and took the moon away with him and hung it up in Heaven.

THE SPAN OF LIFE

W hen God had created the world and was appointing all creatures a span of life, the donkey came and asked, "Lord, how long shall I live?"

"Thirty years," answered God. "Does that suit you?"

"Oh, Lord," answered the donkey, "that is a long time. Consider my hard existence: carrying heavy burdens from morning till night, hauling sacks of grain to the mill to provide bread for others to eat, getting nothing but kicks and blows for comfort and encouragement! Remit a part of such a long span."

Then the Lord had pity and took away eighteen years. The donkey went off consoled, and the dog appeared.

"How long would you like to live?" God asked him.

"Thirty years was too long for the donkey, but you will be satisfied with it."

"Lord," answered the dog, "is this Your will? Consider how I have to run—my feet will not hold out that long. And once I've lost my voice for barking and my teeth for chewing, what will be left for me except to run from corner to corner, growling?"

God realized that he was right and took away twelve years.

Next came the monkey.

"I suppose you'd like to live thirty years," the Lord said to him. "You don't have to work like the donkey and dog, and you are always merry."

"Oh, Lord," he answered, "that's what it may look like, but it really isn't so. When it's raining cereal, I'm the fellow without a spoon. I'm supposed to play amusing tricks all the time and make faces to get people to laugh, and when they give me an apple and I bite into it—it turns out to be a sour one. How often sadness is concealed behind a mask of gaiety! I can't stand thirty years of it."

God was merciful and released him from ten years.

Finally man appeared, happy, healthy, and youthful, and told God to appoint him his lifespan.

"You shall live thirty years," said the Lord. "Will that be long enough for you?"

"What a short time!" cried man. "Just when I have built my own house and the fire is burning on my own hearth, when I have planted trees that are blossoming and bearing fruit, and when I look forward to some joy in my life—that is when I must die! Oh, Lord, extend my time."

"I will add on the eighteen years of the donkey," said God.

"That isn't enough," answered man.

"You shall also have the twelve years of the dog."

"That still isn't enough."

"Very well," said God, "I will give you the ten years of the monkey, too, but you won't get any more."

Man went off, but he wasn't satisfied.

And so man lives seventy years. The first thirty are his human years. They pass quickly. He is healthy and happy, works with a will, and rejoices in his being. Then follow the eighteen years of the donkey. One burden after another is heaped on him; he must carry grain to feed others, and kicks and blows are the rewards for his faithful service. Then come the twelve years of the dog. He lies in the corner, growling, and no longer has teeth to chew with. And when that time is gone, the ten years of the monkey make up the end. Man becomes silly and fool-

ish, plays idle pranks, and becomes a laughingstock for children.

THE UNEQUAL CHILDREN
OF EVE

░░

After Adam and Eve were driven out of Paradise they had to build their house on barren ground and to eat their bread in the sweat of their brows. Adam hoed in the field and Eve spun wool. Each year Eve gave birth to a child. However, the children varied: some of them were beautiful and some were ugly.

After a considerable time, God sent his angel to announce to the two of them that He was coming to look over their household. Eve was glad that the Lord was so gracious, and she busily cleaned her house, decorated it with flowers, and strewed rushes on the floor. Then she fetched her children, but only the beautiful ones. She washed and bathed them, combed their hair, and dressed them in fresh linen, and she warned them to behave nicely and properly in the presence of the Lord. They must bow politely, offer their hands, and answer his questions with modesty and good sense.

The ugly children, however, were to keep out of sight. She hid one in the hay, the second in the loft, the third in the straw, the fourth in the stove, the fifth in the cellar, the sixth under a tub, the seventh under the wine barrel, the eighth in her old fur coat, the ninth and tenth under the material she used to make clothes for the children, and the eleventh and twelfth under the leather out of which she made their shoes.

She had just finished when there came a knock at the front door. Adam peeked out through a crack and saw that it was the Lord. They opened the door reverently, and the Heavenly Father stepped inside. There in a row stood the beautiful children, who bowed, offered their hands to Him, and knelt.

The Lord began blessing them. He laid his hands upon the first and said, "You shall be a mighty king," and to the second, "you a prince," to the third, "you a count," to the fourth, "you a knight," to the fifth, "you a gentleman," to the sixth, "you a burgess," to the seventh, "you a merchant," to the eighth, "you a scholar." Thus He divided his blessings among them all.

When Eve saw that the Lord was so kind and gracious, she thought, "I will go fetch my ugly children—perhaps He will give them his blessing too." So she ran off and got them out of the hay, the straw, the stove, and all the other places where they were hiding. There came the whole rough, dirty, scurfy, sooty pack.

The Lord smiled and said, "I will bless these too." He laid his hands on the first and said, "You shall be a farmer," and to the second, "you a fisherman," to the third, "you a smith," to the fourth, "you a tanner," to the fifth, "you a weaver," to the sixth, "you a shoemaker," to the seventh, "you a tailor," to the eighth, "you a potter," to the ninth, "you a carter," to the tenth, "you a sailor," to the eleventh, "you a messenger," to the twelfth, "you a servant for the rest of your life."

When Eve had heard all this, she said, "Lord, how unequally you divide your blessings! After all, they are all my children, and I bore them. Your favor should be parted equally among them all."

God, however, answered, "Eve, you do not understand these things. It is right and necessary that I must provide for the whole world with your children. If all men were princes and masters, who would raise the crops, thresh, grind, and bake? Who would forge, weave, frame, build, dig, cut, and sew? Each must fill his place so that one will support the other, that all may be sustained like the members of the body."

Then Eve answered, "Oh, Lord, forgive me. I was very rash to speak out of turn. May your divine will be done also upon my children."

THE HARE
AND THE HEDGEHOG

T his sounds like a made-up story, children, but it's true all the same because my grandfather, from whom I got it, enjoyed telling it and would always say, "It's bound to be true, son, because no one could have made it up." Anyhow, this is how the story went.

It was a Sunday morning in harvest when the buckwheat was just blooming. A bright sun had risen in the sky, a warm morning breeze was blowing over the stub-

ble, the larks were singing in the air, the bees were buzzing in the buckwheat, and the people were going to church in their Sunday best, and all creatures were happy, including the hedgehog.

The hedgehog was standing in front of his door with his arms crossed, facing the morning breeze and humming a little song to himself—no better and no worse than a hedgehog generally sings on a fine Sunday morning. While he was thus softly singing to himself, the idea suddenly occurred to him that he might as well take a little walk in the fields to see how his turnips were doing while his wife was washing and dressing the children. Since the turnips grew very close to his house and he and his family always ate them, he regarded them as his property. No sooner said than done. The hedgehog shut the door behind him and took the path to the field.

He hadn't gone very far from his house and was just rounding a thornbush by the edge of the field on the way to the turnip patch, when he met the hare, who was out on similar business, namely to inspect his cabbages.

When the hedgehog saw the hare, he wished him a friendly good morning. The hare, however, who was in his way quite a gentleman and terribly lofty about it, didn't answer the hedgehog's greeting but instead said to the hedgehog, giving himself a mightily scornful air, "How do you happen to be running around in the fields so early in the morning?"

"I'm taking a walk," said the hedgehog.

"Taking a walk?" laughed the hare. "It seems to me you could find some better use for your legs."

This answer greatly offended the hedgehog, because he will put up with everything except remarks about his legs, precisely because they're crooked by nature. "I guess you think," said the hedgehog to the hare, "that your legs are worth more than mine?"

"I think so," said the hare.

"That has to be proved first," said the hedgehog. "I bet that if we run a race I'll leave you behind."

"That's ridiculous—you with your crooked legs," said the hare. "But as far as I'm concerned, let's go ahead, since you're so eager. What will you bet?"

"A gold *louis* and a bottle of brandy," said the hedgehog.

"Agreed," said the hare. "Let's shake hands on it and start right away."

"No, I'm not in that much of a hurry," said the hedgehog. "I haven't had a thing to eat yet. First I'd like to go home and have a bit of breakfast. In half an hour I'll meet you back here at this spot."

The hare agreed, and the hedgehog left. On the way the hedgehog thought to himself, "The hare is counting on his long legs, but I'll put one over on him. He may be a fine gentleman, but he's a stupid fellow all the same, and he'll have to pay in spite of everything."

When the hedgehog got home, he said to his wife, "Wife, get dressed right away. You have to come out to the field with me."

"What's going on?" said his wife.

"I've bet the hare a gold *louis* and a bottle of brandy. I'm running a race with him, and I want you with me."

"Oh my God, husband," the hedgehog's wife started to scream, "are you crazy? Have you lost your mind completely? What on earth could make you want to run a race against the hare?"

"Shut up, wife," said the hedgehog. "This is my concern. Don't meddle in men's affairs. Hurry up, get dressed and come along."

What could the hedgehog's wife do? She had to obey, whether she wanted to or not.

As they were on their way, the hedgehog said to his wife, "Now pay attention to what I tell you. Do you see that long field? That's where we're going to run our race. The hare will run in one furrow, and I'll run in the other, and we'll start from the top of the field. All you have to do is to stand down here in the furrow, and when the hare arrives at your end, you call out to him, "Here I am already.""

With that they reached the field. The hedgehog showed his wife her place and then went on up the field. When he got to the top, the hare was already there.

"Can we get started?" said the hare.

"Certainly," said the hedgehog.

"Then let's go!"

And with that each one got ready in his furrow. The hare counted, "On your mark, get set, go," and he was off down the field like a whirlwind. The hedgehog, however, ran about three steps, then ducked down in the furrow, and calmly sat there.

Now when the hare, running full tilt, reached the other end of the field, the hedgehog's wife called out to him, "Here I am already!"

The hare stopped short, not a little surprised. He had no idea that it wasn't the hedgehog himself calling out to him, for it's a well-known fact that a hedgehog's wife looks exactly like her husband.

However, the hare thought, "There's some trick about this." He called, "Race you back again!" And he was off once more like a whirlwind, so that his ears streamed behind his head. But the hedgehog's wife stayed calmly where she was.

When the hare got to the top of the field, the hedgehog called out to him, "Here I am already."

But the hare, utterly beside himself with anger, cried, "Race you back again!"

"I don't mind," answered the hedgehog, "as many times as you like as far as I'm concerned."

So the hare ran another seventy-three times, and the hedgehog always won. Every time the hare got to the top or bottom of the field the hedgehog or his wife said, "Here I am already."

But the seventy-fourth time the hare didn't finish. He collapsed in the middle of the field, the blood gushed out of his mouth, and he was dead in his tracks. The hedgehog, however, took the gold *louis* and the bottle of brandy he had won, called to his wife to get out of the furrow, and the two of them went happily home together. And if they haven't died, they're still alive.

So it happened on Buxtehude heath that a hedgehog ran a hare to death, and since that time no hare has ever dared to run a race against a Buxtehude hedgehog.

The moral of this story is, first, that nobody, no matter how grand he thinks he is, should allow himself to make fun of a lesser person, even if it's only a hedgehog. And, second, that it's a good thing for a man choosing a wife to take one from his own class, one who looks just like him. A hedgehog should make sure that his wife is also a hedgehog, and so forth.

THE MASTER THIEF

|||||||||||||||||||||||||||||||||||||||||||||||||||||||||||||||||||||||

O ne day an old man and his wife were sitting in
front of their poor cottage in order to rest a little from their labors. Suddenly a magnificent carriage drawn by four black horses drove up, and a richly
dressed gentleman stepped out. The farmer rose to his
feet, approached the gentleman, and asked what it was
he desired and how one might serve him.

The stranger gave his hand to the old man and said,
"All I want is to enjoy some country cooking for a
change. Prepare some potatoes for me just the way you
always have them. Then I'll sit down at your table, and
it will give me pleasure to eat them."

The farmer smiled and said, "You are a count or
prince, or perhaps even a duke. Fine gentlemen sometimes have cravings of this sort. But your wish shall be
fulfilled."

His wife went into the kitchen and started to wash and
peel potatoes to make some dumplings such as farmers
eat. While she was busy with her work, the farmer said
to the stranger, "In the meantime, won't you join me in
the garden, where I still have some work to do?" He had
dug holes in the garden, and now he was going to set
some saplings in them.

"Have you no children," asked the stranger, "who
could help you with your work?"

"No," answered the farmer. "I did have a son," he
added, "but he went out into the wide world a long time
ago. The boy turned out badly—shrewd and clever, but
he refused to learn anything and was always up to some
kind of mischief. Finally he ran away, and I've never
heard of him since."

The old man took a sapling, set it in the hole, and

drove a stake into the ground beside it. And after filling
the hole with dirt and stamping it down, he tied the trunk
to the stake with straw cords at the top, the bottom, and
in the middle.

"Tell me," said the gentleman, "that gnarled and
crooked tree in the corner that's bent almost all the way
to the ground—why don't you tie it to a stake, too, like
this one, so that it will grow straight?"

The old man smiled and said, "Sir, that's all you know
about it. One can easily see that you've never had much
practice in gardening. That tree over there is old and
twisted—no one can ever make it straight again. Trees
have to be trained while they are young."

"Just the way it is with your son," said the stranger.
"If you had trained him while he was still young, he
wouldn't have run away. By now he too will have become
hardened and twisted."

"Yes," answered the old man, "but he's been gone for
a long time. He must have changed."

"Would you recognize him again if you were to see
him?" asked the stranger.

"Hardly by his face," answered the farmer, "but he has
a token, a birthmark on his shoulder that looks like a
bean."

When he heard this, the stranger stripped off his coat,
bared his shoulder, and showed the farmer the bean.

"Good heavens," cried the old man, "you really are
my son." And the love for his child stirred in his heart.
"Yet," he added, "how could you be my son? You have
become a great lord living in wealth and luxury. How
did you manage to do it?"

"Oh, Father," answered the son, "the young tree was
not tied to any stake, and grew up crooked. Now it's too
old—it will never grow straight again. How did I acquire
all of this? I became a thief. But don't be frightened—I
am a master thief. Locks and bolts mean nothing to me:
whatever I desire is mine. Don't believe that I steal like
a common thief—I only take from the rich who have
more than enough. Poor people are safe from me. I'd
rather give to them than take anything from them. Also,
I won't touch anything that does not require effort, cunning, and skill."

"Oh, my son," said the father, "I still don't like it. A thief is a thief. I tell you, no good can come of it." He led him to the mother, and when she heard that it was her son, she wept for joy. But when he told her that he had become a master thief, two streams of tears flowed down her cheeks. Finally she said, "Even if he did become a thief, he's still my son, and my eyes have seen him once more."

They sat down at the table, and he joined his parents once again, eating the poor fare he had not tasted for a long time. The father said, "If our master, the count, over in the castle, finds out who you are and how you earn your living, he won't dandle you in his arms as he did when he held you at the font. He'll swing you at the end of a rope instead."

"Don't worry, Father, he won't harm me, because I know my business. I intend to call on him myself this very day."

As evening drew on, the master thief got into his carriage and drove to the castle. The count received him courteously because he took him for a man of rank. But when the stranger identified himself, the count grew pale and remained completely silent for a while. At last he said, "You are my godchild, and therefore I will temper justice with mercy and will deal leniently with you. Since you boast that you are a master thief, I shall put your skill to the test. But if you fail, you shall marry the ropemaker's daughter, and the croaking of ravens shall be your bridal music."

"Your Excellency," answered the master thief, "devise three tasks, as difficult as you please, and if I cannot solve the problems you set me, do what you like with me."

The count thought for a few moments, then said, "Very well. First, you must steal my favorite horse out of the stable; second, you must steal the sheets out from under my wife and me after we've gone to bed, without our noticing, and you must also steal the wedding ring from her finger; third and last, you must steal the parson and the sexton out of the church. Mark my words well, for your neck is at stake."

The master thief went to the neighboring town. There

he got an old peasant woman to sell him her clothes, and he put them on. Then he stained his face brown and also lined in a few wrinkles, so that no man could have recognized him. Finally he filled a little keg with old Hungarian wine that he had mixed with a strong sleeping potion. He laid the keg in a carrier, strapped the carrier on his back, and with measured and faltering steps he went to the count's castle.

When he got there it was already dark. He sat down on a stone in the courtyard and started coughing like an old consumptive woman and rubbing his hands as though he were cold. Before the stable door the soldiers were lying around the fire. One of them noticed the woman and called to her, "Come closer, Granny, and warm yourself at our fire, for you haven't got a place to spend the night and must take what you find."

The old woman shuffled over, asked them to lift the carrier off her back, and sat down among them beside the fire.

"What have you got in that little keg, old biddy?" one of them asked.

"A good drink of wine," she answered. "That's how I earn my living. For money and a few kind words, I'll gladly give you a glass."

"Let's see," said the soldier, and when he had tried a glass, he cried, "If the wine is good, I always drink a second glass." He let her pour him another, and the others followed his example.

"Hey there, comrades," one of them called to those in the stable, "here's a little old woman who has some wine that's as old as she is. Have a taste yourself—it will warm your insides even more than our fire."

The old woman carried the little keg into the stable. One of the soldiers was sitting on the count's horse, which was saddled, a second had the bridle in his hand, and the third one was clutching the tail. She poured out as much as they wanted until the supply was exhausted.

In a little while the bridle dropped out of the hand of the one, and he sank down and snored. The second let go of the tail, lay down, and snored even louder. The third managed to stay in the saddle, but his head bent forward until it almost touched the horse's neck, and he slept with his mouth puffing like a smith's bellows. The soldiers outside had fallen asleep long ago and were lying motionless on the ground, as if they were made of stone.

When the master thief saw that he had succeeded, he gave the one a rope to hold instead of the bridle. The one who had been holding the tail got a wisp of straw. But what was he to do with the one sitting on the horse's back? He didn't want to throw him down for fear that he might wake up and give the alarm. But he thought of a good plan. He untied the saddle belt, fastened the saddle to a pair of ropes that were looped through rings in the wall, and hoisted the sleeping rider up, saddle and all. Then he wound the ropes around a post and tied them fast. He soon got the horse off the chain, but if he had ridden over the cobblestones in the courtyard, the noise would have been heard in the castle. Therefore, he first wrapped the horse's hooves in old rags, carefully led it outside, jumped on its back, and galloped away.

Early the next morning the master thief spurred to the castle on the stolen horse. The count had just gotten up and was looking out of the window. "Good morning, my lord," the thief called out to him. "Here's the horse, which I managed to fetch out of the stable. Just go see how nicely your soldiers are lying there asleep, and you'll see how your watchmen have made themselves cozy."

The count had to laugh. Then he said, "You've succeeded once, but the second time won't turn out so lucky for you. And I warn you that if I encounter you as a thief, I will treat you as a thief."

After the countess had gone to bed that night she closed her fist tightly around her wedding ring, and the count said, "All the doors are locked and bolted. I'll stay up to wait for the thief. If he tries to come in by the window, I'll shoot him down."

The master thief, however, under the cover of darkness went to the gallows and cut down a poor sinner who was hanging there, and carried him on his back to the castle. There he leaned a ladder against the bedroom, set the dead man on his shoulders, and started to climb up. When he got high enough so that the dead man's head appeared in the window, the count, who was lying in ambush in his bed, fired his pistol at him. Immediately the master thief let the poor sinner fall to the ground, jumped down from the ladder, and hid in a corner.

The moon was bright enough for the master thief to see clearly how the count stepped out of the window onto the ladder, climbed down, and carried the dead man into the garden. There he started digging a grave for him.

"Now the right moment has come," thought the thief. He stole lightly out of his corner and climbed the ladder right into the countess's bedchamber.

"Dear wife," he began, imitating the count's voice, "the thief is dead. But he was my godson, and more of a rascal than a criminal. I'm not going to hold him up to public shame, and I also feel sorry for the poor parents. I intend to bury him in the garden before daybreak so that this business won't get noised about. Give me the sheet and I'll shroud the corpse so as not to bury it like a dog."

The countess gave him the sheet.

"Do you know what?" the thief continued. "I've had a sudden impulse of generosity—give me the ring, too. The unfortunate fellow risked his life for it, and so let him take it along into the grave."

She didn't wish to cross the count, and so, albeit unwillingly, she removed the ring from her finger and handed it to him. The thief escaped with both items and got home successfully before the count had finished his grave-digging in the garden.

What a sour face the count made the next morning when the master thief came to him with the sheet and the ring. "You're quite a magician!" he said to him. "Who got you out of the grave into which I myself laid you, and who brought you back to life?"

"It wasn't me you buried," said the thief, "but a poor sinner from the gallows." And he told him in detail how he had done it, so that the count had to admit that he was a clever and cunning thief.

"But you haven't finished yet," he added. "You still have the third task to perform, and if you don't succeed, all the rest won't save you." The master thief smiled without answering.

After nightfall he came to the village church with a long sack on his back, a bundle under his arm, and a lantern in his hand. The sack contained crabs, and the bundle, little wax candles. He sat down in the churchyard, took out a crab, and stuck a candle on its back. Then he lit the candle, put the crab on the ground, and let it crawl away. He took the second out of the sack, did the same with it, and continued until he had emptied the sack. Thereupon he put on a long black garment that looked like a monk's habit, and pasted a gray beard on his chin. At last, when he was completely disguised, he took the sack that had contained the crabs, went into the church, and climbed into the pulpit.

The clock in the steeple was just striking twelve. As the final stroke died away, he cried in a loud, piercing voice, "Hear me, you sinful people, the end of all things has come. The last day is near. Hear, oh, hear! Whoever wishes to go to Heaven with me, let him crawl into the sack. I am Peter, who opens and shuts the gates of Heaven. See the dead wandering in the churchyard to gather their bones. Come, come and crawl into the sack. The world is coming to an end."

His cries rang through the whole village. The parson and the sexton, who lived closest to the church, were the first to hear them, and when they saw the lights wandering around in the churchyard, they realized that something extraordinary was going on and went into the church.

They listened to the sermon for a while. Then the sexton nudged the parson and said, "It might not be a bad idea if we took advantage of the opportunity and took an easy way to Heaven before the coming of the Last Day."

"Yes indeed," answered the parson, "that's just what I was thinking. If you want to, let's get started on the way."

"Yes," answered the sexton, "but you, Parson, should go first, and I will follow."

So the parson went ahead and climbed into the pulpit, where the master thief opened the sack. The parson crawled in first, and then the sexton. Immediately the master thief tied up the sack tightly, grabbed it by the neck, and dragged it down the pulpit steps. Every time the heads of the two fools struck the steps, he cried, "Now we're already crossing the mountains." In the same way he dragged them through the village, and when they went through puddles, he cried, "Now we're already going through the damp clouds." And finally, as he was dragging them up the steps to the castle, he cried, "Now we're going up the celestial stairs, and we'll soon arrive at the outer court." When he got to the top, he shoved the sack into the pigeon house, and when the pigeons fluttered around, he said, "Can you hear how the angels are rejoicing and flapping their wings?" Then he shot the bolt and went away.

The next morning he went to the count and told him that he had solved the third problem, too, and had kidnaped the parson and sexton out of the church.

"Where did you leave them?" asked the count.

"They're lying up in the pigeon house imagining that they're in Heaven."

The count climbed up there himself to make sure that he was telling the truth. After the count had freed the parson and the sexton from their prison, he said, "You are an arch-thief, and you have won your wager. For this time, you'll escape with a whole skin, but see that you get out of my domain, for if you ever set foot in it again, you can be sure of being promoted to the gallows."

The arch-thief said farewell to his parents, went back into the wide world, and no one has ever heard of him again.

APPENDIX

Two Early Versions of "Snow White"

The following versions of "Snow White" illustrate early stages in the development of the *Kinder- und Hausmärchen*. The first is the earliest form of the story known to have been in the possession of the Grimms and has been preserved only through a lucky accident of literary history. The Grimms' own manuscripts of the tales prior to the first edition of 1812 have not survived. However, in 1809 Clemens Brentano, the good friend of the brothers and one of the chief collaborators on the ballad collection *Des Knaben Wunderhorn*, asked the brothers for copies of the tales they had collected for use in a volume of folktales that Brentano himself was contemplating. Nothing ever came of Brentano's project, but the manuscripts of the tales that the Grimms generously provided him with have come down among Brentano's literary remains. They are preserved today in a Trappist monastery in Alsace, and were brought out in 1927 in a handsome edition by Professor Joseph Lefftz. The translation below of Jacob Grimm's manuscript version of "Snow White" has been made from this edition with the kind permission of Professor Lefftz.*

The second version translated below is that of the first edition of 1812. Although it preserves certain features of the earlier version, it is based for the most part

---

*For the present edition the translation has been checked against Heinz Rölleke's definitive edition of the manuscripts, *Die älteste Märchensammlung der Brüder Grimm* (Cologny-Genève: Fondation Martin Bodner, 1975).

on a different source. Even before the Grimms undertook their collection, "Snow White" was one of the most popular stories in oral tradition, and several different versions were known to them. "Snow White" is one of the stories that was reworked and polished in every one of the seven editions of the *märchen*. A translation of the final form of the story is, of course, given above on page 155.

I. "Snow White": *Earliest Version**

Once upon a time when it was winter and the snow was falling from the sky, a queen was sitting by a window of ebony wood, sewing. She wanted so very much to have a child, and while she was thinking about it, she carelessly pricked her finger with the needle so that three drops of blood fell on the snow. Then she made a wish and said, "Oh, if only I had a child as white as this snow, with cheeks as red as this blood, and with eyes as black as this window frame!"

Soon after that she bore a wondrously beautiful little daughter, as white as snow, as red as blood, as black as ebony, and the little daughter was called Snow White. The queen was the most beautiful woman in the land, but Snow White was one hundred thousand times more beautiful, and when the queen asked her mirror,

> "Mirror, mirror on the wall,
> Who is the fairest woman in all of England?"

the mirror answered, "The queen is the fairest, but Snow White is one hundred thousand times more fair."

For that reason the queen could not endure her anymore, because she wanted to be the most beautiful in the kingdom. One time when the king had gone off to war, she had her carriage hitched up and gave orders to drive into a distant and dark forest, and she took Snow White along. In the same forest many very beautiful

*Translated from *Märchen der Brüder Grimm. Urfassung nach der Originalhandschrift der Abtei Olenberg*, ed. Joseph Lefftz (Heidelberg, 1927).

roses were growing. When she and her little daughter arrived there, she said to her, "Oh, Snow White, please get out and pick some of the beautiful roses for me!" And as soon as Snow White got out of the carriage to obey her command, the wheels began to turn and rolled off at top speed; but the queen had arranged it all that way because she hoped that the wild beasts would soon devour the girl.

Because Snow White was now all forlorn in the great forest, she wept a great deal and kept going on and on, getting very tired, until at last she came to a little house. In the house lived seven dwarfs, but they weren't home just then, and had gone off to the mines. When Snow White entered the house, a table was standing there, and on the table were seven plates, and beside them seven spoons, seven forks, seven knives, and seven cups, and there were also seven little beds in the room. Snow White ate a few greens and a bit of bread from each plate and drank a drop from each little cup, and finally wanted to lie down to sleep because she was so tired. She tried out all the little beds and none of them suited her until the last; there she remained lying.

When the seven dwarfs came home from their daily work, each one said:

> "Who has been eating from my plate?
> Who has taken some of my bread?
> Who has been using my fork?
> Who has been cutting with my knife?
> Who has been drinking out of my cup?"

And then the first dwarf said, "Who has been lying in my bed?" And the second said, "Why, someone has been lying in mine, too." And the third also, and likewise the fourth, and so on until they finally found Snow White lying in the seventh bed. But they liked her so well that they let her go on lying there out of pity, and the seventh dwarf had to share the sixth dwarf's bed as well as he could.

The next morning, after Snow White had slept enough, they asked her how she had got there, and she told them everything—how the queen, her mother, had abandoned her in the forest and driven off. The dwarfs were sorry for her and invited her to stay and cook their meals for them when they went to the mines, but they warned her to beware of the queen and to be sure not to let anyone into the house.

When the queen found out that Snow White was staying with the seven dwarfs and had not perished in the forest, she dressed herself as an old peddler woman and went to the house and asked to be let in with her wares. Snow White didn't recognize her at all and said at the window, "I may not let anyone in."

Then the peddler woman said, "Oh, just look, my dear child, what beautiful laces I have, and I'll let you have them for a good price!"

Snow White thought, "I just happen to need laces. It can't do any harm to let the woman in. I'll get a good buy." And she opened the door and bought some laces. And when she had bought a few, the peddler woman began, "Why, how slovenly you're laced. How ill it becomes you. Come, I'd like to lace you up properly for once." Thereupon the old woman, who was really the queen, took the lace and laced Snow White so tight that she fell down as if dead. Then the queen went away.

When the dwarfs came home and saw Snow White lying there, they suspected right away who had been there, and quickly unlaced her so that she recovered consciousness. But they warned her to be more careful next time.

After the queen found out that her little daughter had come back to life, she could not rest and went back to the little house again in disguise and tried to sell Snow White a splendid comb. Now since Snow White liked the comb so exceedingly well, she let herself be taken in and opened the door, and the old woman entered and began combing her yellow hair, and left the comb sticking in it until Snow White fell down as if dead. When the seven dwarfs came home, they found the door standing open and Snow White lying on the floor, and knew right away who had caused this misfortune. Immediately they pulled the comb out of her hair, and Snow White came back to life. But they told her that if she let herself be deceived once more, they would no longer be able to help her.

The queen, however, was furious when she discovered that Snow White had come back to life, and disguised herself a third time as a farm woman and took along an apple, half of which was poisoned, and that was the red half. Snow White did not dare to let the woman in, but she handed her the apple through the window and acted her part so well that one couldn't notice a thing. Snow White bit into the lovely apple where it was red and fell to the ground dead.

When the seven dwarfs came home, they could not help anymore and were very sad and made great mourning. They laid Snow White in a glass coffin in which she kept her former appearance completely, wrote her name and ancestry on it, and carefully kept watch over it day and night.

One day the king, Snow White's father, was returning to his kingdom and had to pass through the same forest where the seven dwarfs lived. When he discovered the coffin and its inscription, he felt great sorrow for the death of his beloved daughter. In his retinue, however, there were some highly experienced physicians. They asked the dwarfs to give them the body, took it, and tied a rope to the four corners of the room, and Snow White came back to life. Then they all went home. Snow White was married to a handsome prince, and at the wedding a pair of slippers were heated red-hot over a fire. The queen had to put them on and dance in them until she was dead.

* * *

According to others, the dwarfs knock thirty-two times with little magic hammers and bring Snow White back to life that way.

II. "Snow White": *First Edition of 1812**

Once upon a time in deep winter, when the snow-flakes were falling like feathers from the sky, a beautiful queen was sitting at a window with a black ebony frame, and she was sewing. And as she looked up from her sewing at the snow, she pricked her finger with the needle, and three drops of blood fell upon the snow. And because the red looked so beautiful against the white snow, she thought to herself, "Would that I might have a child as white as snow, as red as blood, and as black as this frame." Soon after that she bore a little daughter who was as white as snow and as red as blood and as black as ebony, and therefore she was called Snow White.

The queen was the most beautiful in the whole country and was very proud of her beauty. And she owned a mirror before which she stepped every morning and asked:

> "Mirror, mirror, on the wall,
> Who is the fairest woman of all?"

The mirror always replied:

> "You, Lady Queen, are the fairest woman of all."

Then she knew for certain that there was no one more beautiful in the whole world.

Snow White, however, grew up, and when she was seven years old, she was so beautiful that she surpassed even the queen in beauty, and when the latter asked the mirror:

> "Mirror, mirror, on the wall,
> Who is the fairest woman of all?"

the mirror said:

> "Lady Queen, you are the fairest here.
> But Snow White is a thousand times more fair than you!"

*Reprinted by Friedrich Panzer (Munich, 1913).

When the queen heard the mirror saying this, she turned pale with envy, and from that hour she hated Snow White. And when she looked at her and thought that Snow White was to blame that she was no longer the most beautiful in the world, she felt a violent pang in her heart.

Her envy would not let her rest, and she summoned a huntsman and said to him, "Take the child out into the forest to a distant and desolate place. There stab her to death, and bring me her lungs and her liver as proof. I will boil them in salt and eat them."

The huntsman took Snow White and led her away, but when he had drawn his hunting knife and was about to pierce her with it, she began to weep and begged him very hard to spare her life. She would never go back but would run away into the forest.

The huntsman took pity on her because she was so beautiful, and thought, "The wild beasts will soon have devoured her. I'm glad I need not kill her." And since at that moment a young boar came rushing by, he killed it, cut out the lungs and the liver, and took them to the queen as proof. She boiled them in salt and ate them, thinking that she was eating Snow White's lungs and liver.

But Snow White was left all forlorn in the great forest, so that she was very much afraid and began running and running over the sharp stones and through the brambles the whole day long, and at last as the sun was about to set, she came to a tiny little house. The little house belonged to seven dwarfs; however, they were not at home but had gone to the mines.

Snow White went inside and found everything small but dainty and clean. There stood a little table with seven little plates, and beside them seven little spoons, seven little knives and forks, and seven little cups. Against the wall stood seven little beds in a row covered with clean sheets. Snow White was hungry and thirsty, ate a few greens and a bit of bread from each plate, drank a drop of wine from each little cup, and because she was so tired she wanted to lie down and sleep. She tried the seven little beds one after another, but none of them suited her until the seventh. In that she lay down and went to sleep.

When it was night, the seven dwarfs returned from their work and lit their seven little candles. Then they realized that someone had been in their house.

The first one said, "Who has been sitting on my chair?"

The second, "Who has been eating from my plate?"

The third, "Who has taken some of my bread?"

The fourth, "Who has eaten some of my greens?"

The fifth, "Who has been using my fork?"

The sixth, "Who has been cutting with my knife?"

The seventh, "Who has been drinking out of my cup?"

Then the first turned around and said, "Who has been lying on my bed?" The second, "Why, someone has been lying on mine, too." And so did all the rest until the seventh: when he looked at his bed, he found Snow White lying there asleep.

Then the dwarfs all came running up with cries of astonishment, fetched their seven little candles, and looked at Snow White. "Ah, dear God! Ah, dear God!" they exclaimed. "How beautiful she is." They were delighted with her and didn't wake her up but let her go on lying in the little bed. The seventh dwarf slept one hour with each of his comrades, and then the night was over.

When Snow White woke up they asked her who she was and how she had got to their house. Then she told them how her mother had wanted to have her killed but the huntsman had spared her life, and how she had run the whole day and finally come to their little house.

Then the dwarfs took pity on her and said, "If you will look after our household, do the cooking, make our beds, do the washing, sewing, and knitting, and keep everything neat and clean, you shall stay with us, and you shall lack nothing. At night when we come home, dinner has to be ready, but during the daytime we shall be digging for gold in the mines, and you will be alone. Beware of the queen, and don't let anyone in."

But the queen thought that she was once again the

most beautiful in the land. In the morning she stepped
before the mirror and asked:

> "Mirror, mirror, on the wall,
> Who is the fairest woman of all?"

But the mirror again answered:

> "Lady Queen, you are the fairest here.
> But beyond the seven mountains,
> Snow White is a thousand times more fair than you!"

When the queen heard that, she started back and
realized that she had been deceived and that the huntsman had not killed Snow White. However, since there
was no one living in the mountains besides the seven
dwarfs, she knew right away that Snow White had escaped
to them. And now she began to plot anew how she might
kill her, for as long as the mirror said that she was not
the most beautiful in the whole land, she could not rest.

Since nothing else seemed sure and certain enough,
she disguised herself as an old peddler woman, smeared
paint on her face so that no one could recognize her,
and went out to the dwarfs' house. She knocked at the
door and called, "Open up, open up. It's the old peddler woman with fine wares for sale."

Snow White looked out the window: "What have you
got?"

"Laces, dear child," said the old woman, and got out
one that was woven out of yellow, red, and blue silk.
"Would you like that one?"

"Oh yes," said Snow White, and thought, "I'm sure I
can let in this good old woman. Her intentions are
honest." So she unbarred the door and purchased the
lace.

"But how slovenly you're laced," said the old woman.
"Come, let me lace you up properly for once."

When Snow White stood in front of her, she took the
lace and laced and laced it so tight that Snow White
could not breathe and fell down as if dead. Then the
queen was satisfied and went away.

Soon thereafter it was night, and the seven dwarfs came home. They were very frightened when they saw their beloved Snow White lying on the floor as if dead. They lifted her up, and then they saw that she had been laced too tight and cut the lace in two. First she started to breathe and then she came back to life. "That was none other than the queen," they said. "She wanted to take your life. Be careful and don't let anyone else in."

But the queen asked her mirror:

> "Mirror, mirror, on the wall,
> Who is the fairest woman of all?"

The mirror answered:

> "Lady Queen, you are the fairest here.
> But where the seven dwarfs stay,
> Snow White is a thousand times more fair than you!"

She was so startled that all the blood ran to her heart, for she realized that Snow White had come to life again. Then she brooded the whole day and night how she might still surprise her, and she made a poisoned comb, disguised herself in a completely different form, and went out again.

She knocked at the door, but Snow White called, "I may not let anyone in." Then she got out the comb, and when Snow White saw it gleaming and saw, besides, that this person was a total stranger, she opened the door anyway and bought the comb from her.

"Come and I'll comb you, too," said the peddler woman, but hardly had she stuck the comb in Snow White's hair than the girl fell down and was dead. "Now you'll stay lying there," said the queen, and her heart felt light and she went home.

But the dwarfs came in time, saw what had happened, and pulled the poisoned comb out of Snow White's hair. Then she opened her eyes and was alive again, and she promised the dwarfs that she would under no circumstances let anyone else in.

But the queen stopped in front of her mirror:

"Mirror, mirror, on the wall,
Who is the fairest woman of all?"

The mirror answered:

"Lady Queen, you are the fairest here.
But where the seven dwarfs stay,
Snow White is a thousand times more fair than you!"

When the queen heard this once more, she trembled and quivered with rage: "Snow White must die even if it should cost me my life!" Then she went to her most secret chamber, where no one was permitted to come to her, and there she made a poisonous, poisonous apple. On the outside it was lovely and red, and everyone who saw it desired it. Then she disguised herself as a farm woman, went to the dwarfs' house, and knocked.

Snow White looked out and said, "I don't dare let in a soul. The dwarfs have absolutely forbidden it."

"Well, if you don't want to, I can't force you," said the farm woman. "I'll have no trouble selling my apples. There, I'll give you one to try."

"No, I may not even take any presents. The dwarfs won't allow it."

"Perhaps you're afraid. There, I'll cut the apple in two and eat this half, and the nice red half shall be for you!"

However, the apple was so skillfully made that only the red half was poisoned.

When Snow White saw the farm woman herself eating from it, and since her longing for it kept increasing, she finally allowed the other half to be handed in to her through the window and bit into it. But she had hardly taken a bite than she fell dead to the ground.

The queen was glad, went home, and asked the mirror:

"Mirror, mirror, on the wall,
Who is the fairest woman of all?"

It answered:

"You, Lady Queen, are the fairest woman of all!"

"Now I can rest," she said, "since I am again the most beautiful in the land, and this time Snow White will surely stay dead."

At night when the dwarfs came home from the mines, Snow White was lying dead on the floor. They unlaced her and searched for poisoned objects in her hair, but it was all in vain. They couldn't bring her back to life. They placed her on a bier, and all seven sat beside it and wept and wept for three days. Then they were going to bury her, but they saw that she still looked fresh and not at all like a dead person and that she still had her beautiful red cheeks. They had a coffin made of glass, placed her inside so that one could see her, and wrote her name and ancestry on it in gold letters. One of them stayed home every day to keep watch over it.

Thus Snow White lay a long, long time in the coffin, and her freshness did not fade, and she remained as white as snow and as red as blood, and had she been able to open her eyes they would have been as black as ebony, for she lay there as though she were asleep.

One time a young prince came to the dwarfs' house and wanted to spend the night. When he came into the room and saw Snow White lying there in the glow of the seven little candles, he could not gaze at her beauty enough, and he read the gold inscription and learned that she was the daughter of a king. He asked the dwarfs to sell him the coffin with the dead Snow White, but they wouldn't for any amount of gold. Then he asked them to give it to him as a present, for he could not live without seeing her, and he would keep and honor her as his dearest possession on earth.

Then the dwarfs took pity on him and gave him the coffin. The prince had it carried to his castle and set in his bedroom. He would spend the whole day sitting beside it and could not take his eyes away. And when he was forced to go out and could not look at Snow

White, he was sad, and he could not eat a bite if the coffin was not by his side.

However, his servants, who constantly had to carry the coffin around, resented it, and once one of them opened the coffin, raised up Snow White, and said, "For the sake of a dead girl we get harassed all day long." And he hit her on the back with his hand. Then the deadly piece of the poisoned apple that she had bitten off flew out of her throat, and Snow White came back to life. She went to the prince, who didn't know what to do for joy now that his beloved Snow White was alive, and they sat down to dinner and ate together in happiness.

The wedding was set for the next day, and Snow White's wicked mother was invited too. In the morning when she stepped in front of the mirror and said:

> "Mirror, mirror, on the wall,
> Who is the fairest woman of all?"

it answered:

> "Lady Queen, you are the fairest here.
> But the young queen is a thousand times more fair than you!"

When she heard that, she was startled, and she became so terribly afraid that she could not express it. But her envy made her want to see the young queen at the wedding, and when she arrived she saw that it was Snow White. Two iron slippers were heated red-hot in the fire. She had to put them on and dance in them, and her feet were miserably burned, and she was not allowed to stop dancing until she was dead.

AFTERWORD

When they entitled their collection of folktales *Kinder-und Hausmärchen* (Children's and Household Tales), the Brothers Grimm did not mean to suggest that they had compiled a book of children's stories. It was in part their purpose that, as has actually happened, each new generation of children should read their book and that it should become a household work. But the title implies a great deal more. For the Grimms it meant that the stories preserved the simplicity and innocence that their generation—the first generation of romantic writers—associated with children and with the family hearth. "These stories," Wilhelm Grimm wrote in the preface to the first volume of 1812, "are pervaded by the same purity that makes children appear so marvelous and blessed to us." A childlike sense of wonder and a moral simplicity were also qualities that the Grimms attributed to the past, and it was primarily for what remained in them of the spiritual heritage of the past that the Grimms collected folktales. In the study and preservation of the literature of the past the Grimms were striving to make their own generation and future ones conscious of the national soul that, so they believed, had lived on subconsciously in the traditional stories of the folk.

Their interest in fairy tales was, therefore, historical, just one aspect of their broader interest in ancient Germanic languages and literature. The greater part of their lives was devoted to their work in philology and medieval literature, and of the three columns about them in the *Encyclopedia Britannica* only a paragraph is allotted to their collection of folktales. To understand why the Grimms collected folktales and also how they went about recording and, in many instances, revising the stories they had collected, it is necessary to see the *märchen* as part of their lifework—the restoration of the German literary past.

The Grimms appeared at exactly the right moment for the accomplishment of this task, and it exactly suited their temperaments and talents. In them two main currents of their time, seemingly incompatible but not really so, come together: a passionate and romantic nationalism and a painstaking historical scholarship. Their career began just when the French Revolution and the Napoleonic invasions had aroused a keen sense of nationalism among German intellectuals and focused their attention upon their own literary tradition. At the same time new standards of accuracy were developing in the editing of historical and literary documents. Not only did the past seem worth preserving; it seemed essential to preserve it as it had actually been.

Jacob Grimm was born in 1785 and Wilhelm a year later. Their father, who died when they were children, had been a lawyer, and it was at his wish that they studied law at the University of Marburg. At Marburg they were befriended by one of their professors, the distinguished legal historian Karl Friedrich von Savigny. From him they first learned historical method, and to him they owe their first contacts with medieval literature and with folklore. It was in von Savigny's library that Jacob came upon a volume of medieval poetry that inspired him to study medieval literature, and it was von Savigny who introduced the Grimms into a small but influential circle of writers and artists where they encountered romantic theories of art and history that were to color their own philological and literary theories and practices. They became good friends of the poets Clemens Brentano and Achim von Arnim and worked with them on *Des Knaben Wunderhorn* (The Boy's Magic Horn), a collection of poems based on folk songs. Through this collaboration they began to develop their own ideas about folk literature, which differed essentially from those of Brentano and von Arnim, and they began collecting on their own.

The Grimms would have liked nothing better than to pursue their studies in peace and quiet in Kassel, the little town in Hesse where they had gone to school and where they had settled after leaving Marburg, but their poverty prevented them. They had studied law in the expectation of holding positions in the Hessian civil service as their father had before them, but with the occupation of Germany by Napoleon's troops, this employment was closed to them. Instead they became librarians, at first for Jerome Bonaparte, who was then King of Westphalia with his capital in Kassel, and later, after the defeat of Napoleon, for the Hessian Elector. The library posts actually gave them more time for their own work than the civil service would have, and as they published the results of their research, they became quite well known in scholarly and literary circles.

The Grimms reluctantly left Kassel in 1830 after the accession of an Elector who had no appreciation of their work and who refused them promotions they thought they deserved. Many universities had offered them positions before this, and now they went to Göttingen, Jacob as professor and librarian and Wilhelm as an assistant librarian. They were forced to resign these positions when, along with five other professors, they protested an unconstitutional act of the new King of Hanover. After three years of retirement in Kassel, they were invited by the King of Prussia to Berlin, where they spent the rest of their lives lecturing at the University of Berlin and continuing to publish revisions of the fairy tales and studies in medieval literature and philology. They began work on their final project, the monumental *German Dictionary*, on which they were still engaged when they died, Wilhelm in 1859 and Jacob in 1863. The dictionary was finally completed in 1954.

The Grimms always regarded their years in Kassel as their happiest, and it was their family life that made the place so dear to them. Their mother had died soon after

they left Marburg, and they had assumed the responsi-
bility for the younger members of their family—three
brothers and a sister. Their portraits by the artist brother
Ludwig show them to have been an attractive group,
and they were an affectionate and loyal one. The relationship between Jacob and Wilhelm was especially close.
When Wilhelm married at the age of forty, Jacob, a
confirmed bachelor; kept on living in the same house.
In his commemorative address to the Berlin Academy
after his brother's death, Jacob described their life
together:

> While our school years slipped slowly by, we slept in
> the same bed and worked together in the same little
> room at one and the same table. Afterward at the
> university two beds and two tables stood in the same
> room; in later life there were still two desks in
> one room; and finally, until the end, in two adjoining
> rooms, we kept our belongings and our books in
> complete, uncontested, and undisturbed common own-
> ership . . . Our last beds, too, shall in all probability
> be made close beside one another.

The Brothers Grimm not only shared the same house
and the same books, but they shared the same tastes and
ideas. Jacob's first publication was a discussion of the
relationship between the meistersinger of the late Middle
Ages and the minnesinger of the twelfth and thirteenth
centuries; Wilhelm had translated medieval Scandinavian
poetry. Both of them collaborated on other editions
and translations of medieval texts, and while they were
working on the second edition of the *märchen*, Jacob
brought out the first part of his grammar of the Germanic languages, a work of enormous philological significance. It contains the description of certain patterns
of sound change in the Indo-European languages that
have come to be known as "Grimm's Law."

All of these labors, whether they involved comparing
different versions of fairy tales or word stems in ancient
Germanic languages, were inspired by the belief that
there is a spiritual force in nature that finds expression

in literature. The ancient poets, the Grimms and their fellow romantics felt, had lived closer to nature, and their works were therefore imbued with fundamental truths and values. These truths and values had been given their noblest embodiment in the ancient epic poetry, much of it lost, but they were still present in the humbler form of the folktale. Such ideas are recurrent themes in the prefaces to the early volumes and editions of the *märchen*. In justifying their efforts in collecting these simple tales, Wilhelm Grimm wrote in the preface to the first volume:

> . . . their very existence is sufficient to defend them. Something that has pleased, moved, and instructed in such variety and with perpetual freshness contains within itself the necessity for its being and surely comes from that eternal fountain that quickens all living things with its dew, even if it be but a single drop, clinging to a small, tightly folded leaf, sparkling, nevertheless, in the first light of the dawn.

The "eternal fountain" was for them the mystical power of nature, the source of all good. Anything partaking of nature must be good, and so the Grimms saw a natural morality in stories that told of "faithful servants and honest craftsmen, above all, fishermen, millers, charcoal burners, and shepherds who live close to nature." The fairy tales gave expression to natural human instincts: the desire of parents for children, as in Tom Thumb's mother who wishes for ". . . just one . . . even if it were terribly small, only the size of a thumb . . ."; the affection of brothers and sisters like Hansel and Gretel; the loyalty of servants like Iron Henry and Faithful John; and the natural courtesy and compassion shown by so many younger brothers.

The animism of nature in fairy tales was for the Grimms evidence of an innate spiritual power, and they were impressed by the mysterious bond of sympathy that links the heroes and heroines of fairy tales to nature:

As in the myths that tell of the Golden Age, all of nature is alive; the sun, the moon, and the stars are approachable and bestow gifts . . . the dwarfs mine for metals in the mountains; the nymphs sleep in the water; the birds (the doves are the best-loved and the most helpful), the plants, and the stones are able to speak and know how to express their fellow feeling . . .

In both "The Juniper Tree" and "Cinderella" the guardian spirit of the dead mother passes into a tree that magically protects her children. The briar hedge is the symbol of nature guarding her rose, the princess who sleeps inside the castle; when the right prince comes along, the briars turn into flowers that separate of their own accord to let him pass. On the other hand, nature punishes whatever is unnatural and evil. The doves who help Cinderella peck out the eyes of her wicked sisters, and the proud brothers in "The Water of Life" are imprisoned by the mountains.

In the many parallels between the fairy tales and Germanic mythology and legend the Grimms detected the traces of a primitive natural religion. The sleeping Briar Rose surrounded by the hedge of thorns is like the sleeping Brunhild surrounded by the ring of flames; the three spinners are the Norns, the Fates of Germanic mythology; the boy who goes to Hell to bring back the Devil's three golden hairs is like all the legendary heroes who travel to the Underworld. Even ostensibly Christian figures like God and Saint Peter wander over the earth as Odin did. Such parallels suggested to the Grimms that the fairy tales were not merely delightful stories but had a deeper religious significance:

They preserve thoughts about the divine and spiritual in life: ancient beliefs and doctrine are submerged and given living substance in the epic element, which develops along with the history of a people.

Thus the Grimms applied romantic theories of nature and art to the folktale. Their prefaces reflect the thought

of Rousseau, who had argued that man is naturally
good but had been corrupted by the artificial values of
society. Primitive man, children, and also rustics are
morally superior to the rest of mankind because they
are closer to nature. Schiller had expressed essentially
the same idea in his essay "On Naive and Sentimental
Poetry," which begins:

> There are moments in our lives when we respond
> to nature—in plants, minerals, animals, and land-
> scapes, as well as in human nature, in children and
> in the customs of country folk and primitive peoples—
> with a kind of love and affectionate regard, not
> because she pleases our senses, nor because she
> satisfies our reason or our taste . . . but simply
> because she is nature.

In such a view folklore, the literature of "common
folk" and "primitive peoples," appeared as something
that had been produced, as it were, by nature itself
working through human instruments, and romantic writers everywhere turned eagerly to folk literature for
inspiration. Wordsworth declared in the preface to the
Lyrical Ballads that he had chosen subjects from "hum-
ble and rustic life . . . because in that condition the
passions of men are incorporated with the beautiful and
permanent forms of nature." Moreover, the emergent
sense of nationalism gave men a further reason to cherish not only what grew from the soil but especially from
native soil. Thus Sir Walter Scott collected the ballads
of the Border Minstrelsy, and in America, Washington
Irving attempted to celebrate the legendary past of a
country that had barely had time to acquire one.

The Grimms, then, shared a widespread interest in
the preservation and use of native culture. The original-
ity of their contribution lay in their respect for oral
tradition. Collections of folktales had been made before, but the earlier collectors had relied primarily on
literary sources and had not scrupled to recast material
that they regarded as crude or naive into a more learned
literary style. The Grimms, too, often relied on literary

sources, which they also felt free to revise, but the aim
of their retellings was to restore the simplicity and naiveté
that they believed to be essential elements of such tales
in the oral tradition of the folk.

They also set about recording tales told within their
social circle in Kassel. Their informants consisted for
the most part of young women of their own age, who
shared the brothers' enthusiasm for folklore. Among
them were the four daughters of the Wild family (one of
whom, Dortchen, was to become Wilhelm's wife) and
their mother, and the three daughters of the Hassenpflug
family. The Grimms' methods of collecting were long
misunderstood, partly because they themselves in the
preface to the first edition of the *Kinder- und Hausmärchen* had not been clear about their procedures, and
partly because Grimm scholars accepted without question the recollection of Wilhelm's son Herman, then in
his late sixties, that the "Marie" referred to by the
brothers among their informants was an old servant in
the Wild family—"die alte Marie"—not, as has only
recently been proved, young Marie Hassenpflug.* A
comparison of tales in the first edition of *Kinder- und
Hausmärchen* with manuscript versions, not available
until this century, reveals that they freely revised the
stories they had taken down with respect to both style
and content.**

The fact that the *märchen* are not pure examples of
oral tradition as recorded from unlettered old peasants
and servants but were mediated by educated young
middle-class women has caused consternation in some
quarters. One iconoclastic book accuses the Grimms
outright of deliberate lies and fraud.***

It cannot be denied that the preface to the first edi-

---

*Heinz Rölleke, "The 'Utterly Hessian' Fairy Tales by 'Old
Marie': the End of a Myth," in *Fairy Tales and Society*, ed.
Ruth Bottigheimer (Philadelphia: University of Pennsylvania
Press, 1986), pp. 287–300.
**See appendix, pp. 279–291.
***See John M. Ellis, *One Fairy Tale Too Many* (Chicago:
University of Chicago Press, 1983).

tion to some degree misrepresents the authenticity of their texts and the license that the Grimms permitted themselves in presenting them. "We have taken pains," they wrote, "to collect these *märchen* in as pure [*rein*] a form as possible. . . . No newly invented circumstance has been added nor has anything been embellished or changed, for we would have shunned piecing out tales in themselves so rich with analogues and reminiscences implicit in them; they cannot be invented." The statement seems to be saying that the Grimms faithfully reproduced their sources, something that is not borne out by the facts. The Grimms, however, did not believe that what they called the "pure" form of the *märchen* could be found in most existing versions, be they written or oral. Their intention was rather to restore, *so far as possible,* an ideal form of each story, freed of such impurities and artificialities as had crept into individual versions in the process of oral or literary transmission.

Such an ideal form might not exist and may never have existed. Nevertheless, the Grimms possessed models that they believed came very close to perfection. Two of the most brilliantly told tales in the first volume, "The Juniper Tree" and "The Fisherman and His Wife," had been set down in low German dialect by the painter Philipp Otto Runge. Wilhelm Grimm scrupulously transcribed these from Runge's manuscript, and these tales, unlike most of the others, were never altered in subsequent editions. They seemed to the Grimms to represent the ideal they were aiming at and strongly influenced their own redactions of their sources. The concept of an "ideal" *märchen-* form or -style is, of course, a phantom. A trained folklorist today can easily see that Runge's masterful stories are highly literary renderings of folk material, but they conformed exactly to the Grimms' romantic notions of what pure German folktales should be like.

Wilhelm's preface to the second volume of the first edition (1815) greatly clarifies the Grimms' procedures, especially in the description of a new informant who also influenced not only their notion of the genuine oral style of the folktale but also of the ideal German teller of such tales. In response to the brothers' public appeal for help in their collecting, stories had begun to pour in from different parts of Germany. But the most interesting new contributor was Frau Katherina Dorothea Viehmann from the neighboring village of Zwehren, of whom Wilhelm drew this striking portrait:

> This woman is still vigorous and not much over fifty . . . she has firm, pleasant features and a clear, sharp expression in her eyes; in her youth she must have been beautiful. She retains these old legends firmly in her memory—a gift that she says is not granted to everyone, for some people cannot remember anything. She tells a story with care, assurance, and extraordinary vividness and with a personal satisfaction—at first with complete spontaneity, but then, if one requests it a second time, slowly, so that with a little practice one can take down her words.

This oft-quoted passage, too, contains certain misrepresentations. Frau Viehmann was not, as Wilhelm had stated, a "peasant" but the wife of a tailor, the child of a thoroughly bourgeois family. Moreover, her ancestors were French Huguenots and she herself spoke French, a fact that explains why some of the tales she told the Grimms are not German folktales at all but derive from the French tales of Charles Perrault. Nevertheless, she, like the Grimms and their other informants, had doubtless heard peasant or servant storytellers from whom she would have acquired her manner of telling a tale. Frau Viehmann's portrait, as engraved by Jacob and Wilhelm's artist brother Ludwig for volume two of the second edition, came to represent in the imagination of the brothers and their growing readership the archetypal storyteller of the *Kinder- und Hausmärchen*.

It is apparent that until they met Frau Viehmann, the Grimms had not been in the habit of taking down the stories word for word. At first they had been chiefly interested in making an accurate summary of the plot. It is the plot of the stories that Wilhelm is thinking of in a well-known passage (this time from the preface to the second edition of 1819): "As for our method of collecting, our primary concern has been for accuracy and truth. We have added nothing of our own, nor have we embellished any incident or feature of the tale, but we have rendered the content just as we received it." He is careful to distinguish this aspect of the collection from the matter of style:

> That the mode of expression and execution of particular details is in large measure our own is self-evident; nevertheless, we have tried to preserve every characteristic turn that came to our attention, so that in this respect, too, we might let the collection retain the diversified forms of nature. Moreover, anyone who has engaged in similar work will realize that this cannot be regarded as a careless and mechanical sort of collecting; on the contrary, care and discrimination, which can be acquired only with time, are necessary in order to distinguish whatever is simpler, purer, and yet more perfect in itself from that which has been distorted. We have combined different versions as one wherever they completed each other and where their joining together left no contradictory parts to be cut out; but when they differed from each other and each preserved individual features, we have given preference to the best and have retained the other for the notes.

From this description of their method it can be seen that the Grimms did not make free use of their materials as had been the practice of Brentano and von Arnim in *Des Knaben Wunderhorn*. The Grimms felt that such reworking would destroy not only the historical value of their collection but the inner "truth" of the stories. However, this did not mean that they felt obliged to retell the stories exactly as they had heard them, or that they might not combine different versions of a story in an attempt to arrive at the "best" form. They were thus not inventing details but simply drawing, like the original storytellers, on the vast stockpile of traditional material in an effort to approach the ideal form of a story, "present and inexhaustible in the soul."

Wilhelm Grimm had stated that the ability to distinguish the true folk material from the false was a gradually acquired skill, and it was natural that as he heard and recorded more and more stories, especially those told by Frau Viehmann, he should have become conscious of a definite fairy-tale style and attempted to imitate it. This style became, especially for Wilhelm, an intrinsic part of the value of the *märchen* and an objective test for what in a story was "true" or "false." This gradually developing sense of style was applied not only to new stories, but many of the older ones, already printed in the first volume, were revised in the light of it. The history of the *Kinder- und Hausmärchen*—seven editions during the Grimms' lifetime—is a constant polishing and refinement of the style. Some of the favorite stories like "Snow White," "The Wolf and the Seven Kids," and "The Brave Little Tailor" were revised in almost every edition. The difference may be seen by comparing any of these tales with a story like "Jorinda and Joringel," which has hardly changed since the 1812 volume and seems mysterious, choppy, incomplete, and yet strangely powerful.

The labor of revision fell chiefly to Wilhelm Grimm while the more scholarly Jacob pursued his linguistic research. It is obvious today that the style of the Grimm tales is in large measure the original creation of Wilhelm. They are neither genuine folktales nor literary fairy tales like those of Hans Christian Andersen, but comprise a unique genre somewhere between the two, which Heinz Rölleke, the foremost Grimm scholar today, has designated as the "Grimm genre" (*Gattung Grimm*).* It is difficult to say to what degree Wilhelm was conscious of how much "of his own" he was contributing to the stories. But if he has received more than his due as a folklorist, he has rarely received due recognition as an artist—except for the tribute of being universally read.

Die Märchen der Brüder Grimm (Munich: Artemis, 1985), p. 36.

The gradual development of the tales into the form in which they are known today may be illustrated by comparing the final version of "Snow White" with two earlier versions that are printed as an appendix to this anthology. "Snow White" was evidently a favorite of the Grimms as well as of their readers, and there are some changes in almost every one of the seven editions.

The earliest version known to have been in the possession of the Grimms already contains the basic motifs: the mother's wish for a child as white as snow and as red as blood, the queen's jealousy, the friendship of the seven dwarfs, and three attempts to murder the child, the glass coffin, and the queen's being punished by having to dance in red-hot slippers. It comes as a surprise, however, that Snow White is a blonde, that her father and not the prince discovers her in the coffin, and that the jealous queen is not a stepmother but Snow White's own mother. A number of details, like the huntsman who spares Snow White's life, are not found in this version, and the narrative reads like a bare outline of the plot, with practically no description or dialogue. There are several loose ends; for example, the method used to bring Snow White back to life at the end is completely puzzling.

For the first edition the Grimms chose another version, which introduces the huntsman and the prince and which has an ending that is at least logical, though it is not the final one. What makes the story seem strikingly different, however, is the filling in of vivid details and the use of dialogue to replace indirect discourse, both changes that were to be carried even further in the later editions. In the earliest version, as the story opens, "the snow was falling from the sky"; this becomes, "the snowflakes were falling like feathers from the sky." Many of the charming and specific details that delight the reader—and are the despair of the translator— are the result of years of polishing. The use of dialogue adds a dramatic quality to the story, and the characters come increasingly alive through the successive revisions. The character of the queen is made blacker through her reactions when she thinks that she has succeeded in

poisoning Snow White. In the earliest version these are
not mentioned. In the first edition we are told that she
"was satisfied," that "her heart felt light," and that
she "was glad." In the final version she gloats, "Now you
were the most beautiful," "You paragon of beauty . . .
now it's all over with you," and the third time, "White
as snow, red as blood, black as ebony! This time the
dwarfs can't revive you again."

The most interesting changes, however, are those in
which the Grimms modified the stories to conform
with their theory of nature. No doubt this is why in
the second edition Snow White's mother becomes a
stepmother. The Grimms would have felt justified in
such a change because of the many wicked stepmothers
in other stories; in any case, a mother's jealousy of
her daughter would have clashed with their romantic
belief in the purity of the love that mothers in folk
literature should show for their own children. Similar
revisions of other stories have resulted in occasional
inconsistencies so that the same person may sometimes be called "the mother" and at other times "the
stepmother."

Although they claimed that they did not invent details,
the Grimms selected and added folk motifs that empha-
sized the sympathy of the world of nature for Snow White.
Her coffin, instead of being kept in the dwarfs' cottage lit
by candles, is transferred to a mountainside, and there
she is mourned by the owl, the raven, and the dove. Fur-
thermore, in the final version the piece of the poisoned
apple is ejected not by having a servant thump Snow
White on the back, like a petulant child punishing a
doll, but by having the servants carrying the coffin trip
over a bush. Here it is almost as if nature itself had a
hand in restoring Snow White to life and marrying her
to the prince.

Many small touches underline the moral qualities of
the tales. Thus when the queen at last feels at peace
after she has poisoned Snow White with the apple, the
Grimms later added, "so far as a jealous heart can ever
be at peace." Because they found deeper spiritual meaning expressed with childlike purity in the fairy tales, they

believed that their collection could serve "as a book of education," as a book that would develop the moral character of children. They were sensitive to objections, apparently raised against the first volume, that certain details and stories were not suitable for children. To these criticisms Wilhelm replied in the preface to the second volume with the argument that what was natural could not be harmful. He compared the stories to flowers that might, for exceptional reasons unconnected with nature, give offense to a few: such a one "who cannot enjoy their benefit may pass them by, but he cannot ask that they be given a different color or shape."

Yet the Grimms themselves must have felt a few colors were too strong to be natural. The first volume had contained two stories in which children play "butcher" and one child slaughters another. These tales were suppressed in the second edition. In the original version of "The Twelve Brothers," the brothers actually carry out their vow to kill every girl that they meet, and when their sister comes to the house in the forest, her youngest brother orders her to kneel: "Your red blood must be shed this instant!" It is not that the Grimms objected to the horror of such scenes—there is nothing here to match the horror in "The Juniper Tree." But the action of the twelve brothers, who are intimately associated with nature in the story, would tend to contradict the Grimms' idea of nature, whereas "The Juniper Tree" perfectly confirms it. The tree is the symbol of nature, and through it the murdered boy is brought back to life and his unnatural stepmother is destroyed. More than any other story, this mysterious and primitive tale reveals the connection that the Grimms perceived between fairy tales and ancient mythology and religion.

The success of the *Kinder- und Hausmärchen* had gradually brought about a new purpose not truly compatible with the Grimms' original purpose of faithfully preserving the heritage of German folklore. Initially they had not thought of their collection as a children's book, but as the work came to be received as children's literature their attitude toward it began to change. Not only did they eliminate stories that they themselves acknowledged as unsuitable for children, but Wilhelm's revisions exercised censorship over the rest, especially with regard to explicit sexual references.* In the first edition, for example, the witch finds out about the prince when Rapunzel innocently complains, "Do tell me, Godmother, why my clothes are getting so tight and don't fit anymore"; this was changed to "Do tell me, Godmother, why you are so much heavier to pull up than the young king's son." As has been shown in the revisions of "Snow White," Wilhelm added moralistic comments intended to point out the nature and the consequences of good and evil.

Of course, children do learn from fairy tales, and the question of what they learn from the Grimm tales has been a subject of debate ever since their first appearance, a debate that is still going on. They have been both praised and denounced for their conservative and nationalistic tendencies. The Nazis claimed them as works of impeccably Aryan purity and made them required reading in the schools. It is hardly surprising, therefore, that the violence of tales has also been interpreted in other quarters as a sinister influence on German militarism. The tales themselves cannot be blamed for such simplistic political exploitation, but the rejection of children, the cruel punishments, and the mutilations that occur in many of the stories do raise questions about their effect on children. The eminent child psychologist Bruno Bettelheim makes a compelling defense of the stories he loved: "The child intuitively comprehends that although these stories are *unreal*, they are not *untrue*; that while what these stories tell about does not happen in fact, it must happen as inner experience and personal development; that fairy tales depict in imaginary and symbolic form the essential steps for growing up and achieving an independent existence."** In the

---

*See Maria Tatar, *The Hard Facts of the Grimms' Fairy Tales* (Princeton: Princeton University Press, 1987), pp. 7–11.
**Bruno Bettelheim, *The Uses of Enchantment: The Meaning and Importance of Fairy Tales* (New York: Alfred A. Knopf, 1976), p. 73.

imaginary world of fairy tales the problems that seem overwhelming to the children in the real world are happily resolved, and thus the stories bring a message of reassurance and hope.

The fact that fairy tales have always functioned to socialize children, however, leads to the question of whether they perpetuate stereotypes that are no longer acceptable to many. Sandra Gilbert and Susan Gubar point out that the voice of the mirror in "Snow White" is that of the absent father, judging woman's worth by the standard the male imposes on the female: "You are the fairest one of all." Both the wicked stepmother and Snow White are seen to be the victims of male attitudes— the passive heroine enshrined in her glass coffin until the prince awakens her; the queen enslaved to her magic looking glass. "What does the future hold for Snow White?" ask the authors. "When her Prince becomes a King and she becomes a Queen, what will her life be like? Trained to domesticity by her dwarf instructors, will she sit in the window, gazing out on the wild forest of her past, and sigh, and sew, and prick her finger, and conceive a child white as snow, red as blood, black as ebony wood?"* Clearly the Grimms' fairy tales are products of both nature and society. In them the timeless world of the folktale intersects with the historical and social moment of German romanticism at the beginning of the nineteenth century.**

Whatever their effects may be, fairy tales still speak to us and tell us about ourselves—about our hopes and dreams as well as about our fears and anxieties.

*The Madwoman in the Attic: The Woman Writer and the Nineteenth-Century Literary Imagination (New Haven: Yale University Press, 1979), pp. 36–42. On the recurrent theme of women who must redeem themselves or others through silent suffering, see Ruth M. Bottigheimer, Grimms' Bad Girls & Bold Boys: The Moral and Social Vision of the Tales (New Haven: Yale University Press, 1987), pp. 71–80.

**See Jack Zipes, Breaking the Magic Spell (Austin: University of Texas Press, 1979), pp. 30–33, and The Brothers Grimm: From Enchanted Forests to the Modern World (New York: Routledge, Chapman & Hall, 1989).

They have not lost their power to please, move, and instruct. What Wilhelm Grimm said about them in 1812 can still be maintained today: their very existence justifies them.

—*Alfred David and*
Mary Elizabeth Meek
1964, 1988

SELECTED
BIBLIOGRAPHY

1. SELECTED WORKS BY
THE BROTHERS GRIMM

JACOB GRIMM

Über den altdeutschen Meistergesang, 1811
Deutsche Grammatik, 1819–1822
*Wuk Stephanovitsch's kleine serbische Grammatik,
   verdeutscht mit einer Vorrede, 1824*
Deutsche Rechtsaltertümer, 1823
Reinhart Fuchs, 1834
Taciti Germania edidit, 1835
Deutsche Mythologie, 1835
Geschichte der Deutsche Sprache, 1848

WILHELM GRIMM

*Altdänische Heldenlieder, Balladen, und Märchen
   Übersetzt, 1811*
Über deutsche Runen, 1821
Die Deutsche Heldensage, 1829

JACOB AND WILHELM GRIMM

*Das Lied von Hildebrand und das Weissenbrunner
   Gebet, 1812*
Der Arme Heinrich von Hartmann von der Aue, 1815
Deutsche Sagen, 1816–1818
Irische Elfenmärchen aus dem Englischen, 1826
Kinder- und Hausmärchen, 1812–1815
Deutsches Wörterbuch

2. EDITIONS OF
KINDER- UND HAUSMÄRCHEN

Grimms' Kinder- und Hausmärchen. Ed. Friedrich von
    der Leyen. Jena, 1912.
*Märchen der Brüder Grimm. Urfassung nach der Original-
    handschrift der Abtei Olenberg.* Ed. Joseph Lefftz.
    Heidelberg, 1927.
*Die Kinder- und Hausmärchen der Brüder Grimm:
    Vollständige Ausgabe in der Urfassung.* Ed. Friedrich
    Panzer. Wiesbaden: Emil Vollmer, 1953.
*Die älteste Märchensammlung der Brüder Grimm: Synopse
    der handschriftlichen Urfassung von 1810 und der
    Erstdruck von 1812.* Ed. Heinz Rölleke. Cologny-
    Genève: Fondation Martin Bodner, 1975.
Brüder Grimm. Kinder- und Hausmärchen. Ed. Heinz
    Rölleke. 3 vols. Stuttgart: Reclam, 1982 (7th edition).
*Kinder- und Hausmärchen. Gesammelt durch die Brüder
    Grimm.* Ed. Heinz Rölleke. 2 vols. Göttingen:
    Vandenhoeck & Ruprecht, 1986 (1st edition).
Die Kinder- und Hausmärchen der Brüder Grimm. Ed.
    Reinhold Steig. Jubiläumsausgabe 1812–1912, Berlin
    and Stuttgart, 1912.

3. ENGLISH TRANSLATIONS

German Popular Stories. Trans. Edgar Taylor. London:
    John Camden Hotten, 1969.
Grimms' Fairy Tales. Trans. Margaret Hunt and James
    Stern. New York: Pantheon, 1944, 1972.
Grimms' Tales for Old and Young. Trans. Ralph
    Manheim. New York: Doubleday, 1977.
The Complete Fairy Tales of the Brothers Grimm. Trans.
    and with an introduction by Jack Zipes, New York:
    Bantam, 1987.

4. WORKS ABOUT THE BROTHERS GRIMM
AND GRIMMS' FAIRY TALES

Auden, W. H. "Some Notes on Grimm and Andersen."
    New World Writing, II, New York, 1952. Reprinted as
    the introduction to the Modern Library *Tales of Grimm
    and Andersen.* New York: Random House, 1952.

Bettelheim, Bruno. *The Uses of Enchantment: The Meaning and Importance of Fairy Tales.* New York: Alfred A. Knopf, 1976.

Bottigheimer, Ruth B. *Grimms' Bad Girls & Bold Boys: The Moral and Social Vision of the Tales.* New Haven: Yale University Press, 1987.

Crane, T. F. "External History of the Grimm Fairy Tales." *Modern Philology* 14 (1917): 129–162 and 15 (1917): 1–12, 99–127.

Dégh, Linda. "*Grimms' Household Tales* and Its Place in the Household: The Social Relevance of a Controversial Classic." *Western Folklore* 38 (1979): 83–103.

Ellis, John. *One Fairy Story Too Many: The Brothers Grimm and Their Tales.* Chicago: University of Chicago Press, 1983.

Gilbert, Sandra, and Susan Gubar. *The Madwoman in the Attic: The Woman Writer and the Nineteenth-Century Literary Imagination.* New Haven: Yale University Press, 1979.

Lüthi, Max. *The European Folktale: Form and Nature.* Trans. John D. Niles. Philadelphia: Institute for the Study of Human Issues, 1982.

———. *Once Upon A Time: On the Nature of Fairy Tales.* Trans. Lee Chadeayne and Paul Gottwald. New York: Ungar, 1970.

Michaelis-Jena, Ruth. *The Brothers Grimm.* London: Routledge and Kegan Paul, 1970.

Peppard, Murray B. *Paths Through the Forest: A Biography of the Brothers Grimm.* New York: Holt, Rinehart and Winston, 1971.

Rölleke, Heinz. "The 'Utterly Hessian' Fairy Tales by 'Old Marie': The End of a Myth," in *Fairy Tales and Society: Illusion, Allusion, and Paradigm.* Ed. Ruth B. Bottigheimer. Philadelphia: University of Pennsylvania Press, 1986, pp. 287–300.

Tatar, Maria. *The Hard Facts of the Grimms' Fairy Tales.* Princeton: Princeton University Press, 1987.

Zipes, Jack. *Breaking the Magic Spell.* Austin: University of Texas Press, 1979.

———. *The Brothers Grimm: From Enchanted Forests to the Modern World.* New York: Routledge, Chapman & Hall, 1989.